Praise for Kate Thompson

'Inspiring tales of courage in the face of hardship'
Mail on Sunday

'A brilliant novel'
Daily Express

'A compelling saga set around the tenacious
women of the East End'
Daisy Styles

'Beautifully written, well drawn characters and a plot that
had me guessing. I could really feel the emotion'
Fiona Ford

'A lively authentic social history . . . a hair-raising,
but always warm-hearted tale'
My Weekly

'A riveting and wonderful read'
Mary Wood

'The way Kate Thompson writes . . . made me feel
that I was reading about old friends. I just had to
keep the pages turning'
Pam Weaver

'Kate Thompson writes books that make you laugh and
make you cry, sometimes at the same time. You cannot
put them down. I advise you to read them all!'
Anita Dobson

Kate Thompson

Kate Thompson is an award-winning journalist, ghost-writer and novelist who has spent the past two decades in the UK mass market and book publishing industry. Over the past eight years Kate has written ten fiction and non-fiction titles, three of which have made *The Sunday Times* top ten bestseller list. *Secrets of the Lavender Girls* is her eleventh book.

KATE
THOMPSON

Secrets of the
Lavender Girls

HODDER

First published in Great Britain in 2020 by Hodder & Stoughton
An Hachette UK company

2

Copyright © Kate Thompson 2020

A CIP catalogue record for this title is available from the British Library

Paperback ISBN 9781473698147
eBook ISBN 9781473698154

Typeset in Plantin Light 12/15.25 pt by
Palimpsest Book Production Limited, Falkirk, Stirlingshire

Printed and bound in Great Britain by Clays Ltd, Elcograf S.p.A.

Hodder & Stoughton policy is to use papers that are natural,
renewable and recyclable products and made from wood grown in sustainable
forests. The logging and manufacturing processes are expected to conform
to the environmental regulations of the country of origin.

Hodder & Stoughton Ltd
Carmelite House
50 Victoria Embankment
London EC4Y 0DZ

www.hodder.co.uk

In memory of:

Louise Acampora, aged 5
Alfred Batt, aged 5
Leonard Bareford, aged 5
John Brennan, aged 5
William Challen, aged 5
Vera Clayson, aged 5
Alice Cross, aged 5
William Hollis, aged 5
George Hyde, aged 5
Grace Jones, aged 5
Rose Martin, aged 10
George Morris, aged 6
Edwin Powell, aged 12
Robert Stimson, aged 5
Elizabeth Taylor, aged 5
Rose Tuffin, aged 5
Frank Wingfield, aged 5
Florence Woods, aged 5

PROLOGUE

Wednesday 20th June 1917

Queen Alexandra's open landau slides along the wide elegant thoroughfares of Knightsbridge, past the cheering crowds waving paper and silk roses in celebration of the annual Rose Day procession. Thousands have been bought by the time Her Majesty's carriage sets out from Marlborough House, raising funds for the sick and needy.

Their petals drift through the blue skies, getting caught in the smart hats of the gentry. They coat men, women and children up from the provinces, and skitter through the London parks. Smiling flower sellers in bonnets throng the crowds, pinning roses to sailors on leave, children's straw boaters and washerwomen's aprons. Hawkers on bikes sell ices and sarsaparilla to keep the onlookers cool. It is quite the spectacle of pomp and pageantry.

But further east, through the city, past the Aldgate pump and into the guts of Whitechapel, a very different procession winds its way through the cobbled quarters. Here the streets are narrow and the buildings blackened. The stench of horseshit curls through the hot air on a gusting westerly. Every window has its blinds pulled closed, even in the middle of the day.

Residents of Poplar and the surrounding boroughs have taken to the streets in their thousands, filling the highways, in some places so thick it slows the progress of the fifteen tiny coffins, each covered in a blanket of pink and white blossom.

This part of the East End has never been so quiet. Even the endlessly toiling docks have stopped work for the day. Grief has wrapped its bony fingers around the whole community.

Usually it's trucks, loaded down with goods, which rattle their way from the docks along the East India Dock Road. Today, it's bodies.

Hundreds of floral wreaths line the road. Simple offerings of sweet wild flowers from remote rural villages, cherry blossom from the Workers' Suffrage Federation, an elaborate harp fashioned from carnations from the Women Workers of the Woolwich Arsenal. Even a primary school from New Zealand has sent its condolences on a wreath of white roses.

It is an extraordinary outburst of feeling from every corner of the Empire.

At the graveside, as the tiny coffins are lowered into the ground, the mourners watch in a horrified hush at the ghastly spectacle, kept back by a wide ring of three hundred wounded soldiers home from the battlefields. The noise of weeping is drowned out only by the drone of two military aeroplanes circling overhead, keeping a watchful eye on proceedings.

This is a mass coming-together of humanity, a powerful global outpouring of love and grief, as if flowers alone can close over the dark empty space in the heart of the East End. No one will ever forget the day the newspapers have dubbed 'The slaughter of the innocents'.

The world shudders at the murder of all those children, but even the smell of flowers cannot mask the deeper stench of fear. For who will be next?

Before dawn broke over the docks, a solitary man hastened under cover of darkness to place a tiny bouquet of orange blossom beside the freshly dug earth of the open gravesides. Now, his simple flowers are buried under the avalanche of elaborate wreaths.

His note contains just one word.

Sorry.

PART ONE

Twenty-six years later

I

Esther

At 4 a.m., Esther finally gave up on sleep. A twinge of excitement reminded her that today was the day. She pulled on her old dungarees, tied a headscarf over her curling rags and crept from the house.

Outside, all was still, as the residents of the Shoot slumbered. It wouldn't be for long. Give it an hour and this place would be a riot as the race began to see who'd be out first whitening their doorstep and bashing the daylights out of their rag rug.

Odds on it'd be Nell Gunn, Esther's landlady at number 10. But Mrs Povey at number 14 – since she'd got herself an American lover, she was enjoying a new lease of life thank you very much! Then would come the coal man, the cat's meat woman and the beigel seller, making their way noisily through the Shoot, all adding to the daily theatre of life in this straggly elbow of the East End.

Esther smiled as she walked towards the Dig for Victory allotment in the centre of the square. She'd found the doorstep etiquette bewildering when she had first arrived in Stratford.

It was only now, after four years of living here, that Esther finally felt she belonged among the grimy back alleys of the Shoot.

But the place she loved the most was here, in the sanctuary of the allotment. The enthusiasm and skill cockneys had shown in transforming every spare patch of land had stunned the authorities! Hitler and his Huns thought they could break East Enders' spirits by bombing their homes in the Blitz. Instead, they had simply stuck two fingers up and planted veg.

Even the most uninviting soil had yielded – bombsites and playgrounds, railway sidings and factory yards – but it was this plot, in the grounds of the cemetery around the Shoot's church, which concealed all their secrets.

Esther pushed open the wooden gate and breathed in the smell of creosote. The sky over the jumble of rooftops was striated with bands of palest lemon and peach as a new day dawned. Snowball's compost lay gently steaming in the morning mist.

And there was the alchemist himself, digging over the soil around the rhubarb.

'Can't sleep?' she called.

Snowball turned around, his face obscured by the gloaming.

'I ain't slept in ten years, love,' he replied, digging his pitchfork down into the soil. Sometimes it was hard to see where the earth ended and Snowball began.

'Ain't brides-to-be supposed to be beautifying themselves with curlers and wot not?'

'Not this one,' she shrugged. 'You don't think Walter'll mind if I get hitched in these?' she asked, pointing down at her crusty old dungarees.

'Ooh love . . . I don't think . . .'

'Don't worry,' Esther laughed. 'I know women in slacks isn't the scandal anymore, but I think brides in dungarees would be a step too far!'

'Thank the Lord for that,' he replied, his lovely smile lighting up every corner of his craggy face. 'I'm just brewing up. Want one?'

'Ooh, not many,' she replied, following him into the shed.

Somewhere among the tomato plants, tools, packets of seeds and Dig for Victory gardening pamphlets, Snowball kept an old primus stove and a caddy of tea.

'Sit yourself down, love,' he said, brushing the earth off a small wooden bench made of old Yardley's pallets. 'How you feeling? Nervous?'

'If I had my way, I'd get hitched on the quick and not make a fuss.'

'And rob your mum, Nell and the women of the square of the chance for a knees-up? To say nothing of your future mother-in-law!' he remarked. 'Now, I know you're brave girl, but you ain't stupid.'

Smiling, Esther took the cup of tea from Snowball.

'True. You know what they say about Maureen Smith?'

'She's the only woman who can go on holiday and come back with a sunburnt tongue?'

Esther chuckled.

'Maureen's met her match in my mother though. Do you know the difference between a Rottweiler and a Jewish mother?'

'Enlighten me.'

'The Rottweiler eventually lets go! I dared to mention to Mum that I may wear my old blue frock and I haven't heard the end of it.'

Snowball burst into laughter.

'Oh dear. It's been that bad?'

Esther smiled at him through the steam, breathing in the comforting tangy smell of tomato plants and tea leaves.

'It's to be expected. It's taken Walter nearly three years to convert and we can't let that go without a big shindig. And it's mine and Mum's chance too, to say thank you to Nell and the women of the neighbourhood for taking us in, making us feel like family.' She hesitated, trying to find the words to articulate what he, Snowball, meant to her too.

'And I've never properly said thank you to you either. When we moved here from Vienna and then getting that dreadful news . . .' she hesitated. 'I . . . I was so scared. I couldn't imagine ever being free of fear, but you . . . You've been so kind to me.'

Snowball waved a hand in front of his face.

'I only treated you as any decent human would.'

Esther knew he was uncomfortable discussing emotions, but some things needed to be said.

'Since my father died, I've come to look upon you as a kind of a father. I . . . I hope that's not too forward to say?'

'Not at all, love,' he said. 'You know I think the world of you too.'

'You remind me of him,' she persisted. 'You're kind and gentle, selfless and . . .'

'No, I'm not,' he interrupted stiffly.

There it was. That look where he suddenly seemed to lose himself, drift off to an unknown place where no one, not even Nell Gunn, the woman he loved, could reach him. Esther longed to shake out his secrets, because no one really knew about the old soldier's past.

When Esther had first arrived in Stratford at the outbreak of war, she'd been a frightened fifteen-year-old refugee, on the run from the dark force of fascism. Snowball's enemy was invisible, but no less ruthless. Back then, he had been a dosser, leading a largely peripatetic existence, invisible to society.

'A disgrace', her mother Julia had called it, when she had seen him and the other veterans of the Great War, washed up like flotsam on the foreshore. When Snowball returned home from the trenches, it was supposed to have been to a 'Home for Heroes', as all the returning soldiers had been promised. Those promises never came to much in the finish, but that's politics for you. Men who had fought the most terrible war the world had ever seen were reduced to picking mouldy veg out of the gutters and queuing for soup. The sun apparently never set on the British Empire, which was odd, as Esther had seen enough broken men slumped in its long shadows.

One of those broken men was Snowball. Until three years ago, his home had been the church porch or whatever dry doorway he could find down Angel Lane Market.

But over the years, as Esther had found her feet at Yardley's, blossomed through work and Walter's devotion, so too had he.

The love of Nell Gunn, the Shoot's chief female, had been his salvation. That and this allotment had been balm to his troubled soul, offering not just a use for his hands and a roof over his head, but a return to society. They'd all found that in surviving the Blitz, but of all the transformations, Snowball's had been the most profound.

Perhaps bound by their uncertain pasts, she and Snowball had grown and twisted closer together, like the roots of a tree.

'What happened to you, Snowball?' Esther probed now. 'Why did you end up on the streets? Only you've never said . . .'

She knew she was pushing her luck, but something about the golden dawn light, the breaking of a new day, her wedding day, felt symbolic. How could she move on to a new life, when the man she had come to regard as a father was still haunted by his past?

Snowball's eyes flickered to his tomato plants.

'Do you know I read the other day in the *Stratford Express* an allotment thief was fined fifty pounds for nicking some tomatoes under the new Defence Regulations, what about that then?'

'I don't want to talk about tomatoes! I want to talk about you!'

Snowball said nothing, just pulled out an old button from his pocket and turned it over between his fingers. A strange old thing it was, shaped like an anchor, fashioned from ivory or perhaps shell, the gloss long worn away.

'Please, you can trust me.'

Her voice hung in the soft gloom of the potting shed. Snowball stared down at the button in his fingers, then at the compacted soil beneath his feet as if searching for the strands of his story.

'I'm not who you think I am.'

'You are,' she insisted. 'What you went through in the Great War makes you a hero in my eyes.'

She laced her fingers through his.

'I only want to help.'

'What the hell are you doing hiding away in this dirty, smelly shed?'

Nell's voice was like a klaxon. Snowball jumped, dropping the button as the large, aproned figure of his good lady filled the doorway.

'Oh hello, love,' he flustered. 'I was just having a cuppa with the bride-to-be.'

Nell Gunn's bulk filled the tiny potting shed. She was a formidable-looking woman at the best of times. Not fat; more like a solid brick wall, with a voice that sounded like a laugh and a shout at the same time. She had shrewd green eyes with a built-in bullshit detector.

'None of your chicanery you. It's her wedding day! She don't want to hang out in a shed!' Nell scolded, before clamping her hand on Esther's arm.

'Come on, you, I've fixed you a nice bit of egg and fried bread and I've got the hair tongs heating. We need to get you out of them dungarees and looking like a bride.'

Esther was hustled from the shed. She turned back to see Snowball hunting among the flowerpots for his button and it occurred to her: she still didn't know his real name.

*

Eight hours later, Esther stood with Walter before the rabbi as he read the ketuba in Aramaic. She could tell by his frozen top lip how nervous Walter was, but as he turned to make his declaration to her, his whole face softened. Above them hung the Jewish wedding canopy; behind them, half of Stratford. But as Walter spoke, the space between them melted away.

Walter's freckled face shone as he pledged his love, and Esther felt overwhelmed with gratitude. Just nineteen years old and she had already been tested so much in the dips and swells of her short life, but Walter was her one constant. He had never let her down, not from the moment they had first met at the Yardley factory when she was fifteen. He'd been by her side when they had worked together to save Yardley's from burning in the Blitz, and he had comforted her when her good friend Renee Gunn had been killed in the bombings. The thought of the beautiful blonde livewire caused a sudden ache in her heart. How she would have loved today.

But Esther felt her there in spirit, right beside her under the chuppa. She forced a smile. Today was about looking forward, not back.

The rabbi said the blessing over the wine before passing the goblet to first Esther, then Walter. He nodded at Walter, who brought his foot firmly down on the wine glass at his foot. The glass exploded into pieces and the guests erupted.

'*Mazeltov! Mazeltov!*'

'May the Lord bless you and keep you,' said the rabbi over the noise.

The ceremony was over and the guests descended on them. Her mother was first up on her feet, squeezing Esther.

'Aren't you pleased you wore that dress now?' she whispered. 'A bride should always wear white. Make sure you tread on his feet on the way down the steps, that way you'll always have the upper hand.'

Esther rolled her eyes at the old wives' tale. 'What if I don't want to have the upper hand?' she went to answer, but she was drowned out as the others pushed forward.

'Welcome to the family, ducks,' said her new mother-in-law. Maureen Smith looked like she'd been ironed and starched into one immovable package. 'I must say, I never thought we'd have a Jew in the family.'

Walter extracted himself from an elderly aunt and raised an eyebrow at his mother.

'I'm Jewish too now, mother, remember? And Esther's husband.'

'But still my son!'

Esther's head began to spin from the attention.

It was a relief when Nell and Snowball finally reached her. Snowball kissed her gently on the cheek. Esther smiled at the sight of him. Out of his tattered old gardening clothes and cardie, and manhandled into a serge suit, he looked uncomfortable but proud. With the grime of the garden washed away, he had brown, leathery skin and a pink scar that ran the length of his right eyebrow.

'You scrub up well, Snowball.'

'You don't look so bad yourself, love,' he grinned.

'Not so bad? She looks an absolute picture,' said Nell.

Esther was glad now that she'd saved some of the white silk from a Jerry parachutist who'd been shot down over the factory during the Battle of Britain. From it, her mother had made her the most exquisite dress, cut on the bias, which shimmered under the candlelight. Her long, dark hair cascaded down her back, threaded through with jasmine from the allotment.

'This is the only thing I'm going to say on this matter,' Nell went on, her voice unusually quiet, 'but I feel my Renee here today. Weddings were her favourite thing, that and jawing. Cor, she was a chatterbox, weren't she?'

Esther smiled.

'Yes, she was a force of nature. I feel her presence too, Nell . . .' Esther hesitated. 'She would have been proud of you. For moving on with your life.'

The loss of Nell's youngest daughter was not the only tragedy to have struck at the heart of the Shoot during the Blitz. Nell had also lost her husband, Pat, in the bombings, leaving her to raise their youngest son Frankie alone – until Esther and her mother Julia had moved in that was, shortly followed by Snowball.

Tramps, refugees and widows. They were an unorthodox wartime family at number 10, but for the past three years, it had worked.

Esther glanced over at her new husband. He stood stoically as Maureen scrubbed at a lipstick stain on his cheek with her handkerchief.

'I'm going to miss you so much,' Esther said suddenly, throwing her arms around Nell. The lavender-scented bulk of her was so reassuring. The thought of leaving Nell's warm and cosy home to move in with Maureen Smith was not one she relished, but Walter's mum had insisted. She had a larger home a few streets away with two whole rooms for the newlyweds to start their married lives in. It made sense on a practical level.

'Don't be crying over that, you daft little article. Come on, the girls have been decorating the square, wait until you see it.'

Walter led her from the wedding car and up Cat's Alley, with his hands over her eyes.

'Can't I look? I'm going to break my neck on these cobbles,' she laughed.

'Wait a minute . . . All right . . . now you can.'

Esther blinked.

'Oh my!' Her hand flew to her mouth.

'Ta-da! Wotcha think then, girl, you like it?'

'Lou!' Esther exclaimed. 'Did you do all this?'

'Not on me own no, I had a little help from the girls.'

Esther's good friend Lou Button stood in the middle of the square with half the lipstick and soap department of the factory where they all worked.

All the crew was here. Betty, Joanie, Joycie, Little Irene (Big Irene had joined the ATS years ago, but the name had stuck), Mavis and a dozen more Yardley girls – or, as they preferred to be known, the Lavender Girls. Out of their red-and-white overalls, they looked the business. The more the privations of war had been thrust upon them, the more they had hit back with bold glamour. Elaborate hairstyles had become badges of honour. Elegant pompadours, with hair pinned up at the sides and swept high on to the top of the head in a striking Eugene wave; gleaming victory rolls, chignons and pin curls. Lips were stained a rich red with carmine, eyes dark with kohl or, more often than not, boot polish.

Esther felt a burst of pride. The factory girls hadn't let clothes rationing cramp their style, and old clothing had been renovated and recycled with amazing ingenuity. East End girls had style, swagger and a magic way with a needle and thread. She was still amazed how they could copy the latest styles from the West End and be wearing them within days. To anyone else, sixty-six coupons' clothing allowance a year was disheartening, but to the girls, it had become a matter of personal pride to see who could put together the best rig-out.

'I don't know what to say!' Esther cried.

'Fanks'd be a good start,' piped up Little Irene. 'I nearly broke me bleedin' neck getting that bunting up.'

'Thank you, Irene,' she gushed. 'Thank you all, in fact.'

Little Irene blushed. 'It was nuffink. Thank God it ain't rained. I prayed for a fine day.'

With weather reports forbidden since the start of war, it had been anyone's guess how the day would turn out. But Esther smiled as she looked at the July sunshine drenching the square. 'Your lips to God's ear,' she uttered.

Faded red, white and blue bunting – dug out from the old King's silver jubilee – had been strung from gas lamps, ribbons streamed from the sweet pea bushes in the allotment, and fat bunches of lilac sat in jam jars on trestle tables.

Even the square's shabby window boxes were sprouting red geraniums. At least two pianos had been rolled out on to the cobbles, and most of the women of the Shoot were already at the drinks table handing round what looked like Scotch.

And the spread! All the guests had contributed a dish and all of Esther's favourite foods, such as smoked salmon beigels, wallies, rollmops and hot latkes, were mixed in with cockney wedding classics like pork pies and sausage rolls.

'How much did you pay on the black market for that?' Esther asked.

Nestled in the middle of the table was a huge bowl of peaches smothered in cream and a bowl of cherries. She hadn't seen food like that in years.

'Nah, no fences. We've got them lot to thank for the nosh,' Joanie said, nodding to the far side of the Shoot. 'And the Scotch.'

As one, the girls' gaze turned to where Mrs Povey, a widow from the start of the war, was standing chatting to half a dozen men in the sharpest cut uniforms Esther had ever seen.

'Who invited the Yanks?' muttered Walter.

'Mrs Povey and praise the Lord,' said Joanie. 'She's having it off with one of them by all accounts.'

'She ain't the only one,' muttered Lou, gesturing towards Mrs Mahoney. 'Rumour has it she's doing the double shuffle with a Polish airman.'

'I heard it was a Yank,' said Joycie.

'Either way, I don't reckon her husband will care when he gets released from that prisoner of war camp to find he's miraculously fathered another kid,' remarked Little Irene.

They hadn't called it the friendly invasion for nothing. Esther had seen the American GIs around Stratford a lot since the spring of '42; they were a common enough sight as they set to work helping to rebuild the bombed areas and visiting children's schools and hospitals on morale-boosting trips. But up close, Esther had to admit, they made a fairly awesome spectacle of glamour.

'Who'd have thought? Lucky old Mrs Povey – I'd love an American boyfriend,' said Joanie. 'Look at their smart uniforms. They're another class, ain't they? All shiny and new. Even their buttons.'

'Play your cards right, Joanie,' nudged Mavis.

'It ain't the buttons I'm looking at,' said Lou, with a lairy look on her face. Esther braced herself. Lou, or Fat Lou as she was more commonly known in the factory, had a right mouth on her.

'It's the bums. Check out that one with his back to us. Like cream on strawberries.'

'I'd pluck him any day,' Joanie quipped.

Walter's mouth tightened as the girls fell about.

Esther knew it wasn't Lou and Joycie's potty mouths he objected to. It was the presence of handsome males in his territory that ruffled his feathers. Despite proving himself in the Home Guard during the Blitz, Walter still felt ashamed that his poor eyesight had prevented him from going off on active service like his pals at Yardley's.

Their laughter tailed off as Mrs Povey's boyfriend snaked

his arm around her waist, drew her into his arms and kissed her so hard on the mouth, her fascinator fell off. A chorus of wolf-whistles flew round the square.

'Watch out, Mrs P!' yelled Nell Gunn.

'Yeah, one yank and your drawers'll be down yer ankles!' hollered Lou.

'Just as well you're leaving this place, dear,' said a disapproving voice in Esther's ear.

'Maureen,' said Esther, swinging round to face her mother-in-law.

'Mum to you now! What a disgrace, she's making a right show of herself.'

'Why's that then, Maureen?' asked Nell, who had also joined them. Nell saw herself as having responsibility for the women of the square and didn't take kindly to outsiders passing judgement.

Maureen's eyebrow shot up, making her look like a plump little owl.

'You have to ask? Her with her husband barely cold.'

'Her husband killed himself the day after war was declared and I've sat with that woman while she's cried oceans into her fireside,' Nell snapped. 'She's worked her socks off this past four years to keep her nippers fed, so if she wants to have a bit of fun, good luck to her.'

'Thought you might take that stance, Nell,' Maureen said flintily.

'Meaning?'

'Well, it weren't long after your Pat died that you took up with that old tramp, was it? Got a thing for dossers, have you?'

'How fucking dare you!' Nell thundered, drawing nervous glances from round the square.

'Mum!' gasped Walter. 'Snowball ain't a tramp. He's a war hero who fell on hard times, and I think Mrs Gunn is the best judge of who to share her home with. Let's not forget how kind she's been to Esther and her mum.'

'Well, when your father died, I swore no man would ever take his place,' Maureen replied.

'You're getting right up my bugle,' Nell snapped.

'Just saying it as I see it.'

'How about you keep your trap shut for a change?' Nell replied, knuckles twitching.

'Shall we enjoy this lovely wedding?' interjected Esther's mum, Julia. 'Look at all that good food going to waste. Let's go and tuck in.'

'I intend to,' said Lou, who, along with the rest of the Lavender Girls, had eagerly been watching Nell and Maureen's showdown. 'Come on, girls, let's go and introduce ourselves to those nice boys while we're at it.'

'Ooh, before you go, girls, can you keep an eye out for the new girl who's starting at work tomorrow?' Esther called. 'She's called Patsy Jacks. I invited her today to meet us all informally, make her feel less nervous about starting. She's moved into number twelve.'

'Course we can darlin',' said Lou. 'What's she look . . .'

Lou's voice was drowned out by the scraping of a sash window up above. An elderly lady poked her head out of number 16.

'You'll never believe it, I just heard on the wireless, Mussolini's only been arrested.'

An enormous cheer rang out through the wedding party.

''Bout bloody time!' yelled Nell Gunn over the hubbub. 'Our lads got 'em on the run again.'

No one dared to hope this was an end to the war, or even close, but at the very least the news had broken the strained atmosphere, Esther thought in relief. She silently wondered how on earth she was going to live with someone as domineering as Maureen Smith. Mussolini had nothing on her mother-in-law.

From that moment on, the celebrations went into full throttle as the wedding party kicked up their heels and did what East Enders do best. The news of the Italian dictator's arrest, coupled with the syrupy summer sunshine, to say nothing of all the food, booze and the presence of so many good-looking men, had raised everyone's morale. Blind Eric, who usually played the piano in the Yardley canteen at dinner-time, had kindly agreed to perform at the wedding and was belting out an enthusiastic version of 'Knees Up Mother Brown'.

Esther weaved her way in and out of the crowds, hand in hand with Walter, making sure to chat to all her guests.

Maureen and Nell were now on separate sides of the square. Nell was sitting back expansively, the queen of the Shoot, ready to hammer out some gossip. Maureen, meanwhile, looked a little more relaxed after a few port and lemons and was offering an opinion to whoever would listen on the Allied advance and the future of the 'Eye-talian fleet', as she called it.

Esther caught sight of Lou and the rest of the Lavender Girls and laughed out loud. Lou was holding court with the Americans, draped over the piano, showing them her best Mae West impression with one of their cigars clamped between her red lips. Joycie, Joanie, Betty and Mavis were perched on the knees of four GIs in a fug of smoke.

'She's a case, our Lou,' Esther chuckled. 'Them GIs won't know what's hit them.'

'I still don't think Mrs Povey ought to have invited them,' Walter said. 'Honestly, Esther, to listen to them, you'd think they was all film stars from California; penny to a pound most of 'em are from a shack in Hicksville.'

Esther stared at him, dismayed, and on impulse, grabbed his hand and pulled him over to the allotment.

'Are you going to tell me what's wrong? You're not the

jealous type, so I know something else is bothering you. This isn't you, Walter.'

'Nothing is all,' he said, folding his arms.

Esther stroked the soft patch at the back of his neck, where his red hair curled in tendrils over his collar. Poor Walter, no matter how much brilliantine he put on his hair, his curls refused to lay flat.

'Really?' she said, playfully poking his ribs until, at last, a smile spread over his face. 'Only we're married now, and you can't keep secrets from your wife.'

'Oh, Esther,' he said, turning to look at her with a crooked smile. 'I don't mean to come over like an old grouse. It's only, I wanted so much more for my new wife than a spare room at me mum's and utility furniture. I should be out there helping to beat the Boche, sending you home enough money to keep a nice house and rising up through the ranks . . .'

'Oh Walter. Not this again. I didn't want to marry a war hero. Besides, you've already proved you're no coward. It's not like it's been plain sailing on the home front, has it?'

'No one's going to be pinning any medals on my chest for putting out a few incendiary bombs, are they?'

'The Blitz was more than that and you know it,' she replied. 'And had they invaded after Dunkirk, you and the Home Guard would have stopped them.'

'Would have, should have, could have . . . Hardly the stuff of family folklore, is it?'

A silence smothered the allotment. From the distance came the deep rumble of American laughter, followed by a whoop and a squeal.

'No, I have to face facts,' he said, scuffing at the earth with his shoe. 'There are two types in this world, their sort and mine.'

Esther gripped his face in her hands.

'Now you listen here, pal. I'll take your sort anytime – the brave, loyal and kind type, thank you very much.'

She pulled his face to hers and kissed him for a long time.

'I'm already so very proud of you, you silly berk.'

As she rested her forehead against his, the sun was beginning to bend to the horizon, and a soft mauve light deepened to indigo over the jumble of chimneys.

'Come on, we'd better get back to our own wedding,' said Walter, looking a little brighter. 'Before it's blackout time and gawd knows what mayhem will happen after dark.'

Esther stood up, dusting down the back of her dress as Little Irene came running up the path.

'Oh, there you are,' she said breathlessly. 'Come on, you've got to do a first dance and pretend to cut the cake before the light goes. It's quarter past ten. Blackout's at ten twenty-six. Oh, and I've met Patsy, the new girl.'

Out in the square, an enormous cheer went up as they emerged from the allotment.

'Oi oi, Walter my old son! Can't you keep yer grubby mitts off your new wife for one minute?' shouted a voice. 'You've left your hat in the potting shed.'

Walter's hand flew to his head before remembering he wasn't even wearing one.

'Cretin,' he mumbled under his breath.

Blushing, he led his wife into the middle of the square.

He whispered something in Blind Eric's ear before folding Esther in his arms.

As the smooth silky notes of 'When the Poppies Bloom Again' floated through the crowd, he murmured in her ear.

'This silly berk will always love you, Mrs Smith.'

Then he waltzed her round and round, until the white silk of her dress flew up and jasmine petals tumbled from her dark hair. Esther saw the faces all round her soften, as each and every one dreamt of a missing sweetheart and an end to this war.

'Love is all that matters,' he murmured, echoing their favourite saying.

And he was right. Who cared that there was no honeymoon, the cake was made of cardboard and married life would be two rooms at his mum's? It was a start.

As the music stopped, Snowball tapped his glass with a spoon and the crowd fell silent.

'Most of you know what this young woman has been through since she arrived here. I don't think there's too many of us could leave behind their home city, with their life in tatters, and find the guts to start all over again. From the moment we all met Esther, she has surprised us over and over, with her remarkable spirit . . .' Snowball's eyes misted over as he smiled at her. 'You are cunning, courageous and compassionate. And you deserve nothing less than magic!'

'Hear hear,' murmured the crowd.

'Will you all please join me in a toast to the bride and groom. They embody British courage, London pride, East End fortitude!'

As the crowd applauded and drinks were charged, Esther weaved her way towards Snowball, but as she did, an odd thing happened.

His smile slipped and froze. He was staring, dumbstruck, at the far side of the Shoot. Esther felt a peculiar sensation crawl through her as she looked in the direction of his gaze.

There, on the doorstep of number 12, stood Patsy Jacks, the Gunns' new neighbour and Yardley's latest recruit. Beside her was a woman Esther took to be her mother. An extraordinary looking creature she was, cloaked head-to-toe in black. Her arms were folded and her dress sleeves rolled up, revealing heavily tattooed forearms.

Only Esther saw it – the look that passed between her and Snowball as she stood on the doorstep. His mouth opened and his lips mumbled something Esther could not make out.

She glanced back, but with a rustle of her black skirts the woman was already gone, the door closing softly behind her.

Esther turned back and scanned the crowd, but Snowball seemed to have vanished too.

'Come on, girl, conga line time,' whooped Fat Lou, who was clinging to the back of a Yank. 'Bride up front, groom at the back. By order of the Yardley girls.'

Esther surrendered and found herself at the head of a giant conga line that snaked round the square and through the allotment. A sneaking feeling of disquiet crept up on her as the sun set over her wedding, and she resolved to speak to Snowball as soon as she could. Since the Blitz, she'd developed a sixth sense when it came to trouble.

2

Patsy

Queenie Jacks had learnt to smoke aged nine. She'd had her first tattoo at fifteen, was a regular on the music hall scene by eighteen and scandalised Poplar by eloping with a mixed-race sailor in her twenties.

Now, at fifty-one, Patsy's mum was a buttoned-up member of The Public Morality Council. But what had happened in between was something of a mystery.

'Mum,' mumbled Patsy, hopping about the kitchen with a piece of toast clamped between her lips while she tried to pull up her stockings. 'You really don't need to come into Yardley's today. I don't need you to speak for me.'

'I'll be the judge of that,' Queenie remarked, eyeing her only daughter through the steam from her teacup. Tea and nicotine seemed to be the only thing that passed her mother's lips these days. Patsy remembered when she had flesh on her bones, curves that her father used to run his hands over as he danced her round the kitchen to his favourite jazz records. Now her dad was dead and her mum had a face like a knife.

Patsy gripped the antimacassar on the back of the chair to steady herself.

'It's a very respectable place, Yardley's,' she persisted. 'I'm on a bursary scheme and everything. All the girls are nice sorts. S'pect I'll get a free chastity belt with me clocking-on card . . .'

Queenie's dark eyes thinned into narrow black slits.

'That's funny, 'cause I heard Yardley's has a reputation for being the local knocking shop. Did you see them lot cavorting about yesterday evening?'

'You mean Esther's wedding?'

'If you can call it that. Looked more like a Roman orgy from where I was standing. Girls whose morals have gone south like their knickers. Flaunting themselves with . . .' she shuddered, '. . . Americans.'

'I had a chat with a lot of them after you turned in, they seem a decent enough bunch,' Patsy protested. 'Why don't you go and introduce yourself to our new neighbour, Nell Gunn, once you've finished the unpacking? She's the auntie round these parts. Her fella runs the allotment in the middle of the square. Got a funny name . . . Snowman, or Snowball, summit like that.'

'That what he's calling himself these days, is it?'

Patsy had finished hoiking up her stockings and moved to the range to refresh her hat over the kettle. She glanced at her mother curiously through the steam.

'Do you know him, then?'

'Once upon a time.' Queenie mashed out her fag and moved to the kitchen window, which looked out over the square. Pale rays of sunshine filtered through the tape that criss-crossed the window. Patsy couldn't see her face, but her voice had its usual brittle edge.

'I knew it was a mistake moving here.' Her shoulders tensed and Patsy could see the tiny bones in her neck. Her mother was like a little bird. A little, hard, angry bird, pecking away at everything.

'Mum, we had no choice.'

Since an unexploded bomb had been discovered four doors up from their old home in Poplar, the council had relocated them here.

'At the very least, I should never have brought you and your brother back from the countryside.'

'Mum,' sighed Patsy. 'I'm seventeen! I was the oldest evacuee in Britain!'

'But you and your brother was safe in Suffolk.'

She felt a sharp pang of fear tug at her guts. If only.

Patsy wanted to yell at her mother, tell her the countryside wasn't all rose-covered cottages and ruddy-faced farmers' wives. Instead, she walked up behind her mother and laced her arms round her waist.

'Mum, me and Jimmy Junior, we missed you . . . And Dad.'

At the mention of their father, she felt Queenie's wiry body tense.

'I know nothing can ever bring Dad back.'

'He should never have been on them convoys, I told him not to enlist. He was too old.'

'Mum, you could never have stopped him.'

Patsy thought of her oh-so-handsome father. Tall, broad-shouldered, brown-skinned with laughing eyes, Jimmy Jacks – born to a white Irish mother and a West Indian father – was a man who turned heads wherever he went. There was prejudice, of course there was, even in Canning Town, which had the largest black community in Britain. But her dad had known how to handle them.

'It's safe here now,' Patsy went on. 'There's eight hundred kids coming back from the countryside every week I heard on the wireless.'

Queenie whirled round.

'It ain't safe here. It's never safe in the East End.'

Patsy sighed. 'That's as may be, Mum, but I can't stay cooped up in the countryside. I've got to start living and I'm starting today. At Yardley's.'

'Suit yourself,' she said. 'I'm coming too then. I need to pick up our new ration books from the town hall. Least the government's finally seen sense and put all clothing and food coupons under one cover.'

Of all the government departments her mother liked to grouse about, the Ministry of Food was the one that came in for the least criticism. She had a certain amount of grudging respect for Lord Woolton, the Minister of Food.

She picked up her string bag and some leaflets from the Public Morality Council. 'It'll also give me a chance to start handing out some of these.'

'Oh Mum, save the sermonising. Not today.'

'Jimmy!' Queenie yelled up the stairs, ignoring her daughter's words. 'I'm going out with our Patsy. You can play outside, but don't go outside the square if you know what's good for you. Bread and marge on the side.'

'What's for tea later, Mum?' he called. When it came to food, Patsy's brother was a forward planner.

'Air pie and windy pudding!' Queenie yelled back, before turning back to Patsy. 'What's he think this is? A bleedin' restaurant?'

'Don't be too hard on him, Mum,' Patsy said as Jimmy clattered down the stairs and went straight to Patsy, slipping his hand though hers.

'We were spoilt for food in the countryside weren't we, Jimmy?'

Instinctively, for Patsy had spent the past few years caring for Jimmy more like a son than a brother, she took out a comb from her bag and brushed it through the tuft of hair that always stuck up on the top of his head.

'I'll bring you back some pie and mash after work, Jimmy, would you like that?'

'With parsley liquor?' he asked, his little face lighting up.

'Yeah,' she laughed.

'You're the best, sis!' he whooped.

Over his back, Patsy saw a shadow pass over her mother's

face. Jealousy, pain and a darker emotion Patsy couldn't quite decipher coloured the air around her.

'It'll take a bit of time for Jimmy to adjust is all,' she said, untangling herself from his embrace.

Patsy had meant it as a peace offering, to soothe her mother's insecurity, but her face soured even more.

'Adjust? You've both been spoilt in the countryside. Well, the party's over now,' Queenie retorted, jamming a fag in her mouth and wrenching open the door.

Patsy pinned on her hat, kissed Jimmy goodbye and followed her mum out into the square. She breathed in the hot, dusty smell of East London, the foul drains, carbolic and asphalt. It was good to be back!

The morning after the night before, and the square looked a little jaded. It was still early, and the women of the Shoot were out, scrubbing their doorsteps, folding up trestle tables and cleaning up homemade confetti from the cobbles.

Living in the countryside, Patsy had been insulated from the reality of the bombings and it was still a shock to see the damage up close. She'd been back six months now, and she didn't think there'd ever be a time when she'd get used to the sights of smashed-up streets and roped-off rubble.

The Shoot in Stratford hadn't come off as badly as the neighbouring docks. She gazed round curiously at their new home. Tall, dilapidated slum housing, coated in centuries of industrial soot, all bowed inwards into a central square, in the centre of which stood a tiny church and Snowball's allotment. It was a funny little thing, a patch of green in and among all the dirt. The smoke from so many chimneys hung like a net in the windless air, smudging the horizon grey.

'The Shoot' referred to not just the square, but the complicated maze of streets, alleys and cold-water tenements that threaded off from it, all stewing in poverty. It kept outsiders out and insiders in, a place where lost tribes of the world could protect one another. A place where everyone knew everybody else's business and woe betide if you didn't play by the rules.

Mind you, Patsy mused, Hitler hadn't played by the rules when he started bombing helpless civilians. Number 26 and 28 were dust and the houses either side had no roofs, only a bit of tarpaulin slung over the top.

As they walked past the gate to the allotment, a young couple emerged, looking like they'd slept all night under the raspberry canes – a GI with his arm slung round a pretty young blonde woman in a red dress Patsy recognised from the wedding party. The wedding had officially wrapped up shortly after the blackout came into force, but clearly some revellers had carried on behind closed doors . . . or in the allotment.

'Morning ma'am,' the GI said, tipping his hat towards them. He took one look at Patsy and seemed to sober up instantly, his eyes slithering appreciatively up and down her body. He whistled under his breath. Patsy hadn't been so sheltered in the countryside not to know the powerful effect she had on men.

'And a *very* good morning to you, miss.' He grinned wolfishly at Patsy.

'You can fuck right off,' Queenie snapped, her face set in a hard mask of disapproval. 'Take your eyes off her. Some people might be taken in by you Yanks but I ain't one of 'em!'

'And you ought to know better,' she said to his companion. 'Whoring yourself for a pair of nylons. Yankee bag!'

Patsy groaned inwardly as they cut through Cat's Alley and out on to Angel Lane Market.

'She's no better than she ought,' Queenie muttered as they walked. 'No better at all.'

'Mum,' she hissed. 'That was so rude. Remember when people used to spit at Dad in the street.'

'That's different,' Queenie replied, threading her arm protectively through her daughter's as they weaved their way through the market stalls. 'Your father was a God-fearing man.'

Angel Lane was the true shopping heart of Stratford, a long, narrow, bending road, teeming with shops, barrows, life and commerce, a place where housewives could buy anything from cat's meat to corsets, so long as they were prepared to haggle.

There was Joseph Rosin the bakers for your fresh bread at number 17; you could get a haircut at number 84, Benjamin Phillips' hairdressers; then nip along to Gertrude's the milliners at number 52 if you wanted to pop a hat on. An ironmongers at number 127. A cat's meat seller at number 40. If it was fish you were after, there were three establishments to cater for your needs. And if you couldn't afford any of it, a Sally Army Hall at number 25 dished out free soup. Pies, pubs and pawnshops. Angel Lane had the lot.

'Reminds me of Chrisp Street,' Patsy said, determined to cheer her mother up. 'Smells the same anyhow.' She breathed in the smell of spices and overripe veg. 'Ooh, look, they've got an eel and pie shop. Oh, I love this city!'

Like the bomb damage, another thing Patsy couldn't wrap her head around since her return was the lack of women in the streets. Seemed like every other woman was employed in war work these days, since conscription for women had been introduced. Unemployment was at a record low, so they said, with women replacing men in the factories and workplaces, and making a bloody good fist of it as well.

Every market stallholder turned to stare as Patsy strode past. Since she had been away, there was no denying that Patsy's looks had ripened. She was as tall as her father had been, with a mass of long, wavy, black hair, a wide, sensuous mouth and her mother's arresting green eyes.

'Morning,' she smiled to a coster whose sign declared him to be the King of the Fruit Sellers.

'Where have you been all my life, darlin'?' he said, eyes flashing as he jogged backwards, alongside Patsy.

'Poplar . . .'

'I bet you are darlin'.'

Queenie glared at him as he slipped a bag of apples into the string bag she was carrying.

'For you, mother,' he said, without taking his eyes off Patsy, 'to sweeten you up so I can take your beautiful daughter out.'

Wordlessly Queenie took the bag of apples and rammed them hard into his privates. He doubled over in pain and surprise.

'Go near my daughter and I'll have your balls for a necktie.'

'Sorry,' Patsy mouthed to the speechless coster as she ran after her mother.

Queenie's mood hadn't improved by the time the tall wrought-iron gates of Yardley's hove into view. What an astonishing place Carpenters Road was. Seven different types of air rushed down the street, so the Lavender Girls had told her the previous evening, and looking at the diversity of industry, she could see why.

It was bedlam. Steam cranes crashed and screeched as they unloaded raw goods from the factories and on to barges on the canal that ran adjacent. Girls in turbans streamed past, giggling and smoking, others clung to the back of lorries as they trundled past, and over the top of it all was the incessant blasting of a dozen or so factory hooters.

'Half a mo, Mum,' said Patsy. 'I just wanna touch up my face before we go in.'

Nervously, she pulled out a compact from her handbag and inspected her flawless skin.

'Since when did you start trowelling that muck on your face?' Queenie demanded. 'Girls that wear make-up look like they play fast and loose.'

'Oh, Mum, everyone's wearing it these days. Didn't you

hear? Beauty's our duty now, ain't it? Good looks and good morale are close companions, or summit like that.'

'Codswollop!' Queenie announced. 'More bloody government propaganda.'

Patsy rolled her eyes as Queenie turned her back on her. She wondered if her mother still imagined her to be the thirteen-year-old she'd been when she'd left the East End at the outbreak of war.

'What the . . .?' Queenie muttered.

On the other side of the road, sealed off from the street by a roll of barbed wire, there was a scrubby patch of land filled with makeshift huts.

'Hello, Patsy, Mrs Jacks,' sang out a voice. Patsy immediately recognised the friendly-looking blonde from Esther's wedding party the night before.

'Oh hello, Lou.'

'Call me Fat Lou,' she said with a cheerful grin. 'Everyone else does.'

'What's that place over there?' asked Queenie, curiosity overcoming her usual rudeness.

'That? Oh, that's a prisoner of war camp,' said Lou. 'Used to be a wood yard until it burnt down in the summer of 1940. Now they use it to keep Jerry POWs in.'

A crowd of kids was assembled outside, shouting something unintelligible through the barbed wire.

'What are they saying?' Patsy asked.

Lou roared with laughter. '"We're winning" in German. Little sods. They're always over there giving them verbal.'

Patsy couldn't help but laugh.

'Well, I don't think it's very funny,' said Queenie. 'It's a disgrace in fact, keeping the enemy so close to decent folk.'

Lou glanced at Patsy and raised her eyebrow.

'I best clock on, they dock you fifteen if you're late. You'll want Miss Rayson's office, three floors up, next to the canteen. Ta-ta.'

'Thanks, Lou,' said Patsy. 'Hope I'll be working near you.'

Gripping her mother's arm, she guided her through the cobbled yard and the crush of girls all clamouring round the big clocking-in board in the entrance hall, and up to the personnel office.

Patsy knocked softly.

'Enter,' came a voice.

In the office, Miss Rose Rayson and Esther Smith smiled up expectantly.

'You've brought your mother, what a good idea,' said Miss Rayson. 'Please sit down.'

'Good morning,' said Patsy, determined to make a good impression. 'And congratulations again, Esther – I mean, Mrs Smith. You made a beautiful bride.'

'Thank you, sorry we didn't get much of a chance to chat last night,' she replied, staring curiously at Patsy's mother. 'I saw you on the doorstep to number twelve.'

'Yardley's have permitted Mrs Smith to take a honeymoon, but she refused, just in case you're wondering why she's here,' smiled Miss Rayson. 'Though I can't deny I'm not relieved. Mrs Smith started here as a service girl four years ago and, through diligence and hard work, has worked her way up to being a room supervisor. She's a crucial member of staff here at Carpenters Road. Virtually stopped the factory from burning to the ground during the Blitz.'

'Stop it,' said Esther, blushing. 'It wasn't just me and I'll take a honeymoon once the war's over. Besides, there's not much point, not when most of the beaches are behind barbed wire. Also, we are terrifically busy at the moment.'

She smiled brightly at Patsy. 'Which is why we're thrilled you're able to take up our new bursary scheme, named after one of the former workers tragically killed in the bombings—'

'Renee Gunn,' interrupted Patsy. 'Yes, I've heard all about her. She was our new neighbour's daughter.'

'Yes, Nell Gunn is a dear friend of mine,' smiled Esther. 'You'll love living down the Shoot, I miss it already.'

'Let's talk about the work, shall we?' said Queenie.

'Of course,' said Esther, looking taken aback. Patsy nudged her mother under the desk.

'Like I say, we are terribly busy, and we need willing hearts and busy hands to beat Hitler. Your name was suggested to us by Kamal Chunchie of the Coloured Men's Institute, of which I believe your late father was a member.'

'Yes, that's right, my father was killed in 1940. He was in the merchant navy, his convoy was hit by a German U-boat.'

'My deepest sympathies,' said Esther. 'My father died in 1940 too. Not in action, in a Jewish ghetto in Poland, so I understand your pain.'

'I'm so sorry to hear that,' Patsy replied. The two young women locked eyes and, in that brief moment of connection, Patsy knew she had an ally in Esther.

'We're very short-staffed here at Yardley's,' Miss Rayson went on. 'As well as losing half our workforce to the services, we are now undertaking emergency war work.'

'That's right,' said Esther. 'Our premises have been requisitioned by the Board of Trade, making as we are luxury items. The Limitation of Supplies Order has severely curtailed our output. There are half a dozen different firms now working out of our premises. As well as cosmetics and toiletries, two of our largest floors are given over to the manufacture of components for light aircraft, aircraft flare tubes, anti-radar devices and sea water purification tablets, so we can all do our bit—'

'To kill humans,' interrupted Queenie coldly.

'I beg your pardon?' replied Miss Rayson sharply.

'Mum, calm down,' Patsy muttered, before turning nervously to face her new supervisors.

'My mum is a conscientious objector,' Patsy explained to

the flabbergasted women on the other side of the desk. 'Since the first war.'

'A conchie!' gasped Miss Rayson.

'I dislike that term,' Queenie replied haughtily. 'I'm registered with a tribunal and have officially notified the authorities of my objection to the wholesale murder of a generation of our young men. Neither I, nor my daughter, will do anything that could lead directly to the death of another human being, and as such Patsy will not be helping to produce munitions or aircraft components.'

'I see,' said Miss Rayson, wearily removing her spectacles. 'At seventeen, Patsy is not yet old enough to fall within the scope of the extended Military Service Act, but as an employee of Yardley's—'

'She packs lipstick and soap only, or we're leaving,' said Queenie, making to stand up.

'Mrs Jacks, please sit down and we can talk about this like sensible adults,' urged Esther.

'Please, Mum, do as Mrs Smith says,' begged Patsy. 'I really want this job.'

Personally, Patsy didn't count herself as a conchie, not now or ever, but that was another row for another time. She needed this job, if only to get away from her mother.

'We'll need Patsy to undertake factory civil defence duties, like every other employee here, but we have enough work on the lipstick and soap belts to occupy her,' said Miss Rayson, sensing they had reached an impasse. 'I'll keep a note of your objections on record.'

'Make sure you do,' said Queenie, rising up in a rustle of black and tapping a long finger down on the desk. 'It's lipsticks only, not bullets for my girl.'

She eyed them both.

'Or you'll have Queenie Jacks to answer to. And trust me, you don't want to have a row with me.'

With that, Patsy's mother swept from the room. The poisonous odour of mothballs lingered in her wake. Patsy slumped back in her seat and waited until she heard her footsteps fade.

'I'm so sorry about me mum, she's worse than the Gestapo when she gets going,' she joked weakly.

'Clearly,' said Miss Rayson, looking shell shocked. 'She certainly has robust opinions. My personal opinion of conchies is that the only conscience they have is directed at saving their own skin. I do wish you'd informed us of this before now, Miss Jacks.'

'I'm so sorry, Miss Rayson, but I promise to work hard. You won't regret it. I'll even do all the earlies if you like.'

Fat Lou had warned her to try and not get saddled with the 5 a.m. until 1 p.m. early shifts, but she could see she needed to curry favour.

'Very well,' sighed Miss Rayson. 'But I'm going to insist you take part in our fundraising drives for Wings for Victory. All of Stratford's doing its best to raise money to fund new Spitfires and Lancaster Bombers for the RAF, as well as our efforts for the Red Cross food parcels for prisoners of war. Saving here is second only to production.'

'That's right,' agreed Esther. 'Our motto here at Yardley is "Beauty from Order Springs".'

'Beauty is playing an important role in this war, as I'm sure you're aware, Miss Jacks. Beauty is a woman's duty and we wholeheartedly believe that now, of all times, we need to defend the little luxuries. It's a woman's right to want to make the best of her assets, to feel beautiful when she is worn and tired.'

Try telling her mother that, Patsy thought grimly.

'Absolutely,' she said instead, smiling brightly. 'I'm a huge fan of Yardley's, I've always wanted to work here, right from when I was a nipper. Used to get the bus from Poplar all the way to Stratford when I was younger, just so I could smell the lavender and roses.'

'Yes, our lavender-scented air is famous locally,' said Miss Rayson. 'When the air's blowing the right way, that is.'

'Well you can start now,' Esther smiled, handing her a white tunic and turban. 'Lou Button will be your chargehand in the soap room. I'll take you down there.'

Patsy reached the door. 'Miss Jacks,' called Miss Rayson. 'You'll need your clocking-in cards. Please don't make me regret your appointment.'

Despite being a chargehand, Lou was giving it both barrels down on the soap floor. Patsy had changed into her white overalls and had just about managed to pile her long dark hair under a white turban, before Esther had led her down to the ground floor. As the door swung open, the terrific heat and smell of lavender hit her first, then the deafening racket of machines and singing.

'*Fuck 'em all, fuck 'em all . . .*'

It was the most astonishing sight she had ever seen. Teams of girls, all in white, sitting at conveyor belts as bars of soap sailed past, singing as they worked.

'*All the long and the short and the tall . . .*'

'I've never heard George Formby sung that way before,' Patsy laughed as Esther led her past the machines.

'Sorry, the language can be a little colourful.'

'No need to apologise to me, Mrs Smith,' Patsy grinned, trying to gather her senses as she gazed about the place. 'Don't you mind them singing though?'

'No,' Esther grinned, 'makes them work faster!'

The room was huge, filled with great clanking machines with conveyor belts attached. At the end of each belt was a desk where a girl in an orange tunic sat, checking over the work and keeping an eye on production.

'They're the chargehands,' Esther explained. 'Lou, who I think you've already met, will be yours.'

Outside the windows flowed a stagnant-looking canal, known locally as the Cut. The same boys Patsy had seen earlier taunting the POWs were fishing something out of its foul, poisonous depths.

'The brickie kids,' said Esther. 'Don't be surprised if you see them swimming naked in it later.'

A small pedestrian bridge led over the canal to a large factory on the other side of the Cut, and was that . . .

'Yes, maggots,' said Esther, following her gaze over the Cut to where streams of maggots wriggled and glistened in the gutter outside the firm. 'That's a fishmeal manufacturer. And that one there,' she said, gesturing to their other neighbour, 'is Hunt's the soapmakers. It can get terrifically smelly when they boil up the bones, but I expect you're used to the smells of East London, Miss Jacks.'

Esther showed her round the room, pointing out the huge, stainless steel vats churning up masses of creamy liquid. As they walked, the smells became overpowering. Patsy held a hand to her nose.

'That's the soap,' Esther grinned. 'Doesn't smell too good until we add the perfume. Don't worry, you'll get used to it. Then you'll hardly notice it.'

Patsy doubted that.

'Yardley's Old English Lavender Soap is our most popular,' Esther went on. 'We used to do so many other ranges, but obviously war has brought a halt to that. We only produce a fraction of what we used to.' She sighed, gesturing to a table where teams of girls were parcelling up the soap.

'Waxed containers now for everything, instead of metal and tin. We've seen so many changes over the past four years. Next door was the talcum powder room, but that's the factory air-raid shelter now. Upstairs was all creams and brilliantines, but that's now shared with aircraft components. Top floor was perfume and now that's shared with Crookes Laboratories. A lot of our production has been moved to Borehamwood for safety purposes. Or Boreham Stiff as the girls call it.'

Esther carried on giving Patsy the rundown of changes war had wrought upon the factory, but Patsy wasn't listening.

'What's that?' she asked, looking down into the nearest soap machine.

The creamy white soap that was cooking up was streaked with red and tufty bits of what looked like hair.

'Not again,' Esther grimaced, slamming her hand down on a button that immediately stopped the machinery.

'Lou, get one of the service girls to fetch an engineer. We've got a Jerry in the machine.'

'A Jerry?' queried Patsy, half wondering if one hadn't made their way over from the POW camp and toppled into the machine.

'Rat. A dirty great big rat,' said a loud voice behind her.

Lou Button had joined them and was grinning broadly as she stared down into the machine.

'We call 'em Jerries for obvious reasons. Looks like a big 'un too. Curse of being next to the canal, they sneak in here all the time during the summer.'

'Lou, can I leave Miss Jacks in your capable hands? I have work to tend to.'

'Of course.' Lou slung her arm around Patsy, and led her towards her section. 'We're a friendly bunch down here in Stink Bomb Alley, so long as you pull your weight and don't come over too kippers and curtains.'

Patsy shook her head, desperate to fit in. 'I may've lived in Suffolk for the past four years, but I'm a cockney all right, Lou.'

They reached the conveyor belt and Patsy could feel herself being scrutinised by half a dozen pairs of curious eyes.

''Ere. You ain't a conchie, are yer? 'Cause rumour has it your mum is,' piped up the very same blonde Patsy had seen staggering out of the allotment that morning with a GI.

'God, no!' she gasped. 'I ain't on the conscientious! But me mum is and she'll have a blue fit if I do war work. Personally, I couldn't give a monkeys what work I do, so long as I'm earning.'

'In that case, I reckons as how your face'll fit,' Lou declared.

Patsy nodded, trying to forget about her mum's mortifying behaviour.

'Cheer up, sausage,' grinned Lou, patting her stool on the conveyor belt. 'You're a Lavender Girl now.'

A man walked past, carrying a box containing the torso of a dismembered rat, which he gleefully waved under their noses.

'Oh, fuck off, Bert,' Lou laughed, cheerfully punching him on the arm. Suddenly the room seemed to close around Patsy. It could've been the heat, the fecund smells or the sight of the rat, but in that moment, she knew she was going to be sick.

'Out those doors, turn left,' Lou said, spotting her expression.

Patsy made it just in time. After she'd emptied the contents of her stomach, she felt rather fragile and stood for a full minute running her wrists under cold water. She hoped Esther was right and she would get used to it. Not that she had much choice.

With trembling fingers, she pulled down the roller towel and dried her hands. Just above someone had scratched something into the painted brickwork.

*Long and thin slips right in
But short and thick does the trick.*

Patsy raised an eyebrow. Yardley was going to be a baptism of fire.

3

Lou

The morning crawled by, the smell of sweat mingling with the stench of sweet lavender and stale booze. Despite the copious amounts of alcohol consumed at last night's wedding, and the late night, the girls had all managed to clock in on time, but it was a relief when the bell rang for the mid-morning tea break and the machines shut down with a shudder. Usually, the Lavender Girls stayed on the floor and tucked into crusty dripping-filled rolls brought round by a tea lady, but it was so hot, no one had much of an appetite, and everyone headed outside to sit on the bridge by the Cut for a quick puff with their morning cuppa.

As they sat swinging their legs over the filthy canal water, smoking roll-ups and drinking tea from enamel mugs, Lou gazed curiously at the new girl. She was more than beautiful; she was a smasher. That body! The face, the smouldering green eyes . . . She oughtn't have been working in a factory, Lou thought, she should be in Hollywood!

'I don't mean to be rude like,' Joanie said. 'But did your dad have a touch of darkie?'

'Joanie!' Lou exclaimed.

'What? I'm not being rude, I promise, just curious.'

'S'right,' Patsy replied. 'Yes, he's, sorry he *was*, half-caste. His dad was from Antigua and his mum Irish, but he was born here. Met my mum. She's white, and well, here I am, me and my little brother, Jimmy.'

'You from Draft Board Alley then?' Mavis asked her.

Patsy laughed. 'Nah, not Canning Town, Poplar.'

'So where you been working before now?' asked Betty.

'I only come back six months ago, I was evacuated out to the sticks.'

'What all this time, since the start of war?' Joanie gaped.

Patsy rolled her eyes. 'My mum's overprotective.'

'Mine too,' said Mavis, 'except she wouldn't let me go. Reckons as how if we was going to die, we should all die together, which in the finish I'm not sure how I feel about.'

'You must've had plenty of fellas sniffing round you in the countryside, Patsy,' said Betty. 'My sister's in the Land Army. She says every haystack has a couple humping behind it.'

The girls fell about.

'Betty,' Lou sighed.

'What? I'm interested is all. Fresh air makes people randy, stands to reason blokes'd be queuing up to date Patsy.'

Patsy smiled tightly. 'Not really.'

'But you're beautiful,' breathed Little Irene. 'You must've been standing in the giants line when they was handing out looks!'

'Shut up,' Joanie laughed, getting her in a headlock. 'She'll think you're one of them women what love other women.'

'I think you mean a lesbian, Joanie,' Lou replied, flicking her fag butt in the canal.

'Don't worry,' joked Patsy with an insouciant grin. 'She ain't my type.'

Everyone laughed and Lou could tell the new girl was going to fit in fine. It wasn't easy being an outsider around such a mouthy, opinionated bunch, but Patsy could hold her own. By the looks of her mother, she'd clearly been raised not to take any shit.

At the thought of mothers, Lou felt her heart sag. She must remember to go home on her dinner break.

'Anyway, there's no need for women to resort to other women,' said Joanie. 'There's a dance on tonight, at the town hall. Johnnie's invited all of us to join his unit there. Meet at the Two Puddings first for a sharpener, then head to the dance. Who's coming? He's promised to teach me the jitterbug.'

'Looks like you was doing the horizontal jitterbug last night,' Mavis teased.

'We fell asleep,' Joanie protested, blushing. 'I didn't let him cross the dotted line. I ain't stupid.'

'But you'll all come this evening, won't you?' Joanie persisted. 'I promised him I'd bring all me pals. They've only got another few days left of their leave.'

Betty stifled a yawn. 'Think I'll be ready for my bed by clocking-off.' Everyone nodded.

'They're bringing nylons,' Joanie added. 'And chocolate!'

'Why didn't you say?' Betty laughed.

'What time do you want us?' Little Irene asked.

'Will you come, Patsy?' asked Joanie, mashing out her fag on the cobbles.

'Not sure I'll get it past me mum.'

'Tell her you're joining that new sewing circle the WVS are running in the evenings on the Barking Road. They're knitting comforts for the troops,' said Mavis.

'Comforts for the troops,' snorted Little Irene. 'It's not even a giant whopper when you put it that way.'

'I'll try,' Patsy laughed.

'What about you, Fat Lou?' asked Joanie, poking her in the ribs. 'Though we're gonna have to start calling you Skinny Lou if you keep losing weight.'

Lou rolled her eyes. 'Behave. I don't think I can; I think I've got a date tonight.'

'You never have, why didn't you say, you saucy cow?' squealed Joycie.

The girls all rounded on her, eyes sparkling in the bright summer sun. The end-of-tea-break bell sounded.

'Saved by the bell,' Lou joked, heaving herself up and dusting down her orange overalls.

'No more jawing, let's get back to work.'

The rest of the morning passed by in a hot blur. When dinner break came along, Lou was out the factory gates like a greyhound out the traps.

As she pegged it past the factories of Carpenters Road, back in the direction of home, she wondered why she'd lied to the girls about having a date that evening. She took a shortcut past the men's urinal and cut through the roped-off remains of a bombsite, before rounding the corner into the row of terraced houses along Gibbins Road. She glanced at her watch. Four minutes flat. A record. No wonder she was losing weight.

She pushed open the door and a sharp oniony odour hit her, making her eyes smart. The stagnant air in the passage was dim, at odds with the dazzling summer light outside.

She could tell already her mum, Flo, was having one of those days. The step hadn't been scrubbed, and the air smelt stale. It had rained in the evening and the women had put their aspidistras out on the pavement to give them a wash. In fact, the women of the neighbourhood had been busy all morning. In backyards all along Gibbins Road, clean sheets flapped in the breeze and steam rose from dolly tubs. All except her backyard.

This. This was why she had lied about an imaginary date, why she wouldn't be going out dancing, not this evening, nor any other evening for that matter. Her mum was sick, kidney disease the doctor had told her, but it wasn't just that crushing the life out of her.

Lou painted on an artificial smile.

'Cooey, Mummy, I'm home.'

'In here, darling,' called back a voice.

She found her mum sitting in an easy chair by the kitchen fireside. As soon as Lou walked in, she struggled to get to her feet.

'Hello, Tin Ribs, what you doing home?'

Tin Ribs was the daft name her mum had given her when she was a skinny rake of a kid. The nickname no longer suited, but Flo Button had clung to it out of sentimentality, Lou supposed. She'd clung to a lot of things out of a sense of duty to the past; her good-for-nothing husband, chiefly.

'Don't get up, Mum. You sit and rest. It's Monday, so I thought I'd nip home and make a start on the washing.'

She kissed her on the head before heading straight out into the yard to make a start on scrubbing the sheets she'd stripped off the beds that morning.

As the eldest of six girls, Lou's childhood had been spent cradling bawling infants. Now twenty-one, for as long as she could remember, she was more of a mother than a sister to the Button brood. She'd learnt to whiten the step, make a stew, fetch the coal in the pram and keep toddlers away from the fire.

It was Lou to whom her mother turned for comfort when she realised another nipper was on the way. Lou whose eighteen shillings a week from Yardley kept the family going. Lou who stood up to the spiteful bastard her mother had had the misfortune to marry.

Honest John – of all the ridiculous nicknames! Outside number 38 Gibbins Road, her father was a respectable pillar of society. Former mayor of East Ham back in 1935, now he worked in the accounts department of the local council. In '39, he'd even been awarded the Honorary Freedom of the Borough. Her mother didn't even have the freedom to walk to the end of the road.

Just the thought of him curdled Lou's insides. As she fed the sopping wet sheets through the heavy mangle, the raw blister on her finger threatening to burst, Lou imagined it was him she was squeezing through the ringer. That would stop him treating her mother like some sort of breeding cow.

'Leave it there, love, I'll peg it out in a bit.' Her mother's voice drifted out into the backyard from the scullery.

'No, it's all right, Mum, I'll do it.'

Lou pegged out the sheets, nice and white after a good scrubbing in the dolly tub. If there was one thing Lou could do, it was scrub.

Ducking under the forest of gently swaying linen, she found her mother up by the stove, engulfed in clouds of steam, stirring something over the pot. She'd made it out of her chair and was pretending not to be in pain.

Lou wanted to scream out loud. Yardley was busy telling the nation's women to 'put your best face forward'. She and her mother had been doing nothing but that for years. Hell, she'd almost made it into an art form. Fat Lou. The factory clown, always good for a giggle. She'd perfected the act of walking with a swagger, made a character of herself to hide behind. God, it was tiring pretending to be someone you weren't.

'How many life cycles that stew been through?' Lou joked.

Her mum cocked her head, pretending to count.

'I think I started it before the war broke out.'

The two women burst into laughter, and Lou lit up two cigarettes and patted the kitchen chair.

'Come and have a tickler, Mum.'

The way they behaved together was more like two sisters than mother and daughter.

'Where are the girls?' Lou asked.

'School, or playing out front. Seen this?' remarked her mother, pushing the latest copy of the *Stratford Express* under her nose.

'The Battle of the Babies Has Been Won,' Lou said, reading the headline out loud.

'Apparently for the first time since war's began, the birth rate has risen and the maternity ward of St Mary's has reopened,' Flo said.

'I don't think the birth rate has ever gone down round here,' Lou remarked, drawing smoke into her lungs. Gibbins Road was known locally as Incubator Alley. The sounds of a skipping chant drifted in through the open window, as well as the thud of a ball on the cobbles.

The article was accompanied by a photograph of proud mothers standing outside the hospital in front of a semicircle of Silver Cross prams, stuffed with bonny babies.

'And how many of them have a Yank for a daddy, I wonder?' Lou smirked.

'Louise,' scolded her mum, tapping her on the hand. 'Don't be so cynical.'

'No lie,' she replied. 'Them Yanks are everywhere. Joanie at work is having a bit of fun with one now. Wants us all to meet the rest of his unit at some dance this evening.' She flicked her ash into the ashtray. 'Like I wanna do that!'

'Oh, love, you should go,' urged Flo. 'Do you good to have a bit of a fun.'

'Mummy, I've only got through half that washing, I'll need to do the rest when I get home. Plus, I said I'd help our Betsy with her homework.'

'Don't worry about that, my darlin', Mrs Taylor from five doors up has offered to run some stuff up the bag wash for me. Please love, you must go,' she urged. 'Your father'll help Betsy with her homework if he's back from work on time.'

Lou raised one eyebrow.

'He's very busy in the office,' Flo replied loyally. 'But honestly, love, we're all under control here. You deserve to let your hair down.'

Lou stared at her mum. There was a feverishness about her, a strange look in her eye she recognised from . . .

'Oh Mummy, you're not. Please tell me it ain't true.'

Flo Button sighed and folded away the photo of all those babies in their prams.

'You always did know me better than I know myself.'

'So you're carrying?'

She nodded.

'Are you sure, Mummy?' Lou asked.

Flo tapped her tummy.

'Trust me, I know the signs, love.'

Lou felt mute with frustration and anger.

'I'm so sorry, love,' her mum said, reaching for another cigarette. 'What can I say? He's only got to hang his trousers up and I'm caught.'

Tight fingers of rage clamped themselves quite suddenly round Lou's neck.

'More like he forced you.'

'Please, love,' said her mum, her hands shaking as she tried to light her cigarette.

'Sorry, Mum,' Lou said immediately, desperately trying to calm herself down, 'but you remember what the doctor said. You're too frail to have another baby.'

That wasn't what he said. What he'd said, quite explicitly, was that another birth would more than likely kill her.

'It's me who should be apologising.' Flo blew the smoke out on one big sigh. 'I know how this will affect you. Elsie will have to move in with you and our Lily and Poppy.'

'Forget it, I've always slept with someone's feet in my face,' Lou joked weakly, trying to quell the silent scream that was building inside her.

'Oh Tin Ribs, I always wanted something better for you than this.' Flo cast her eye despairingly around their home, with its damp washing steaming over the fireguard, and the remnants of a five-day stew. 'This place and life in the factory. You got brains . . . Not like me. I should've fought for you to stay at that school, should have dug my heels in, but I weren't strong enough.'

At the mention of school, Lou felt a tears gathering, but she forced them back to where they had come from. She didn't want her mum to ever see how much she grieved for the loss of her place at grammar school. But behind closed doors, she wept for what might have been. Her father had pulled her out after one year, saying they needed her income, but despite working all the hours at Yardley's for the past five years, she was hard-pressed to say where her wages went.

Lou stared at the worn lino, the cracked windows shaken out of their frames by the Blitz. Not one thing in this house was new. Even the flies stuck to the ginger strip of flypaper hanging from the bare bulb were last summer's.

That bastard hadn't just robbed her of an education; he'd stolen her future.

'Why don't you leave him, Mum?'

'Oh, love, and where would I go?'

Lou lapsed into silence.

'But look, don't worry, I'll sort it.' Flo lowered her voice. 'I reckon it's still early days. Mrs Taylor, who's popping over later – she doesn't just run stuff up the bag wash, if you catch my drift. She's, er . . . handy.'

Silence. Then the penny dropped.

'Oh Mum, no . . . *No, no, no*! Don't you dare! Remember all that trouble with Nell Gunn before the Blitz? 'Sides, the old man'll cut up rough if he finds out.'

Lou stared out the window. Her mother had been so pretty. Hair as rich red as brandy and skin the colour of cream. All the life and joy in the world poured out of her once. She was such a caring woman too. She'd give the rings off her fingers for any woman in need. The kind of woman who bought broken biscuits for all the nippers in the street, warmed Lou's nightie by the fire so it was toasty for bedtime and made up stories in which Lou was always the queen of the castle.

Now, she was ravaged, her breasts sucked dry, her kidneys failing. Her life had been one long round of childbearing, child rearing, worry, hunger, exhaustion, cold, poverty and now sickness.

'I don't see as how I've got a choice, love.'

'Mum, we'll sort it, together. I'll come with you to see the doctor tomorrow. I'll get the morning off work somehow. We'll take his advice. Just don't do anything stupid, you must promise me.'

Lou mashed out her mother's cigarette and took her puffy fingers in hers. In the distance, she heard the hooter go for the end of the dinner break.

'Only if you promise me to go out to this dance this evening,' Flo said.

She turned and pulled something from the drawer behind her and slid it over the tabletop.

'I was saving these for your birthday, but why wait?'

It was a pair of fine Ballito silk stockings. Rarer than chocolate, coal or hen's teeth. Flo kicked the cupboard door shut on her tallyman's secrets.

'Don't tell your father about that drawer.'

Lou smiled. Her mother might have been downtrodden, but she still had her crafty ways. Mind you, they could do with a separate cupboard for the pawnshop secrets, and another for the secret list of items on tick down the corner shop. There weren't enough cupboards in Stratford for the Button family secrets.

'Here, do you remember when the tallyman used to knock when I was little?' Lou asked.

Flo's body rocked with laughter.

'Yeah, and you used to answer and say: "Mum says to say she's not in right now."'

Lou shook her head.

'Dropped you right in it, didn't I?'

'You've made up for it since. Now about this dance . . .'

'All right, Mummy. I'll go this evening, so long as you promise to come to the doc's with me tomorrow.'

Flo nodded.

'Cross my heart.' She licked her finger, touched her chest and gave a thin smile. Satisfied, Lou stood up and reached for her bag. Her mother stood too, her ankles painfully swollen as she made her way unsteadily to her easy chair.

Lou had just reached the door when Flo called her back.

'Love you, Tin Ribs,' she whispered.

Her mother looked tired, her eyes were already closing. The light from the window made a halo of her fine-spun grey hair. She was so frail. Lou clicked her eyes and photographed her, captured her image in her mind's eye forever.

She gazed at the woman whose whole life was devoted to her kids, who never stopped giving, and realised she loved her with a pang so fierce, it was like a pain.

'Love you too, Mummy.'

Lou closed the door softly behind her and made her way back to the factory.

4

Esther

Later that afternoon, Miss Rayson attempted to make her voice heard over the din of demob-happy girls, most of whom were busy comparing notes over what frock they were planning to wear for the dance that evening. A blowsy soup of smells, Evening in Paris and other black market fragrances, hung over the scent of lavender and boiling bones.

'Stop jawing!' Esther screamed and a silence fell over the soap room.

'Yes, well thank you, Mrs Smith,' Miss Rayson murmured. 'I wanted to let you know that we have a very important visitor to Yardley's tomorrow.'

'Ooh, who is it? Someone dishy, I hope. I got me eye on Errol Flynn,' piped up Little Irene.

'Or is it an actress?' Betty asked. 'Rumour has it Gracie Fields is gonna be at the Theatre Royal soon. I prefer Betty Grable, or better yet, Marlene Dietrich.'

'Behave, as if Marlene Dietrich's gonna be swanking her way up Angel Lane Market anytime soon!' Joanie scoffed.

Esther laughed. The Lavender Girls had a fixation on Hollywood stars that bordered on obsession, and they copied everything from their hair to their make-up.

Garbo. Dietrich. Harlow. These women were their gods, offering them the holy grail of glamour and a means of changing their identity. When Veronica Lake changed her trademark peek-a-boo hairstyle last year to a more sensible pageboy roll, they'd all followed suit.

Copies of their beauty bible *Vogue* and the pre-war magazine *Film Fashionland* often made their way through thirty or more pairs of hands, as the girls scrutinised the pages for the latest beauty dodges and insights into the luxury lifestyles of their favourite actresses.

Everyone treasured each available drop of scent and make-up. *Woman's Weekly* promoted the natural look and advocated the use of Elizabeth Arden's Burnt Sugar, a pretty coral which was supposed to go well with khaki. But the Lavender Girls would give their back teeth for a tube of spanking vermilion red lippie, preferably Tangee, or one of the new wartime shades like Homefront Ammunition or Regimental Red.

Who wanted safe pink when you could have bold, punchy, glamorous red?

'I'm afraid Miss Dietrich isn't available, Betty,' Miss Rayson said. 'It's Sir Stafford Cripps.'

Stony silence.

'Minister of Aircraft Production. He wants to make a speech and thank all the workers who have helped make aircraft components.'

'A good Labour man he is and a damn good rival for Churchill,' said Lou. 'I think it's bloody marvellous he's prepared to come here in person.'

'If you say so, Lou,' sniffed Betty. 'I'd still have preferred Marlene Dietrich.'

'Miss Rayson, mind if I clock off?' Esther asked. 'Only Snowball's getting some sort of award at the allotment soon, and I promised my mum and Nell I'd be there to support him.'

'Of course, dear.'

'You coming to the dance later?' Lou asked.

'I thought you weren't going?' Esther replied.

'Me mum's changed my mind.'

'Oh, I'd love to go too, but I'm an old married woman now, I'd only cramp your style.'

'More like your mother-in-law wants you at home under lock and key,' Lou laughed.

Esther grimaced. There was more truth in Lou's joke than she knew. Maureen had been horrified when she'd told her she wouldn't be giving up her job at Yardley's, and was only pacified when she said she'd leave as soon as the war was over.

'Oh, Lou, I meant to give this to you earlier.' She pulled a brown envelope from her bag.

'This is Yardley's contribution towards the Wings for Victory fund. Is your dad still the borough trustee?'

Lou nodded.

'Lovely, would you mind giving him this?' she asked, handing her the envelope. 'Be careful with it. There's quite a bit of cash in there.'

'Guard it with me life,' Lou winked.

'Thanks, Lou. You're a pal. Have fun later.'

As Esther weaved her way through the Carpenters Road clocking-off crowd, she felt a seed of doubt take hold. Walter had sided with his mum suggesting that she should give up work, which had stunned Esther. They'd worked side by side at Yardley's for the past four years. He, of all people, knew what this place meant to her; how thrilled she'd been when she'd been promoted to room supervisor. It was only work that had stopped her from going completely doolally after her father's death. That and Walter of course. The last thing she needed was her new husband going all macho on her now.

As she slipped through Reeves Alley and into the Shoot, she spotted Snowball and smiled. Mild-mannered and introverted, Snowball was at his happiest knee-deep in compost, tending to his beloved vegetables. Now, surrounded by officials in suits, he looked uncomfortable, and was plucking the starched collar of his shirt.

'Oh, here you are, love,' said Nell Gunn, who was stood beside Esther's mother.

'Doesn't he look smart?' Esther beamed, slipping her arms through Nell's and Julia's.

'Starched that shirt meself and took up the hems on some of Pat's old trousers,' Nell remarked. 'Fit him lovely, don't they?'

'Hush. They're starting,' said Julia.

'It gives me enormous pleasure to award this certificate of merit today,' explained the official, handing Snowball a fancy embossed certificate.

'Inspector from the Ministry of Agriculture,' whispered Nell.

'This community allotment, which produces food all year round, does a tremendous job of feeding families. There are officially two thousand and eighty-six allotments in West Ham now, but we at the Ministry are particularly impressed with the imagination and resourcefulness of this particular plot.

'Fresh vegetables are plucked from the soil and handed straight into the back door of this church hall, where I understand local women run a communal cost-price restaurant that helps feed the entire neighbourhood. Ingenious. The savings involved, financially, and in fuel and food wastage by feeding families collectively, are huge.'

'The grub's pretty good an' all!' called Nell. 'If I do say so myself.'

The inspector laughed.

'I dare say. Would you like to give me a tour?'

The inspector, followed by half the women of the Shoot, squeezed into the tiny kitchen at the back of the church hall.

'Soups, stews, puddings . . . You name it, we cook it here,' remarked Nell, grinning as a photographer from the *Stratford Express* trailed after them taking pictures.

'The oven and chimneys were blasted during the bombings,' said Julia. 'But Snowball collected old drainpipes, caulked them together with dough and mended them, then we applied for a catering licence from the town hall. We're nowhere near on the scale of the British Restaurants popping up everywhere, but we do our bit.'

'I should say,' remarked Nell. 'Where else you gonna get a decent, fresh, home-cooked meal, like pea soup and a roll, followed by corn beef hash, a sweet and a cup of tea for a shilling?'

She patted the side of her turban with mock pride.

'No Blitz broth here, thank you very much.'

'You're making my mouth water,' laughed the inspector.

'We've even applied for a licence from the Ministry of Health to turn the other side of the church hall into an official wartime day nursery,' said Julia. 'Nell looks after the children of the neighbourhood in her own home while the women go out to do war work, but now so many are working we could use some extra space for children to play.'

'What do you do with any glut of seasonal vegetables?' the inspector asked, pointing to some spare lettuces and cucumbers stored in the cool, dry passage.

'Snowball sells the surplus and donates the proceeds to the Red Cross prisoner of war food parcels funds,' Julia replied. 'There are lots of women in the Shoot whose husbands are POWs abroad, so it helps to know we're feeding them too.'

The inspector shook his head in admiration and clamped an arm around Snowball, who so far hadn't managed to get a word in edgeways.

'Snowball's beating the Squander Bug,' he declared, grinning as the photographer's flashbulb popped. 'Tell your editor he can have that one.'

'Oh, please don't use that headline,' Snowball protested. 'It's a group effort.'

They all wandered back outside, where cold lemonade and fresh mint was being served in the allotment.

'I say, I've a friend on the council in West Ham who tells me they're opening a hostel in Loughton for aged homeless men and women soon,' the inspector said to Snowball. 'They're concentrating on the welfare of the older people in the borough, not just those made homeless by bombs either. About time, shame it took the Blitz to make them realise it was necessary.'

He lowered his voice.

'Hope you don't think I'm speaking out of turn, old chap, but I understood you once slept rough?'

'Yes,' Snowball replied quietly. 'Until Mrs Gunn gave me sanctuary.'

'He'd lost his way and all's I did was show him back,' Nell replied, reaching over and squeezing his hand.

Esther felt a sudden lump in her throat. She'd done more than that. Losing her daughter and husband in the most brutal way imaginable would be enough to tip most women over the edge, but in her loneliness and grief, Nell had reached out to the one person most people avoided. She had always told Esther that down the Shoot, everyone mattered and that, in times of trouble, neighbourhoods could only survive by pulling together. Nell Gunn may have come over rough and ready, but beneath that apron, she was solid gold.

'How about we get you on the committee for the hostel, come and tell us what you think would work?' the inspector went on, smiling at Snowball and Nell. 'Perhaps you could even get the hostel to start their own Dig for Victory allotment?'

'That's a smashing idea,' Esther enthused. 'Snowball, you'd be terrific at that.'

'Oh . . . I . . . I don't know,' Snowball mumbled. 'I'm very busy with this allotment.'

'Tell your pal at the council he'll do it,' Nell remarked, jutting her chin out. 'It's about bloody time lessons were learnt over the welfare of decent folk round these parts.'

'I understand, Mrs Gunn, and trust me, I share your anger. We were slow to respond to the need for shelters and rest centres, but lessons *have* been learnt. The health and welfare of the working classes are improving daily, thanks to the Citizens Advice Bureau, the War Damage Bureau, British Restaurants and War Nurseries, to name but a few. Shelters have been reinforced, renovated and kitted out with bunks, canteens and entertainment. There's more money flowing into the borough than ever before, thanks to our friends overseas, and we all have great hopes for the plans laid out in the Beveridge Report. Reform will ameliorate living standards, you wait and see.'

'It's all a bit late for my Renee though,' Nell replied bluntly when the inspector had finished his little speech. 'I queued up like everyone else and paid my two shillings to read his proposals.' She crossed herself over her apron. 'Please God it comes to pass, but for now I'm the closest thing the Shoot has to social welfare!'

At the far side of the square, a loud shriek rose up.

'Now if you'll excuse me, I'm needed elsewhere.'

Esther ran after Nell.

'Are you all right, Auntie?' she asked, touching Nell's arm.

Her pale green eyes filled with tears, but Esther knew Nell would never shed a tear in public. She wished she would. She didn't think Nell had cried once since Renee died. Bottling in all that grief had to do something to a woman. As it was, her hair had turned from blond to grey in the weeks after Renee's body was pulled from the rubble of a school in Canning Town. She hadn't just lost her youngest daughter either – Renee had been expecting a baby when she'd been killed.

'It's been three years now, but it might as well have been yesterday,' Nell said softly.

'It's true,' Esther agreed. 'I feel the same about my father. They say time heals, but that's not my experience. You're allowed to talk about Renee, you know.'

'But what would that do, Esther?' Nell replied. 'Who here hasn't lost someone or something?' She gazed about her, her green eyes bewildered. 'I sometimes feel as though I could walk along any street and stretch out my arm, and I'd touch someone who has lost a lover, a mother, a child or a friend. We are a nation in mourning and it ain't done yet, so no time to sit and wallow.'

'But . . .'

A loud banging drowned Esther out, as she followed Nell's gaze to the far side of the square where the shrieking was growing louder.

'Who is that woman about to knock down Mrs Povey's door?' Nell asked.

'Oh Lord. That's Queenie Jacks, your new neighbour. Her daughter Patsy started at Yardley's today. She's quite combative, just to warn you, Auntie.'

Nell's eyes narrowed as she watched Queenie spanking the door knocker and yelling through the letter box.

'Well she's met her match!'

Nell called out to Queenie as they drew close. 'If there's any trouble round these parts you come to me, love, all right? I'm Nell Gunn. The guv'nor.'

Queenie whirled round. Her mouth was as tight as a white-knuckle fist and her eyes were threaded through with cold, hard rage. It seemed she hadn't calmed down a whole lot since her earlier encounter in Miss Rayson's office.

'I don't care if you're Genghis Khan of the Mongol Empire,'

Queenie retorted. 'The only person who looks out for my kids is me.'

Mrs Povey finally opened her door and looked out in surprise. 'Yes?'

'Your son called mine a black bastard. He needs to get out here now and apologise.'

Mrs Povey's mouth fell open.

'Go on, tell her Jimmy Junior, what her precious son said to you,' Queenie ordered.

For the first time, Esther realised a boy was hiding behind Queenie. He couldn't have been more than seven or eight.

'Mum, leave it,' he begged. 'Please. We've only just moved in.'

'You let it go, even once, and they'll have you down as a victim. And if there's one thing I ain't, it's a victim. Now tell them!'

The boy's shoulders sagged in shame.

'He said: "God made little niggers, he made them in the night. He must've been in a hurry, because he forgot to paint them white."'

Queenie rolled up her sleeves to show off her tattooed forearms.

'Niggers . . . Niggers!' she spat. 'Always with the fucking N word. That word has been used for centuries to denigrate . . . Well, we didn't ever stand for it in Poplar, and we won't stand for it here neither.'

Mrs Povey looked like she might keel over at any moment.

'I'm ever so sorry. If he did say that, he'll be getting six of the best, I can assure you. I don't stand for any of that.'

'None of us do,' Nell interjected. 'We don't judge people on the colour of their skin down the Shoot. We never have. Black, white, purple, it don't matter.'

Queenie didn't look appeased, her eyes glinting as she turned back to Mrs Povey.

'Maybe if you spent more time teaching your kids manners and less time cavorting with Yanks, he might know right from wrong.'

'Now you look here . . .'

But Queenie wasn't done.

'Yeah, I saw your lot last night. You hanging off that fella, with your come-hither eyes and your rouged-up cheeks. Then there's that slut whose kid should be talking Polish.'

Esther glanced round and realised a hushed crowd had assembled, including the photographer and the inspector.

'That's enough now, Mrs Jacks,' Nell ordered in a low voice. 'Let's take it inside, I'll make us a cup of tea and Mrs Povey's son can apologise properly.'

'Tea?' Queenie exclaimed. 'The world's going to hell in a handcart and you wanna sit down and drink tea?'

She gestured to the whole square.

'This place needs a proper clean-up, if you ask me. Women out making bombs, affairs, illegitimate kids . . . it's a moral cesspit round here. And as for that place.' She gestured to the communal restaurant and Esther wondered what on earth she could find to object to about that.

'The scourge of communal dining is leading to the breakdown of traditional family life. And that allotment . . .' she pointed a bony finger to the other side of the square, 'why, it's nothing more than a soft bed for local girls and Yanks. I'll be conducting nightly patrols from now on in my capacity as observer for the Morality Council. This place needs a bloody good clear-up.'

She turned to the photographer. 'And you can stick that in your paper.'

Her eyes narrowed to slits and Esther shuddered to think what the world looked like through her narrow, censorious gaze.

'Right, I've had enough of this rubbish. Show's over,' Nell ordered, but Queenie had obviously been saving the best for last.

'The rot's clearly set in from the top.' She took a step closer to Nell.

'You see, I know all about you, Mrs Gunn. I keep my ear to the ground. I heard about your little spell inside. Your abortion practice. You've got a son who's weak in the head too, ain't yer? Little wonder living round here.'

Nell's fist moved like lightning, but Queenie was faster, and gripped her bunched knuckles tight in her hand, her eyes glinting with triumph.

'That's enough, Queenie!'

Esther turned, stunned to see Snowball push his way out of the crowd.

'You look like you've come up a few inches in the world since I saw you last,' Queenie taunted. 'You never wore fancy suits when I knew you. Any of these lot know your real name?'

Snowball's face drained of colour, his hands shaking so violently that the cigarette he was holding shed ash over his knuckles. It was extraordinary, Esther thought, as if a ghost train were passing through him. Turning, he ran back through the flabbergasted crowd.

'That's it, run away, you always was good at that!'

A heavy silence settled over the cobbles. Esther didn't know what was worse – the scolding humiliation of it all, or that Nell had come off worse in front of everyone.

Esther left her mother with Nell and headed back to her new home, hoping for nothing more than a cup of tea and a sit-down. What an afternoon! After the Blitz, life had been relatively quiet in Stratford, but Queenie Jacks' arrival was like tossing a live grenade into the Shoot. And just what was her connection to Snowball? Whatever it was, seeing her had clearly rattled him.

Esther pushed her key in the lock and called out softly up

the passage. 'Walter. You back?' The wireless crackled in the front parlour.

Walter worked in the Yardley warehouse stockroom and often put in long hours, but suddenly, Esther remembered he was out on his evening shift for the Home Guard. Maureen insisted they pool their rations and, judging by the smell of wet vegetables in the passage, there was some sort of cabbage or marrow boiled to within an inch of its life awaiting her. Unable to face it, Esther decided to just call it a night and turn in. Even five inches of bath water sounded appealing right now.

But when she pushed open the door to her bedroom, she was startled to find her mother-in-law in there smoothing down the coverlet on their bed.

'Maur . . . Mum. What are you doing?'

'Just changing your sheet,' she replied defensively.

'But it's only been on one day . . .' Esther's voice trailed off, for in that moment, to her absolute mortification, she knew precisely what Maureen Smith had been doing. The girls at the factory had joked often enough about interfering women checking the sheets the day after the wedding to see if their new daughter-in-law's virginity was intact. She hadn't actually imagined it really happened.

'You were checking the sheets, weren't you?' Her insides tightened like a small, cold fist as she looked round the room. Maureen had tidied up and all her cosmetics had been neatly arranged. The fussy antimacassar that Esther had removed from the back of a chair had been put back, as had the heavy eiderdown that she'd found too hot to sleep under last night.

'Just making sure everything's as it should be,' Maureen replied, patting her hand on the bed. 'My Walter gets cold at night. Oh, and leave his sandwiches to me to make, eh sweetheart? You forgot to cut the crusts off this morning.'

Esther shook her head and felt like the walls had just slid

an inch further together. The awful realisation dawned on her – she hadn't just married Walter, but his mother too.

Without saying a word, she turned and clattered down the stairs. Maureen's voice called after her.

'Where you going?'

'To a dance!'

5

Patsy

Patsy emerged blinking from the gloom of Piccadilly Circus Underground. She looked about, dazzled, at the many different uniforms hurrying past her. London was a boomtown at the moment, with plenty of troops on leave and with money to spend in this battered old city.

The July air was hot, laced with the threat of a thunderstorm, and the back of her neck was sticky with grime. Mind you, she had just raced here from Stratford via bus and Underground, leaving as soon as the clocking-off bell had gone.

She glanced up at a poster on the side of a grand Portland stone building, her heart thumping. *GUINNESS FOR STRENGTH*. It'd take more than a drop of drink right now to calm her nerves. She scurried past where the statue of Eros once stood. Poor old Eros has been evacuated like her, removed for safe-keeping with the pedestal now heavily sandbagged.

Flecks of rain began to fall from a gun-coloured sky.

Damn, she'd forgotten her hat. She pulled her gabardine mackintosh up over her head and hurried in the direction of London's most famous wartime theatre, The Windmill on Great Windmill Street.

'You can do this,' Patsy murmured under her breath, as

she stood in front of the theatre she had read about so many times during evacuation, the only West End theatre out of forty-one not to dim its lights.

'We Never Closed.' Patsy repeated their Blitz catchphrase under her breath. She felt a shiver of excitement as her eyes travelled up past the sandbagged entrance to the sign above.

'Mrs Henderson presents,' she read out loud. 'Revudeville. A Vivian Van Damm production.'

Just above the sign, the incendiary-scorched face of a carved-stone cherub looked down at her from the top of the wall. She winked. She could've sworn it winked back.

The door swung open and two off-duty Windmill girls waited to pass her.

'You in or out?' an impossibly glamorous redhead asked.

Time to find her chutzpah.

'In . . .' She gave them her best dazzling smile, shook back her hair and walked into the glittering heart of Soho.

'If you're here for an audition, then you're in luck,' said the lady summoned to come and talk to her. 'The Old Man's in. Follow me.'

'The Old Man?' Patsy queried as she clattered up a narrow stone staircase after the smartly dressed woman.

'Sorry, that's what we call Mr Van Damm.'

As they climbed, Patsy was breathless. The smell of grease-paint and sweat, cut through with sweet perfume, clung to the bare brick walls. The front of the theatre might have been all plush red velvet, but backstage, it was anything but glamorous. The sound of the show was relayed through the building by tannoy. There was a faint clatter of a Singer sewing machine – or was it tap-dancing? Patsy felt a powerful sense of belonging in this noisy, vibrant theatre.

In the quiet sanctuary of Mr Van Damm's office, the Old Man didn't mince his words.

'You've got the looks all right, but can you sing and dance?'

'Yes,' she said eagerly. 'I've spent the past four years at Miss Violet's School for Dance in Ipswich.' He kept on staring at her, unimpressed. He had the most intensely challenging gaze, dark eyes unflinching behind his spectacles. She met his gaze boldly.

'Age?'

'Eighteen,' she lied.

'Where you from, Miss . . .?'

'Patsy Jacks, sir. Patsy from Poplar.'

For the first time, a glimmer of a smile.

'I have a soft spot for East Enders. Back in 1932, when I began, I asked the *Star* to organise a competition to find a suitable name for a non-stop variety show. The name Revudeville was dreamt up by a man named Arnold Kite from Bethnal Green. He won five shillings for that. It's a terrific name, don't you think?'

'Not many, sir,' Patsy replied. 'You can always trust an East Ender, quick off the mark.'

He smiled and leant back in his chair.

'Patsy Jacks from Poplar. It's got a ring to it.'

'Canny marketing man like you should have no problem dreaming up a smashing act for me.'

'Slow down, Miss Jacks,' he said, steepling his fingers together and regarding her once more with that hawk-like gaze. 'You're not through the doors yet . . .' He paused. 'But I do like you, I'm going to take a chance on you. I'll start you off as a revudebelle. A lot of the girls start that way and if they show promise, they quickly move up to become all-singing, all-dancing Windmill girls.'

'Revudebelle, sir?'

'Yes, it's what we call our nude tableaux vivants.'

'Aah, yes.'

Patsy had heard of the famous nudes who posed motionless on a pedestal. Just one movement would be enough to get the entire show shut down by the Lord Chamberlain and for The Windmill to lose its licence, so strict were the laws surrounding nudity.

Van Damm mistook her silence for hesitation.

'I'm fiercely protective of my nudes. My own daughter works as a revudebelle. I would never ask a girl to do anything my daughter wouldn't be happy to do.'

'Oh no,' she gushed. 'I'm not ashamed to show my body, sir.'

'Good. And what about your voice?'

'My voice, sir?'

'I'm afraid I can't even consider you for a speaking role until we've done something about that accent.'

'Oh, right-o . . .'

Patsy thought the East End had been scrubbed off her tongue after so long away.

'Don't worry, we'll pay for elocution lessons.'

'Fanks.'

'That's arranged then. I'll have my secretary draw up a contract. You can start tomorrow.'

Patsy had agreed to sign before he even mentioned the seven bob a week.

'Ta very much – I mean thank you, Mr Van Damm,' she grinned as she left his office.

She felt like she was floating on air as she walked back down the stairs. Two jobs in one day. What a touch! It'd be hard going, of course it would. Her early shift at Yardley ran from 5 a.m. to 1 p.m., which gave her one hour to hot-foot it from East End to West End to get here for the rehearsals. Then there were continuous shows until 10.30 p.m. Six days a week. Which, of course, left little time for sleep.

But who cared about that? She was seventeen. She'd sleep when she was old.

An unnerving image of her mother flashed into her mind,

sour and acerbic, and quickly she pushed it from her mind. She'd have to dream up a bloody good excuse to hide her double life from Queenie Jacks, who would have a coronary on the spot if she knew what her only daughter was planning.

Back on the ground floor, Patsy paused as a flock of Windmill girls, frilled and feathered, their lips luscious with carmine, sashayed past and entered the stage by the wings.

The last girl, a blue-eyed blonde with more than a touch of Irish in her, winked at Patsy.

'Crikey. I do hope the Old Man took you on, you're a doll,' she whispered in a husky voice.

Patsy recognised her as blonde Blitz bombshell Margaret McGrath, who last year *LIFE* magazine had called Windmill's number one glamour girl. She was a pocket Venus who'd kept on performing while bombs rained down relentlessly on London. Margaret, along with her friend Annie Singer, was famous for rescuing six panicked horses from a bombed stables and leading them right through the middle of Piccadilly Circus in a raid, while apparently singing 'I've Got Sixpence'.

This alone was reason to love her! Patsy could've sworn she stopped breathing for a full minute as she watched the gorgeous spectacle and stood in the vacuum of glamour they left behind. The echo of laughter and applause drifted back-stage and Patsy's head span. All thoughts of her mother and her life back in Stratford melted to nothing. Boredom, fear, the privations and drab greyness of war – they were irrelevant here in this little theatre of dreams.

The chance to one day become a Windmill girl like Margaret was worth the risk. The glamour; the pure undiluted glamour of it was intoxicating. She was young, full of life and fizzing over with energy. Anything was possible, wasn't it?

As the bus bumped back to the East End and the streets narrowed, Patsy stared out through the anti-splinter nets spread over the window and ran the options through her mind.

It was gone 8 p.m. by the time she slipped through Cat's Alley and into the Shoot. The smell of stew and washing drifted through the open windows.

She drew in a deep breath as she pulled the key attached to a piece of string through the letter box. Why couldn't her mum just leave the door open to let air in up the passage like every other woman in the Shoot?

She found her mother in the kitchen, sitting at the scrubbed tabletop, darning a sock.

'Sorry I'm late,' she said. 'Where's Jimmy?'

'In bed, we had a spot of bother with that old cow at number fourteen. So where you been? I thought your shift finished early?'

'I stayed on to do another shift, then . . .' she took a deep breath, 'I joined the WVS.'

Queenie's gaze was like an X-ray.

'You know, the Women's Voluntary Services.'

Patsy kept her fingers crossed behind her back. She hated lying to her mum, but how could Queenie, with her strict moral judgements, ever hope to understand her hopes and dreams for the future? It was baffling. She'd been a music hall singer once, so Patsy's father had told her, so surely she knew the thrill of performing, had felt the same tingle Patsy had experienced at the smell of greasepaint. Being in that theatre made her feel more alive than she had ever felt in her life. But Patsy also knew there was little point questioning her mother. Her past was sealed off behind a closed door.

'Good for you,' her mother replied with uncustomary softness. 'They do some excellent work, in knitting comforts for the troops and helping bombed-out families. Very respectable lot.'

'So you don't mind that I'll be spending a lot of time there? Only, I've volunteered to do most evenings. You know, do my bit.'

Queenie smiled. A rare thing that peeled years off her.

'Course not. I'm proud of you.'

While her mother was in a good mood, Patsy continued.

'Some of the girls from Yardley's are at a dance at the town hall. Mind if I join them? They're ever so friendly and I really think I ought to show my face if I'm to fit in.'

'Very well. But be back by ten thirty latest.'

'Thanks, Mum.'

As she moved past her to freshen up, her mother caught her wrist and brought it to her lips.

'I know you think I'm an old sour puss, but it's hard. With your father gone, I have to be mother, father and protector all rolled up in one. It was always me and him against the world. Now I'm all alone.'

A vein in her temple flickered and, suddenly, Patsy saw her fragility, her shattered nerve endings, the strain that had seeped and poured into every crevice of her mother's body. Her father's death had cast deep shadows over Queenie's soul and something inside her had calcified, her rage as large and lucid as the moon. The problem was, she wasn't just at war with bigots, she was at war with the whole world.

'I miss him too, Mum,' Patsy replied quietly. 'I'd best go get ready.'

'Patsy?'

'Yeah?'

'You – you're a good girl.'

Patsy smiled sadly. In all her years, her mother had never been able to express her affection for her. It was little wonder Jimmy looked to Patsy for that. This was as close as she'd get to an expression of love.

'Thanks, Mum.' She went to say something else, something

to close the chasm between them, but after four years apart, in many ways, this woman was a stranger to her.

Instead she murmured, 'I'll be quiet when I come in.'

'If you would.'

Queenie went back to her darning and Patsy left the small, silent room.

By the time Patsy pushed open the door to Stratford Town Hall, the dance was already jumping – literally! The sprung floor was bouncing beneath her T-bar heels as several hundred people jitterbugged like their lives depended on it. Heat, noise, moist tobacco air and the fug of hormones blasted her in the face.

The crush of bodies made navigating her way through the dance hall difficult, but eventually she found the Lavender Girls at a round table in the corner lit by a dim lamp. Through the soft red glow, she could see they were flanked on all sides by Americans.

'Blimey, is this what they mean by the friendly invasion?' Patsy joked over the noise.

'Oh here she is, squeeze up, girls,' said Fat Lou. Her breath was laced with gin as she pressed a hip flask into Patsy's hand under the table.

'Smashing rig-out, Patsy,' said Little Irene admiringly, taking in Patsy's pin curls and light, coral-pink summer dress with tiny mother of pearl buttons at the throat, luminous against her honeyed skin.

'Yeah, lovely bit of clobber,' Joanie agreed, dipping her head so her GI date could light her cigarette. 'You run it up yourself?'

Patsy nodded and sat down, taking a large swig from the hip flask. A second later, she coughed, feeling like her eyeballs were on fire.

'Hell's teeth, Lou, what's in that?'

'Dutch courage,' Lou winked, sparking up a Craven A.

Blinking, Patsy gazed through the smoke at the group of GIs. Immediately, she spotted the one who fancied himself the lady-killer.

'Well smack me down, boys, I feel like Hollywood herself has just walked in,' grinned a man whose teeth were too big for his head, as he pulled up a stool next to Patsy.

'I persuaded all my pals to come to the East End because they have the most terrific-looking broads here. Am I right or am I right, fellas?'

'You know what they say, boys,' grinned Joycie saucily. 'Don't go up West if you want the best.'

'Boy, ain't that ever the truth?' drawled Sgt Teeth, draping his arm around Patsy's shoulders. 'But seriously, like I says to my pals here, are we in Hollywood? You girls sure do know how to put on the style.'

As he spoke, he absent-mindedly twirled a curl of Patsy's hair around his finger, drawing her closer to him. The gesture set her teeth on edge and she pulled back.

'Aw come on, sugar, don't get all stiff on me . . .' He leant in closer, his gin-breath soft in her ear, his gaze resting predictably on her breasts. 'Relax, honey. You and me could have a good time. Whaddya say?'

He was far drunker than Patsy had realised. A smudge of pan stick shone gaudily from his cheek.

'Looks like you've already had a good time,' she muttered.

'What's that you say?' he said, but the music was getting louder. The wail of a clarinet soared above them, drowning out all conversation. Patsy hadn't even realised the music was coming from a big band up on the stage. 'Don't Sit Under the Apple Tree' by the Andrews Sisters was a crowd-pleaser, and a flood of people stampeded to the already heaving dance floor, led by Lou and Joanie.

Patsy felt like she'd stumbled into a strange dream as she

watched the dancers. As pleated skirts flew, there were flashes of milky thigh unstained by gravy browning, bumping bodies, men swinging women high into the air and through their legs with furious abandon. The swish of silk brushed against hot wool uniforms. Tangee-stained lips parted in feverish laughter. The intimacy of it all was making her stomach churn. She longed for something softer. Her father's jazz favourites washed through her mind: Fats Waller, Jelly Roll Morton . . .

'C'mon, Dolly Daydreamer,' said the persistent GI, tugging her in the direction of the dance floor with one hand and clicking his fingers impatiently with the other. His palm felt hot. Panic bloomed in her chest.

'I . . . I . . . I don't want to dance . . .'

'You are one uptight broad. Come on, baby, let's swing this . . .' He yanked hard on her arm and started to pull her towards the fray.

A broad-shouldered figure pushed between them. A deep American voice.

'The lady said she doesn't want to dance, so come on, get the hint and scram.'

'Butt out, Blue. This dance is mine.'

'Well, let's ask the lady.'

The figure turned around and Patsy found herself staring into the brightest blue eyes she'd ever seen.

'You wanna dance with this chump?' he asked, mouth twitching with mischief.

Patsy shook her head.

'There's your answer.'

The GI wiped his hand across his mouth and his eyes narrowed.

'Suit yourself, frigid bitch.'

Blue floored him with one punch. Wallop. Patsy stared, stunned, at the crumpled figure on the parquet floor.

'Thanks,' she murmured, 'but you didn't have to do that.'

'Sure I did, he asked for it.'

A flicker of a smile crossed his face.

'I apologise for my fellow countryman. By and large, we're a pretty decent bunch, but this one here's a chump,' he said as he jerked his finger at the man staggering to his feet. 'If his brains were dynamite, he wouldn't have enough to blow his own hat off.'

Patsy burst out laughing as the tension left her body.

They turned as one to the dance floor, where the pace had slowed. The band had switched tempo and were now playing a soothing Glenn Miller tune.

'"Moonlight Serenade", I love this,' said Patsy. 'Want to dance?'

The question came as almost as much of a surprise to Patsy as it did to Blue.

'How can I say no?' he replied, taking her hand gently and leading her into the sea of swaying bodies.

Patsy felt her heart rate slow as he cupped her hand and drew her body closer to his. He was as tall as he was broad, and Patsy had the strangest sensation she was leaning against a solid oak tree. It wasn't unpleasant. He smelt good too. Drifts of woody soap came from his skin.

She felt him searching her face.

'I don't mean to be rude, but were you *born* in the East End?'

She raised one eyebrow.

'I was born in the East End Maternity Home, within the sound of the Bow bells if you must know.'

The GI looked mortified. 'Sorry, that was crass, I just wondered what your heritage was.'

'It's all right. My mum's white, my dad was half-caste, white mother, black father. He was very proud of his West Indian heritage, as am I,' she added smartly. ''Sides. No one's really from the East End, we're all immigrants somewhere down the line. You must know that coming from America?'

'You got me there.'

He stared at her curiously and she met his gaze. He was handsome all right; tall, well built, with thick lashes. His body fizzed with such an energy, he looked like he might burst into flames. But there was something underlying, a chemistry that seemed to draw them together like mercury. He felt it too, she knew it, and suddenly, she didn't know where to put herself.

'No prizes for guessing why you're called Blue,' she grinned, tapping his eyelids softly. The gesture broke the intensity of the moment.

His eyelids flickered as his face creased into a wide smile, the skin at the corners of his eyes creasing into crow's feet.

'My real name is Benny. Benny Delaney from Boston.'

'So, what are you doing here Benny Delaney from Boston, fighting our war?'

'Your war is our war, as they say.' He shrugged. 'Your dead our dead.'

'You really believe that?' she asked, curiously.

'Sure I do. For me, army life has joined up the dots. It's the greatest experience our generation can ever hope to have. Besides, I always wanted to travel.'

'You must be jibbed to have ended up in Stinky Stratford then,' she teased.

'Actually, I'm based in Chipping Ongar. It's about twenty-five miles north-east of here in Essex. We're on a furlough for a few days, but from where I'm standing, Stinky Stratford is the prettiest darn place on earth.'

Patsy rolled her eyes.

'What?' he grinned. 'I'm not joking, you're beautiful.'

He swallowed hard. 'Actually, you're more than beautiful. You're mesmerising.'

She pretended to yawn and he burst out laughing.

'Come on, give a fella a break. I swear I'm not handing you a line, I don't go in for all that.'

Patsy lifted one pencilled brow.

'What do you want me to say?' he grinned. 'You got a face like a squashed tomato?'

Patsy grinned in spite of herself.

'Nincompoop.'

'What in the hell is a "nincompoop"?' he laughed. 'I don't know what it means, but I kinda like the word.'

'Daft sod,' she giggled. 'Look it up.'

'And we're supposed to speak the same language?'

'Maybe it's not so different,' she ventured. 'You'll never believe this, but my dad used to tease me and call me squashed tomato face when I was little, that and titty nose.'

'Where's your daddy now?' he smiled, tracing his finger down her nose.

She cleared her throat.

'Dead. His ship was hit by a U-boat.'

For the first time, Blue looked unsure of himself.

'My God . . . That is awful . . . Just awful. I . . . I'm so sorry . . .' He searched for her name, then realised he didn't even know it.

'How weird is this? I've just met the girl I know I'm going to marry and I don't even know her name.'

A silence fell between them and something inside her hardened. He'd actually talked to her like a human being, but now he was using some corny old line to try and get her in the sack. He was just the same as his pal. They all were deep down. Patsy felt the familiar scorch of shame and began looking for the exit.

''Ere, Cinderella. I hate to break up the party, but ain't you under orders to be home by half past ten?'

Patsy turned to find Fat Lou standing behind her.

'Yeah . . .'

'Well you better get a wriggle on, sweetheart, 'cause it's gone eleven and from what I know of your mum, you won't half catch it.'

Patsy's hand flew to her mouth.

'God, she's gonna leather me! I gotta go.'

Blue's face fell.

'Wait, you can't go yet, I don't even know your name.'

He threaded his fingers through hers and drew her to the side of the dance floor.

'Please. I really want to see you again while I'm on leave.'

'It's not a good idea,' she muttered. His closeness, the press of his hot fingers on hers, was making her feel deeply uncomfortable.

The desire to extricate herself from this situation was suddenly overwhelming. She wheeled round and pushed through the crowds to the cloakroom.

'You can't just leave like this,' he protested, catching up with her as she checked out her coat and bag.

'Watch me,' she said as she did up the buttons on her astrakhan coat.

He looked about frantically and, suddenly, his face lit up. He unpicked something sparkly from his shoulder.

'Your earring, must've come off when we were dancing,' he said triumphantly. 'I'm not giving it back until I know your name and you agree to go on a date with me.'

Patsy shook her head. 'Keep it. It's only a bit of cheap tat off the market.'

'At least let me hail you a taxi.' Patsy laughed at the notion of finding a taxi in the East End.

'No ta. I'll go shanks pony.'

And then she was gone. A flash of light as she wrenched open the heavy doors to the town hall and the darkness swallowed her up. She ran across the High Street, heels tapping as she dodged through the criss-cross of torch beams. Only once she'd crossed the road did she allow herself a backwards glance. Blue was still standing in the doorway to the town hall. She couldn't see his face, but she knew it was him by the silhouette of his broad shoulders. She saw the glow of amber as he lit up a cigarette. Smoke against the moonlight. She felt a momentary urge to run back, but she forced herself to keep moving forward. In the space of one day, she'd got herself two jobs in two very different worlds. She'd have her work cut out keeping on top of those without throwing a fly-by-night GI into the mix. A man, especially a handsome, flamboyant, devil-may-care one, was a complication she could do without right now. Besides, if she was being brutally honest with herself, she didn't know if she'd ever truly be able to be with a man, not in the way she guessed was normal. Trust, intimacy, unconditional love? Notions of these sentiments swirled around her head; foggy, unformed and never quite within reach.

6

Lou

Lou watched enviously as Patsy shrugged off the attentions of her persistent GI and left the dance. She longed to do the same. If she left now, there may be time for a good-night kiss.

She stood in the foyer, torn between friendship and love. She'd watched Patsy dance in the American's arms and felt a horrible twist of jealousy. If only she and her sweetheart could have the freedom to do just that. Society's judgemental gaze was always upon them though – their love was forbidden and that was a fact she would never accept. Somewhere out there in that inky darkness was a person who made her so happy, yet they could never be together, not in the way they each wanted. It would help if there was someone, anyone, whom she could confide in about her relationship.

But how did one go about voicing it? *My name's Louise Button. I'm 21, I work as a chargehand in a factory in Stratford packing lipstick and soap . . . oh and I'm in love with a woman!*

Lou was surrounded by a circle of female solidarity: a whole tribe of understanding, wise, warm and witty women, and yet she didn't dare open up to any of them about her true feelings. The fear of condemnation, of being rejected by the people she loved most, was unbearable. Some secrets were just too vast, and had to be shouldered alone. Better all round to go on making up imaginary dates and being 'loud and lairy'. Not easier, but safer, more sanitised somehow.

'You look how I feel,' said Patsy's blue-eyed American, turning from the doorstep. He lit up two Lucky Strikes and placed one between her fingers.

'Love,' said Lou, drawing deeply and shaking her head.

'Lousy, isn't it?' he agreed. 'And yet, we never give up on it. That girl . . .' He whistled under his breath.

'She is sensational,' he breathed, drawing out every syllable.

'If I were you, I'd forget about our Patsy,' Lou said, blowing out three perfect smoke rings. 'Trust me. I've met the mother. You'd be playing with fire going there.'

'Patsy . . .' He smiled, sounding out her name. 'I can tell you now, sweetheart, I am *never* gonna forget about Patsy.'

He held an earring up to the light with a smile before slipping it in his pocket and threading his arm through Lou's.

'What say we get a little lubrication and have a toast to love?'

By midnight, Lou found herself well and truly lubricated. With gin and adrenalin snaking through her veins, she had danced, smoked, laughed and danced some more with the Lavender Girls.

'I have to go home,' she said, draining her drink.

'Noooo!' A chorus of boos went up.

'Spoilsport. Things are just warming up, eh fellas?' said Joanie, who had spent most of the evening wrapped around her GI Johnnie.

'That's right, I insist you don't go until you've had at least one more dance with me,' said a man whose friends called him Budgie. He was handsome enough, if you liked the tall, dark, swarthy sort of look, which Lou didn't.

'Come on, sugar, what you got to lose? Unless you reckon you can't keep up with me?'

He drained his beer and held out his hand just as 'Take

the A Train' started up. An uncomfortable image of her mum, tired and broken, spun through Lou's mind, along with the bitter memory of her promise to get her to the doctor's tomorrow, or come to think of it, looking at the hour, today! Oh Lord! She hiccuped loudly.

A swaggering recklessness took hold; the music was so loud and energetic, the dance floor a wet pulpy mess of tangled limbs.

Bugger it, she was too drunk to worry about it now. Her responsibilities could wait! Right now, she was a young woman who just wanted to dance.

'Right, chum, you better keep up!'

A great cheer went up, as Lou grabbed his hand and headed to the dance floor. She jitterbugged with as much abandon and disregard for injury as she could.

Budgie turned out to be a worthy adversary and as the lights came on inside the dance hall, they were the last two dancers still going.

'You are one hell'va girl; you dance just like the girls back home in Little Rock,' he grinned, his hair plastered with sweat. 'You know we gotta swap tops now, right?' Lou was never one to shy from challenging convention. Without pausing for breath, she whipped her white blouse free from the waist of her slacks and threw it at him, covering her ample breasts with her hands.

'You're barmy!' screamed Little Irene. 'I can see your bra. It's the size of a bleedin' barrage balloon!' The Lavender Girls clung to each other, screeching with laughter at Lou's antics. A minute later, Lou had the GI's shirt on and was tying the bottom up in a knot.

'The very latest in GI chic,' she said, swaggering and skidding her way across the soupy dance floor.

'Come on you lot,' said a grumpy caretaker, pushing a broom across the floor. 'Ain't you got homes to go to?'

The girls spilt out into the blackout in a great cloud of smoke and laughter and bid loud farewells to each other. Budgie and Blue were larking about, piggy-backing Joanie and Joycie up the High Street to the hilarity of all.

Lou felt herself elbowed to one side. The GI who'd been coming on strong to Patsy earlier staggered past, clearly even more drunk than he'd been before Blue had landed one on him.

He stood swaying gently on the steps to the town hall, attempting to light a cigarette.

An off-duty Tommy ran past to catch the bus that had trundled to a stop further up the road.

'Hey, limey, is that the way you ran at Dunkirk?' the GI slurred. Lou didn't think the man had heard him, but he stopped in his tracks and swung round, face rigid.

'Yeah, and when we ran out of ammunition, we used this weapon.'

'What, your white flag?'

'No . . . This.'

With that, he raised his fist and socked the GI right in the eye. Lou winced. He hit the ground like a sack of spuds, and Blue and Budgie came running over.

'Not your night tonight, Ed,' Blue grinned, hauling him to his feet.

'You need to pull in your ears,' said Budgie.

Ed slithered out their grip and staggered up the street like a marionette puppet, collapsing in the doorway of the Two Puddings pub.

'Say, Ed, I think you mislaid your feet,' Blue laughed.

'Go on, get out of it and go home,' ordered a passing ARP warden, who'd seen enough wars not to find the fun in them anymore. 'This is Stratford, not the bleedin' Wild West.'

Esther came out buttoning her coat.

'We better do as the man says.'

'Say, would you like me to escort you ladies home?' Blue asked.

'No, we know our way round this manor,' Lou replied, 'but thanks for asking, Blue.'

'You're a caution, you are,' said Esther, grabbing Lou and hugging her tightly. 'Thanks for this evening though, I needed that.'

'Go on, you soppy sod,' Lou laughed. 'Get on home before that husband of yours wonders where you are. It's fucking taters out here.'

Lou was still smiling to herself as she weaved her way through the network of silent terraced streets. Say what you like about the Yanks, they had brought with them glamour, colour and money to this bedraggled elbow of East London. Cor, would her mum love these stories or what? She couldn't wait to tell her about the GI who'd copped two black eyes and her jitterbug dance-off.

As she walked up Gibbins Road, the darkness folded in around her and after the noise of the dance, her ears felt like they were screaming. The night was as black as pitch. She stopped outside number 49, stared up at the window and fought the urge to throw a stone up. It was too risky. *Loose Lips Sink Ships* was the government message rammed into them from every information hoarding. Hold back, keep secret, stay silent for the good of the society. Hadn't she done that all her life?

As she drew closer to home, Lou felt she was being swallowed up into her own suffocatingly parochial patch of East London, like a Russian doll shedding its skins, getting smaller with every step. Larger than life Lou with her high jinks and painted lips was left behind in the dance hall.

Nailing on a compliant smile, she pulled the string through the letter box and slid the key into the lock. The dark passage smelt powerfully of carbolic, and something altogether sharper and sweeter.

'Mum,' she whispered, pushing open the kitchen door. 'You still awake?'

She knew she would be. Lou's mum reckoned she could never sleep until her eldest was safely home. Besides, she got such a kick out of hearing her daughter's stories. 'Living vicariously', she called it.

'Mum, you won't believe what happened, I swapped tops with a . . .' Her voice trailed off. Her mum's chair by the fire was empty, the room cold.

He slid from the shadows and Lou felt herself take a jerky step back.

'Louise,' he said coolly.

'D-Dad. I thought you'd be asleep. Where's Mum?'

'Gone to bed, she weren't feeling too clever.'

Lou stared up at her father for a long time. He was all sharp edges, with a nose so straight it looked like it had been cut with cheese wire.

He looked her up and down.

'State of you . . .' he muttered, pulling a box of snuff from his top pocket. 'No wonder you ain't got a chap.' He paused. 'Follow me . . .'

Abruptly, he turned and marched through into the scullery. Lou followed obediently. The back door to the tiny yard was open. The moon was hidden, but the shapes of white outlines seemed to glow from the floor. It took a moment for Lou to work out what it was.

'The washing!' she exclaimed.

All the sheets, towels and clothes she had painstakingly washed that very morning and finished off after work had been pulled off the line and trampled into a filthy, sodden mess on the floor of the yard.

'Call that washing?' he sneered, pulling a pinch of snuff and rolling it between thumb and forefinger. The smell fouled the crisp night air.

'It's a disgrace. You're supposed to be helping your mother. Instead, you rush through your jobs so that you can gallivant off to a dance. No wonder people talk about you.'

He stepped closer and gripped her chin tightly.

'You'll do this again in the morning, only this time you'll wash them properly.'

'But I've got to take Mum to the doctor's before work,' she protested.

His fingers tightened and Lou winced, but she hid her pain. She wasn't going to give the bastard the satisfaction.

'This is more important than pandering to your mother. Thick as thieves you two, aren't you?'

He ran his tongue over his teeth, as if to cleanse them of an unpleasant taste.

'It's unnatural.'

With that, he sniffed and walked back into the house, leaving Lou among her trampled washing.

No tears came as she picked up the sheets; just a quiet, stealthy rage that sobered her up instantly. Her father was a sociopath, a sly, spiteful shit of the highest order. Not only that but he was jealous, jealous of the closeness she and her mother enjoyed. She searched the exhausted spaces of her mind for any pleasant memory that involved her father, but found none.

Aged seven he had punished her for taking too much bread at tea by threatening to take her after dark to Wheler Street arch and leave her there for the ghost of Jack the Ripper. Farcical now looking back, but as a child it had a fearful impact.

Lou caught a couple of hours' sleep, before she was up and back out in the yard at 4 a.m. scrubbing sheets again. Did people really talk about her? Did the neighbourhood know her secret? Her heart began to beat fast, but she pushed down her panic, plunging her hands deep into the soapy water and scrubbing until her skin grew raw and her mind emptied.

The first skeins of pinkish light were breaking in the eastern sky by the time she pegged out the washing again.

Out front, she heard the clanking of bottles and the familiar comforting sound of horses' hooves. Wiping her hands on her apron, she stepped out on to the deserted street.

The milkman hopped down and tightened the girth straps of his horse, who took the chance for a quick doze. Lou had never seen so many horses on the streets. A lot of vehicles must have been requisitioned by the army she supposed, along with iron railings, saucepans and anything else that could be turned into Spitfires.

'You're up with the sparrows, love,' the milkman grinned, as she scooped the bottle of milk up from the doorstep.

'No rest for the wicked, Bill,' she joked.

'I must be bleedin' Satan in that case,' he joked, slipping an extra bottle into her hand.

She liked Bill, the wiry old milkman who'd kept on delivering his rounds right through the bombardment, even delivering milk through piles of still-smoking rubble. How he made any money, Lou had no idea, since he seemed to give away more than he sold.

Inside, while the tea was brewing, she prepared some bread and marge and laid it all out carefully for her sisters along with their uniforms, before pouring her mother a cup. Upstairs, she knocked softly on the door.

The door opened a crack. Her father's hand shot out and took the tea.

'How's Mum feeling? I want to see her.'

'Leave her be,' he ordered. 'I told you last night, she's not feeling well.'

'Dad,' said Lou carefully. 'She needs to see a doctor.'

'We can't afford to run to the doctor for every little ache or pain. Run along now and don't forget that washing.'

'Tell Mummy I'll be back on my dinner break,' she said,

trying to look behind her father's head into the fetid gloom of the bedroom. 'I'll fix her some—'

Bang! The bedroom door slammed shut.

'—soup.'

In the kitchen, Lou rummaged through the dresser drawer. A baby on the way and kidney disease was a little more than an ache or a pain, she thought as she took out a treasured Yardley refill lipstick in poppy red, and studiously applied a coat to her lips. She studied her reflection, hoping that the lipstick would act as a panacea to all her ills. What was it the Yardley advert had said last year?

> *The slightest hint of a drooping spirit yields a point to the enemy. Never must careless grooming reflect a 'don't care' attitude . . . We must never forget that good looks and good morale are the closest of companions. Put your best face forward.*

This was a sentiment echoed in all the women's periodicals and government propaganda. What was the one that had caused a wry smile to pass Lou's lips? Oh yes, *Vogue*'s assertion that a woman past caring was a woman past repairing. Cold comfort to women like her mother.

Wearily, Lou reached for her bag just as the Yardley clocking-on hooter blasted up the street. The sudden noise dislodged a thought in her head and she ran back up the stairs, opening her mother and father's bedroom door without knocking.

'I nearly forgot, this is from Yardley's for the Wings for Victory fund.'

'I'll take that,' her father said, grabbing the brown envelope and hustling her from the room. It was dark in the room with the blackout blinds not yet drawn, but as Lou's eyes rested on the crumpled bed, it looked empty. And at her feet, a trail of something dark and sticky had seeped over the green lino. The airless, flannel-like atmosphere of the room seemed to close in around her.

'Your mother's spending a penny. Now get to work or you'll be late,' ordered her father, watching her carefully.

Lou felt sick with exhaustion and foreboding by the time she reached the factory. Something was wrong. She stood rooted to the spot by the clocking-on board, frozen in indecision. The strange fetid odour in the house, her father's odd behaviour . . . He had insisted her mother was in bed, but Lou just knew she wasn't in the house. She was so connected to her mum that she felt her absence like a physical sensation. But if not there, then where on earth was she?

'Oh good, you're early,' said Esther, tapping her on the shoulder. 'We have the Minister of Aircraft Production visiting today at dinnertime, so it's all hands on deck. You and your team are on lipsticks today. Miss Rayson wants all room supervisors and chargehands in her office now for a briefing . . . Lou, are you all right? You look ghastly.'

'Sorry, what?'

Esther grinned. 'Are you suffering from last night? It was a late one. I didn't drink, thank goodness, but you look as if you might have over-indulged.'

'Yeah, yeah, that's it, overdid it on the sherbet.' Lou smiled weakly. 'I'll be right as rain after a strong cuppa and a ciggie.'

'That's my girl.'

Lou and Esther clocked on then climbed the wrought-iron staircase up to the top-floor offices.

'About dinnertime,' Lou said, tucking her hair under her turban. 'Do you mind if I miss it, only I promised Mum I'd nip home.'

'Again?'

'Sorry, she ain't feeling too well and looking after my sisters is a handful.'

'I sympathise, Lou, but not today, I'm afraid. Three-line whip from Mr Lavender. All personnel in the canteen at dinnertime. They've even invited workers from the neighbouring factories, so all Lavender Girls have to attend.'

Back on the floor and with production on the lipstick line in full throttle, Lou found release from her thoughts by the high spirits of the Lavender Girls, still buoyed up from the dance.

'Did I tell you Johnnie's coming round for tea at mine tonight?' said Joanie, as she levelled off the end of a lipstick with a sterilising flame. 'Keen as mustard he is, even prepared to miss some big night out at The Windmill in Soho with his unit this evening. Reckons he wants to see as much of me as possible before his leave's up.'

'I bet he does, mucky sod,' quipped Joycie.

'Do you mind?' she said with mock offence. 'My Johnnie's not like that. He's given me all sorts of things you know. Chocolate, tinned peaches, crystallised fruit . . .'

'. . . the clap,' winked Lou.

'Right, that's it, I ought to give you one round the chops for that,' Joanie said huffily.

'Don't get your arse in a sling,' said Joycie, poking her in the ribs teasingly. 'You know we love you really.'

'And what about that dish you was dancing with, Patsy?' asked Little Irene. 'You two looked like Errol Flynn and Betty Grable dancing together, it was ever so glamorous. He had the dreamiest eyes and the whitest teeth. You could fall in love with a fella like that teeth first.'

'And a knock-out punch too from what I remember,' Lou laughed.

Patsy looked up and smiled. Lou felt a twinge of envy. She looked radiant, her skin dewy and lovely eyes sparkling. Her back and shoulders were so straight, all her cares seemed to slide straight off.

'Not interested,' she said, holding up a lipstick refill case for inspection.

'Why ever not?' Little Irene asked. 'If I looked like you, I'd be on a different date every night.'

'More to life than boys, Little Irene,' Patsy replied enigmatically.

'Blowed if I know what,' Joanie quipped.

The girls' banter went back and forth all morning and, for once, Lou was happy to lose herself in their lively voices. What on earth would they say if they knew the truth about her?

When the bell went for dinner, Patsy was up and out of her seat.

'That's me, thank God for earlies. See you tomorrow, girls,' she said, whipping off her turban and overalls and stuffing them in a string bag.

'Ta-ta.'

'Where's the fire?' asked Joycie as she watched Patsy run from the room with her clocking-off disc in hand.

'What's the betting her mum won't let her listen to that fella, the Minister of Aircraft Production, because it's all about bombing and that?' remarked Little Irene.

In the canteen, Lou was surprised to see the large top-floor room overlooking all the factories of Carpenters Road jam-packed with workers in overalls.

'Blimey, half of Stink Bomb Alley in here,' she remarked.

'Smells like it an' all,' said Little Irene, wrinkling her nose.

Munitions workers mixed with fishmeal producers, paint factory workers, furriers, confectionery producers and dog food makers, all of whom had now found their hands and work benches directed towards the war effort.

The crush of so many people was producing a damp,

earthy heat, and the glass between the anti-blast tape on the windows was steamed up.

Lou felt a deep weariness seep like treacle through her body as she perched herself up on a windowsill, and rubbed a Yardley's freesia cologne stick over the sticky sweat under her turban.

Yardley's had rolled out the red carpet for Sir Stafford Cripps, the popular Minister of Aircraft Production. In ordinary life, Lou would have been thrilled to be up close to a man she admired so much. She'd followed his politics and found much to like. A man who'd served as a Red Cross ambulance driver during the first war, he had founded and led the Socialist League in the early thirties and had also opposed the appeasement of Nazi Germany.

With his patent-leather hair and penetrating gaze, he looked unnervingly like her father, but when he opened his mouth and began to speak from a makeshift podium, she could see that was where the similarities ended.

'As we approach the final victory, we need to make a great effort. I should like to thank each and every one of you. We are building an ever-growing bomber force.' He paused, seeming to connect with every worker in the room. 'You are integral to that. Go to work with fresh vigour, so we can support our boys in the RAF. These aircraft components you are helping to produce aren't isolated parts; they keep the Spitfires and Lancasters up in the air. They form a vital part of our defences as we go to bomb Germany.'

Applause and cheers echoed round the canteen.

As he went on to discuss the social order that would follow the war, Lou's gaze roamed over the milling crowds, and it was then that their eyes connected. Lou felt a deep emotional punch within. It was obvious working as she did in a woodmill further up Carpenters Road that she would be here, and yet Lou felt scared and exposed as she and Martha locked eyes. She felt the same leaping happiness she did every time, and the same guilt and shame.

Martha! Sweet, thoughtful, devoted Martha Robertson. The girl she had grown up playing knock down ginger with on their street. The woman she loved, maybe had all her life.

Lou smiled briefly, lifted her hand, but something in Martha's expression froze it mid-air.

That sickening feeling she had worked hard to shake off all morning lurched back up. Slipping off the window ledge, Lou eased her way through the crowds, until she reached Martha's side.

'Hi, Lou Lou.'

'Don't call me that here,' Lou muttered. 'What's wrong?'

'I came to try and find you last night, but I couldn't, then by the time I knocked this morning you'd already left for work . . . Only, it's your mum. There's a rumour up the street that she's in hospital.'

A cold fear clamped Lou's heart.

'I knew it. I just knew that bastard was lying to me.'

And then she was hurrying out, weaving her way through the crowded canteen, panic mounting.

'Lou, whatever's the matter?' Esther called after her. But there was no time to explain.

Outside, she began to run up the long twisty road, past the prisoner of war camp with Martha close behind her, her breath ragged in her throat. The stench of boiling bones from the soap works caught in her lungs and she gagged, but she carried on, eyes streaming.

As she reached the street shelter at the end of Gibbins Road, Martha caught up with her and gripped her wrist.

'Lou calm down . . .' Martha's fingers brushed her own. 'You have to calm down.'

Lou's heart was beating so fast and, for one dreadful moment, she felt the world tilt and slide.

'Sit down.' Martha pulled her into the gloom of the shelter and they sat on the long wooden bench. Neither of them had used this awful dank place since they were forced to shelter in it during the 1940 bombings. 'What do you know?' Lou wept.

'Not much, only what my mum said, which was that there was some sort of business, about ten-ish last night, an ambulance was seen up your end of the street. Of course, everyone's saying it was your mum but no one knows for sure. We'll go to yours now, and then to all the hospitals in the area. Don't worry, we'll find her. It'll all be all right, you'll see.'

Lou smiled gratefully and stood up, feeling calmer. Martha rose too and put her arms around Lou. What lay ahead was frightening, but here in this brief moment she savoured the feeling of being held by Martha.

'I love you,' she whispered into the gloom of the shelter.

Martha pulled her closer. 'I love you too.'

Her cool, slender arms snaked around Lou's neck, her hot breath whispering in her ear. 'I can't stop saying it. I want to tell everyone I meet: I'm in love with Lou Button.'

By the time they reached Lou's front doorstep, she was surprised to see the door already open. As they drew closer, her father emerged with another woman out on the street. Their heads were drawn close together and they appeared to be laughing. Lou felt the tight knot of anger ball in her throat.

His smile tailed off when he spotted Lou and Martha.

'Good, you're home. I was just about to come to the factory to find you.'

'Who's she and what's she doing in our home?' Lou demanded, taking in the woman's dyed straw-blond hair and scarlet-painted nails.

'This is my friend from the accounting department, Nancy, and don't be so rude.'

He cleared his throat.

'Your mother's been taken up to Whipps Cross Hospital.'

'So I hear, no thanks to you. We're going up there now.'

'No need.'

'Wh . . . what do you mean, no need? Mum's sick, she needs me there.'

'She's dead.'

Lou stared ahead, dumbfounded, unable to compute her father's words.

'She died this morning. Her kidneys finally gave up on her . . .' he fiddled with his cufflinks. A fly circled his bald head. 'Sad but, you know, not unexpected.'

Heat prickled up her back, the hot scruffy street began to spin. Lou staggered backwards, felt Martha's hands reach out to grab her.

Devastation. Shock. Agony. And a hot, bright-white anger that sliced through her.

'Oh Mummy,' she wept, crumbling to her knees. 'Mummy.'

'For God's sake, get off the floor,' her father seethed. 'You're making a show of yourself in front of the whole street.'

She stared up her father, bewildered, praying that this was all some sort of sick joke.

'I have matters to tend to, but be sure to be here when your sisters get back from school. You'll need to tell them.'

And then he was gone, walking briskly up the street with Nancy from accounts.

All the women of the street were out on their doorsteps, arms folded over their aprons, watching this bizarre show play out.

Anger swallowed her whole and in seconds, she was on her feet, clutching the doorframe.

'It wasn't her kidneys what killed her, it was you!' she bellowed, her voice quivering with rage. 'You've been killing her slowly since the day you met.'

Her father didn't even turn around. Martha unhooked her fingers from the doorframe and pulled her into the passage.

Lou fell into her arms, sobbing, and wondered how on earth she was ever supposed to live in a world without her mum.

She couldn't breathe. The tiny passage couldn't contain her anger, her grief. Gasping, she pulled back from Martha's embrace.

'Oh Lou . . . I don't know what to say.'

Lou turned to look at Martha and passed her hand slowly over her mouth as an awful realisation swept over her.

'I was out jitterbugging with a GI while Mum lay dying.'

7

Esther

Esther stared out of the fly-blown window. From Miss Rayson's office you could see straight down into the prisoner of war camp on Carpenters Road. The German prisoners sat in the yard, seemingly lost in thought. Occasionally, they'd get up and slowly walk round the perimeter fence, ignoring the taunts of the local kids. The sun was hot today, a shimmering haze of acrid heat that hung like a steaming flannel over their heads, carrying with it the smell of acid from the nearby Berk Spencer factory.

Esther could have laughed out loud. The pride of Hitler's Aryan army, languishing behind barbed wire, sandwiched between Spratt's the dog food firm and an abattoir. If they survived the war, she wondered what they'd tell their children about their time in Stinky Stratford.

But at least they would survive the war, unlike Renee. Was one of them the same man who dropped the bomb on the school Renee Gunn had been sheltering in during the Blitz, killing her and six hundred other innocent civilians? Or the same pilot whose Messerschmitt had been shot down and crashed into the wood yard, on the very spot where the POW camp had been built?

She remembered the night the yard had burnt to the ground and the terrible sequence of events that had unfolded afterwards. Nell's husband and daughter, Esther's own father and countless other innocent men, women and children had lost their lives to this cruel, barbaric war. How many more people in their small corner of East London were unknowingly walking in the shadow of death? The notion of Hitler's secret weapon was, by and large, scoffed at, but if war had taught her anything, it was to expect the unexpected.

Esther trailed a finger down the windowpane and the grief hit as unexpectedly as it did every time. How could life in all its mundanity go on? How could she clock on to work, barter for vegetables down Angel Lane, trade jokes on the factory floor, when her lovely father was dead?

'My dear, did you hear me?'

Esther turned around.

'Sorry, Miss Rayson, I don't know what's wrong with me today, what were you saying?'

'It's this heat,' the older welfare officer replied from behind her desk. 'It turns one's thoughts to soup. Now where was I? Oh yes . . .'

The frown line between her eyes deepened.

'I'm concerned about Lou.'

Esther sat down heavily. It was a Thursday dinnertime, and Lou's mother had died on Monday evening while they were all at the dance. The terrible news had floored them all. Such a short time ago, but already, Lou was back at work.

'Can't you persuade her to have a little more compassionate leave?' Miss Rayson asked. 'Her mother's death was quite out the blue. Nobody can be expected to carry on in those circumstances.'

'You know Lou,' Esther sighed, tightening the knot on her white turban. 'She's as stubborn as they come, and proud. Doesn't want to be seen as though she's not coping. Besides, she needs the money. Her wage has to spread to many mouths.'

'But surely her father's job at the council covers that?'

'Between you and I, Miss Rayson, I don't think they get on.'

'Why ever not? He's a very respectable man.'

'Search me.' Esther shrugged. 'She's quite private about her life. But I do know all the care of her younger sisters will now fall to Lou, as she's the oldest.'

'Yes, well, that I can believe, it's called a woman's lot. It's why I chose to put my job first,' Miss Rayson remarked in a rare moment of candour.

'Really? Is that why you never married?'

'I'm married to my profession, which includes the welfare of you young girls, so please, if you can't persuade Lou to take more time, then tell her Yardley's will support her all we can.'

'Of course. I've already told her she's exempt from fire-watching shifts and granted her permission to go home on her dinner break so she can shop for an evening meal for her sisters. Getting to the front of the queues down Angel Lane can take the best part of a hour.'

'Very good. And start a collection for her, would you? And tell her we will all be attending her mother's funeral. I'll arrange a wreath from Yardley's.'

For one moment, Esther thought the usually buttoned-up older lady might cry.

'Lou's the backbone of the lipstick room. She always has a smile and a kind word for everyone. It's dreadful . . . So very dreadful to lose one's mother.'

'I agree, what's the point in working with such a large team of girls if we can't support one another?'

Miss Rayson fell silent, and began to tap her pen against her thumb, something she did when she was about to broach a thorny topic.

'On the subject of the girls . . .

'In all the sadness of Lou's mother's death, it's rather slipped my mind, but news reached me of a spot of bother outside the town hall after the dance on Monday. It's the talk of Stratford apparently.'

Esther's face fell.

'So you were all there?'

'Just a bit of horseplay.'

'Rather more than that according to my cousin, who was the ARP warden on duty that night. He says the American soldiers were behaving like Stratford High Street was the "Wild West", as he called it, with brawling and drunkenness.'

'It was just one who had a bout with British beer and lost. The rest were rather nice.'

'That's as may be, but Lavender Girls should not be seen piggy-backing up the High Street on the backs of Americans.'

'I'll have a word with the girls,' Esther said.

'Please do. It's not for me to say how they conduct themselves outside these factory walls, but they are representing Yardley's.'

Her face softened.

'I know the Americans seem very glamorous, with their easy talk and their free-spending ways, but they will go back to their worlds, leaving our girls to theirs.'

Esther shifted uncomfortably.

'Over the years, you can't imagine the trouble I've mopped up, Esther. It rather comes with the territory when you work with young women. But these GIs, they are young, the sap is rising, it's all a big adventure to them. But they are here to prepare for the invasion of Fortress Europe, not romance the locals.'

'Is that all, Miss Rayson?'

She nodded.

'Just remember, it's always the woman who's left with the mess.'

With Miss Rayson's warnings ringing in her ears, Esther returned to the lipstick room and a rather sombre-looking group of girls stood waiting for the machines to restart after tea break.

'Where's Lou?' Esther asked, glancing about.

Joycie looked nervous. 'Her little sister come up the factory, said there were some fella from the funeral parlour at the house. She had to clock out and dash home . . .'

'She won't be long, Esther,' interjected Joanie. 'Don't be cross with her.'

'I'm not cross,' Esther sighed. 'In fact, while she's not here, I'm going to pass round this envelope, if you'd like to chip in something towards the cost of the funeral.'

'Smashing idea,' said Little Irene. 'I only wish there was more we could do.'

'Also, while I have your attention girls . . . I'm not lecturing, I promise, but Miss Rayson's back is up over the kerfuffle outside the dance on Monday. Just watch yourself around the Yanks, that's all she's asking.'

'Bloody Nora! Cheek of her,' Joanie exclaimed. 'There's a war on and we're just trying to find a bit of fun.' She sniffed. ''Sides, everything's respectable between me and my Johnnie. Me mum and dad loved him when he came round for tea. He brought a tin of peaches for me mum and cigarettes for me dad, and feast your pork pies on these . . .'

She stretched out one long, slim, bronzed leg, turning her ankle this way and that to show off a spanking new pair of nylons.

'No gravy browning here, thank you very much!'

'Ooh mark you, *my* Johnnie now is it?' teased Mavis, licking her finger and running it up Joanie's leg. 'Lovely, Oxo?'

'Behave, you saucy cow,' Joanie said, shrieking with laughter as she made a grab for Mavis's turban. Her thick, blond hair tumbled from beneath the white headwear. Competition for

Yardley's highest turban was fierce among the girls, and in a bid to look the most glamorous, they had not only taken their burgundy overalls home and taken them in so they skimmed every curve, but they'd also taken to filling out their turbans with smalls and socks.

'There's more socks in there than a WVS sewing circle!' Joanie shrieked, taking the headpiece and lobbing it to Little Irene, who threw it to Patsy.

Esther shook her head. These girls were irrepressible.

'Here, Patsy,' said Joanie as she handed Mavis back her turban. 'My Johnnie was telling me how all Blue can talk about is you. Won't you write to him? They're only based in Chipping Ongar, it ain't so far away, but he's a long way from home.'

'Sorry, ain't interested.'

'But why?' probed Little Irene. 'He was the most handsome of the lot. Where's the harm in a bit of fun?'

'You've met my mum, right?'

'Fair comment,' she replied and they all fell about laughing.

'What's the joke?'

Esther and the girls all turned as one and a silence fell over the conveyor belt.

'Lou!' Esther murmured. 'You're back.'

'Why you all looking at me like a tit in a trance?' she asked.

No one replied. Lou looked awful, hollow and desolate. She'd already lost weight in just a few days and the skin under her eyes was paper-thin and dark as bruises.

'Listen,' she said bluntly. 'My mum's died, you don't need to treat me with kid gloves. Life goes on.' She turned to Esther.

'And you're to dock my wages fifteen. I had to sort the order of service with the funeral director, but it won't happen again.'

'Oh, Lou, I wouldn't hear of it. Besides, it's tea break.'

'No one leaves the factory during tea break. I don't want special treatment.' Her lip quivered, like a drop of water suspended from a leaf.

She bit down hard and buttoned her overalls, eyeing the small envelope that was earmarked for the funeral contribution.

'And I don't need charity.'

The bell for end of tea break sounded.

'Right, pull out, girls, we've got a lot to get through,' Lou ordered, taking up her place as chargehand at the top of the belt.

It was a relief when 3.30 p.m. rolled around and *Workers' Playtime* came on.

Singing didn't just keep flagging morale up, it also meant the girls seemed to work harder, all of them singing along, their sweet voices meshing as one in the harmonies. The classics worked their magic: 'The White Cliffs of Dover', 'At Last' and 'Don't Fence Me In' saw fingers work faster and hearts lift. Even Lou relaxed, her shoulders loosening.

Esther squeezed Lou's arm as she passed. Lou reached up and threaded her fingers through Esther's, just for a moment. It was the briefest of gestures, but it was a symbol of solidarity. Because sometimes, words weren't enough.

Just then, the tempo changed and Esther felt a tremor run through Lou's hand.

The soft melody ached with emotion.

'"As Time Goes By",' Lou murmured as Dooley Wilson's deep, soulful voice filled the lipstick room. 'This was Mum's favourite, ever since I took her up to the Regal to watch *Casablanca* last year. She loved that film, I promised her we'd go back and see it again.'

Lou's hands covered her mouth, her eyes haunted.

'Oh God, she had so little joy in her life, so bloody little of anything.'

'Turn the wireless off,' Esther whispered to Patsy.

'No, don't,' Lou blurted. 'In fact, could you sing it, Patsy?'

The girls had quickly realised that the youngest among their number had the most smashing voice.

Patsy obliged, and an awed silence fell over the belt as her sweet seventeen-year-old voice filled the room, searching out the notes. Esther could feel the pure, raw aching emotion, which seemed to reach a sweet spot in her heart. When Patsy finished and the last note trailed off, Lou stared at her, spellbound, a single tear tracking down her cheek.

'She had you, Lou,' Patsy said, blowing her a kiss.

Back at home after work, Esther pushed the key in the lock, still humming the notes to Patsy's beautiful song.

'Someone's in a good mood,' said Walter, coming down the passage with a tea towel over his shoulder. He threaded his arms around her and pulled her close, kissing her firmly on the lips.

'I'm not the only one,' said Esther pulling back, amused.

'Well, the sun's shining, I'm not on any kind of rota for anything this evening. My beautiful new wife is home from work, and with Mum at her WI meeting, we've got the whole place to ourselves for once.'

'What's that smell?' Esther asked, sniffing the warm, spicy scent curling up the passage.

'Aah, your mum popped by earlier, think she's worried my mum's not feeding you properly.' Esther laughed and bit back a reply about soggy marrow.

'So she brought a tureen of her special chicken soup and fresh-baked bread, and I popped down the Shoot's canteen and bought up the last of Nell Gunn's bread and butter pudding.'

'Oh I've just died and gone to food heaven,' Esther murmured as she followed Walter into the kitchen and watched him ladle out bowlfuls of steaming soup and place them on the kitchen table.

'How's Fat Lou holding up?' asked Walter as he slurped back his soup.

'I really think we should stop calling her that.'

'But everyone's called her that in Stratford since we was all knee-high.'

'Maybe so,' said Esther thoughtfully. 'But I've never liked it. 'Sides, it's not even accurate. Grief seems to be hollowing her out. Patsy – you know, the new girl?'

'Oh yes, lovely bit of crumpet, the one with the legs and the . . .' Walter's voice trailed off when he saw Esther's face.

'Walter!'

'Yeah, I mean, she's all right and all, not a patch on you, darling, obviously.'

'Anyway, Patsy sung her the most beautiful song earlier. She really does have the most terrific voice. Truth be told, with a voice and a face like that, she should be on stage with ENSA, not working in a factory.' She stopped, looking pensive.

'What is it, you don't like her?' Walter queried. 'I hear her mum Queenie's a force to be reckoned with!'

'No, she's lovely and all, only . . . Oh, I don't know, I'm being daft is all.'

'Go on.'

'Maybe she's just shy, but I feel like she's holding back, like her heart's elsewhere. And she tears out the factory when her shift's over like her feet are on the fire.'

'Listen, if I had a mother like Queenie Jacks, I wouldn't be late home either.'

'True, anyone that can take on Nell Gunn . . .'

'. . . is a woman you don't wanna cross,' finished Walter.

'And I got the most terrific dressing-down from Miss Rayson earlier about the girls' conduct around the Americans.'

Walter's face stiffened.

'I can't say as I blame her, Esther.'

'What do you mean?'

'Mum told me all about them, one of them got knocked out by a soldier on leave. Probably asked for it. They ain't half got people's hackles up. Drunk the Two Puddings dry, they did.'

'So?'

'Well, I went in there for a pint after shift the other day, sold out of beer!' Walter exclaimed. 'Damn Yanks drunk the lot. Well, they can afford it, can't they? Seeing as how they're all earning a fortune compared to the pittance our lads are on.'

His face took on a sour expression.

'Oh yeah, they're living well and laying warm all right. Meanwhile the rest of us chumps get nothing . . .

'You know what they saying about 'em, don'cha? "Overpaid, overfed, oversexed and over bleedin' here."'

Esther felt a hot flush of anger.

'What's all this us and them? They're on our side, Walter.' She scraped back her chair. 'You're starting to sound like . . . like . . . your mother!'

'And what's wrong with that?' he yelled, throwing down his spoon. 'At least she ain't carrying on like some sort of Yankee bag. I just don't feel comfortable with their sort round here.'

'Their sort!' Esther cried, aghast. 'Do you know how dangerous that kind of rhetoric is?'

Walter's face reddened.

'That's how it always begins,' she went on. 'Dividing people on the basis of their faith, their country of birth, their accent. Separate someone as "other" because they're not like us, and you set off on a very dangerous path . . . I ought to know.'

Esther worked hard to keep the exasperation from her voice, but she was stunned at Walter's ignorance.

Anger pulsed in the chasm between them.

'Oh God, Esther, you're right,' said Walter. 'Forgive me, I'm a silly twerp.'

'Yes, you are. They're our allies, not our enemies,' she snapped, gathering up their bowls and taking them out to the scullery. Walter followed, and she felt his arms snake round her waist as she began the washing up.

'Have we just had our first row?'

She turned to face him, her hands covered in soap suds.

'Yes, I think so,' she replied.

'Please forgive me,' he whispered, bending down and kissing her softly on the forehead. 'I always knew you'd make me a better man. I love you so much, Esther, I can't bear to think of us fighting.'

Esther gazed at the man she loved and wondered why there seemed to be more tension since they married than in the whole three and a half years of their relationship prior to that.

Out the back door to the yard, she spotted Maureen's beloved fat ginger cat Marmalade sunning himself on the top of the toilet block. He glared at her and yawned, showing off rows of little sharp white teeth, then turned his back on her. Behind him, the sky was full of ragged clouds.

'Leave the washing up,' Walter murmured.

'Why, you going to do it?' she grinned, flicking a blob of soap on to his cheek.

'Right, you've had it now,' he grinned, scooping her off her feet.

'Put me down!' she yelled, laughing as her hair fell free of its headscarf. 'You're not flaming Tarzan.'

In the bedroom, he kicked shut the bedroom door and laid her down gently on the eiderdown.

'He certainly sees more action with Jane than I do with you.'

Esther giggled as she stroked back his hair.

'Some honeymoon, huh.'

'Yeah,' he grinned. 'Sorry I fell asleep.'

'And I've been out or working since then.'

'Let's make up for it then,' Walter replied, his voice growing husky as he began to undo the buttons on her shirt.

'Have you got a French letter?' she murmured, reaching over to the bedside table drawer.

'I never bothered to get one,' he replied. Esther sat up.

'Why not?'

Walter looked baffled. 'Well, we're married, ain't we? We don't need it.'

'Walter,' she said carefully, feeling her desire abandon her. 'We talked about this. It's not the right time to bring a new baby into the world. I don't want to start a family until after the war's over.'

He held her hand and looked at her imploringly.

'That magic phrase. "After the war". It's all we talk about, but hang it all, why don't we live for today? Please, Est. You and I, we came through the Blitz together, we fought so hard for everything, for our lives, to be together. A baby would be the perfect celebration of our love.'

Esther froze, massaging the back of her neck as she stared at a fly repeatedly butting the windowpane.

'I love you so much. Becoming a father means everything to me.'

The look in Walter's eyes tore her heart in two. She knew what it meant to him. But she also knew how constrained she would feel here. It would mean leaving behind her life in the factory, the company of the girls, a life she loved, to sit in confinement in these four walls with her mother-in-law watching her like a hawk.

She thought of the Dutch cap her mother had managed to buy for her, a secret wedding present she had called it, hidden in a box under the bed. She hadn't wanted to use it, but now she knew she had no choice.

'I . . . I . . .' she started to try and explain.

A sudden breeze as the bedroom door flung open.

'Whatever are you two up to in bed at this hour? Gracious, it's hot in here.'

Maureen marched into the bedroom and wrenched open the sash window.

'It's unhealthy! Can you believe my WI meeting was cancelled because Marjorie Fletcher forgot the minutes from last time? I ask you.' Her chins wobbled as she expostulated.

Esther found herself on the verge of a dangerous hilarity.

'And I don't know what you're sniggering at, madam. There's lights on downstairs and a dripping tap. Switched-on lights and turned-on taps make happy Huns and joyful Japs. Don't you know there's a war on?'

Esther stared bleakly out the cracked window at the sheer broken shabbiness of the street. Anything that didn't move had a sandbag stuck on it.

Of course I know there's a fucking war on, it killed my dad! she wanted to scream at her meddling mother-in-law, before strangling her with one of her own lace antimacassars.

Instead: 'Sorry, Mum, I'll be more careful.'

'Good,' Maureen said.

She reached for the door and turned back.

'Oh, and that woman's downstairs for you.'

'What woman?'

'Nell Gunn,' Maureen replied through gritted teeth.

She stomped out and Walter fell back against the cushion, biting the back of his hand in exasperation.

Esther couldn't help but laugh.

'Sorry, Walter, this wasn't the evening you had planned. Maybe we don't need contraception after all.' She winked to show she was joking. 'Not as long as we live with your mother!'

Downstairs, Nell Gunn was hovering on the doorstep. Out of her territory, she looked unsure of herself.

'I hope you don't mind me coming, love, only I need you home,' she wept. 'It's Snowball. Something's wrong!'

Esther didn't reach for her coat, or even shut the door behind her. She ran off immediately in the direction of the Shoot.

They found Snowball in the allotment digging. Nothing so unusual in that, except he was repeatedly driving his shovel down into the soil and had dug a hole so deep, you could hide a grown man in it.

Esther stared at Nell, flabbergasted. 'He's been out here all afternoon,' Nell whispered. 'He won't listen to me, he ain't making sense. Maybe he'll listen to you.' Nell pushed Esther forward with a gentle shove.

'Snowball.' She placed her hand softly on his shoulder. He jumped and whirled round. But it was the look on his face that took her breath away. Usually so placid and ready with a smile, his features were a rigid mask, but his eyes were as wide as windows.

Esther couldn't pin down the swirling emotions she saw there. Pain? Regret? Fear? The air around him swirled purple and crimson.

'You trying to tunnel your way out of Stratford?' she joked, staring at the hole which, at any second, looked like it might engulf the raspberry canes.

'Y-you don't understand,' he stammered, turning back to continue his digging, 'I mustn't stop.'

'So help me understand, Snowball,' she pleaded. 'Whatever are you digging for?'

But he ignored her and, with a superhuman strength, kept driving his shovel down into the earth.

'I've had enough of this,' muttered Nell, close to tears, making a grab for his shovel. 'Your tea's ready so come on inside, you silly old man. You're making a right show of yourself.'

But he wrenched the shovel back so hard, Nell toppled backwards.

'Snowball!' she cried, pulling herself to her knees and brushing earth off her apron.

'Auntie, go and fetch the doctor. Now,' muttered Esther. A small crowd of women from the Shoot had gathered and were watching in a kind of horrified fascination. Julia broke through. 'What's going on?'

'Mum, take Nell inside, make her a cup of tea and someone please fetch Dr Goldie.'

Without a word, Julia led a shaken Nell back to number 10.

The crowd dispersed and Esther took hold of Snowball. Half restraint, half hug, she held him tightly, whispering softly in his ear, over and over: 'You're safe. You can stop now. You're safe.'

His body was like concrete to the touch, but suddenly, he seemed to soften in her arms and all the breath left his body in one enormous sigh. And then he was sobbing and clinging to her.

She felt his forehead.

'You're running a fever. Let's get you inside.' To her astonishment, she realised he had wet himself. Now that he was no longer in the grip of hysteria, he was as helpless as a baby.

Snowball allowed himself to be led from the allotment, mute and compliant.

As they walked, Esther sensed net curtains twitching all round the square. Behind the partially closed shutters of number 12, she saw a flash of black. An eye stared out. Esther felt a dreadful sensation crawl up her spine.

Snowball saw it too, and at the sight of Queenie Jacks' shadow, he started to tremble, his fingers curling into a fist.

'I can't leave . . . I mustn't . . .'

'Ssh, come now,' she soothed as she helped him over the doorstep. As she shut the door, the judgemental eye was still at the shutters, peering out. Dark as a crow. As silent as the grave. All-seeing . . .

'Flu,' declared Dr Goldie an hour later, after she had taken his temperature. 'I'll give him a sleeping draught, but what this man needs is rest and fluids.'

'No need,' said Nell, holding up her hand, relieved to find herself in her comfort zone once more. 'I'll treat him with a jollop of Fennings and some syrup of figs. Trust me, the guts are the powerhouse; if your digestion's working, everything else is.'

They walked out the bedroom and on the landing outside, Dr Goldie turned to Esther, Julia and Nell and lowered her voice.

'I only wish it were as simple as digestive problems. Did this man serve in the Great War?'

'Of course,' Nell replied.

'I think he suffered some kind of trauma, or shellshock as they call it. Was he gassed in the trenches?'

All three looked on blankly.

'We don't know, Doctor,' said Esther. 'Possibly.'

'In my opinion,' ventured Julia. 'And I am only a nurse, but I worked for a teaching hospital back in Vienna and by listening one acquires information . . .'

'Never *only* a nurse,' interrupted Dr Goldie, with a wry smile.

'If the brain never lays down a proper cohesive memory of an event, or processes the trauma, the victim can remain locked in this endless torture . . .' She shook her head, searching for the words.

'It's complex, but it may be that guilt at having survived

the trenches is layered over the top. He was homeless for a great many years, before Mrs Gunn gave him a safe place.'

'I wonder what has happened to disturb that feeling of safety?' mused Dr Goldie.

Confusion swirled through Esther's thoughts. It was a curious case, one with as many layers as an onion, and with a heart she felt sure would make them weep.

'Rest assured, Doctor, he will be well cared for here,' said Julia.

'Good,' said the doctor, picking up her large black bag and making her way downstairs to where her old bone-shaker bike was parked. She heaved herself on.

Her dark eyes were candid. 'He's not alone. There are many souls who have returned to the East End but whose minds remain in France.'

With that, she pedalled off.

'Shellshock?' said Nell, looking bewildered. 'But he's been happy here for years.'

'You better get off too, back to that husband of yours,' said Julia to Esther.

'I think I'll stay here tonight, Mama, just until Snowball looks a little brighter. I'll only worry otherwise.'

Esther stared out across the square, filled with kids playing. It was still light with double summertime in force. Blackout wasn't for a good hour yet, but already the blinds were up at the Jacks'. The house lay masked behind a veil of darkness. Dr Goldie may have diagnosed shellshock, but Queenie Jacks was a piece in this curious puzzle, of that Esther was certain.

8

Patsy

Seven miles west of Stratford, in the sultrier streets of Soho, Patsy's heart was going at the double.

'Th-this evening?' she stuttered. 'But I've only just started my rehearsals.'

'I know, Patsy, my dear,' said Mr Van Damm from the other side of his desk, his expression inscrutable. 'But a revudebelle has just called in sick and we've a full house. Lot of Americans in this evening . . .'

Patsy swallowed hard.

'You won't let me down,' he said smoothing down his tie and returning to the letter he was dictating to his ever-faithful secretary, Anne.

'No course not, sir,' said Patsy, realising the question was rhetorical. 'Very good, sir.'

Patsy had reached the door when Mr Van Damm called her back. 'One more thing. Did you bring your tin hat?'

Patsy's green eyes widened.

'Don't forget it in future, I insist my girls never leave here without one.'

'I won't forget again, sir.'

'Don't. We had a great many near misses during the Blitz.'

As Patsy's long legs clattered down the endless flights of

stairs, tin hats were the last thing on her mind. She waved to Ben, the affable stage doorman, and he smiled back warmly. All the girls loved Ben. With his silver hair, rounded Edwardian collar, waistcoats and watch chain, he was a benign presence in his cubbyhole by the door. But woe betide any stage door Johnnie who tried to get past him to the girls.

The hot basement dressing rooms were alive with activity. Patsy didn't think she'd ever get used to it. The girls were all drop-dead beautiful. Patsy wondered how she'd ever match up to such talent, beauty and class.

Plump lips the colour of cherries, smooth, sculpted bodies, gleaming waves and long, slim limbs moved about in a haze of cigarette smoke and gossamer. Over it all hung the scent of greasepaint, disinfectant and expensive perfume.

Patsy had been relieved to see there was no bitchiness. The girls were a smashing lot, always on hand to support one another; in many ways, the same as at Yardley's. Despite the lure of naked flesh, The Windmill offered wholesome, professional fare and the girls reflected that.

'Hullo, darling,' said Kitty as she walked in. Patsy had liked Kitty Beauvoir from the moment she first met her. Kitty was a tall, elegant blonde who smoked like a train. Privately educated, from Sevenoaks in Kent, Kitty came from a very different world to Patsy, but she'd shown her nothing other than kindness.

'Are you on this evening?' she asked.

Patsy nodded and sat down next to her at the plain wooden trestle that passed for a dressing table.

'Oh poppet, you'll be fine,' Kitty smiled, lighting two cigarettes and handing one to Patsy.

'Ravishing girl like you.' She touched her gently on the cheek. 'What say I do your make-up?'

'Oh, would you?'

As Kitty set to work on her face, Patsy noticed the scar

and dimpled skin at the top of her left thigh, faintly visible even through the coating of pan stick. Kitty caught her looking and smiled.

'Admiring my war wound are you, darling?'

Patsy nodded, as Kitty used a camel hairbrush to slick a coating of vermilion red on to her lips.

'Happened the last night of the Blitz, would you believe? Managed eight months without a scratch, then on the last night, I was having a salt beef beigel in the deli over the road – utterly divine they are – anyway, there I was minding my own business when a bomb came down.

'Mags pulled me out, had to stuff her fist in the wound to stop me bleeding to death. Honestly, darling, now I've had shrapnel pulled from an open wound, I'm prepared for child-birth. Never did get to finish that beigel either.'

Instinctively, Patsy winced and Kitty laughed, a great gritty laugh as dirty as a drain.

'Sit still, silly, see now, you've smudged your lipstick . . .'

Kitty took out a tissue and blotted Patsy's lips gently.

'What happened?' Patsy asked when she'd finished.

'Four skin grafts and a lot of recuperation. Took a dashed long while to recover and finally I was back on stage. I worried I'd never dance again.'

'What kept you going?' Patsy asked, looking at the carefree blonde in an entirely new light.

'This place mainly.' She exhaled a long lazy steam of blue smoke that rose slowly up to the ceiling, which strangely seemed to be covered in foreign bank notes.

'The Old Man, the girls and Mrs Henderson of course.' She pulled a stray strand of tobacco from her lip. 'We're a close-knit team. We had to be during the Blitz. We held each other's lives in our hands. Slept down here night after night in our negligees and tin hats. Me, Valerie, Joan, Jay, Charmian, Rosemary, Moy and of course Maggie.'

'Negligees and tin hats?'

Kitty laughed. 'Catchy isn't it? Perhaps when I write my memoirs when I'm a little old lady I'll call them that.'

'Tell me more,' Patsy urged.

'It was the people who made those times unique. Not just the girls either, the backroom boys, the Windmill Boys, the comedians, ballet dancers, the dressers, machinists, cleaners, the canteen workers, even the women in the shop over the road who keep us aside vermilion. We're a family. And like all good families, we stick together.'

Patsy nodded sadly. Oh, but that were true of hers.

'This little theatre shook to its foundations every night by ack-ack fire,' Kitty went on, 'but . . . Oh, I don't know, Patsy, we had a purity of purpose, I suppose one might call it. We never closed, as you will have heard, and I for one am very proud of that fact.'

'But weren't you scared?' Patsy asked.

Kitty's fingers absentmindedly traced the scar on her leg.

'Why?' Her gravelly laugh made Patsy jump. 'I honestly think I'm having the fucking time of my life, darling. I shall miss this war when it's over. Until it is, I intend to sing and dance my way through the rest of it.'

She cupped Patsy's cheek.

'I found a strength I didn't know I had and so, little Patsy from Poplar, will you. So will you.'

She rose abruptly.

'Now you've got your face on, tell me about your midlands.'

'Midlands? I'm from the East End.'

Kitty fell about.

'Oh Patsy, you're a scream. I mean have you seen to down below – you'll need to shave.'

The penny dropped.

'Aaah.'

'Yes, our nude tableaux vivants need to look as close as

possible to a statue. You'll be softly lit and side-angled, but you need to make sure everything's smooth and peachy.'

As they talked, the revue was in full swing. Every fifteen minutes or so, a fresh flock of effervescent girls would come breezing in, resplendent in feathers, gauze and gossamer.

'The Yanks in?' asked Kitty, as a Windmill girl dressed as an underwater goddess hitched up her mermaid tail and fanned her face.

'Not many!' she laughed. 'Quite the crowd tonight, a woman vacated her seat in the front row, and golly, such a steeple-chase stampede, I thought the seats would break.'

'It's what they call it when customers hurdle the seats to get the best spots,' Kitty explained to Patsy. 'Sometimes it's so bad, the handyman has to tighten the bolts of the seats in the front row.'

'Don't look frightened, dear,' said the Windmill girl as she performed a rapid change.

'These GIs might come across as brash . . .' She adopted a broad American accent: '"Take it off!"'

Kitty roared. 'Don't forget: "Shake it, sister!"'

'But what you have to remember is that deep down, they're frightened and lonely. And a long way from home.'

Joanie's words about Blue from earlier echoed through Patsy's head.

'That's right,' agreed Kitty. 'We're everything to these boys. We're a photo tacked to the wall of a Nissen hut, a picture cut from a magazine, an impossible dream, a fantasy to keep them going while they're flying into enemy territory. I've had piles of letters since the Yanks came last year. Marriage proposals, the works, darling. Some of them on the back of banknotes.' She gestured upwards.

'But – and take my advice on this, Patsy – don't get involved. Write back, smile, be polite and friendly, sure. We're here to keep their morale up, after all. But don't get tangled up, darling. The Old Man is very protective of his girls, especially you revudebelles. That's why you're first name only on the billing.'

'Indeed he is, my dear, treats them like pearls. Doesn't want them dating any old hoofer.'

At the sound of an older woman's voice, Patsy turned and found herself looking at an elderly lady with hair as white as candyfloss. Patsy gazed curiously in spite of herself. Everything about the legendary owner of the theatre screamed wealth, from the jewels at her throat to the silky voice. But there was a shrewdness in the pale blue eyes behind the spectacles.

'Mrs Henderson,' exclaimed Kitty, jumping up. 'Please take my seat.'

'Thank you, my lovely,' she said, patting Kitty's arm, 'but I'm not stopping. Just came to wish you good luck and to meet the new cockney sparrow, see whether her looks merited her reputation.'

She turned to Patsy, eyes twinkling.

'Oh my dear, you are a peach, a perfect peach. You shall fit in here nicely with all my other lovelies.' She gazed at Patsy for what felt like a very long time. It was curious. Behind the syrupy voice and twinkly bonhomie, Patsy sensed an iron will and something else; a secret sorrow to match her own.

Rumour had it that it was Mrs Henderson's powers of persuasion that had convinced the Lord Chamberlain to grant the theatre a licence for nudes, provided they didn't move. Buying a theatre seemed an odd thing to do with her wealth at her advanced years. She must have been eighty if she was a day, but she had a youthfulness Patsy's own mother didn't possess.

Patsy didn't know why she did it, but she curtsied, bobbing down in front of the doyenne of the theatre. Mrs Henderson's sudden laugh lit up her whole face.

'Oh, you are too marvellous for words, Patsy from Poplar.'

When she left, Patsy groaned.

'Why did I do that?'

'Don't worry,' Kitty laughed. 'She likes you.'

'How can you tell?'

'Trust me, you would know if she didn't. Right, darling, hurry up. It's nearly showtime.'

A few minutes later, Patsy followed Kitty, blinking, on to the famous illuminated glass stage, shivering with excitement in a silk robe.

In the moments before the red curtain was pulled back, as she took her place on the pedestal, a strange calm descended. Her heart was beating so loud, she could hear nothing but the hiss of blood in her ears.

The stagehand respectfully averted his eyes as she handed him her robe and he seemed to melt into the wings.

Beneath the robe, Patsy was wearing nothing but a silk purple ribbon, tied up in a pussy bow at her throat, and a sweeping purple silk hat. The ribbon trailed between her naked breasts and skimmed her thigh. The dazzling rich colour gleamed against her honeyed skin.

She adopted the pose exactly as shown to her by the director who, rumour had it, had worked at the Folies Bergère in Paris. One arm aloft, eyes gazing into the middle distance. Patsy had never felt so exposed – she was about to show her naked body to three hundred and twenty strangers – but she'd also never felt so alive, so in control.

Patsy Jacks. Not quite a Windmill girl, but on her way.

Kitty, standing in the chorus line, glanced back and winked.

The curtain swept back, Patsy raised her chin a fraction, a heat washed over her and the roar and applause thundered through the little theatre. She sensed the presence of the Americans beyond the footlights, their whoops and banter filling the darkness of the auditorium, stealing life back from the war.

Twelve minutes and thirty-seven seconds passed in the blink of an eye, before the next performers came on, a comic drag duo by the name of Biddy and Fanny.

It was all a blur, a wonderful heady blur of quick changes and posing, dashing from the underground changing room back to the stage. Theatre life was intoxicating, thrilling, and by the time the final curtain had fallen, Patsy doubted she'd sleep that night. As the girls dressed back into their civvies, lit cigarettes and bade their farewells, Patsy half wished the Blitz was still on, so that she could bunk down in the changing room and keep real life at bay.

She dreaded the thought of returning to Stinky Stratford, to her damp terraced home, the smell of cabbages and drains, her mother's bitterness leaching the oxygen from the air. And somewhere deeper below that feeling lurked the ever-present fear, the memories that tainted everything, had her running from dance halls and came calling to her in her sleep like a foul-winged serpent . . .

'Don't look so glum, you were fabulous this evening,' breezed Kitty as she belted her fawn mackintosh round her tiny waist before taking a bottle of Schiaparelli Shocking out of her bag and dabbing some of the pungent scent on her wrists.

'Pre-war, darling, rumoured to smell like a woman's sex organs.'

Threading her arm through Patsy's, she led her out the changing room and back up the stairs to where Ben was holding back a small army of GIs jostling round the stage door on to Archer Street. Their voices blurred into one.

'Over here, sugar… Say, baby you wanna go dancing . . . You girls are swell . . .'

Patsy hung back as Kitty signed autographs and chatted easily to the men, the smile never once slipping from her vermilion lips.

Across the street, a sleek-looking staff car purred to a stop and a tall man in an RAF uniform got out.

'Fabulous show, Kitty, but do hurry, they're holding a table for us at the Savoy.'

Kitty finished signing a programme with a flourish and smiled dazzlingly at the officer.

'Coming, darling.'

Patsy stared at her, incredulous. Kitty gently tapped closed her jaw.

'Do as I say, darling, not as I do.' She winked and disappeared off into blacked-out night.

Patsy was still laughing at Kitty's bravura as she walked down Archer Street. It was late, nearly midnight, but Piccadilly pulsed with intent. Every doorway, every turning, offered the promise of entertainment. In the dark cobbled estuaries of Soho, all life existed. She passed a late-night boxing gym, heard the thwack of leather behind the blacked-out glass. Two doors up, the bombed remains of what looked like a cafe – Kitty's beigel bar? – lay dark and silent, jagged debris, smashed brick stark against the moonlight. Her footsteps echoed off the pavement. In the bombsite, a flurry of movement as two fused figures sprung apart. The crackle and flare of a match. Two amber cigarette tips glowed like eyes through the smoke-filled night. There was something elemental about these figures, coming together and copulating under cover of the blackout.

A gang of GIs loomed suddenly out of the darkness, laughing loudly, and out of the shadows of the bombsite slid a shapely ankle lit up by torchlight.

'Hello, Yank. Looking for a good time?'

Patsy crossed the road and, keeping her eyes locked to the white arrows on the kerb, kept moving, edgy and alert. The back streets were empty save for the occasional cab, creeping along like an insect with hooded eyes.

She didn't see the figure until she collided with it. The breath left her body and she gasped as she stared up at the face, lit by a sliver of moonlight.

'Hiya, baby. It's your nincompoop.'

'B-Blue!' Patsy stammered. 'How . . . Why . . . Say, are you following me?'

He looked amused and pulled something from his pocket. Her earring glittered as it twisted and turned in the breeze.

'Not at all. I was out with my buddies. Last night of our freedom deserved a night at the famous Windmill Theatre. Imagine my surprise when I saw you on stage!' He whistled under his breath. 'Boy, are you ever a sight for sore eyes. Two jobs? I'm impressed at your . . . Your work ethic.'

Patsy cringed and suddenly felt inexplicably vulnerable, staring down at her hands. God she despised feeling like this. *You're not that girl anymore.*

She turned sharply and started to walk off, but Blue caught her arm.

'Aah, please don't be like that,' he said softly. 'I didn't mean to embarrass you. I've been carrying this round, hoping to see you again. I'll admit, I didn't expect to see you here, but when lady luck hands you an opportunity . . .'

She sneaked a look at his face, trying to see whether he was mocking her. But there was no trace of irony, just those burning blue eyes, framed by thick lashes, staring down at her.

'Come for a drink.'

'No I don't think so, I've got to get home.'

'At least let me walk you to the Underground.'

'I'm fine, really.'

Laughter and raised voices broke the tension between them. The GIs Patsy had passed moments before had turned around and were coming back up the street.

As they drew closer, a bolt of alarm crossed Blue's face and he pulled her in his arms.

'Pretend to kiss me,' he whispered in her ear.

'Eh, what's your game?' she shrieked, pulling back.

He pressed his forefinger to her mouth. 'Sssh. There's someone I need to avoid, please just let me kiss you.'

'I . . . I don't know . . . '

But her words fell away, as suddenly his lips were on hers, soft and gentle, his hands stroking down her arm until his fingers found hers and curled round them. She felt the rush of her breath, her blood, her senses dizzying as his lips probed hers.

Patsy's heart was pounding fiercely in her chest. To her horror, she realised her hands were actually shaking. The sudden unexpected intimacy of the moment had caught her completely off guard.

'Phew they've gone,' he said drawing back. 'Thanks.'

Patsy shook back her hair and thrust her trembling hands into her pocket, hating the way her body betrayed her.

'I ought to box you one in the chops for that,' she blazed.

'Oh please don't be angry. I can explain.'

'I'm waiting!"

'On the crossing over, it was kinda boring so I got into a game of blackjack with a wannabe hustler from Texas. He'd bet on anything, turn of a card to a seagull's flight. Turns out he was pretty lousy, I cleaned him out and boy was he mad. I needed a bodyguard for the rest of the trip over.' He grinned. 'Fortunes were made and lost on that voyage.'

'So was that him?'

'Maybe . . .' he shrugged.

'Blue!' she laughed in spite of herself, punching him on the arm. 'You're a flamin' caution.'

'So I'm told. Now that we've got our first kiss out the way, what say we go for that drink and you can tell me all about yourself?'

She shook her head.

'You've a nerve. One cup of tea, that's it! And no more funny business.'

He saluted.

'On my honour.'

'I must want my head read,' she muttered, as she took his arm. The sudden laughter had diffused the tension.

Together, they walked into the heart of Piccadilly, past Rainbow Corner, the famous Red Cross club for American servicemen. One of the Windmill girls had told Patsy that when the club had first opened in November 1942, the key had been thrown away in a symbolic gesture to indicate that as long as US troops were fighting the war in Europe, Rainbow Corner would keep its doors open twenty-four hours a day.

The door opened and slammed shut, releasing a blast of Glenn Miller's 'Chattanooga Choo Choo'.

'They've got a dance on tonight,' Blue explained.

'Wouldn't you rather be in there with your pals?'

'Not without you.'

'Are women not allowed?'

'Sure, but you have to submit their names forty-eight hours before a dance, so they can be screened to check they're suitable.'

Patsy raised her eyebrows sardonically. 'Fancy.'

'Anyways, I've travelled all this way here to England, why do I wanna sit around drinking coffee, playing pinball and eating doughnuts? I can do that at home. I wanna experience English culture, not suitable women.'

'Are you saying I'm unsuitable?' she bristled.

'I'm saying you're interesting, Patsy revudebelle slash Lavender Girl.'

They reached Piccadilly Circus and Patsy spotted a mobile WVS van.

'If you really want to experience English culture you can start with a cup of tea you can stand your spoon up in!'

After they'd purchased two cups of creosote-strong tea and two cheese and tomato sandwiches, they found a spot on the steps where the Eros statue once stood. All of Piccadilly had faded into an inky pit, the only light the changing green and red crosses of the masked traffic signals, and tiny flashing torches.

'Tell me about yourself, Patsy. I want to know everything there is to know.'

Patsy longed to tell him everything, the two halves of her life. Before war. And after. When she was evacuated. The crawling, never-ending ever after . . .

She closed her eyes and willed back a wave of panic. Why did these attacks keep coming? Hot, fierce and prickling, turning her thoughts toxic and causing her chest to constrict.

His fingers suddenly felt hot, burning in fact, and she pulled back her hand with a jerk, spilling her tea.

'Sorry,' she mumbled, 'butterfingers.'

'Heh, it's all right,' he said softly. 'You can tell me on our next date.'

She raised an eyebrow.

'Or the one after?' he grinned.

She laughed and shook her head. It was impossible to stay down around Blue and, encouraged by her, he began to tell her about his life. As he talked, she learnt he was born and raised in Boston. He had a life mapped out at his father's insurance firm, until the skies had darkened over Pearl Harbor.

'I wanted to fight in this war before that though,' he told her thoughtfully. 'I was a faithful listener to Ed Murrow, the CBS correspondent who used to broadcast nightly from London during the Blitz. He used to take his microphone out on to the streets, and I remember listening to sounds of bombs crashing, people screaming, sirens wailing.

'"This is London," he always used to start. I remember after one horrific night, in December 1940, all these historic places getting burnt to the ground; good, innocent folk getting killed. My mom turned to me, she didn't need to say a word, I already knew I was going to enlist.'

Patsy smiled as he talked. He reminded her of a dog with a permanently wagging tail.

'I came on the Queen Mary, loaned by your Churchill, sailed right outta Boston filled to the brim with doughboys. I never forget when I saw the great old lady looming out the fog. I walked up the gangplank fully laden, and I never looked back. This is the greatest experience my generation could ever hope to feel.'

'You really believe that?'

He nodded. 'Sure I do, I never say anything I don't mean. I know I freaked you out at the dance, when I said I'd met the girl I was going to marry.'

Her gaze fell to a piece of chewing gum welded to the concrete step at her foot.

'I'm sorry for unnerving you, but it wasn't a line, Patsy.'

Patsy found herself believing him this time. Blue was such an easy person to talk to, as open as a book.

His life, so different to hers, was intriguing.

He was a navigator embedded with the United States Army Air Forces 387th Bombardment Group with the 9th Airforce in Chipping Ongar, where he slept in a draughty steel Nissen hut that smelt like a 'festering goat hut'. The diet largely consisted of sprouts and boiled mutton, 'which causes problems at 30,000 feet'.

He flew in a B-17 Flying Fortress, which he described as a 'Big Bird'. The crew had nicknamed it 'Hot Garters', and he had to get on a 'kid's bike' to cycle to the nearest pub and drink 'warm beer'.

Patsy laughed out loud at his wry observations of life on their little island.

'I've never felt so alive in my whole life,' he concluded.

'Aren't you scared?'

Blue shrugged.

'Ask me again next month; we haven't flown our first combat mission yet.' He cracked his knuckles. 'We're itching to get over there, join your Bomber Command boys over the skies of occupied Europe, make it a round-the-clock effort.'

'Be careful what you wish for,' she murmured.

Blue was like no one she'd met before: loose-limbed, talkative and wise-cracking. Nothing like the tough-chinned cockneys she'd been raised among, or the silent, closed-shop country folk she'd been billeted with. And it was here she suddenly realised, with his easy swagger, that he reminded her of her father.

'I've got to go,' she announced suddenly, standing up and brushing crumbs off her skirt. 'It's really late.'

'I'm seeing you home.'

'But I'm a tube and a bus . . .'

'No excuses, lady.'

Blue stood up and offered her his arm. 'Bye, Eros. When the war is over, I'm going to kiss you again, Patsy, right here on these steps.'

'Don't you ever give up?' she groaned, taking his arm. ''Sides, Eros ain't even here no more. He's gone and so should I be.'

Blue stepped in front of her, barring her way down to the tube, his eyes sparkling with mischief.

'Please, Patsy. Humour a silly Yank. Promise me that when the war is won, you'll meet me right here on these steps and kiss me.'

Patsy sighed. 'You're bananas you are. But yes, I promise. Now can we get going?'

As the escalator slid down into the softly lit gloom, creaking and groaning as it descended into the bowels of London, a soft fetid breeze ran over her shins. She felt Blue behind, his arm protectively on her shoulder.

As they stood on the platform, Patsy stared at the Bovril advert and wondered how it was so many people had slept underneath that, night after night, crushed into this strange subterranean world, while bombs screamed down overhead. As hellish as it sounded, she'd still rather have been here, sleeping by the tracks, than . . .

The train rumbled into the station with a hot blast of air.

'Hey, where did you go then?' Blue asked once they found a seat.

'Nowhere, I'm tired is all.'

'There's something about you,' he said quietly. 'A layer of grief, as fine as ash, just below the surface.'

Patsy looked up, startled.

'Sorry. I'm being too American for you, aren't I?'

'Maybe . . . A bit . . .' she replied, folding her arms across herself.

Blue changed the subject and kept up his easy conversation as the tube rattled along the tracks.

In Stratford, he insisted on seeing her to her front door, but as they turned into Cat's Alley, she put a hand against his chest.

'This is where you and me say our goodbyes. Thanks, Blue. It's been fun. Ta-ta.'

'That's it?' he said, all doe eyes. 'Ta-ta?'

'Don't give me the puppy-dog look,' she laughed.

'Patsy,' he breathed, stepping closer to her. 'I've never met anyone like you before in my whole life. This can't be goodbye. When can I see you again?'

'You hardly know me.'

'This is war, Patsy, life has to be lived at double speed.'

Patsy watched as a skinny cat slunk up the alley and weaved its way through Blue's legs. The fractured tenement rooftops stood out, motionless and black against the smoky mauve sky. The moon was a slim and perfect crescent. All the smells of Stratford hung suspended in the soft, silvery night.

'We're from different worlds.'

'We're all fighting the same war.'

'I'm only seventeen.'

'I'm only twenty.'

'I'm British, you're American.'

Blue went to open his mouth, but Patsy got in there first.

'And my mum hates Americans. Loathes them.'

Without a word, Blue took her hand, kissed it and stepped back.

Against the dark and grime of the wall, she saw his toothpaste smile, the strong sweep of his jaw.

'We're in for one hell'va ride then.'

He turned and walked to the end of the alley, but spun backwards, sauntering with his hands in his pockets.

'Watch this space, Patsy Jacks. You and me, we're getting married. You can't fight what's written in the stars.'

The skinny cat ran after Blue, purring.

'See. She knows it.'

His voice echoed up the deserted courtway and Patsy shook her head, desperately scanning to see if anyone had overheard. But the alley was deserted, there were no signs of life. Except when she turned into the square, where she spotted Snowball, hard at work digging like a man possessed in the allotment, even at this hour. Men, Patsy concluded as she pushed her key in the lock, were all completely barmy.

And yet, as she slipped between the sheets and the dark, silent house folded around her, the joy of her magical first performance at The Windmill was eclipsed by Blue's face, his smile, those eyes dancing through the darkness.

The memory of his lips on hers was vivid. That kiss was like nothing she had ever experienced before. It was tender and sweet. She sighed and beat the lumps out of her horsehair mattress to dislodge the thought. For there was no way she and Blue could *ever* be together. And it had nothing whatsoever to do with age or nationality and everything to do with her, and the darkness that had seeped into her soul.

Conflicting thoughts churned around her mind until finally sleep was too strong and she let herself fall into it.

9

Lou

'Come on, Lou, you gotta come,' begged Little Irene, her face flushed peachy pink beneath her turban.

'Yeah, go on, Lou,' urged Joanie. 'It'll be a last hurrah before double summertime ends . . .' she threw up her arms in mock fright, whispering in horror-film tones, 'and the darkness descends.'

'Before you know it, we'll all be wrestling with metres of black bombazine around teatime,' added Joycie gloomily.

''Sides,' sniffed Little Irene. 'We always go every bank holiday Monday. It's tradition.'

Lou shook her head. The way the girls were going on, it was as if Glenn Miller was appearing down the Stratford Royal, not the poxy East Ham Civil Defence Sports Gala over at Loughton.

'I . . . I don't know, girls. We only buried Mum yesterday, it don't feel right to be out having fun.'

Lou recalled the pathetic little ration-book funeral with a lump in her throat. All the Lavender Girls had come, as well as the neighbours, and their kind donation of flowers had brightened up the dark recesses of the graveyard. Her dad had begged wartime austerity – the gravestone was so small, it looked like half of it had already sunk into the ground, and the pathetic spread of meat paste sandwiches was embarrassing. Thank God for the neighbours rallying round, or else she'd have had nothing to offer. Had her mother really meant so very little to her father?

As she'd watched her mother's body being lowered into the ground, it had dawned on Lou that she had never really stood a chance. She'd begun life in deficit merely by virtue of being born working class. Every new pregnancy had ground her down that bit further into the hole from which she would now never emerge.

'So wotcha say, Fat Lou?'

Little's Irene's shrill voice snapped her out of her reverie.

Lou looked round the table. Only Esther remained strangely quiet, staring out the window into the flat waters of the Cut.

'I dunno, what do you think, Esther?' Lou asked.

'Lou, I think your mum would be horrified if she knew you weren't going. I think you ought to take your sisters and try and have a break.'

'Really? You don't think it seems . . . disrespectful to her memory?'

Esther closed her hand softly over Lou's.

'Your lovely mum was at her happiest when you and your sisters were having fun.' And then, in a quieter voice: 'You are allowed to be happy again, Lou. You'll never stop grieving for her, I know that, but you can start celebrating her.'

Esther was right. Flo Button was always the life and soul of street parties, first to kick up her legs and let down her hair, before life – or more accurately, her husband – had broken her.

'You're right! I'll go,' Lou declared. 'But only if you come, Patsy.'

Patsy inspected a fingernail. 'I'm not sure.'

'You have to, Lavender Girls' law,' stated Joycie. ''Sides, the factory's closed Monday for bank holiday, so what else you gonna do?'

Joanie smiled slyly.

'Unless, that is, you've finally agreed to meet Blue.'

Patsy rolled her eyes.

'Let's not start all that again. Right-o, I'll come, but I'll have to leave early.'

'Why, you gonna turn into a pumpkin?' asked Little Irene.

Patsy looked uncomfortable.

'No . . . It's me mum, you know what she's like.'

'Gordon Bennett! It's a bleeding sports gala, it couldn't be more wholesome.'

'Say, Esther,' said Patsy, changing the subject. 'Day before yesterday, I looked out the window, middle of the night it was, and I saw Snowball out there digging in his allotment. I know he's a keen gardener, but that's taking it a bit far, ain't it?'

To the girls' surprise, Esther burst into tears.

'Hey,' Lou soothed. 'I thought there was something up, whatever's the matter?'

'It's Snowball, he's not himself. He's been acting very queer. He was out there Thursday afternoon. We put him back to bed, but he must have sneaked back out.'

'What's he digging for?' asked Little Irene. 'Buried treasure?' Joycie silenced her with a look.

'Doctor reckons he's having some sort of memory of the first war,' Esther sighed, scrubbing her face wearily.

'But that don't make sense,' said Lou. 'He was fine when Hitler bombed the hell out of us eight months straight. Why now?'

'I only wish I knew,' Esther sighed, drying her eyes on Lou's hankie. 'Sorry, girls. I don't want to be a wet blanket, it's just that I'm so worried about him, I've been over there every day after work helping Mum and Nell look after him, and Walter's . . . Well, Walter's . . .'

'Feeling neglected?' asked Lou sympathetically.

'You could say that,' Esther replied.

'Talk of the devil,' said Joycie.

Walter was striding across the canteen floor carrying a large wicker basket fastened up with an extravagant pink bow.

'Present for your wife?' grinned Joanie.

'No actually,' he said putting the hamper down on the table, 'it just got delivered. It's for you, Patsy.'

Patsy looked surprised.

'You sure?'

'Well, it's got your name on it.'

'Go on, open it up,' said Little Irene eagerly.

Patsy lifted the lid, and nestled among shavings was a cornucopia of treats. Hershey bars, tins of peaches, nylons, cigarettes, Kirby grips, soap.

'Who's it from?' Esther gasped.

'I think I know,' Patsy sighed as she took out a single earring attached to a small white card and read out loud.

> 'To my darling squashed tomato face. One day I'll give you the whole world, but this is a start. I'll wait for you, forever if needs be. Your loyal, devoted Nincompoop xxx.'

'Who the hell's that?' screeched Joycie.

'Blue! That man never gives up,' Patsy snapped, tearing the note in half and letting the pieces flutter on to the table top.

A cry of uproar went up round the table.

'You're dotty,' Joycie exclaimed. 'I'd be there like a rat up a drainpipe. You heard the man, he wants to give you the world . . . You can rinse him for loads more.'

'Oh, eff off, Joycie,' laughed Joanie. 'It's not all about nylons. He's smitten with her. My Johnnie – did I mention him?'

'Yes!' everyone groaned in unison.

'All right, keep your knickers on. Anyways, he says Blue talks about Patsy non-stop. Vows she's the only girl for him. Love at first sight apparently.'

'Pie crust promises,' sniffed Patsy. 'Easily broken. Besides, he's only trying to butter me up so he can get in me drawers. How's it go? Oh yeah . . .

> *'It's a different town – a different place*
> *To a different girl – a different face*
> *I love you, darling – please be mine*
> *It's the same old Yank – the same old line.'*

Patsy did a little curtsy after her mocking song, and the girls hooted and roared.

'Well, I think it's quite romantic,' protested Esther over the clamour. 'Have you considered that he might genuinely like you?'

'He doesn't know me, Esther,' Patsy protested. 'Here,' she gestured to the open hamper, 'I don't want any of it. Help yourself, girls.'

'Don't mind if I do,' said Little Irene, diving in.

Lou felt her heart break all over again. There were more gifts in that one hamper than her father had given her mother over twenty years of marriage.

As the girls rifled through the hamper, Lou became aware of a growing tension between Esther and Walter. He had bent down on his haunches where she was sitting, shoulders strained in tension. Esther was flushed red, her tremulous voice growing louder.

'Just one more night, then I'll be home.'

'And what about my needs, as your husband!' Walter cried, throwing a copy of the *Stratford Express* down on the tabletop before storming from the canteen. Esther blew out slowly.

'Husbands,' remarked an older woman on the next table, nodding sagely. 'You cook for 'em, clean for 'em, then when their working day's over, yours ain't 'cause you still gotta have sex with them.'

Esther smiled weakly as the whole table cracked up. Then something happened to make the laughter stop.

'Lou,' said Little Irene carefully. 'I think you better take a look at this.' Slowly she slid across the table the newspaper Walter had thrown down.

'How dare you lie to me?' Lou thundered. Every cell of her body was vibrating with a white-hot anger. She must have covered the space from the factory to her father's office at the town hall in record speed.

'Not here,' he seethed, gripping her arm and steering her through the polished entrance hall to the steps outside.

Out on the pavement, Lou's anger had not abated.

'Is it true, what they're saying in here?' She slammed the paper into her father's chest.

He closed his eyes as if he were dealing with a truculent child.

'I was hoping to spare you the scandal, Louise.'

'Th . . . the scandal?'

'Yes, your mother's crime.'

The world crumbled around her, silent tears soaking her face.

'Crime? What crime did Mum ever commit?'

'She took the life of our unborn child and she paid with her own life.'

'She died of a bloody botched abortion, according to this article.'

Her father wiped a speck of imaginary dust from his sleeve and said nothing.

Lou wrenched the article back and began to read out loud.

'Stratford Justices committed two women for trial on

a charge of manslaughter and for using an instrument to procure an abortion. The women, Mabel Brown, a forty-four-year-old bottle-washer, and Emma Whatley, a twenty-eight-year-old bus conductress, pleaded not guilty to manslaughter but guilty to the second charge. The evidence for the prosecution was to the effect that Mrs Flo Button, a mother of six from Gibbins Road, Stratford, was admitted to Whipps Cross Hospital on Monday 26th July suffering from peritonitis and was immediately operated on but died later.'

Lou could feel herself growing hysterical.

'Y-you let me believe she was asleep, but she wasn't, she wasn't asleep, she weren't even in the house. She was in hospital while I . . .' She covered her mouth in horror. 'While I scrubbed sheets outside. Oh God . . .'

Lou clutched the side of the building for support as the traffic on Stratford High Street spun into a sooty blur. 'She died alone.'

Outside the Two Puddings, a few doors up from the town hall, two sinewy men in leather aprons were unloading barrels and rolling them down into the cellar.

'Everything all right, love?' one asked, but Lou was speechless with pain.

'Keep your voice down,' her father hissed. 'This is my place of work, for goodness' sake.'

'Oh well, God forbid I embarrass you.'

She gave a wild little laugh at the unreality of it all.

'How dare you lie to me?' she repeated again. 'About my own mum.'

'I told you, I wanted to spare you.'

The inside of her head felt swollen, muddy, as she struggled with the truth.

'You didn't spare Mum, did you? And now . . . Now, she's gone.'

Lou's mind replayed the last time they had sat together, having a smoke and a jaw, like they'd done so many times before.

'I told her, begged her not to get rid of it.'

'Seems she didn't listen to you. Maybe you weren't as close as you imagined you were.'

Her father's smile was so sly, so triumphant, Lou found herself wanting to ram her fist in his face. A thick, treacly clot of hatred caught in her throat.

He glanced impatiently at his wristwatch.

'Now look here. I really must be on my way. I'm away this weekend. Civil defence business, I'll be back Monday. Look after your sisters.'

Lou tugged off her white turban as she stared at his retreating figure.

There was no point going back to the factory now. How could she face anyone? She thought about visiting her mum's grave, but that pitiful headstone was not how she wanted to remember her. Instead, she walked home in a trance, oblivious to the twitching curtains and the conversations that tailed off as she passed doorsteps. News of her mother's abortion would be halfway round Stratford by now.

Inside, she drew the blinds and allowed her tears to come. She gave in to the emotion, and sobbed, screamed and punched the floor with such ferocity, her knuckles bled. She raged at the injustice of it all, at a society that allowed a woman to die because she couldn't cope with birthing another child. And then, at exactly 5 p.m., she drew herself up, and brushed herself down.

'Enough,' she told herself. She heard her mother's voice as clear as a bell in her ear.

Hold it together, Lou. Put on your lippy, put your best face forward. You're all those girls have got now.

Lou walked up the creaky stairs and picked up her only photo of her mother from its usual place next to her bed.

She smiled as she studied it. It had been taken on a beano to Brighton when Lou had been eight. Flo was larking about on the beach, the pier stretched out behind, giggling like mad as foamy white water gushed between her toes.

Lou closed her eyes. She could hear the rush and suck of seawater over shingle and the calling of the birds; could smell the chip fat and candyfloss.

Downstairs, she took out a cloth and carefully polished the glass, before putting it on the sideboard. She lit a candle and placed it next to the photo, so that the warmth from the flame made the seawater shimmer. This was how she was going to remember her mother. This shrine would remind her of the times when her mother had known joy, albeit fleeting.

Lou had always been her mother's shadow, folded into her coat, which smelt of sweet talc and Woodbines. She felt nostalgia grip her, a yearning for a lost life. Had her mum not met her dad, she'd be like every other woman in the street right now. Grousing to the neighbours about rationing, peeling her veg on the doorstep, longing to be a grandmother, but now . . . that future was unavailable.

And she knew exactly who was to blame. It wasn't Mabel Brown or Emma Whatley. It was that wicked bastard who had driven her mother into their hands. Outside the terrace windows she heard the murmur of the clocking-off crowds and realised the girls would be home soon. The war had afforded them such freedom, and most of their days were spent roaming through the willow herb of the bombsites. They were as confused and shattered by their mother's death as Lou, so it was imperative she keep some sort of routine and normality in their lives. But before she started on their tea, she opened a drawer and took out her mother's lipstick, a treasured tube of Homefront Ammunition. The irony hadn't been lost on either of them when Lou had given it to her. Slowly and deliberately, she slicked on a thick glossy coat of red. Picking up the back of a knife to check it hadn't smudged, Lou smacked her lips together and turned to her mum's photo.

'That better, Mum? I won't let you down. You have my word. I'll keep this family together.'

From the moment the girls got in for their tea, the rest of the weekend flew by at such speed that come Monday morning, Lou had clean forgotten about her promise to take her sisters and meet the Lavender Girls at the sports gala over at Loughton. She'd been up since 5 a.m. making a start on the mountain of washing. Most of her sisters had pitched in to help, all except thirteen-year-old Elsie, who was winding the rest of the Button sisters up a treat.

'Lou, tell her,' demanded eight-year-old Maisy, marching into the yard, 'she's gone and nicked my good ribbon.'

'Els,' Lou mumbled from the yard, through a mouthful of pegs, 'behave.'

'Give it back or I'll clump yer! Oh leave off . . . Cry baby . . .'

Their voices reached a fever pitch in her head. Then Elsie pushed her little sister, sending her sprawling across the yard. Maisy's scream could've been heard over on the Wanstead Flats. Something flicked inside Lou and she dropped the clean, wet washing on the ground and grabbed Elsie by the shoulders.

'How dare you push her?' she screamed. 'We don't use violence in this house. You hear me?'

Lou took in Elsie's frightened face and immediately felt guilty.

'I hate you,' Elsie cried, tears streaming down her cheeks. 'I want Mum back.'

She wriggled free and ran from the yard.

'Elsie . . . Els, I'm sorry!' Lou called after her. The upstairs door to her bedroom slammed so loudly, the whole house shook. Lou flipped the old tin bath tub over and sat down, fighting back tears. The girls were grieving for their mum every bit as much as she was; yelling at them wasn't the answer.

'Shitty morning?' said a soft voice.

'Martha!' Lou exclaimed. 'I didn't even hear you come in.'

Martha was stood at the door to the scullery dressed in scruffy dungarees, patched at the knees, her wild curls bursting out from under a dusty turban covered in faded spitfires.

'You like my Sunday best?' she laughed, patting the side of the turban. Her laugh quickly dissolved into a yawn. 'Oh hang on, it's Monday, ain't it?'

'You just come off a night shift?' Lou asked, patting the space beside her on the tin tub.

Martha nodded and pulled a bag from behind her back.

'Your favourite. Apple doughnuts, fresh out the oven from that Jewish baker you like down Angel Lane. Thought you could use some support . . . and sugar!'

Lou looked at Martha and felt her heart give a thud of applause.

'I'm a lousy girlfriend, ain't I?' she sighed, taking the doughnut from her. 'I'm either crying, moaning or surrounded by crowds of arguing kids. I wouldn't blame you if you ditched me for some glamorous ATS sort.'

Martha took a big bite of her doughnut and laughed.

'Who'd have me? Look at me. I stink to high heaven.'

Martha had been working for Briggs woodmill down Carpenters Road for a full year. The mill had taken on a raft of female workers to replace the men who'd been called up.

'That wood don't half pong. Half it comes from Singapore and South America, stinks something rotten when we're cutting it. I've been on the dipping machine all night, coating it in green paint to preserve it.'

Martha's face was speckled with green and the hair that had sprung free from her turban was flecked with wood shavings. She had never looked so beautiful. Lou longed to kiss her, but she was aware of old Mrs Moon pottering around in next door's yard.

'Why don't I help you finish the washing, then we'll make ourselves respectable, sort the nippers and head over to Loughton to meet the girls?'

'But don't you want to grab a bit of shut-eye? You're back at work later. You must be shattered.'

Martha wiped the sugar from her fingertips on the bib of her dungarees, pressed them to her lips and then touched them softly on Lou's. Lou tasted wood stain and sugar.

'Life's a funny old game as my mum says. I'll sleep when I'm dead, so come on, girl. Let's face the world. Show 'em Lou Button's flag's still flying.' She stood up and held out her hand.

Lou followed her and, on impulse, pulled Martha into the cool of the scullery and pressed her mouth to hers. Martha's lips were soft and warm, and she felt her heart give a soaring lurch for this beautiful woman.

'I don't deserve you,' Lou whispered, drawing back.

'Course you do,' Martha replied, resting her forehead against Lou's. 'And we're gonna grow old together, like two old maids.'

'But at what cost? I can't give you anything, I'll never be able to give you security or children.'

Martha's face broke open with a smile that lit up the gloom.

'What you talking about you soppy sod, you've got a house full of 'em.'

They stayed that way, savouring the moment of peace in the darkness, hip to hip. Lou's eyes flickered shut as she relished the warmth of her lover's limbs, pressed against hers.

'Miss Robertson, you're here. Again.'

Her father's thin voice broke open the darkness and the two of them sprang apart.

'Dad! What you doing here?'

'I live here,' he said, crisply.

'You said you were away for the weekend.'

'And now I'm back. Did I interrupt something?' he said, eyeing them both.

'No, Martha's helping me get the girls ready before we head to the sports gala.'

The tension was unbearable. Lou could see Martha was frantically thinking the same thing. Had he been watching them, had he seen them kiss?

Maisy ran into the scullery.

'Martha!' she cried, throwing herself into her arms. 'Will you do my hair?'

'Course I will,' Martha smiled, hoisting her up. 'Give us a hand hanging up the rest of this washing, then I'll plait your hair.'

Martha shot Lou a pointed look. 'You go and make your peace with Elsie and get ready. I'll finish off down here, get the girls together and we'll head off.'

Her father went out into the yard to wash, but Lou could feel his eyes on her.

An hour later, Lou, Martha and the girls were scrubbed up a treat and they piled out into the bank holiday sunshine to find all the Lavender Girls striding up Gibbins Road towards them. Betty, Joanie and Joycie clattered down the street, heels tapping on the cobbles, followed by Esther, Little Irene and Patsy.

Lou immediately felt herself switch into factory clown mode.

'Oi-oi! Up the Yardley girls!' she hollered, lighting up a cigarette.

'Wotcha, Fat Lou, Martha, all right girls,' they chorused back.

'You two are joined at the hip,' remarked Little Irene.

Martha smiled easily. 'Just helping Lou out.'

'You're a real pal to her,' Esther said.

'Don't you all look the business,' Lou said, swiftly changing the subject, though they really did look ravishing. Faces all made out, curls gleaming with Vitapointe, everyone all in their best clobber. Handbags matched headscarves and shoes. In the East End, glamour wasn't just about prettiness, it was about personality, swagger and attention to detail.

'Say what you like about East End factory girls, but we won't be bettered on glamour,' said Joanie proudly, fluttering her eyelashes.

'Wherever did you get your hands on mascara?' Martha asked. Make-up was now so strictly rationed, mascara was more precious than gold. 'You didn't get that black market stuff, did ya? It's got lead in it,' Martha warned.

'Course not. Melted a candle down, welded blobs of wax on to the end of my eyelashes and touched it up with my dad's boot polish.'

'Cor, it's ever so effective,' Martha replied admiringly.

'Let's just hope it don't melt in the sun,' Joanie laughed, 'otherwise I won't half give Johnnie a fright. Did I mention he's going to be there today with his unit? British War Relief Society of America have a stand and they've been detailed to help out.'

She looked meaningfully at Patsy. 'Including Blue.'

Patsy laughed and rolled her eyes. 'Bloody Nora, you don't give up easy!'

Lou couldn't keep her eyes off Patsy. Even in a crowd of such smashing-looking girls, no one could hold a candle to her. She was wearing a lavender-coloured summer frock, her tiny waist cinched in with a white belt, a white cardigan, a white silk headscarf tied in a knot round her dark hair and sunglasses with pale plastic frames. Her lips were stained to a deep red. The paleness of her clothes against the lush red lips and smooth honey tone of her skin was striking. She looked like a film star, not a factory girl.

'Come on, let's get going,' said Esther, slipping her arm through Lou's. As they walked in a great crowd towards the bus stop on the high street, Esther lowered her voice.

'Are you all right, Lou? I've been worried about you ever since we found out what really happened to your mum on Friday.'

'Keep your voice down, I can't have my sisters find out.'

'Of course,' Esther whispered. 'It's the most terrible thing . . . I just can't imagine how you must be feeling.'

'Not the first time it's ever happened round here and it won't be the last I dare say. After the war, they'll drain the lake in Vicky Park and you can imagine what they'll find. Bloody men. My father ought to have had it chopped off years ago.'

Esther stared at her in shock.

'I'm sorry, Esther, but I can't bear to think of Mum dying alone and in pain . . .'

She broke off, blinking back tears.

Esther squeezed her hand. 'If there's anything I can do, you only have to say the word.'

Lou smiled. 'I know, and thank you. So what about you and Walter? I gather life on the homefront ain't all rosy.'

Esther's face fell. 'That's the point. I haven't really been at home much. Between work and looking after Snowball, I think he's feeling a bit neglected. But I can't leave Snowball when he's suffering so much. He's been like a father to me and whatever he's going through is pushing him to the brink of his sanity.'

'You don't have to explain yourself to me, Est,' Lou soothed. 'That's the problem for us women. We're expected to be all things to all people. Maybe Walter ought to try and look at it from your perspective?'

Esther sighed. 'Doesn't help with his mother sticking her oar in every two minutes.'

'Aah, the mother-out-law,' Lou chuckled. 'How is Maureen?'

'You know Walter's mother, she has some robust opinions and she likes to . . .'

'Know the ins and outs of a cat's arsehole?'

Esther shrieked with laughter. 'That's one way of putting it. Do you know the day after we got married, I caught her checking the sheets! And when I came home the other day to get some fresh clothes before I headed back to the Shoot, I found her in our bedroom again on her hands and knees looking under the bed. Least she had the good grace to look guilty when she saw me.'

'What was she doing?'

'God only knows.'

'You wanna tell her to back off and keep her nose out of yours and Walter's marriage. At the very least out of your bedroom.'

'Ha. Easier said than done.'

'How's Nell doing?'

'She's scared and she don't know what to do about Snowball. It feels like he's a ticking timebomb. He refuses to say what's wrong. He's supposed to be resting, but every chance he gets, he's out in the allotment digging. I also realised that next month, it's the third anniversary of Renee's death.'

The pair lapsed into silence. Three years since Yardley's was rocked by the death of its golden girl, and none of the Lavender Girls were any closer to understanding the terrible atrocity.

'I thought we should hold a memorial by her graveside.'

'Isn't that a bit creepy?' Lou replied.

'Why? We could light candles, share our favourite Renee stories. It might encourage Nell to talk about her. Also, Yardley's are releasing a new shade of red next month and I suggested we have a lipstick-naming competition, in honour of Renee, with all proceeds going to the RAF Wings for Victory fund.'

Lou smiled, feeling a surge of hope at Esther's humanity. Despite the horror and revelations of the past forty-eight hours, there was some light in the dark. Out of all the girls, Esther was the one who had undergone the most profound change. She still remembered when she had arrived in Stratford at the outbreak of war, a terrified young refugee. Four years on, she had blossomed into a strong young woman, and Lou suspected they still hadn't seen half of what she was capable of. Lou adored Walter, but she hoped marriage to him wouldn't clip Esther's wings. She and Esther had always shared a closeness, born out of a mutual respect. After losing Renee, they had reached out to each other in their grief. Esther was a kind, gentle and generous soul who embraced life, even in the face of tragedy. Suddenly, Lou had an overwhelming urge to confide in her, tell the whole truth about her relationship with Martha. She sensed instinctively that if anyone could cope with her choice, it was Esther.

'Are you all right, Lou?' Esther asked. 'You've gone quiet.'

'I . . . Er . . . I need . . .'

'Hurry up and get a shift on, the bus is coming!' shrieked Little Irene, gesturing wildly as the red trolley bus trundled into view.

Esther grabbed Lou's hand and they ran. The whole of the top deck was filled with Clarnico girls, laughing and smoking.

Lou grinned.

'Oh here we go . . .'

The rivalry between the Yardley lot and the famous sweet factory girls based up the road was legendary.

'Cor, suddenly stinks in here,' announced one, flinging open the window. 'Here, Lou, ain'cha got anything else to wear apart from cat's nats?' asked the mouthiest of their number.

'State of you,' smiled Lou sweetly. 'I've seen smarter bags wrapped round coal.'

The whole top deck fell about.

'You ain't got nuffin' to crow about, Lou Button. Least I don't dress like a docker,' she said, staring pointedly at Lou's slacks. 'I wouldn't wear that to a dog fight!'

Lou sat down behind her and blew on her fox-fur stole.

'Knew it,' she sniffed. 'All fake fur, no knickers.'

The banter went back and forth until they pulled up outside the sports ground.

'What did you want to tell me earlier?' Esther said as they stood up.

'Nothing, forget it.'

East Ham's Civil Defence Sports Gala was terrifically busy, with what felt like half of East London crowded in trying to enjoy the bank holiday sunshine.

Beside the sporting events, there was no end of entertainment. A boxing ring had been set up with local lads slugging it out, there was a coconut shy, a fun fair, a bonny baby competition, tug-of-war and a realistic demonstration of fire-fighting and lifesaving by National Fire Service Area 36, who had proved their worth in the Blitz.

'I've got to go and find Walter,' said Esther over the noisy crowds. 'He's agreed to compère and is announcing the sports line-ups.'

Esther left and soon the rest of the Lavender Girls, and the Button sisters, had also melted into the crowds.

'Do you mind if we just sit here?' Lou yawned. 'I'm shattered.'

'You read my mind,' Martha replied.

They found a spot by the side of the running track and Martha pulled a picnic blanket, two apples and two bottles of ale from her bag.

'Where d'you get those?'

'Your dad's secret stash in the cold box in the yard,' she replied with an impish grin. Lou roared with laughter.

'I knew there was a reason I loved you.'

Lou popped open the top of her bottle with her key and laughed as beer foamed over her knuckles. She drank greedily, before stretching back, propped up on her elbows.

Martha clinked her bottle against Lou's and lay back too, using Lou's cardigan as a pillow. Within moments, her breathing slowed and Lou could tell the lack of sleep had caught up on her.

Lou let Martha sleep in the drowsy sunshine and cast her eye over the crowds. Tommies on leave were having a swell time with their girls, eating winkles on pins and knocking Hitler's block off, three shies for a penny. A GI was doing his best to impress a young blonde Clarnico girl by swinging a wooden mallet down on the high striker game. When he sent the puck shooting up to strike the bell, he whooped and gathered the girl in his arms, kissing her.

In a tent by the racetrack, Esther looked up proudly as Walter stood behind a podium and microphone announcing the upcoming races.

How easy it was for men and women to express their love. They could kiss, hold hands, flirt, argue, and no one batted an eyelid. Whereas she and Martha . . . She ached to reach out, thread her fingers through Martha's, but she would never be allowed even that tiny act of public affection.

Even now, in the fourth year of war, when all sorts of love seemed to be fair game, hers was still forbidden. It would be less scandalous for her to have an affair with three married soldiers than it was to be with Martha. Would there ever be a time that their love would be acceptable? The question seemed impossible, the future cloudy and unformed. Martha's joke earlier that they would grow old together, like two maiden aunts, hadn't seemed so implausible to Lou.

Lou felt the movement of beer in her veins, and the closeness of her secret lover was suddenly intoxicating. In her grubby dungarees, her mass of curly dark hair fanning round her face, Martha had never looked so beautiful. Her creamy skin had a lustre to it. Martha never wore make-up, black market or otherwise. She didn't need to.

Lou remembered the one and only time they had spent a whole night together, at Martha's when her parents were away. She remembered the glorious nakedness of her, their limbs entwined. Even the simple act of watching Martha get ready for work the next day, padding round the bedroom naked, dusting down her body with talc, scooping back her hair under her headscarf, was golden.

She stored the memory away like a precious pearl. The fragments of her life, their youth, were rushing away. Hadn't Renee's death and now her mother's sudden passing taught her how fragile life was?

Lou spotted Little Irene and Betty at the top of a big wheel, waving frantically, and she waved back. Their painted red lips were wide open in laughter, Betty's polka-dot dress billowing round her slender ankles. It would never occur to the Lavender Girls that she wasn't like them. The only clue to her real identity was in the discreet little gold signet ring on the smallest finger of her left hand, which matched Martha's.

Suddenly the ground beneath her legs seemed to rumble and she sat up abruptly. A deep throbbing sound cut over the sound of the fairground squeals. The throbbing became a roar and the crowds strained their necks upwards. A blur of black scratched the eggshell blue of the sky.

Martha opened her eyes blearily and followed Lou's gaze.

Overhead, flying in formation, so low it looked like they were scraping the rooftops, was wave after wave of bombers.

The air offensive directed against Fortress Europe had really picked up pace this year and the skies over southern England were like one vast roaring aeroplane. But it was unusual to see them here, and in broad daylight.

'American planes by the looks of them,' Martha remarked, squinting against the sun. 'Must be coming out of Essex.'

'Nice to see 'em heading out instead of in, for a change,' Lou replied, picking up her beer bottle and raising it aloft in a salute to the crew.

'Wish them luck,' said Walter's amplified voice over the microphone and the crowds cheered, clapped and made 'V for victory' signs.

Lou's gaze lazily roamed the crowds before settling on a familiar figure a hundred or so yards from them, standing by the beer and seafood stall. Her father was busy scooping a winkle out of a shell before popping it in the mouth of a blonde woman by his side. She couldn't use her own hands as they were clamped around Lou's father's arm.

'I don't bloody believe it,' Lou gasped, jumping to her feet. 'Look over there, by the seafood stall.'

Anger rose in her for the second time in as many days.

'So now I really know where you were this weekend!' she yelled at the top of her voice.

Groups of people, clutching pints and cartons of whelks and winkles, fell into silence, eagerly anticipating a juicy row with Yardley's motormouth at the centre of it.

'Civil defence business, my arse. Dirty weekend away with your brassy bit on the side more like.'

Her father walked over, his mouth a tight white slit in his face.

'Louise. This is Nancy from—'

'I know, accounts.' Lou stared flintily at Nancy.

'He tell you our mother died of a botched abortion? You are aware he's married, love, and he's got six daughters, or don't you care?'

'Your father has been a dear friend for many years and I've been comforting him since your mother died,' she said defensively.

'I'm sure you have, love,' Lou scoffed.

'That's enough, Louise,' her father ordered. 'You'll show Nancy respect. She'll be moving in next week.'

'You're moving your fancy woman in?' Lou gaped. 'We only buried Mum on Friday!'

'Like I said, Nancy has been an enormous support. We need a more feminine, respectable influence in the house to guide your younger sisters. After all . . .'

He looked from her to Martha and curled his lip.

'You two are hardly setting a good example. You look like a couple of eunuchs, and why's she always lurking round the house? I've warned you, people are talking.'

Lou flung herself at her father, but Martha grabbed her.

'Leave it, Lou,' she hissed.

Lou locked eyes with her father. 'Over my dead body is that lousy tart moving into our home.'

The blue sky span and she staggered back. It took a moment to realise her father had struck her, a solid backhander that left her reeling.

He leant forward and hissed in her ear, his sour breath soiling the air.

'I'm being polite because we're in public, but when we get home, I'm going to tie you to a post and leather you!'

Behind his shoulder, she could see the crowds had stilled. She picked out the astonished faces of the Lavender Girls. Her father meant to humiliate her in front of half of Stratford.

'So why not do it here,' she cried, blinking back tears. 'Show the whole world what sort of man you really are!'

'Very well.' He drew back his arm, but nothing happened. His face contorted from malice to confusion. A man in uniform had leapt forward and had his arms pinioned behind his back.

'With respect, sir, my daddy brought me up never to raise a finger to a woman.'

'Blue!' Lou cried in astonishment.

'Get your wretched hands off me, Yank,' her father grunted, his cap flying on to the ground.

'Not until you promise not to strike your daughter.'

'I'm leaving,' Lou's father snarled through gritted teeth.

Blue released his arms, then placed himself protectively in front of Lou.

Her father scooped down to pick up his hat from the ground and shot Lou a look of pure poison. He had been humiliated and Lou knew he would never forget or forgive. Grabbing Nancy's hand, he strode away, the crowds parting to let him pass.

There was a moment's stunned silence broken by the sudden screech of feedback from the microphone by the sports field.

'Please, Walter, just listen. You're not being fair.'

Esther's trembly voice echoed out round the whole ground.

Martha was the first to realise.

'Est!' she cried. 'The microphone's still switched on!' But it was too late, for a moment later, it was followed by Walter's angry voice.

'I want a baby, Esther. I'm your husband, I have rights you know.'

'Oh for pity's sake, grow up, Walter. I'm starting to wish we'd never got married.'

Esther's voice blared from every single tannoy around the playing fields and seemed to bounce off the trees, stunning the crowd into silence.

By the time they realised what had happened, it was too late. The entire sports gala had been privy to their bust-up.

'Oh Esther!' Lou's hand flew to her mouth, her own worries momentarily forgotten.

But Esther was already running from the sports tent, her face as pale as bone as she pushed her way through the amused crowds. The East End was used to a bank holiday bust-up, but this one was in another league. Humiliated, Esther fled in the same direction in which Lou's father had just left.

A frozen silence cloaked the still summer air and Lou looked around in disbelief. What was happening to the Lavender Girls?

10

Patsy

Patsy stood by the seafood stall and watched the whole thing unfold, filled with admiration at the way Blue had leapt to Lou's rescue and mortification for poor Esther.

'Oh flamin' hell,' she murmured. If things weren't dramatic enough, it was about to get a whole lot worse. There was her mother, Queenie Jacks, cutting through the bank holiday crowds in a sweeping floor-length black dress, like a spectre at the feast.

In the silence that followed Esther's departure, Queenie flipped over an old orange crate and stood so she was head and shoulders above the crowd. She looked like a dark crow about to flap off into the skies. Her reedy voice carried high over the sports field.

'FORNICATION! ADULTERY! ABORTION!'

The crowd, already geed up, turned to stare at the strange woman on her soapbox.

'What we have observed here reflects the dismal state of our wartime society.'

'Cor,' muttered the man beside Patsy, with obvious relish. 'Who knew a sports gala could be so entertaining?'

Patsy closed her eyes. *Please stop. Please stop.*

'I have signed the temperance pledge and I abstain from drink, from vice, from carnal sins of the flesh, from fornication and warmongering . . .'

'Bloody boring if you ask me,' sniffed Little Irene behind her.

'This is not our war to fight. Let Churchill and Hitler slug it out away from us. You must turn your back on this evil war, as we must also turn our back on sin and vice. No one need be shanghaied, you can claim your right as a conscientious objector—'

'With respect, love, I'm in employment for the first time in years,' heckled a man with one arm. 'It's only the war what's cured the Depression.'

'You're a crackpot!' called another. 'If we ignore it, it'll only be a matter of time before Jerries are marching down your street, then see how your conchie status'll go down.'

Queenie ignored him, raising her voice a pitch.

'I know there are fornicators among us; those who seek pleasures of the flesh, homosexuals, women who break their marriage vows and, as we have just heard, deny their husband his right to a secure family life.' Her eyes flashed and she pointed a long bony finger at the crowd. 'There has been a change in morality around these parts and you cannot afford to turn your back on it any longer.'

Patsy looked around, mortified. People were openly laughing at her mother, others getting ready for a good heckle. She couldn't stand it any longer. Turning, she pushed her way through the crowds. Finally, she spotted him, standing by the War Relief stand recounting his tangle with Lou's father to his buddies. When he spotted her, his face melted from surprise to pleasure.

'Blue . . .'

'Patsy . . .'

They spoke at the same time.

'I didn't think you were here,' he said.

'I was avoiding you. Can we get out of here?'

'Sure, baby,' he replied, looking confused. 'Where do you wanna go?'

'Anywhere, I don't care. As long as it's far away from here.'

Blue took her hand and together they ran. A sort of madness took hold and Patsy found herself laughing in relief as they left the sports ground and, by some miracle, Blue managed to hail a taxi.

Sitting in the back of a taxi, Blue stared at her, dumbfounded.

'Not often you're lost for words,' Patsy remarked, getting out a compact to check her appearance.

'You are just so astonishingly beautiful. You look like some sort of film star in that, what do you Brits call it? *Rig-out.*' He patted down his jacket pretending to look for a pen. 'Can I have an autograph?'

'Daft sod,' Patsy giggled.

'But seriously, why did you want to leave with me?'

'My mother was there, making a show of herself. And as for you . . .' Patsy knew it was because watching him leap to Lou's defence was just about the most heroic, attractive thing she'd ever seen a man do. But she didn't want his head to swell. ''Cause Cary Grant weren't available.'

'So where do you want to go?'

'Somewhere central. I have to be at The Windmill later, so I'll leave it up to you.'

'Your wish is my command. Say, did you get my hamper? I had it delivered to the factory last Friday.'

Patsy took off her sunglasses and turned to him.

'Let's get one thing straight. Do you know how many English girls get a reputation for being a Yankee bag when they accept all these gifts? I am not *that* kind of girl.'

Blue's face fell.

'I didn't mean to insult you, Patsy. It's just that you girls have so little what with rationing. I just want to share what I have with you.'

Patsy's face softened.

'I'm sorry, Blue. I didn't mean to sound chippy, it's just that you don't have to. It sends out the wrong signals when you send me gifts to the factory and spend lots of money on me.'

'So I guess dinner somewhere swanky is out the question?'

'Correct. We could go to the theatre?' Patsy suggested. '*Make it a Boy* with Tessie O'Shea is on at the moment. I love her.'

'But I want to be able to talk to you,' Blue insisted. He thought for a while then tapped the driver's shoulder.

'Say, pal, set us down at Tower Bridge.'

As they pulled up at the famous landmark, Blue tipped the delighted driver handsomely.

'We're going to see some of London's famous sights and then we're gonna have a picnic in the park.' He held out his arm. 'For a couple of hours, I'm going to make you forget there's a war on, Patsy Jacks.'

Patsy laughed as she replaced her sunglasses and tucked her arm through his. 'You'll have your work cut out, but I'm game.'

For the next couple of hours, Patsy saw London as she had never seen it before, through Blue's eyes.

It began as he gazed, spellbound, at the Tower of London. 'I can't believe it's nearly nine hundred years old,' he marvelled.

From there, they walked over Tower Bridge as Blue had promised his mum he would, but had to wait on the other side while the bridge was raised to let a gunboat slide through the oily waters beneath. Vast clouds billowed overhead and as Patsy gazed east towards her home, all she could see was the decimated docklands, fractured and stark against the sky.

Suddenly, a memory popped into her head and she laughed out loud.

'What is it?' Blue smiled.

'Oh you'll never believe it.'

'Try me.'

'When I was growing up in Poplar, down our turning, a lot of the mums had right mouths on them. Serious foghorns, the lot of 'em. When they used to call us in for our tea, it was like thunder rolling up the street.'

Blue chuckled.

'So the fella who ran the corner shop, Mr Buckhurst, one day arranged a competition to see which mum had the loudest voice! All the mums down our turning stood on one side of Tower Bridge and had to sing or shout, and the winner was whoever's voice Mr Buckhurst could hear loudest standing on the other side of the bridge.'

Blue's eyes widened. 'Get out of here. So who won?'

'You have to ask?' Patsy grinned. 'Did you not hear my mum on her soapbox earlier?'

Blue shook his head.

'No, I didn't have that pleasure.'

'Trust me, you didn't miss much.' She sighed.

'Sad really. Before we lost my dad, Mum was forever singing and now . . .' She broke off and turned her head to look west up the river.

'And what happened to the women of your street – the other, what did you call them, "foghorns"?'

Patsy shrugged. 'God knows. A third of the street was wiped out by a UXB left over from the Blitz. Poor Mr Buckhurst was killed.'

'That's tragic.'

'Nothing's the same anymore,' she sighed, picking at a patch of blistering paint on the bridge.

'Come on,' he said. 'I'm supposed to be helping you to forget the war.'

Next they wandered along the river to Westminster Abbey

and Blue's eyes misted over when he saw the stained-glass windows. He laughed like a boy as they walked through the flocks of pigeons in Trafalgar Square, sending them flapping into the skies.

Blue even talked her into visiting the Royal Academy, which was hosting the London County Council Housing Plan. Patsy felt herself grow cold as they stared at the futuristic plans; acres of suburban living setting out the post-war dream, with indoor plumbing and hot and cold running water.

'Little premature, if you ask me,' she remarked.

'Maybe one day we can get a place?' he joked.

'I don't want to live in a box behind a hedge, thank you very much,' she said, turning her back on the vision of the future.

'I'd live in a cardboard box if it were with you.' She felt his blue eyes on hers, scrutinising her for a reaction. She knew enough about Blue by now to know his intentions weren't as basic as she had first imagined. He was a good man. He'd proved that by the way he'd stepped in to help Lou earlier. But this intensity of his, coupled with his candid openness, was completely alien to her. The men she'd met before didn't talk about their feelings or emotions. And that suited her fine, because that way, she didn't have to either. That was a lid she never wanted to open. Because what would come pouring out? Shame, humiliation, guilt at her own pathetic feebleness? She felt her eyes fill with tears.

'Come on,' she said, furiously blinking them back. 'I'm famished.'

'Me too. I know just the place.'

Blue led her in the direction of Piccadilly. Working there, Patsy was used to the area now dubbed Little America, but today was ridiculous. There seemed to have been a small invasion of GIs. They watched in astonishment as a dray cart filled with American soldiers and their girls, drawn by two white shire horses, clattered past them at full speed, the passengers all singing 'Idaho'.

'Where do you stay when you're on leave?' she asked.

'We call it a furlough. I stay at Washington Hotel in Curzon Street.'

'And what about the black GIs?' she asked, spying two young black soldiers walking on the other side of the street.

'They usually stay at the Duchess Club.'

'Black and white don't mix in the American Army, huh?' she queried, narrowing her eyes.

'I don't agree with segregation, Patsy.'

'Well, make sure *you're* decent to them. Bad enough being in a strange land, fighting a war, without their own side discriminating against them.'

'I'm not prejudiced, Patsy,' Blue said quietly.

They walked to South Audley Street, the mood suddenly somewhat sombre.

'We call this Miniature Fifth Avenue,' Blue remarked as they stopped outside an American Army PX store. 'Wait here, I'm going to get some provisions.'

'Get us a needle and thread while you're in there, please,' she asked.

'Sure thing.'

Blue emerged with a feast. Two bars of Hershey chocolate, candy, two bottles of beer, seven packs of Camel cigarettes and other goodies for their picnic. Not only that, but he'd got a couple of comics for her brother Jimmy.

'*Looney Tunes* and *Captain Marvel*. My favourites when I was growing up. Hope you don't draw the line at gifts for your brother?'

She shook her head. 'No, course not. Thank you, Blue. He'll love them. He's had so little of anything, he deserves to be made a fuss of.'

'You really love the little guy, huh?'

She nodded. 'Since our dad died, he's the most important thing in the world to me.' Blue smiled as he handed the gifts to her, unable to keep his gaze from hers.

'Then if he's important to you, he's important to me.'

Patsy shook her head as she looked at the wealth of provisions available to American soldiers, compared to the meagre supplies the women of Stratford survived off.

'I'm not sure I'm going to have time for a picnic,' she frowned suddenly. 'I don't want to be late for rehearsals.'

'Please, Patsy. This is my last day of my furlough. I've got my first active mission coming up in the next fortnight and I don't know when I'll see you next . . .'

Blue looked so crestfallen, Patsy relented.

'Come on then.'

They picked Green Park, but as soon as they walked in, Blue's face clouded over.

'What's wrong?' she asked, gazing about the bucolic scene. Flocks of sheep were grazing in the park as part of the government's Produce More Food scheme.

'It's the sheep,' he muttered.

'Don't tell me a big tough man like you is scared of sheep!' she exclaimed.

'It's the way they look at you with those beady eyes. I'm telling you, Patsy. They're bad news.'

Patsy hooted with laughter, a great big belly laugh that had her doubled over.

'Oh this is priceless,' she laughed, taking off her sunglasses to wipe her eyes. 'You can take on Lou's dad, to say nothing of the Luftwaffe, but you're scared of a little flock of sheep.'

Blue started to laugh.

'I guess it does sound a little screwy when you put it like that. What can I say?' he grinned, spreading out his arms and dazzling her with that smile of his. 'I'm a pantywaister.'

She slapped his arm playfully. 'Let's hope Hitler's new secret weapon isn't Little Bo Peep!'

'Perish the thought,' he grinned.

They were still laughing as they walked into Hyde Park and Blue laid out his jacket for Patsy to sit on in a shady spot under a tree.

All about them was the detritus of war. A team of Yanks was playing baseball in the shadow of anti-aircraft rockets, and as far as the eye could see there were great scrolls of barbed wire. Silver barrage balloons bobbed over their heads like a shoal of big bloated fish.

At times, Patsy felt like it was only those barrage balloons keeping the British Isles afloat: cut the cables and the whole country would sink into the sea under the weight of all the extra troops and machinery of war.

'Guess you can't really escape,' she shrugged, unknotting her headscarf and leaning back against the trunk of the tree.

'This will help,' he said, unscrewing a jar and digging out a big spoonful of something brown and sticky.

'What is it?'

'Try it.'

Patsy opened her mouth and Blue fed her the unctuous gooey mixture.

Her taste buds exploded and her eyes closed as she swallowed.

'That is delicious!'

'Peanut butter,' he smiled. 'Have some more.'

The peanut butter was followed by ripe peaches, thick hunks of cheese and fresh bread, washed down with cold beer. After years of Spam, powdered egg and stuffed marrow, it was the food of the gods.

Warm, content and full – possibly for the first time in her life – Patsy lay back against the grass. Blue picked a blade and traced it against her lips. With her blood red lipstick now faded, she looked younger, more naked somehow.

'I can't tell you how good it is to see you happy, Patsy.'

'Happy's a bit of an abstract concept in wartime, isn't it?' she asked.

'Maybe. When was the last time you felt truly content?'

She thought.

'Camber Sands, 1934.'

A smile played across her face.

'Tell me about it.'

She propped herself up on one elbow.

'Great crowd of us went, must have been a hundred at least. I was only eight and it felt like the day to end all days.'

'Really?' he exclaimed. 'Gee, you East Enders don't do things by half, do you?'

'Actually, we used to call ourselves the "other East Enders".'

'How so?'

Patsy thought for a moment, then pulled out a battered black-and-white photo from her purse. The creases were worn, the paper so thin her father looked like he was fading from the photo, as he had from life.

'Look at you,' he exclaimed. 'Is this you on your daddy's shoulders?'

She nodded, suddenly filled with pride at the sight of the man she had grown up worshipping.

'He sure is a handsome fella. And who are all these other folk in the photo?'

Patsy was perched on her father's shoulders, eyes bright as a summer day, hair flowing behind her in the salty breeze. All around them were other families of all creeds, colours and faiths, mainly white women with Indian Lascar seamen and West Indian men. And dozens of children born from their unions.

'Mixed-race families like ours weren't so readily accepted,' she admitted. 'Like I told you when we first met, Dad was half-caste, he had a West Indian father and white Irish mother.

He never really felt like he belonged anywhere. He met my mum at a pub she used to sing in down the docks, two years after the first war ended. Mum took one look at Dad and it was love at first sight.

'I can see why,' Blue said, intrigued by the photograph. 'He's a got a terrific smile.'

'Oh, everyone loved my dad. Could he hold a tune! And he was hardworking too, polite, loyal. He made you feel the centre of his world. It's just a shame . . .' She tailed off.

'Don't clam up on me now, Patsy,' Blue urged.

'Well it was hard for Mum. She faced a barrage of abuse to be with him. There was terrible discrimination.

'Her mum, my nan, disowned her. I've never even met her. So these people, in the photo, the "other East Enders" as we called ourselves, they were like our family.'

'Say, who's this fella?' Blue asked, pointing to a man in the centre of the photo. 'He's got a presence about him.'

'That's Kamal Chunchie, Dad's friend and a social campaigner,' she said proudly. 'He set up a group called the Coloured Men's Institute in the Docklands between the wars, to promote brotherhood between the white and coloured people of East London. To young families, like my mum and dad, ostracised from their communities, it was a lifeline. He hated the way people like my dad were treated. So he created a safe place, a sanctuary I suppose, where coloured folk could go to relax, play pool, read the papers, listen to the wireless and so on.'

Patsy knew she was talking too much, but Blue was such a good listener and it was as if a tap had been turned on inside her. Somehow Blue had prised the lid off and was gently teasing out her emotions. To her surprise, she didn't feel self-conscious talking. Just safe. For the first time in a very long time.

'It was him who arranged this trip to Camber Sands. Oh,

it was such a smashing day. Mum parading down the shore-line on Dad's arm, proud as a peacock. Us kids stuffing ourselves on fish and chips, watching Punch and Judy while the men played cricket. That day, I didn't feel scared about being abused or spat on, because for once, there was more of us. We weren't the minority that day.'

Blue listened, rapt.

'You see, Blue, I know no tongue but the cockney one, but I was always the outsider. Looked down on, jeered at . . .'

'Wow,' he breathed eventually. 'I don't know what to say. So what happened to Kamal and all the people in the photo?'

'The Institute was in Canning Town, so like the rest of the Docklands, there ain't much of it left. Not that there's anyone to go there. Kamal's flock is dispersed. We're all scattered to the winds. Mum refuses to visit as it just reminds her of Dad. Most of the men in this photo are probably dead, killed in combat, like my father.'

Blue frowned. 'Where's your mother in this picture?'

'That's her there, the woman next to my father.'

'*That's* your mother?' he exclaimed. 'The same woman I saw today at the sports gala? I only glimpsed her briefly through the crowds admittedly, but she didn't look like this!'

Patsy laughed wryly. 'I know, hard to believe isn't it.'

Dressed in a pretty navy polka-dot summer frock, long legs bare and her hair flowing down her back, she presented a very different woman to the buttoned-up, angry soapbox preacher.

'Dad was so dignified. However low the bigots went, he never stooped to their level,' she explained. 'He used to stop Mum fighting back. Now he's dead, there's no one to hold her back no more; she's at war with the whole world. I worry that one day, that anger'll just eat her alive.'

Patsy sat up and hugged her knees.

'Sorry, I've been rattling on for ages.'

Blue put his arms around her and drew her into an embrace. Patsy went to pull back, but the warmth from his body was comforting and, for once, it felt so good to be held.

'Thank you,' he whispered in her ear, gently kissing the top of her head. 'For opening up to me. For a girl who poses naked on a stage, you hold a lot back. But I think I just saw the real Patsy.'

Patsy said nothing. What could she say? For if he knew the truth, *the whole truth*, he'd run a mile.

Instead, she surrendered to his embrace.

After that, they lay back under the tree. The sinking sun sent shafts of golden light filtering through the green canopy of leaves and its dappled light danced over their faces.

They lay side by side, basking like cats in the drowsy sunshine, content in their own silence. Somewhere nearby, a Salvation Army band had set up and started to play a medley of old-time favourites.

Patsy watched it all through drowsy eyelids. The park keeper in his brown coat renting out deckchairs so people could sit and listen to the band; a group of nurses in dark-blue capes and spotless caps striding past giggling; a blackbird tugging viciously at a worm, before giving up and flying into the sky. She observed all these things, but in Blue's arms, she felt separate from it all, cocooned in the protective warmth of his embrace.

The light softened and Patsy felt the baked earth still warm under the bare skin of her calves. The still, saturated air smelt of dusty lavender and the faint tang of manure from the nearby animal enclosures. Her limbs loosened, her breathing slowed.

Patsy began to drift off, and as her body fell into slumber, she felt his breath, warm against her hair. 'I'm falling in love with you, Patsy,' he murmured throatily.

Patsy looked away. There was no answer she could give

him, leastwise not one that would keep him here. Instead, she sat up. 'I've just remembered something.'

Digging around in her bag, she pulled out a farthing coin. 'You got that needle and thread I asked for earlier?'

Blue reached into his uniform pocket and pulled it out.

'Give me your jacket,' she ordered.

Blue looked perplexed, but did as she said.

Carefully, she threaded the tiny needle and deftly sewed the coin under the shoulder patch of his uniform jacket.

'For luck,' she said when she was finished, handing it back.

Without a word, he pulled her closer, cupped her face with his hands and kissed her. Everything faded away. A soft breeze fingered her hair as his tongue gently probed hers. She waited for her heart to pick up speed, for the panic to crawl its way into her chest, but this time there was no fear. Just a wonderful, sweet pleasure.

She got the feeling that nothing would ever feel as good as this ever again. Right now, being kissed in a summer park by Blue – this was golden. The distant throb of an aircraft droned overhead, its engines filling the sky with a message.

Remember this, remember this, remember this.

'Oh shoot!' she announced, drawing back abruptly.

'What's wrong?'

'I'm late for rehearsals.' She jumped to her feet, hastily brushing grass from her dress and shaking out her white cardigan. 'Not just late, but catastrophically late. I've got to go.'

'I leave tomorrow,' said Blue, standing too, his face distraught in the reddish dusk. 'Can I write, come and see you when I next get liberty?'

She nodded, torn between the desire to run, and one more kiss.

'Yes, I'd like that. And thanks Blue, for today. You were right. I did forget the war.'

She turned to move off, but he caught her fingertips and pulled her back into his arms.

'Wait. Does this mean you're my girl now?' He gazed down, his bright-blue eyes searching hers hopefully.

She laughed, the soft summer breeze ruffling her glossy dark waves. 'Yes, Blue, yes, I'm your girl.'

And then she was running across the shadows of the park, into an uncertain future, leaving the lovestruck American behind her.

At the park gates, she turned and glanced back. Blue was waving her white silk scarf over his head, like he was surrendering.

'Keep it!' she cried.

He pressed it to his lips, then tucked it in his pocket.

'I'll be thinking of you, Patsy Jacks!' he called back. 'You have my heart.'

Seconds later, she slipped on to the busy London street, back in the direction of Piccadilly, and the world became all sharp angles, smoke and wartime traffic again.

Her life was now even more complicated. Dating a Yank, taking her clothes off . . . even her own mother couldn't guess at the depth and duality of her deception. A deception made even more dangerous by the fact that Blue, a young man about to fly into enemy territory, was falling hard and fast. And the ultimate tragedy was that she would never truly be free to love him back, not in the way he deserved.

Patsy was beginning to trust him, and she didn't doubt his sincerity, but what right did she have to expect a calm and settled future with Blue? In the face of war and her turbulent past, this happiness felt as fragile as cheap china. For if Blue knew the secret she was hiding, he'd run a country mile. The real Patsy Jacks was not a girl he would want to marry, not a girl that any respectable man should want as his wife.

By the time Patsy reached the stage door on Archer Street

she was agitated and took a moment to compose herself, to somehow banish the fleeting joy she had felt in the sunlit park to the furthest recesses of her mind. She picked a blade of grass from her hair and reapplied her red lipstick. Patsy the showgirl was a far easier identity to hide behind.

PART TWO

11

Esther

September 1943

Summer faded into autumn and the blackout came earlier every evening. With darkness creeping in, a malaise had settled over Stratford.

There once was a time when autumn was Esther's favourite season, thanks in large part to Nell Gunn's cooking: apples baked with cinnamon, hot potatoes roasting on a fire, the spice in a bread pudding . . . But just lately, it was hard finding the joy in small things.

A bone-sapping exhaustion smothered her, which she put down to double shifts, more fuel shortages and an ever-increasing workload. Each week, they lost another worker who was conscripted into the services, and the production of aircraft components now far outweighed that of Yardley products.

Not only that, but Herbert Morrison, the Minister of Home Security, had recently issued new compulsory fire-watching orders for women, so Esther had to factor that into her complicated shift patterns. The war machine was a thankless mistress. But they were still going, churning out red lipsticks like bullets, thanks to the Beauty is your Duty campaign.

At least they had today to look forward to, with the announcement of the winner of the new Yardley red lipstick naming competition.

Esther finished clearing away the breakfast things just as Walter walked in from the yard.

'You ready, love?' he asked. 'Mum's made our sandwiches. Ooh, that red lipstick looks smashing on you.'

'Thanks, not my normal look, I know. But I'm so haggard at the moment, I thought it might freshen me up. Put my best face forward and all that.'

'You're as beautiful as the day I met you,' he grinned, tightening his braces. 'Stratford's answer to Greta Garbo.'

'Liar,' she grinned.

For once, they were on the same shift pattern, so could walk into work together. Since that dreadful day at the sports gala nearly six weeks ago, an uneasy sort of truce had been called, with Walter promising to give Esther some space, provided she move back in, and Esther promising to think seriously about starting a family. Both sides were bruised and a bit battered from the humiliation of their very public row, but Esther's mum Julia had made them both promise to put their pride to one side and keep talking. It was good advice.

But as long as Maureen Smith was on the scene, Esther had the distinct feeling their peace could blow up in their faces at any moment. At least she had stopped coming into their bedroom. Esther had insisted on that before she moved back in. What Maureen didn't know was that Esther had set up a savings account through Yardley's, where most of her weekly wages were going, in order to save for the rent on a place of their own. If she was going to think seriously about a baby, she was damned if she was having one under Maureen's roof.

The front door banged open and Maureen walked in off the street, clutching a bucket and scrubbing brush.

'You're up, I see,' she remarked pointedly to Esther. 'You've missed the best part of the day.'

'Mum,' sighed Walter. 'It's only seven a.m.'

'Wish I could have a lie-in,' she sighed. 'But the devil makes work for idle hands, isn't that right, Esther? Someone should try telling her next door that. That step of hers hasn't been scrubbed in days and she needs to deadhead her geraniums. Filthy cow . . .'

And she was off. Esther knew Maureen's rants about her neighbours' perceived shortcomings could run on for hours.

'Walter, we have to go.'

'Esther dear, I don't wish to be rude, but are you wearing that red lipstick outdoors? You look like an actress.'

'Oh Mum, everyone's wearing it now. It's patriotic. It makes the girls at work feel nice and glamorous, so where's the harm? Besides, Hitler hates it on women apparently, so all the more reason to wear it I say,' she replied brightly.

Maureen's face puckered as she set down her mop. 'What is it with this generation and glamour? In my youth, we never saw the need. We were content to give up work and raise children. Motherhood is the best job description in the world.'

Esther felt her hackles rise. 'Maybe in peacetime . . .'

'Is that the hooter?' Walter interrupted diplomatically. 'Come on, Esther. We better shake a leg.'

'Be back on time, I've making your favourite, son. Liver and onions.'

His face fell. 'Don't you remember, Mum, we're having a graveside memorial for Renee this evening after work. It's been three years since the Canning Town bomb. I did say I'd be back late.'

Maureen's lip wobbled and Esther stifled her irritation.

'You didn't mention it. Why mourn that Gunn girl? Everyone knows she was only in that hall because she was running away with her bastard unborn child.'

'Mum, please don't start that again.'

'But of course, if you'd rather leave your poor widowed

mother at home on her own, then that's your business.'
Maureen touched her hankie to her eye for dramatic effect.

'Oh, please don't cry, Mum.'

Walter turned awkwardly to Esther.

'You come straight home after work,' she sighed. 'I'll make
an excuse up to Mrs Gunn.'

'Thanks, Esther,' he smiled, relieved.

'You're the best son a mother could ever ask for,' said
Maureen, recovering quickly. 'It's so lonely being here on
your own since your father died, God rest his soul. Course
if I had a grandchild to keep my mind off him . . .'

Esther tried not to roll her eyes. Mr Smith had been dead
fifteen years.

'Come here, Mum,' Walter said, giving her a hug.

'I don't know what I'd ever do if you left me, son.'

'Don't be daft, Mum, as if we'd do that.'

Over Walter's shoulder, Maureen shot Esther a triumphant
smile.

Outside, the air felt smoky blue and autumnal. Esther
gulped it in, relieved to be out from the stultifying terrace.

'The seasons are changing,' said Walter, slipping his hand
through Esther's. 'I'm sorry about this evening. You don't
mind, do you?'

'No, course not,' she lied.

By mid-morning tea break, Esther's lipstick had smudged off
and she felt wrung out. The girls' singing voices were so loud,
she thought her skull was about to split open.

Little Irene was leading the charge, her brassy voice
competing with the loud clanking of the factory machinery.
Though it was September, the heat in the third-floor room
was fierce and the windows were steamed up.

''Itler has only got one ball . . .'

'The other,' roared Lou, 'is in the Albert 'All.'

''Ere,' said Irene, scratching under her turban. 'Do you reckon he really does only have one bollock? I mean, wouldn't he go round in circles every time he salutes?'

The girls rocked with laughter.

'You can't fall to a man with one ball, you know,' Betty said knowingly.

Esther's mouth fell open. 'That's poppycock, Betty.'

'Is it though?' she replied, raising one pencilled brow. 'My older sister, she's in the Land Army now, she told me you can't get in the family way if you do it standing up.'

'And she should know,' quipped Joycie. 'How many haystacks she been up against?' More howls of laughter.

Esther closed her eyes, reached into her overall pocket and wiped a cooling slick of freesia cologne over her forehead. The girls swore by it for headaches, but it didn't seem to touch hers.

'Give me strength,' she whispered under her breath. The girls were driving her round the twist! She knew where this was going to lead. The moment the conversation strayed on to the subject of sex – one of their favourite topics, besides Hollywood actresses, clothes and make-up – some wild theory would usually be bandied about.

'Is it true the baby comes out your bottom?' Little Irene went on from her place at the conveyor belt. A fourteen-year-old service girl pushing past a trolley skidded to a stop.

'Ooh shut up, it never does!' she breathed.

'You dozy cow,' Betty laughed. 'Course not. It's got something to do with that brown line you get down your tummy, ain't it, Lou?'

'No, you nit,' Lou scoffed, looking up from the pallet of lipsticks she was counting. 'Of course you can fall having sex standing up. The baby don't come out your arse, and that brown line is absolutely nothing to do with the birth process.'

'It comes out the same place it went in,' added Joanie bluntly, making a rude gesture with a red lipstick.

Little Irene pulled a face.

'I'm never letting any fella near my minnie, thank you very much.'

'You say that now . . .' laughed Lou, heaving the packaged-up pallet on to a trolley.

Yardley's offered a formidable education in the ways of the world, and often it was left to the older girls and married women to set the younger ones straight. One of these days, Esther planned on bringing her mother in. As a nurse, Julia could offer some much-needed enlightenment. Though somehow, she couldn't see herself getting that one past the welfare officer. Anyway, it would have to wait, as her mother had a new job as a teacher, now that the council had lifted the bar for the duration of the war on married women being teachers.

Only Patsy stayed quiet, a wistful smile on her face.

''Ere, Pats!' screeched Betty, turning from the lipstick churn, where she was stirring up a great vat of churning red liquid. 'I reckon wherever your head is, it's more interesting than what's available in this room. You dreaming of Blue again?'

It was no secret that the factory glamour girl was now dating the GI. According to Lou, he'd written to her every week from his base in Essex. They certainly cut a dashing couple together. But when it came to Patsy Jacks, there was still something more going on. Esther couldn't put her finger on what, but she was out of there like her heels were on fire once her shift finished, and was still refusing to pack munitions on the afternoon shift. Her mother had insisted on it, but Esther also got the distinct impression that wherever it was Patsy tore off to in the afternoons and evenings would not meet with the approbation of that tyrant mother of hers.

Patsy smiled teasingly.

'What could possibly be more interesting than putting a

little red sticker on to the bottom of a lipstick tube, again and again and again?' she joked.

'And remember,' teased Little Irene, flicking Mavis's turban, 'good looks and good morale are close companions . . .'

'So put your best face forward,' chorused all the girls.

'I'd rather have a companion like what Patsy's got,' said Joycie. 'Big smile, big wallet and a great big c—'

'Joycie!' Esther snapped, finally losing her rag. 'Get on with your work.' The mood in the room was febrile and overexcited. Her head couldn't take much more.

'You all right, Est?' said Lou, touching her lightly on the arm. 'They're only having a bit of fun.'

'I know,' she sighed. 'I don't feel too bright.'

'Yeah, you look rotten. You're ever so pale. Want me to take over as room supervisor?'

'No . . . no . . .' Outside, the wind changed direction and the smell of boiling bones from Knights, the soap firm up the road, oozed through the window. Combined with the smell of animal fat from the lipstick churn, it was a ripe aroma. Suddenly, Esther could feel her stomach readying itself to empty its contents.

'Eurgh!' she groaned, clamping her hand over her mouth. She just about made it to the toilet cubicle before she was sick in the lavatory bowl.

She was sick four more times, a delightful mixture of lumpy Garibaldi biscuits and strong tea.

Staggering out, she tried to turn the tap on but the water knocked and spluttered in the pipes. She picked up a wrench kept next to the sink and banged the pipes to make them fire up. The noise reverberated painfully around her head.

She splashed a weak trickle of water on her face and dried her mouth on the edge of a roller towel. She breathed slowly, trying to quell the gathering tide of sickness.

'Drink this,' said a voice, echoey in the tiled room.

'Lou . . . I'm so sorry . . .'

'Don't apologise,' she said, passing her a glass of water. 'We've all been there. Though admittedly, most is down to a hangover. Something tells me yours is down to something else.'

She stared pointedly at Esther's belly.

'What do you mean?' The penny dropped. 'Oh no . . . No, no, no, absolutely not. I use a diaphragm, every time.'

Lou looked at her blankly.

'The Dutch cap.'

'Oh, that! Where did you get that then?'

'My mum managed to buy one from a sympathetic chemist.'

'Does Walter know?'

'Lord no. They're really a very reliable contraception.'

'What, more than standing up?' Lou grinned caustically.

A laugh burst out of her, and she held her knuckles to her eyes, afraid for her mascara, even though that had already gone south.

'Stop it, Lou. You are awful.'

'That's better,' said Lou, pleased to see Esther smiling again. 'Well, you must have a bug then. What you need is a hot water bottle, a couple of aspirin, a gin and a lie-down in Miss Rayson's office.'

She slid her arm round Esther and led her from the toilet.

'Come to think of it, I could use that an' all.'

'How's things at home?' Esther asked as they paused outside the lipstick room.

'Oh, you know. Since he moved his lousy tart in, I can't stick it, Est. She's nice as pie to my sisters, but she doesn't know how to be around me. She leaves the room whenever I walk in.'

'She's probably intimidated by you.'

Lou's icy blue eyes flashed dangerously under her turban.

'And she acts like lady muck. Dolls herself up something proper when Dad comes home, seems to have a different fur coat on each day of the week.'

Her lip curled. 'Still got a face like a suet pudding mind you. Trust me, Est, she's only with him for what she can get out of him. Good luck to her. He's as tight as a gnat's chuff.'

Lou gripped the door handle and Esther got the distinct impression she was so angry, she could've wrenched it off with one hand.

'That woman will *never* replace our mum.'

By clocking-off time, Esther was relieved to be feeling much better. She'd probably vomited out the worst of her tummy bug. To everyone's delight, the winner of the lipstick-naming competition had been none other than the lipstick room's own chargehand, Lou. After the chairman had congratulated Lou in the factory canteen, they'd held a minute's silence in memory of Renee.

Lou was still full of it as they all piled out the factory gates on to Carpenters Road.

'*Renegade Renee*,' said Joycie admiringly. 'However did you come up with that, Lou?'

'I dunno. I looked it up in a dictionary and it said an individual who rejects lawful or conventional behaviour. If ever there was a girl like that, it was our Renee.'

'Well it's the most fitting tribute I can imagine. Renee would be chuffed to bits,' Esther said. 'And it's raised a terrific amount for the Wings for Victory fund. Ought I drop it round to your father at the town hall?'

'No don't worry. He said to pop it in a brown envelope and he'll take it in next week with all the rest of the district collections.'

'Will do,' Esther replied. 'Mrs Gunn and Mum also raised well over fifty pounds from the Shoot's communal dining fund.'

'Dad says that Stratford's raised enough for seven Spitfires,' Lou remarked.

'Apparently Ford's over in Dagenham have bought fourteen,' Betty chipped in. 'But we'll be catching 'em up at this rate.'

'Where we meeting your mum and Mrs Gunn?' asked Joanie.

'Mum's coming straight from her teaching job, collecting Nell and meeting us at outside Boardman's on the High Street.'

'Has she come round to the idea of it yet?' asked Joycie nervously. 'She didn't seem all that keen and, to be honest, Mrs Gunn really ain't someone you wanna upset.'

An unsettled silence fell over them at the thought of getting on the wrong side of Stratford's chief female. Tough as boiled brisket she was. Rumour had it she stabbed Mrs Barnett's violent husband through the testicles with a hat pin after he made a mess of his wife's face.

'She's going to have to trust me,' Esther said. 'Talking about Renee – keeping her memory alive – is the only way to make sense of her death.'

They heard footsteps on the pavement behind them. 'Wait up, girls!'

Patsy was dodging through the sea of factory girls.

'I thought you was busy this afternoon?' said Lou.

'I am, was, but well, you girls have been so kind to me since I started, and I want to support you. I know I didn't know Renee, but the way I see it, she was one of us, which means that bomb could've been for any of us. Lavender Girls stick together, right?'

'Right,' beamed Lou.

They found Nell, Snowball and Julia on the High Street, watching a procession of sea cadets ceremoniously marching up to join the navy, the next generation of West Ham boys to go to war. The steady tramp of boots on asphalt seemed to bore through Esther's head. A brass band accompanied them, playing 'Land of Hope and Glory' as they marched.

'Hello, Auntie, Mum,' said Esther.

'Good to see you out the allotment, Snowball,' she smiled, reaching up to kiss him softly on the cheek. He coughed nervously and Esther realised how much the elderly man hated being out here among such big crowds. He hadn't really recovered from his breakdown at the allotment so it was a mark of how he felt about Nell's daughter that he was here at all.

Mrs Gunn looked almost as wrung out as him, her grey hair scraped beneath a turban.

'I'm not stopping, love,' she said, folding her arms defiantly. 'I'll remember Renee in my own way, at home.'

'Please, Auntie. It's important we remember her together, as a community.'

Nell sighed and the breath left her body in one big rush of air.

'Right-o, let's get this over with then.'

As they walked to the bus stop, they spotted Queenie Jacks standing further up the side of the road, holding up a banner to the parade, which read, simply, *CANNON FODDER*. An ARP warden with a face like thunder was weaving his way through the crowds towards her, so Esther suspected her little anti-war demonstration wouldn't last long.

'Cor, your mum's madder than a bag of frogs, Pats,' Betty piped up.

Patsy flushed.

'Quick please, I don't want her to spot me.'

'There's nothing wrong with standing up for something you believe it, Betty,' chastised Julia. 'This war has many victims and we all choose to grieve in our ways.'

At that moment, Queenie glanced over and saw them.

'Too late,' Betty murmured.

'There you are, Patsy!' she stormed. 'I've been looking all over for you, I needed you at home looking after your brother. What you doing with this shower?'

Nell bristled and Julia placed a firm hand on her arm.

'She's coming with us to pay her respects at my daughter's grave,' she snapped. 'You got a problem with that?'

'I've got a problem with her hanging out with that man.'

She locked eyes with Snowball and her effect on him was once again extraordinary. His whole demeanour shrank. Fear, remorse and guilt clouded his face. Whatever had occurred in the past between him and Queenie Jacks had obviously not ended well. Had they been neighbours? Or something more?

'What's your problem with Snowball?' Lou interrupted. 'He's a decent bloke who's given back so much to our community.'

Queenie's hard mouth tightened. 'He knows!'

They continued staring at one another until, for one dreadful moment, Esther thought Snowball might cry. Every encounter with Queenie Jacks just seemed to bruise him further.

'Mum, please leave it, all right?' Patsy begged. 'I'm going to the grave then I've got to be at a WVS meeting after that. I'll see you later, all right? I'll take our Jimmy out to Vicky Park tomorrow.'

She kissed her mother on the cheek and they walked off, with Queenie staring at their retreating backs.

Her shrill voice called after them.

'He knows, don'cha, Snowball? Or whatever you're calling yourself these days!'

'That woman,' snapped Nell. 'Sorry, Patsy, I know she's your mum, but one of these days, I'm gonna swing for her.'

At Nell's words, they all lapsed into silence, the carnival atmosphere of earlier suddenly evaporating. They stayed that way until they filed into the gates of East London Cemetery in Plaistow.

Renee's grave was unremarkable, one of many hastily dug in the early days of that remorseless period of bombings.

It was a warmish evening, which still felt like late summer, but here in the graveyard, the trees were oddly bare. Just a few fragile leaves clung to the branches, as if new life dare not grow in a place so freighted with violence and loss.

They reached Renee's grave.

'What now then?' said Nell bluntly.

'We talk to her,' Esther said. 'Tell her we miss her, share our favourite stories of her.'

Nell and the girls looked uncomfortable.

'I'll go first.'

Esther took a tube of Renegade Renee lipstick from her purse and placed it beside the gravestone.

'Hi, Renee. Bet you'll be chuffed to bits to know there's a lipstick named after you. It's called Renegade Renee – you always were a bit of rebel. I remember the first time I met you and I was being bullied by that girl in the brilliantine department because I'm Jewish. You didn't stand for any of that nonsense. Knocked her out cold on the floor of the lav, even though you knew it would land you in no end of trouble.'

Esther sat down beside the grave, took a small candle from her bag and lit it.

'You didn't have to look out for me, I was nothing to you, but you cared . . .'

Esther's throat seemed to close with the emotion.

'You put your neck on the line for a fifteen-year-old refugee. After that . . .' she laughed and shook her head at the memory, 'I hero-worshipped you! I used to watch out for you every morning. Bus was far too boring for you as I recall, so you used to hitchhike up Stink Bomb Alley on the backs of the lorries.'

Everyone laughed at the memory of Renee's wild blond curls whipping round her face as she clung to the back of a passing lorry.

'I miss your chutzpah, your bravery, your raucous laugh, Renee.'

Esther hadn't realised while she'd been talking that Lou had sat down next to her. She took a candle from Julia, lit it and placed it next to Esther's.

'You didn't half have a mouth on you, girl! It was easy to tell when you was jibbed. Remember at the start of the war, you spoke up for us Lavender Girls, got us all an extra two shillings a week danger money. Bet you're up there now, putting the wind up them angels, starting up some sort of celestial union if I know you.'

Laughter rippled round the graveside.

'And you was kind. So kind to everyone. An iron fist in a velvet glove. I reckon you got that from your mum.' She glanced up and smiled at Nell. Esther sneaked a peek at Nell's face. She stood frozen by the graveside, her face a mask in the candlelight.

Lou pulled out her own mum's favourite warm wool scarf and wound it round Renee's gravestone.

'To keep you warm, darlin', while you rest. If you see my mum up there, give her a hug, tell her Tin Ribs is looking after the girls and that I love her.'

Tears were streaming down Lou's face, and Esther slid her arm around her.

Betty stepped forward and placed a photo of Renee's favourite Hollywood idol, Betty Grable, next to the scarf and lipstick before lighting her candle.

'You were Yardley's golden girl. You made us think anything was possible. I wrote to the studio in Hollywood, like how you taught me, told them all about you. They sent this back. You'll get a kick out of this, Renee. It's only signed by Betty!' She grinned. 'The real deal before you ask, not me! What about that then? A little slice of Hollywood here in East London.'

One by one, each of the Lavender Girls lit a candle, shared a story and left a token of their love by the gravestone. As dusk gathered, the graveside was lit up by a circle of flickering flames.

Lou pulled a hip flask from her pocket and poured two fingers' worth each of dark liquid into a collection of enamel mugs.

'I liberated these from the canteen,' she said. 'Rum and black. Your favourite, Renee.'

She handed them round the group and, as one, the girls raised their mugs in a toast.

'To Renee and her baby,' said Esther quietly. The dark, potent liquid seeped down her throat. Esther felt her tummy lurch and she closed her eyes, overcome with a wave of dizziness.

'And now, let's have some silence,' Julia suggested. 'So we can all remember her privately.'

As a deep silence folded over the group, Esther found her mind cruelly sneaking to the night of Renee's death.

The heaving crush of shelterers crowded into that godforsaken school in Canning Town. The desperate search for Renee and her brother.

Esther's memory marched her powerfully to the moment the inevitable bomb had hit. *Noise. Chaos. Screams* . . .

Esther remembered it all so vividly. Was it right to be sitting here now, talking about this so openly when, time and again, the authorities had warned them not to speak of it?

Then she swore she heard Renee's voice in her ear. A restless wind flowed over the back of her neck.

Hundreds of women and children had paid for West Ham Council's neglect and incompetence that night. She would never stop talking about this. This war had already claimed too many good lives. Propaganda would tell the rest of the world that East Enders could take it, but she would live to tell another story. For Renee.

Abruptly, her eyes snapped open. She was surprised to see the wind had snuffed out the candles, reducing the group to a seamless circle of dark outlines in the gloaming. How many secrets, Esther wondered in that moment, had the war swallowed up, buried and sucked into silence forever?

Nell's voice came gruffly through the darkness and Esther could see she was crying.

At last.

'Thank you, Esther,' she wept.

Esther smiled back. Nell Gunn would never get over losing her youngest daughter, just as Esther would never recover from the loss of her father. Grief never leaves you, she realised, but rather it shapes you. In that moment, she felt her understanding for the losses of others, her compassion and empathy, was infinite. Grief, in its savage way, had made her more human.

'Come on,' she said, climbing stiffly to her feet and reaching her hand out to Lou. Together, the group walked to the gates of the cemetery. In the west, the sun was finally sinking, a fiery ball of copper sending skeins of crimson floating over the factory rooftops. The red sky was filled with a murmuration of birds.

'That's a Renee sunset if ever I saw one,' piped up Little Irene.

'You're right there,' Esther grinned, ruffling Irene's head.

Outside on the street, they seemed to come to their senses.

'What about a sharpener down the Carpenters Arms?' Lou

suggested, rubbing her hands together. 'It's Friday night, I'm in no rush to get home.'

'I really must be off,' said Patsy. 'I've a WVS meeting I should've been at hours ago.'

'And I must be getting back to my allotment,' said Snowball.

'What, now?' Esther asked.

'I'd . . . I'd rather be alone if you don't mind, but thanks for arranging that. You did Renee proud. See you later, love.' He pecked Nell on the cheek and was off, trudging up the street, shoulders hunched, walking as if he could barely lift his feet from the pavement.

Esther sighed and exchanged a look with Nell. At the grave-side, he had looked at peace, like the old Snowball they knew and loved, but now he had retreated from them once again.

'Anyone get the feeling that Patsy's not really off to a meeting with the women in green?' said Lou, her attentions elsewhere.

Lou had voiced the self-same concerns that Esther had been thinking about over the past six weeks. Something about the newest of their number didn't add up. Just where was it she was always rushing off to? She was only seventeen and just back from the countryside – suppose she was in trouble?

A voice – Renee's? – whispered in her ear.

'We should follow her,' she blurted.

A murmur of agreement went round the Lavender Girls.

'You ain't going without me,' said Nell in a voice that brooked no argument.

'I'm not sure about this,' said Julia, the voice of reason. 'We should respect her privacy.'

'Mama, we just want to check that she's not in any trouble. She's an innocent in a lot of ways.'

'Wonder if she's sneaking off to Chipping Ongar to meet Blue?' said Joycie.

'No chance,' said Joanie, who was still dating Johnnie. 'They won't let girls on to base. 'Sides,' she said as they reached Plaistow tube station and saw her board the District Line. 'She's heading west, not east.'

It was a long way from Plaistow to Piccadilly, but that's where they found themselves an hour later as they followed a surprisingly nippy Patsy, dashing up the steps and out into the busy heart of Soho.

'Whatever's she doing here?' breathed Little Irene as they dodged a sea of demob-happy sailors.

'Well she certainly ain't off home for a mug of cocoa, is she?' Lou remarked, lighting a fag.

'Hurry up, or else we'll lose her,' said Nell.

The blackout was certainly useful for one thing, Esther thought, as they shadowed Patsy up Shaftesbury Avenue. They nearly lost her when she ducked suddenly down Great Windmill Street, but caught up with her just as she turned a sharp right into Archer Street. A flash of light from a door opening up, and then she was gone.

They stood frozen in indecision outside an unremarkable door. It was Nell who plucked up the courage to knock.

A smartly dressed, silver-haired gentleman opened the door and looked at the group. A smile tugged at his lips as he took in the solidly built matriarch in the sensible coat, surrounded by a gaggle of wide-eyed factory girls.

'You're not our usual stage door Johnnies!' he remarked.

'Hello, darlin',' said Nell, all easy cockney charm. 'You mind telling us what this building is?'

'Why yes, Madam. You're standing at the stage door of one of the best little theatres in London, if not to say the world. The Windmill!'

He jerked his head.

'Entrance round the corner if you want to buy tickets for the best revue in town, only you wanna hurry as the show's about to begin.'

'I'm really not sure about this,' said Julia, as Lou and Nell hustled the group round to the entrance.

'Are we actually going in?' said Little Irene breathlessly. 'I heard there's naked women in this.'

Esther had heard of The Windmill, of course. You'd have to have had your head in a hole not to. The Windmill's famous sails hadn't stopped turning, even throughout the Blitz, and rumour had it, they did indeed put on the best show in town. She felt a sneaking excitement build inside as they took their place in the queue of servicemen.

'I reckon Renee's behind this,' grinned Lou, having a last pull on her fag before grinding it out on the floor.

'Yeah,' grinned Nell. 'This would have been right up her street.'

'No wonder Patsy always rushes off at the end of the earlies,' said Betty excitedly. 'She's moonlighting!'

'Probably an usherette, or a souvenir seller,' said Lou, as they paid their fourteen shillings each and made their way towards their seats in the stalls.

'Talking of which,' said Joanie, handing over another four pence for a small printed souvenir.

'Ever such a lot of Americans in here,' said Little Irene, gesturing to the front five rows far beneath them.

'You don't say? I wonder why?' Joycie said sarcastically.

'Ssh, show's about to start,' Esther whispered.

'Bring on the girls!' whooped an unmistakable New York voice, before whistling so loudly, Esther swore her hair lifted off her scalp.

'Oi, mate!' Lou yelled, standing up and leaning over the stalls. 'That ain't a whistle.'

She placed her fingers between her mouth and issued an eardrum-shredding whistle that seemed to reverberate around the theatre.

'That's a whistle, Yankee boy.'

'Way to go, baby,' he called back, blowing her kiss. 'Why don't you come down here and sit with us?'

'No ta, I'll stick with me mates.'

The Lavender Girls fell about in fits of laughter and Esther tugged on Lou's sleeve.

'Sit down, or you'll get us kicked out before we've even found out what Patsy's doing.'

'I told you,' said Lou, 'she'll be selling ciggies at a kiosk or summit.'

'Or maybe she's behind the scenes helping make costumes?' suggested Julia.

'Behind the seams more like,' joked Betty and they fell about once more.

'Sssh,' said an elderly matron dripping in jewels behind them.

The red velvet curtain trembled and a hushed silence fell, followed by a roar of applause as suddenly the stage seemed to burst into life. The air shimmered with excitement.

After the quiet of the cemetery, Esther felt as if she'd entered another world. A troupe of the most drop-dead beautiful women Esther had ever seen danced their way on to the glass stage and it was almost too much for her eyes to take in. Feathers, frills and satin garters shimmered as they high-kicked in perfect time, the smile never slipping from their carmine lips.

It was tremendously athletic and Esther found herself wondering how the troupe kept up such a perfectly timed and strenuous dance act in very little but a slip of chiffon and three-inch heels.

'I think I've just died and gone to heaven,' said Lou, but Esther didn't have chance to ask her what she meant because, all too soon, the opening dance act finished and a magician appeared. The evening went with such a zip and a swing, Esther barely had time to applaud before the next act appeared on stage.

Nell found the comedy drag act so funny, she laughed

louder than the entire audience put together. 'Oh, this is a tonic,' she said to Esther, patting her hand. 'Just what I needed this evening.'

'Is that a man in a dress?' Julia whispered, staring at the comedians.

'Bleedin' hell, there's a stampede below,' Joanie laughed.

One of the GIs in the front row had foolishly vacated his seat to visit the little boys' room and a crowd of men were bundling over the seats behind to get as close to the stage as possible.

'Would customers please refrain from climbing over the seats,' announced a tannoyed voice, which was roundly ignored.

'I still can't see Patsy anywhere . . .' Esther began to say, looking about the theatre. She didn't get a chance to finish her sentence as the lights softened and suddenly the stage seemed to shimmer with great plumes of quivering ostrich feathers.

'This must be the last dance,' said Julia. 'I've read about this, it's the famous fan dance.'

The act was spellbinding and even the Yanks fell silent, straining every optical nerve. The principle dancer coyly and elegantly manipulated the huge plumes of feathers and just as hers slid away, one of the dancers clustered around her would slide her fan into place to save her modesty. It was an awesome spectacle of glamour and the Lavender Girls drank it up, their faces entranced in the dim light.

'Apparently,' Lou whispered into the darkness, 'the Lord Chamberlain'll shut them down if she performs while she's nude.'

'You mean to say she's naked under that fan?' Nell screeched.

'Yeah,' muttered Lou, craning her head. 'Blink and you might miss it!'

'I can't watch,' said Joanie, picking up her souvenir and leafing through it.

Suddenly the lights came on, the dancing girls faded from view and from the back of the stage, a soft plume of golden light lit up two tall marble plinths.

'I think I've just found Patsy,' said Joanie, staring in shock down at the centrefold of her souvenir.

'So have I!' Esther breathed, eyes fixed on the back of the stage. For there, posing as still as statues atop the marble columns, were two strikingly beautiful young women – who were completely and utterly naked!

One was blonde, with skin the colour of milk, the other was . . . well, Patsy.

It was unmistakably her. Her long, slender legs shimmered under the soft lighting. A tendril of her black hair curled over her shoulder and cascaded over her naked breasts.

She stood as still as stone, gazing into the middle distance, but Esther knew that all eyes in the theatre were on her. It was tastefully done, with one leg cocked just so, but her nipples, the soft flesh on her flat belly, the curve and swell of her breasts were all exposed.

Time seemed to stand still. The Lavender Girls sat, for once, stunned into silence.

'She looks like a beautiful painting,' said Lou eventually. 'Or a statue in a museum.'

'She ain't selling fags though, is she?' Joycie remarked.

'Or knitting socks for the troops!' added Little Irene.

'I don't know,' winked Joanie. 'She is providing *some* comforts for the troops.'

Suddenly and inexplicably, Esther became aware of how tightly packed they were in the stalls. It was dark and hot, and as the lights dimmed and the curtain fell, the roar of applause filled her skull. She tugged uncomfortably at her collar.

'You all right, Esther?' asked her mother.

'Is it me, or is it hot in here?' she muttered.

Esther's stomach rose up and quite suddenly, she felt the overwhelming urge to be sick again.

Sitting in a cafe opposite the theatre half an hour later, cradling a hot, sweet cup of tea, Esther felt foolish.

'I think it was the shock of seeing Patsy, you know, in the altogether,' she explained to the girls.

'You weren't well this morning, don't forget, Est,' said Lou. 'Perhaps you should have gone home to bed, slept off that bug.'

'She ain't got no bug,' said Nell gently. She put down her teacup and looked directly at Esther.

'I've been watching you and I can tell you now, girl – I know an expectant woman when I see one!'

Back in Stratford, Esther pulled the string through the letterbox and fumbled in the darkness for the key. Inside the passage, the nauseating smell of cooked liver lingered. Her heart beat fiercely in her chest, as she crept up the stairs as quietly as possible. She didn't want to wake Walter – after all, she didn't know for sure yet. On her hands and knees, she groped for the small box under the bed. Feeling it, she grabbed it, tiptoed back downstairs and lit the tiny gas lamp in the corner of the room.

It was madness. Surely she couldn't have. Only an insane person would do that. But there was really only one explanation for her unexpected pregnancy.

She pulled her diaphragm from its box and held it up to the light. And with that, Esther's whole world shrunk to the size of a pinprick. There in the middle of the yellow rubber cap was a tiny tear. It had been tampered with.

'Of all the devious, wicked . . .'

Esther wanted to believe that it wasn't possible, but this was Maureen Smith, the same woman who checked their marital bedsheets the day after their wedding to ensure her new daughter-in-law's virginity was intact. The same woman she had found searching around under their bed about seven or eight weeks ago.

'Oh God,' she moaned, sinking down into an easy chair and pulling her legs up to her chest. She wanted to feel pleasure, joy, pride. But all she really felt was horribly and inescapably trapped.

12

Lou

'What'll you do?' Lou asked Esther the next morning. They had agreed to meet in the canteen before the shift started to dissect the shocking news of the previous evening.

'Well, I won't tell Miss Rayson or the bosses here, that's for sure. But I want to understand why she's doing it, and whether she's comfortable taking her clothes off for complete strangers. And if her mum ever found out—'

'Not Patsy,' Lou interrupted, 'you, I mean, and the baby!'

'Sssh keep your voice down, Lou,' she said, checking none of the overnight workers having a quick breakfast before they clocked off had heard.

She yawned and brushed the crumbs of sleep from her puffy eyes as she stared out the window. A shaft of sunlight muscled out from behind a sludgy cloud, turning the oily surface of the Cut purple and green. Even with the window shut, the eye-watering stink of chemicals spewn from tanneries, abattoirs, soap works and other firms that lined the Cut oozed in through the cracks.

'Is it just me or is the smell really bad this morning?' Esther asked.

'No worse than usual,' Lou shrugged. 'So, go on, when are you going to tell Walter?'

'I don't even know if I actually am carrying yet, do I? I'll have to go to the doctor's.'

'Is your curse late?'

Esther searched her mind to remember when she'd last had one, and realised with a jolt she couldn't remember.

'I hate to say it, Est, but Nell Gunn is rarely wrong on these matters. My mum reckoned she could smell pregnancy on a woman. You think how many babies she's delivered down the Shoot. Many of which were strained through a cap!'

She looked up puzzled.

'You know, a Dutch cap that's accidentally torn.'

'That hole was no accident,' she muttered. 'That woman sabotaged my contraception so she could be a grandma!'

Lou shook her head.

'I wouldn't put anything past Maureen Smith. All the same, Walter'll be overjoyed, won't he?'

'I know.'

'But you're not?'

'Honestly, I don't know.' She stared up at Lou.

'I love my job here. I love coming to work, being with the Lavender Girls, contributing to the war effort. And I didn't want to bring a baby into the war. Renee's death taught us that random, terrible things are happening to innocent people. We none of us know what's around the corner.'

They fell into silence. Lou thought of her mother.

'You're not wrong there, Est.'

'But Walter, well he hates feeling . . .' Esther inverted her fingers, 'surplus to requirements. He thinks being a father will give him a proper purpose in life.'

Lou smiled sympathetically and closed her hand softly over Esther's.

'The problem being, you've already found your purpose in life?'

'For now, while the war is on, yes. I'm only nineteen, Lou.'

'I know, the youngest person ever to be made room supervisor at Yardley's.'

'Oh, let's change the subject. Maybe I'm just feeling blue because my Ps are about to start and then all this conversation will have been for nothing.'

Esther walked over to the hatch and came back with two more cups of strong tea.

'I'm worried about you, Lou. I don't know how you stick it at home. I really thought your dad was respectable.'

Lou snorted.

'Oh yeah, good old Honest John, pillar of the community. Stands back and does nothing while his wife has no option but to seek out an abortion. Lies about her death, then moves his grubby little tart in.'

'I could ask Miss Rayson to put in a complaint to his bosses at the council about his conduct if you like? He is our official council collector for the Wings for Victory fund.'

'No, don't do that,' said Lou. 'He'd go berserk. No, I have to face facts, Mum's gone. I don't care about him, or his tart for that matter. All that matters is those girls. I just need to stick it at home until they're ready to leave, then I'm out of there.'

'Lou, that's years away. Maisy's only eight!'

'What else can I do?'

'If you were to marry, you could always move the girls in with you?'

Lou stared down at the thick orange tea congealing in her cup.

'I won't be getting married,' she said quietly.

'But you're such a catch, Lou,' Esther insisted. 'You've never had a boyfriend, or even a date that I know of, since I met you.'

A voice screamed in her head: *Do it! Tell her now!* Esther

was the most broad-minded person she knew, but how could she form the words?

I'm in love with Martha Robertson, the girl from the woodmill.

She knew that some of the girls at Yardley's, particularly the younger ones, would never be able to understand the idea of a woman loving another woman.

But Esther was different from Betty and Little Irene. She had been hounded from her country of birth because she was Jewish. If anyone understood about discrimination, it was her.

'I . . . I just don't really like men all that much. I . . .' The words died on her tongue.

'Can't say as I blame you, Lou,' Esther joked lamely. 'Look at the trouble I'm in!'

Lou glanced up and saw Patsy come into the canteen. She spotted them, and her beautiful face lit up. She was as fresh as a daisy. You'd never know she'd been performing on a London theatre stage and probably clocked up no more than five hours' sleep.

'Shall we talk to her now?'

'Yes, we really ought to, before she gets on to the belts. I've told the girls not to make too many wisecracks, but you and I know it's going to be mentioned.'

'Sit down, Patsy,' Esther said, patting the seat.

'What's wrong?' Patsy asked warily, looking from one to the other. 'Am I in trouble?'

'No,' Lou replied. 'But we do need to speak to you about your, er, outside interests.'

Without saying a word, Esther got last night's souvenir programme out and slid it across the canteen table. Patsy's turbaned head slid into her hands.

'Oh God, are you going to tell me mum?'

'No, nor am I going to tell the bosses here, because I can tell you now you'd have your clocking-off cards before you can say "Windmill".'

Patsy looked up between her fingers.

'Please don't say you saw me?'

'We did, Patsy. We weren't prying, we just wanted to know where it is you're always dashing off to. We were worried about you.'

'Well, now you know,' she sighed.

'We all have our secrets in life, Patsy, and I don't judge,' Esther said. 'For what it's worth, we all enjoyed the show, but are you really happy taking your clothes off in front of strangers?'

Patsy cocked her head.

'I know this is hard to believe, but I love being a revudebelle.'

'A what?' Lou asked.

'It's what The Windmill call the nude tableaux vivants. There's nothing smutty or degrading about it. It's like a sort of beautiful art.'

Her eyes shone and, in that moment, she looked so radiant. Patsy was just a girl having the courage to follow her heart, to better herself.

'When I'm up there, girls, I feel alive. One day, I may become a Windmill girl. They've even offered to pay for elocution lessons for me.'

'But I like your accent,' Esther protested.

'Get you, Lady La-Di-Da,' Lou teased, sticking up her little pinky. 'I'm only joking. Good on you, darlin',' she added, raising her tea mug up wearily. 'We're all living on borrowed time; find your happiness where you can, I say!'

'Oh, thanks, Lou,' Patsy gushed. 'I can't tell you what that means coming from you. The Windmill girls are all smashing, so friendly and kind, just like the Lavender Girls. I love my two lives.'

'But therein lies the problem, Patsy,' said Esther. 'How long can you go on juggling two such demanding jobs? I'm already under pressure from the powers that be to have as many hands on the belt as possible. I'm losing girls to conscription every day. Fire-watching shifts are now compulsory. The time will come when you may have to choose between your West End job . . .'

'And your East End one,' Lou finished.

Patsy nodded.

'I understand, and I'm so grateful to you both. I'm so sorry I lied to you. You've treated me with more kindness than I deserve.'

'And tell me, Patsy,' said Esther, 'before we clock on. What's the history between Snowball and your mum?'

She shrugged.

'I wish I knew. Mum mentioned she knew him in a past life, but other than that, she's staying tight-lipped.'

The girls drained their tea just as the clocking-on hooter sounded.

'I feel I should warn you, Patsy,' Lou cautioned as they walked down the stairs. 'It wasn't just Esther and I at The Windmill last night.'

Patsy's face blanched.

'Oh you don't mean?'

''Fraid so.'

She swung open the door and tried not to smile. What had Lou expected? They were fun-loving factory girls, after all. Patsy's nude turn in Soho was never going to pass by without a mention.

Every girl on the belt, from Joanie and Joycie to Little Irene, Mavis and Betty, had, with the help of some white tablecloths and Kirby grips, fashioned their turbans into windmill sails. A round of applause and a good few wolf-whistles went up when they spotted Patsy.

To her credit, Patsy smiled and did an elegant little bow.

'Encore, encore!' cheered Joanie.

'Not on your nelly,' Patsy laughed, taking her place at the conveyor belt. The bell went off, the machinery shuddered into life and another day at Yardley's began.

Come mid-morning, Lou and Esther were walking briskly in the direction of Angel Lane Market with their string bags. Like a number of forward-looking firms, Yardley's gave their female war workers an additional break to allow those responsible for feeding families to do a quick shop. The shops and markets were even busier at dinnertime, especially on a Saturday, when housewives spent a large proportion of their time and housekeeping.

They walked past a mobile shower outside the town hall, funded by the American Red Cross – *A gift from the people of Boston* proclaimed the sign – and turned right into the busy street market.

'Not sure I'd fancy having a wash on the High Street,' Esther remarked.

'I'd rather have some crispy rashers of bacon,' said Lou.

'Toast dripping with butter for me,' said Esther.

'Steak and kidney pudding, piping hot and smothered in gravy . . .'

'My mother's sweet lokshen with cream and cinnamon.'

Back and forth they bandied with their favourite foods until their mouths were watering. Talking about food had replaced talking about the weather these days. They joined the back of the queue snaking out of the butcher's. Grim-faced housewives stood in line, arms crossed. Feeding a large family these days required stamina, guile and cunning.

'Instead, we have . . . Actually what do you reckon that is, Lou?' Esther puzzled, pointing to a small, unidentifiable piece of meat sitting in a tray in the window.

Lou threw back her head and whinnied.

'Behave, you,' Esther giggled.

Lou looked up to see Nell Gunn's youngest, Frankie, racing through the market crowds.

'Esther, please come!'

He tugged their hands and, mystified, they ran after him. They could hear the shrieks and yells as soon as they entered Cat's Alley, the small passage which led to the Shoot.

Nell and Queenie, head to head again. Lou's stomach sank.

Most of the women of the Shoot were gathered in a circle, baying for blood. A shoe flew high up above their heads.

'Let me through,' huffed Lou, elbowing her way through the crowd.

Nell and Queenie were rolling round on the floor in a blur of aprons and stocking tops.

'Nell!' yelled Lou, shoulder-barging her way in between the two warring women. Queenie looked like a woman possessed, hair ripped from her turban, a scratch down her face, her wild eyes flashing.

'Let me at that bitch!' she howled, launching herself at Nell. Lou just about dodged her fist.

'That wicked cow wants locking up in a loony bin!' screamed Nell.

'Enough!' Lou bellowed. 'Everybody calm down, or we'll have the law here.'

Nell doubled over, panting for breath.

'That woman . . .' she wheezed, pointing her finger. 'That woman's got to go.'

'I have as much right to be here as any of you lot,' taunted Queenie, reaching down to pick her turban off the floor.

She waved her bony arm round at the crowd and they all took a step back.

Nell turned to Lou and Esther, a ball of rage.

'First she says something to Snowball again. I don't know what she said because he won't tell me, and now he's taken his things and reckons he's sleeping in the allotment from now on.

'And now she's stirring up trouble for Mrs Mahoney. She's had a telegram telling her her husband's coming home from prisoner of war camp next month.'

Lou knew, like most of the Shoot, that Mrs Mahoney had given birth to a child in the time he'd been away.

Queenie folded her arms, triumphant.

'She's got some explaining to do!' she crowed.

'But that's her business,' said Nell despairingly. 'Why don't you keep your nose out? Neighbours are as close as family. We stick up for one another.'

Her whole face shook with emotion as she pointed to a stricken Mrs Mahoney.

'She didn't know if her husband was dead or alive for two years until he turned up a POW. If she wants to find her comforts where she can, well, good on her. Same for all the women round this square. We've all done stuff I dare say we ought not to, whether it's dabbling in the black market or living for the moment. We're all human and all we're doing is trying to survive this bloody war.'

'There's surviving, and then there's sinning,' shot back Queenie.

'Oh, I'm sure you ain't no angel,' Nell said with a brittle laugh. 'We've all got a past, love. The difference between you and me is, I see life for how it really is, not how I'd like it to be.'

She walked away but, as she reached her doorstep, she turned back.

'This square ain't big enough for the two of us, so why don't you do us all a favour and fuck right off, Queenie Jacks.'

Queenie smiled, a ghoulish pantomime of a grin.

'Oh, I'm not going anywhere, Nell Gunn. You can count on that!' She turned to the crowd. 'I'll find out all your secrets.'

Nell ushered Frankie in the door and slammed it shut so hard, all the sashes rattled. Queenie left too, retreating to her house next door.

'Right-o, show's over!' Lou hollered.

Lou and Esther found Snowball in his shed on the allotment.

'Snowball,' Esther whispered as they pushed open the door, 'you in here?'

A muffled noise came from the corner of the shed.

Behind the tomato plants, Lou made out a tangle of blankets. They pushed back the foliage and there he was, sitting up against the wall, staring blankly ahead.

'What's all this nonsense about you moving in here?' Esther said gently, settling down on to her haunches and rubbing his arm. 'There was some kerfuffle in the square, between Nell and Queenie.'

'She told me I ought to leave, she's right,' he murmured.

'What?' Lou exclaimed. 'Why? The Shoot's your home.'

'The market was my home for longer, or the Cut, or the sea . . .' he gestured vaguely.

'You can't mean you're going on the road again!' Esther cried. 'No, I won't allow it.'

'I think it might be for the best, love.'

The look of bewilderment in his pale rheumy eyes broke Lou's heart. In his fingers, he clutched a button shaped like an anchor, and he began drawing ever-decreasing circles in the dirt with it.

'I'm causing too much trouble here.'

'No!' Esther said. 'That woman is the only troublemaker round here. You can't start drifting again, Snowball. Your life is different now. You said so yourself. You have people who care about you, who need you.'

She started to cry, a tear running down her cheek. 'I need you.'

Snowball looked up from the circle in the dust, an ancient pain boiling in his eyes.

'Please leave me be, girls.'

*

Poor Esther looked desperate for the rest of the day. Whatever happened between Snowball and Queenie Jacks was a mystery, Lou thought. Word on the street was they'd been romantically involved, lovers in a different age. Well, that was all over now. But Queenie certainly had a bigger hold over him than Nell Gunn, that much was certain.

After finishing her double shift at Yardley's, Lou was in dire need of a sit-down and a hot cup of tea, but there was the girls' tea to fetch, to say nothing of the housework.

Reaching the small brick terrace, she heard laughter.

Lou pushed open the door, and pulled her turban off, releasing the scent of lavender and sweat. She worked her fingers through her hair, desperate to be free of the smell of the factory.

Inside the front parlour, Nancy was plaiting Maisy's hair, sitting in her mum's favourite chair by the fire. The intimacy of the scene made her feel sick. Not only that, but Nancy was wearing one of her mum's old rose-printed wrap-around aprons.

A popular BBC music show was playing on the Bush wireless, the melodic sounds of the Joe Loss orchestra wrapping the room in melody. The rest of the Button sisters were gathered round playing cat's cradle or reading books. A fire flickered in the grate.

'This is very cosy,' Lou said and Nancy jumped.

'Oh Louise,' she gasped, putting her hand to her chest. 'I wasn't expecting you.'

'Why? I live here,' she said coldly.

'Come on, girls,' Lou went on, ignoring Nancy. 'Who's coming with me to fetch the pie and mash from Cooke's? Two and two with extra liquor for those that come and help.'

Elsie looked awkward.

'Sorry, sis, we've already had our tea.'

'What? But we always have pie and mash on a Saturday. It was Mum's favourite.'

Nancy had the good grace to look embarrassed. 'Sorry, Louise, your father thought it would be better if I made the girls' tea from now on. I thought with you working double shifts, it might be a help.'

In that moment, Lou knew, with a hard little nugget of certainty, that her father meant to ease her out, erase the memory of their mother and replace it with Nancy.

She did a quick audit of the room and there was something else. Her photo of her mum, the one that was always on the dresser, was gone.

'Where's me mum's photo?' she demanded.

'It's er . . . Well, your father told me to take it down. He thought it might be too painful a reminder for the girls.'

Lou felt a gathering rage build in her chest. 'He did, did he? Our mum's been dead seven weeks and he wants to forget she even existed.'

She clenched her fists. 'You can't replace our mum, she's the girls' mother, not you!'

'Louise, calm down and apologise to Nancy.'

Her father had come through from the scullery.

'Stuff Nancy!' she yelled. 'Now where is it?'

'Where's what?' he asked, looking faintly amused.

'The number twenty-five bus! Mum's flaming picture, what do you think?'

'Help me look, girls,' Lou puffed, and she started flinging open drawers and rifling through Nancy's sewing basket. At last she found it, tucked behind the wireless.

Nancy stood up suddenly, making a grab for the photo and causing a tussle.

'Let go!' Lou roared, wrenching the photo from Nancy's fingertips. The frame slipped from her fingers and crashed on to the iron hearth surround. The glass almost seemed to explode, showering the floorboards with tiny shards. The photo of Flo Button landed in the fire and, with a desperate lunge, Lou plucked it away and blew on it.

'It's ruined,' she sobbed, taking in the blackened, curled edges. 'It's ruined.'

Weeks of pent-up rage, grief and frustration crystallised into a single bolt of fury. Without a word, Lou reached out and slapped Nancy hard round the face.

Nancy fell back into the chair with a cry. A silence fell over the room. Lou was aware of all her sisters' eyes on her. The ticking of the clock cut through the silence.

Her father's voice was icily controlled. 'Get out!'

Without even picking up her coat or bag, Lou fled from the parlour, through the passage and out into the gathering gloom. Heavy, lumbering clouds scudded over Gibbins Street, the smell of whalebone carcasses oozing through the sky from a nearby abattoir.

She began to run in the direction of Carpenters Road until she reached the woodmill. The yard was in darkness, save for the odd shower of sparks from the saw.

Martha was driving a forklift, but when she spotted Lou hanging by the entrance, she parked and hopped out.

'What'sa matter?'

'Can you get a quick break?'

'Guv'nor, all right if I take fifteen?' she called into the darkened work room.

'Make it ten,' called back the disjoined voice.

They walked out on to Stink Bomb Alley and Martha slipped her arm through Lou's.

'I can take fifteen; he's a pussycat. Reckons I'm more efficient than most of the men put together.'

Down by the Cut, Martha rolled them two cigarettes, lit them and handed one to Lou.

'Now, tell me everything.'

They walked alongside the grey waters and Lou shared the whole story.

'I know exactly what that devious weasel's up to. He reckons the girls are young enough that, in time, they'll forget Mum altogether, but me . . . He don't know what to do with me, so he wants me out.'

She stared up at the outline of the high factory walls, behind which lay a dangle of cranes. Brick built upon brick and all smudged with coal dust and grime. Unspeakable dreariness and privation.

'Mum's life may not have amounted to much. Certainly not what she hoped for. But us girls were her whole world. I can't let him wipe out her memory, Martha, don't you see? It would be like killing her all over again.'

The sky had darkened and the moon was hanging over the flat silvery surface of the Cut. The only sound was the soft slap of water against the sides of the factory barges moored up down the banks.

'Come here,' said Martha, sliding her hands round Lou's waist.

She kissed her so softly on the lips, it felt like the brush of a feather.

'Martha, be careful,' Lou whispered, the whites of her eyes showing in the dark. 'We ain't that far from Yardley's, the night workers'll be clocking on soon. And the brickie kids'll be around here somewhere, playing pirates on a barge.'

'I'm browned off with pretending to be something I'm not,' Martha replied, her tobacco breath warm on Lou's cheek. ''Sides, there ain't a soul around. They're all down the Palais at Ilford, or the town hall, doing the Chattanooga Choo Choo with some randy Yank.'

Lou laughed and snuggled in closer to Martha.

'I'm going to kiss you one more time, Lou, but first let me

tell you this.' She flicked her butt in the canal and then traced her thumb down the side of Lou's cheek.

'Together, we'll save every last penny, and when we've saved enough, we're out of here. We'll take the girls to live by the coast in Brighton. Your mum loved it there, didn't she?'

Lou nodded.

'Good. We can run a white-fronted guest house with lacy curtains, like two old spinsters. Cook greasy breakfasts and grumble about our guests. In quiet times, we'll take the girls down the pier, eat rock for breakfast if we bloody well like!'

'That's an impossible dream,' Lou protested.

'Is it? I don't know about you, but thanks to this war, I'm earning more money than I ever have in my life. Me mum's in full-time work, me sisters are out earning. Our house ain't seen a tallyman in months!

'Think about it, Lou,' she urged breathlessly. 'Let's set up a savings account in your name. Yardley's have a special one for workers, don't they?'

'Yeah think so, I can check with Miss Rayson.'

'Let's call it our "escape fund". I'll pay in half my wages each week and you do as much as you can afford. Two, maybe three years, we'll have enough and if what they're saying is true, the war'll be over by then too.'

Lou held her breath, hardly daring to believe it could be possible, but for the first time in years, she felt a golden thread of hope weave round her heart.

'We just have to hold on, my love, bide our time . . .' Martha pulled her closer, until their cheeks were brushing. Lou felt the warmth of her skin, the soft silk of her eyelashes.

'I love you, Martha.'

Their lips touched and Lou surrendered to Martha's embrace. She felt her insides yield, like the churning of cream, until all she was aware of was Martha's taste, touch and scent filling her senses.

'I love you so much,' she whispered into the dusk. They clung to one another. In a world gone mad with war, Lou's love for Martha was about the only thing that made sense right now.

But ten feet away, hidden in the shadows of an Oxo barge, was a figure, silently watching.

Martha smoked another cigarette, gave Lou one last kiss then ran back to her nightshift at the woodmill. Lou decided to walk the long way home. Unlike some, she liked walking in the blackout. The crisp night was calming, allowing her fractured thoughts to still and settle.

Martha had been right, of course; she always was. Now that she had a plan, a crumb of hope to cling to, Lou felt a heaviness lift from her chest.

Indeed, she even started to walk with a certain music hall swagger, imagining her, Martha and the girls promenading down Brighton seafront like a couple of swells. Perhaps she'd learn to seabathe, or join a rambling club and explore the South Downs. Maybe, just maybe, a whole new life with the people she loved *was* possible.

It was gone 10 p.m. when she arrived back on the High Street. A number 25 trundled past her, its headlights dimmed. A giant billboard was plastered on its side, depicting a glamorous blonde draped on a chaise longue.

Keep mum, she's not so dumb. Careless talk costs lives.

'Oh, I will, darlin'. Don'cha worry,' Lou muttered.

She would be the soul of discretion; calm, helpful, obliging. She'd even apologise and make her peace with Nancy, until they'd saved enough that was. Then they'd be out of Stratford, for good.

As she walked up her turning, she spotted something odd on her doorstep. A tatty bundle. For a moment, she half wondered if it wasn't Snowball, but as she drew closer she saw it was her clothes. All heaped in a pile on the pavement.

'What the . . .' She quickened her pace. All right, she oughtn't to have slapped Nancy, but this? Her dismay turned to horror as she picked up her shirt to see it fall to pieces like ribbons in her fingers.

'No, no, no!' she wept, trembling as every piece of clothing she picked up fell apart in her hands.

The divine double-breasted Max Cohen suit, tailored to fit her, splurged on just before the outbreak of war, had the arms sliced off. Her favourite black velvet trilby? The rim had been cut away.

'No,' she cried again, as the hat came apart in her hands. *Of all the twisted, vile . . .*

Lou burst into the parlour to find three faces staring back at her. So hot with anger was she, it took a moment for her mind to process what she was seeing.

'I read a piece today in the *Stratford Express* on the growing rat problem in the borough,' said Queenie Jacks, calmly brushing down her long, black skirt and standing with a rustle. 'They're causing huge food waste, destroying thousands of tonnes of food, according the Ministry of Food. More threatening than the Nazis, would you believe?'

'Queenie,' said Lou warily, looking from her to her father. He was standing very still by the fire, smoking a cigarette, seemingly content to let this woman take the floor. The whole thing felt like a strange Victorian parlour game.

'Apparently, we are all to be rat reporters.' She smiled coldly and in that heart-stopping moment, Lou knew exactly where this was going.

'That's exactly how I see myself in a manner of speaking, you see Louise – patrolling the Cut after dark, ensuring the place is kept clean, free from vermin and disease.'

'How dare you spy on me!'

'Not spying, you weren't exactly subtle. At first I thought it was a man you were embracing, which would have been lamentable enough conduct, but then I realised you were kissing a woman!'

'W-was it you who cut up my clothes?'

'No, it was me,' said her father finally.

His eyes narrowed behind the glass of his spectacles as he dropped his stub into the neck of an old bottle of stout. There was a hiss followed by a thin line of smoke.

'How could you?' he asked.

'How could I what? Fall in love with someone who treats me with kindness and respect?'

'It's no surprise, I suppose,' he sighed, extravagantly. 'I married a trollop who bred a trollop, but this . . . This . . .'

His mouth opened and then closed again, as if there weren't enough words in his vocabulary to convey his disgust.

'You horrible freak of nature,' he said eventually.

She stared at him. How had she ended up with such a foul, evil bastard for a father? She glanced over at Nancy, sitting in the corner, looking stricken.

'My love's more legit than yours.'

Quite suddenly, he spat at her. A goblet of phlegm landed on her left arm and lay quivering. She pulled out a handkerchief and wiped it off.

Her father was actually shaking with rage. 'I want you out of this house and you are not to make contact with your sisters ever again, do you hear me!'

'You . . . you can't do that!'

'Oh, I can and I will. I will not stand by and see them corrupted by you and your . . . your . . .' He shook his head in bewilderment. 'I've heard of nancy boys, but there's not even a name for what you are!'

There was nothing more that she could say or do. With as much dignity as she could muster, Lou picked up the scorched photograph of her mother and walked to the door.

Queenie Jacks moved to let her pass by with a look of triumph.

Lou stopped in front of her.

'I pity you, Queenie.'

Queenie smiled and jutted her chin out. Lou met her gaze unflinchingly.

'I watched you earlier in the square. What is it you're so scared of?'

Queenie sniffed and drew herself upright. Lou saw it again, deep in her green eyes, a flash of fear.

'There's poison in your blood,' Lou whispered. 'What happened to you, Queenie Jacks?'

Lou tried to see past the look of condemnation and the sour tuck of her mouth to see what really lay beneath. Like so many round these parts, Queenie's face was scoured by war and the general knocks of life, but it was the look of mania that Lou found most disturbing.

'Get out,' ordered her father, striding across the floor and wrenching open the door.

'Don't worry.' Lou shot a last look of loathing at her father and his fancy woman. 'I'm going.'

She stepped out into the street and counted to fifteen; not just to acclimatise to the blackout, but to work out what on earth she was going to do next. Her secret was out. Lou had never felt so petrified.

13

Patsy

Winter came hard on autumn's heels and by the third week of November, there was scarcely enough fuel left in Stratford to melt the ice on the *insides* of windows. Damp clung to every bone in Patsy's body, not helped by the fierce winter wind that moaned and rattled through the Shoot. It got in everywhere, freezing buttocks to lav seats and lacing Patsy's feet with purple chilblains.

Despite this, the promise of seeing Blue later was filling her with excitement. She had a rare evening off from The Windmill, which coincided with Blue and his unit being granted their liberty with a three-day furlough. She and Joanie were going on a double date with Blue and Johnnie. Patsy shivered with nervous anticipation. She'd had letters from Blue of course, lots of them, posted from his base in Chipping Ongar, professing his undying devotion, and a snatched cup of tea after her shift in what was now dubbed 'their cafe', over the road from the theatre. But that had been it since their last magical evening in the park in August.

The leaves had drifted from the trees, but Patsy's feelings remained the same. If anything, the longer she went without seeing him, the more her thoughts kept returning to Blue. Since he'd started on active missions, a weariness had seeped into his letters.

'What you wearing tonight, Pats?' Joanie asked, breaking into her thoughts as they tucked into something rumoured to be soup. Yardley's cook had recently attended a food cookery demonstration on the Barking Road, '101 ways with soup'. Though from what Patsy could tell, there were only two: taters and cabbage.

'I've got a natty little navy swagger suit, copied it from a style I saw in the window of John Lewis on Oxford Street.'

'Decent bit of schmutter,' said Joanie, impressed. 'Hair?'

'Left me rollers in overnight so pompadour style, nice and high on the top. Used up my last drop of shampoo last week, so let's hope he don't get too close,' Patsy laughed.

'I washed mine in a teaspoonful of borax in a cup of warm water.'

'Girl Guide badge for you,' Patsy teased.

'Ta. Got no mascara mind, or even a teaspoon of boot polish left.'

'Try this.' Patsy pulled a match from her handbag, struck it then blew it out. She wiped the back of the match head over the back of her hand, then carefully ran the residue under her eyelids and over her lashes.

'Kitty at The Windmill taught me that.' She fluttered her darkened eyes at Joanie. 'Apparently all the French women do it.'

'Ooh la la,' Joanie said admiringly.

'After four months cooped up with a load of men, trust me, Joanie, it ain't your eyes he'll be looking at,' chipped in Joycie, without looking up from the *Stratford Express*.

'Maybe so, but I gotta look the part, it's all about glamour, daaahling.'

Joanie hopped up on the canteen window ledge and patted the side of her turban teasingly.

'*It took more than one man to change my name to Shanghai Lily.*'

'Marlene Dietrich, *Shanghai Express*, 'thirty-two,' shot back Little Irene.

Patsy laughed; she knew what was coming next. The Lavender Girls were obsessed with their favourite Hollywood idols. Every spare hour, and a fair portion of their spending money, was spent watching Hollywood movies in one of Stratford's three picture houses, escaping, dreaming and revelling in its seductive power. There wasn't a factory girl there who didn't secretly dream of being a starlet in Tinsel Town, and a quick round of guess the actress always went down well in the factory's drearier moments.

'I drive a leopard-skin upholstered Lancia, who am I?'

'Easy, Gloria Swanson,' laughed Little Irene. 'Who wore a wig frosted with real diamonds?

'Norma Shearer, in that film about the French queen what got her head chopped off,' said Betty. 'Who wore a costume made of gold coins?'

'I know this one,' screeched Joanie. 'Ginger Rogers. *Gold Diggers of 1933*.'

'VD,' said Joycie, breaking the spell.

'I beg your parsnips?' said Joanie.

'No, that's what it says here.'

Joycie read out loud from the paper.

'*Tainted Goods* is a play for adults only, starring vaudeville star Peggy O'Neil at the Theatre Royal. The theatre sensation, on for one week only, warns about the spread of venereal disease. Thousands of new cases a week according to the Ministry of Health.'

She threw the paper down in disgust.

'Charming. Who the hell wants to go and see that?'

'Watch out, Pats. Your mum'll have her soapbox out again!' laughed Betty.

'Has no one told her apparently we're all sinners in these days of war,' Joycie remarked.

'Chance'd be fine thing,' grumbled Joanie, finally giving up on her soup and lighting a cigarette instead. 'Amount of leave Johnnie gets!'

Patsy felt Lou stiffen next to her.

'You all right, Lou?' she asked. 'You're very quiet today.'

'Yeah,' Betty chipped in. 'Do you know you've got a face like a two bob funeral?'

'No, but if you hum it, I'll sing it,' Lou replied in a dull voice.

'Very funny. What's up?' Betty asked.

'Fine, just tired is all. My new landlady neglected to tell me I'd be sharing my room.'

'Who with?'

'Bed bugs.'

'Eurgh!' Everyone recoiled.

All the Lavender Girls knew that Lou had had some sort of altercation with her dad, and was now renting a room in some bomb-shattered tenement in Canning Town.

'Can't you go home, Lou? I know it would mean going cap-in-hand to your dad,' said Joanie. 'But it's gotta be better than living with strangers down the docks, surely?'

Lou shook her head and joined Joanie in a dinnertime smoke.

'It'll do,' she said, picking a bit of tobacco off her tongue. 'It's just a place to lay me head. I'm in this bleedin' factory more than I'm not.'

'But don't you miss your sisters?' Little Irene asked. 'Swallow your pride, Lou, apologise to your dad and happy endings all round.'

'This ain't some bloody Hollywood picture, Little Irene. Just leave it!' Lou mashed her cigarette out and scraped her chair back. She scooped up her fags. 'Don't be late back from dinner. We've a lot to get through.'

'All right, Lou, no need to get your arse in a sling,' Joanie huffed.

'Sorry. Like I said, I'm tired is all.'

And with that, she stomped from the canteen. A stunned silence fell over the table. Jolly, irrepressible Lou, always ready with the one-liner and easy banter – even during the height of the bombings – seemed to have bleached into a woman they didn't recognise.

'What's eating her?' asked Little Irene.

'Search me,' Joanie replied. 'Maybe she's on her curse? Do you know, Esther?'

Patsy looked up to see Esther and the welfare officer walking towards their regular table at the furthest end of the canteen.

'Do I know what, Joanie?'

'What's wrong with Lou? She just bit our heads off.'

Esther frowned.

'She's having a hard time, so go easy on her.'

'Of course, Est. We all think the world of Lou, you know that. We only want to see her happy,' said Little Irene.

'Well, perhaps this'll cheer her up,' said Miss Rayson. 'Yardley are having their annual Christmas talent show and Miss Homefront beauty contest here in the canteen after work on Thursday the twenty third of December. We'll be telling all the factory workers collectively in a meeting, but I know how enthused the lipstick room gets about this, so I thought I'd let you know first!'

'Yes!' said Betty leaping out of her seat. 'A chance to reclaim the crown.'

Patsy had heard on a number of occasions how Renee had been crowned Miss Homefront in 1939, but for the past three years, it had been scooped by girls from the powder department.

'Do you remember when Lou sabotaged it that year Renee won?' said Little Irene.

'Cor, not many,' laughed Betty. 'She stormed the stage dressed as a pantomime horse.'

'No way,' laughed Patsy.

'Gospel,' said Little Irene. 'She does it every year now, it's sort of a Yardley tradition.'

'Hmm, not sure I like the sound of fancy dress, or the beauty competition. Do we have to enter Miss Homefront?' asked Patsy.

'I'd rather you didn't,' said Little Irene with a toothy grin. 'I'd quite like a fighting chance of winning it!'

'Shut up,' laughed Betty, clumping her round the back of her turban.

'No, why? Did you want to enter the talent contest instead, Patsy?' asked Miss Rayson.

'I should like to give it a go, yes,' she replied. 'I'd sing, if that's all right.'

'Oh, you've gotta hear her voice, Miss R,' breathed Betty. 'Give Vera Lynn a run for her money.'

'In which case, I can't wait to be dazzled,' she replied.

Miss Rayson glanced at Esther.

'And now your room supervisor has some news of her own to share.'

Esther's face coloured.

'Yes, well I do . . . Walter and I are expecting a baby.'

The whole table burst into spontaneous applause.

'Oh, that's wonderful news, Esther,' said Joycie, leaping out of her seat and hugging her.

'Smashing, about time we had a Yardley baby,' said Betty.

'That's terrific, Esther,' said Patsy.

Esther smiled, but somehow, it didn't quite reach her eyes.

'I thought you said you were gonna wait until the war was over to start a family?' asked Joanie.

'A slip-up,' she said tightly. 'But you know, Walter's thrilled.'

'And you, Est?' said Little Irene in her usual blunt manner. 'Are you pleased?'

'Honestly, Irene, what a thing to say, of course I am.'

Patsy wasn't convinced. Something in Esther's demeanour told her that she was far from thrilled.

'Anyway, you shan't get rid of me that easy I'm afraid. Miss Rayson has kindly said I can stay on.'

'Subject to yours and the baby's health of course,' the welfare officer replied. 'I'm not keen on having expectant mothers around the machinery, but we are terribly short-staffed at the moment.'

'I shall be here until at least next May.'

'You are due in June, Esther,' Miss Rayson reminded her. 'I scarcely think your doctor would recommend it.'

'We're packing cosmetics, camouflage cream and small aircraft components, not munitions,' Esther said smoothly. 'I think it's important to remember the personal sacrifices being made on battlefields all around the world. If they can fight on, I can work on.'

She tightened the strap on her overall.

'Let's get the job done.'

The rest of the afternoon passed in a peaceable enough blur. Patsy found the clank and rhythm of the conveyor belt seemed to pick up the loop of her thoughts, and run away with them. She went through the motions like an automaton, but Blue's face, eyes and smile appeared on the bottom of every lipstick she picked up to inspect. When the final bell sounded, she could have cheered.

The machines shut down with a shudder and the sudden silence made her ears ring. All the girls got out their lipsticks and compacts, with the older women rolling cigarettes, all desperate to get the feel and the smell of the factory out of themselves.

Patsy and Joanie got ready in the lavs in a cloud of fag smoke and hair lacquer. After a solid thirty minutes of coaxing the last drop and pinch of make-up out of a fast-diminishing supply, the girls were as ready as they were ever going to be.

'Come here,' said Patsy, spitting on a hankie, and gently smoothing away a fleck of ash from Joanie's chignon. 'A woman past caring . . .'

'Is a woman past repairing,' Joanie replied, arching one pencilled brow. 'How comes you always look so bloody immaculate, and I look like I've been dragged out the Cut?'

'Shut up you daft article and let's get a wriggle on. We don't want to keep Blue and Johnnie waiting.'

'You're right. Oh, I can't wait to see him. I hope they take us dancing up west.'

The girls walked through the cobbled yard to a chorus of wolf-whistles and out on to Carpenters Road, straight in front of a great crowd of Clarnico girls.

'Look at you girls all togged up in yer best schmutter,' said a redhead, looking them over.

'Yardley girls know how to put on the glamour,' Joanie replied flintily.

'Do send your nice Yankee boys our best wishes, girls,' goaded the redhead's pal. 'Tell 'em we had a great time last night.'

'Shove your wishes up your narrow arse,' Joanie snapped.

'Ignore 'em,' said Patsy, sensing a bundle was about to kick off. 'They're only trying to get a rise.'

'Oh I will. Nothing's going to take the shine off my night!'

The girls had agreed to meet the boys at the Carpenters Arms at the end of the road, to have a quick sharpener while they worked out where to go. But when they pushed open the door to the smoky pub, Patsy could only see Blue.

They weaved their way towards him, through the throng of factory workers. Patsy wrinkled her nose at the smell, a stewed miasma of beer, pickles and brilliantine.

'Stinks in here,' Joanie remarked. 'Can't wait to get up west. There's Blue.'

She raised her arm. 'Cooey, Blue.'

As soon as he spotted them, he downed the rest of his pint of Guinness in one go.

'Blue, what's wrong?' asked Patsy.

'And where's Johnnie?' asked Joanie, expectantly. 'Is he in the little boys' room?'

On closer inspection, Blue looked awful. His bright blue eyes, usually so full of mischief, were dull, and he looked like he hadn't slept in days.

'I . . . I'm so sorry, Joanie. He isn't coming.'

'Oh what?' she groaned. 'Why, was he called back to base?'

For a long time, Blue said nothing.

He scrubbed his face, before sitting down again. He clenched and unclenched his fists, as if working up to something.

'God damn it. I'm so sorry, Joanie. I'm so sorry.'

He reached into his pocket.

'Johnnie asked me to give you this, should anything happen.'

'Happen?' she breathed, taking the envelope and staring at it.

Blue slipped his hand through Patsy's. She felt the cold tremor in his fingers.

'Say, baby, perhaps you'd be good enough to fetch Joanie something strong to drink while I sit with her?'

Half an hour later, a shattered Joanie was gone. Her parents had been summoned and had come to collect her, leading her home in a state of dumbfounded disbelief.

'Oh Blue, I don't know what to say,' said Patsy. Just forty minutes ago, she and Joanie were doing their make-up, giggling, gossiping in the toilet and now . . . This horror, this loss. Her brain just couldn't make sense of any of it. Life and death; the line between them seemed suddenly so fragile.

'Wh . . . why didn't you write in advance?' she asked.
'It . . . it . . . Well it was just such a shock.'

Blue shook his head.

'Please believe me, Patsy, I didn't want to have to tell her, not like this, but I didn't want her to read it in a sterile letter either. Was that the right thing to do?'

He stared at her, bewildered and exhausted.

'Is there a right way to tell someone their sweetheart is dead?'

He picked up his glass, but his hand was shaking so much, he had to put it down.

'What happened, Blue?' she asked. 'Sorry. We don't have to talk about it.'

He pushed his fingers through his hair and lit up another cigarette. 'What happened is the same thing that happens every time we go up. If it's not Johnnie, it's some other poor chump.'

He tapped his ash and held out his hand to see whether the nicotine had stopped the tremor. 'It's the law of averages I guess when you're flying through a curtain of flak.'

'Where were you?'

'I can't say, but it makes no difference anyways. Every night it's a different target over some French or German town that was probably a picturesque beauty spot before this war.'

She stayed silent, hoping it would encourage him to talk.

'We were on a mission, somewhere over northern France. We'd just bombed a military construction site when we got hit. There was a fire in the fuselage and right engine. Things looked pretty bad as we dropped out of formation.

'Thinking we were doomed, one of the waist gunners bailed out, inadvertently dragging me with him.'

'No!' Patsy gasped.

'I lost my boots in the slipstream, nearly sucked me clean

out, it was only quick thinking from Johnnie, who managed to cut away the harness, which saved me.'

He laughed. 'I think I used up one of my lives.'

'So what happened to Johnnie?'

'We were laughing, you know, like hysteria at the sheer madness of it all, when all of a sudden . . .'

Blue clicked his fingers. 'He's gone. Flak punctured the fuselage, pierced his flak jacket and hit him straight in the spine.'

He stared down into his pint.

'God it was a mess. I've seen the insides of more men than an anatomy student.'

To Patsy's horror, his eyes filled with tears.

'It's like playing Russian roulette every time the wheels leave the runway, and you wanna hear the worst of it? I find myself wondering, when it comes, will I even know?'

Patsy stared at him, horrified. Before now, she had never really stopped to consider Blue's role in the war. He was here, along with the rest of the Yanks, with their generosity, easy smiles and swagger. But he was putting his life on the line with every mission, to defend a country that at times seemed not even to want him here. The shape of his war was changing and she saw it, right there in those eyes that used to crackle and flare with life, but now seemed resigned to whatever fate had in store.

She pulled out her handkerchief and handed it to him, but he caught her wrist and drew it to his face, inhaling the scent of her, kissing her palm, desperate for her touch.

'You're my lucky charm,' he whispered, patting the space under his shoulder patch where she had sewn the coin.

Patsy feared he would need more than a sentimental keep-sake after what he'd just described. She breathed out slowly, trying to stem her own fear.

'Some swell date I'm turning out to be.'

'Don't be daft,' she said, trying to sound cheerful. 'You're here, with me, that's all that matters for now.' Her words sounded awful, so forced.

'Baby, I don't really feel like dancing . . .'

'No, no. That wouldn't be right,' Patsy agreed.

'Say, can we go to your mom's house? I just wanna be in a home. You know, a house with walls, a kitchen, a roof . . . Just normal stuff.'

'Oh Blue, I'd love to take you home, but I can't. My . . .'

'I know, I know, your mom.' He sighed and in that moment looked like a forlorn little boy. 'God, I miss my mom.'

Patsy chewed her lip.

'There is one place we could go. We'll have to go separately – I'll go first then you follow.'

Some twenty minutes later, Blue was safely ensconced by Nell Gunn's fireplace, being royally fussed over.

The heavens had opened as they'd run from the pub to the Shoot, the rain bashing the bricks. Blue had loaned Patsy his coat and by the time he had made it in, the poor thing was shivering and dripping water on to Nell's floorboards.

'I'm so sorry, ma'am, I love everything about your country – the fish and chips, the humour, your community – but oh boy I do not like the rain. I can't believe I'm in your home and I haven't brought any rations with me.' He sneezed suddenly.

'Sit down, boy and shut up,' said Nell with her usual bluntness, pushing him down on to a seat by the fire and roughly towel-drying his hair.

Patsy and Julia exchanged a look, as Nell busied herself pulling off his boots before preparing a hot towel to drape round his neck. She was in her element.

'You'll need this, and Vicks on your feet else you'll catch your death.'

A cup of hot, thick stew was pressed into his hands.

'Eat up, boy,' she ordered.

Blue looked up at Mrs Gunn through the steam, the twinkle returning to his eyes.

'Mrs Gunn, would you adopt me please?'

Nell roared with laughter.

'Get away with you.'

After a further two bowls of stew, a great lump of bread and butter pudding and two creosote-strong cups of tea, the colour had returned to Blue's cheeks. The frightened young man Patsy had seen in the pub had been banished. For now.

Blue fielded a hundred and one questions about life on base. Nell and Julia seemed genuinely interested to hear about a life so different to their own.

'Wotcha sleep on then?' Nell said, folding her arms over her voluminous chest.

'A biscuit, ma'am. It's what we call the straw-stuffed sack that pretends to be a mattress. We've been sleeping in two inches of water for the past four days.' He began to sing, his lazy American drawl filling the terrace.

> '*You don't know what you're missin'*
> *Until you've heard the rain drops kissin'*
> *On the rooftop of your Nissen.*'

Nell rocked with laughter and Patsy could tell she was taken with Blue's friendly, unabashed nature.

'I got into trouble for pilfering a little extra from the coke stores. They're guarded round the clock, but after evening chow, I took my tin helmet and smuggled some out for the boys.'

Nell nodded approvingly.

'We're fighting a war.'

'We sure are, against your British winters.'

'And what about the unit, is it big?' asked Julia.

'Huge, over two thousands, seven hundred personnel. We have to cycle round base. We have three intersecting runways; the main one is six thousand feet and two of four thousand, two hundred feet. The underlying hardcore is largely Blitz rubble from the East End.'

Nell nodded approvingly. 'So the runways your planes take off from to bomb the enemy are built from the rubble of East End bombsites?'

'That's true, ma'am.'

'So in a way, your runway is built from my daughter's grave?' She heaved herself to her feet to pour Blue another cup of tea.

'Poetic justice.'

At the kitchen sink, Nell pulled back the blackout blind a fraction. Streams of water gushed over the panes and, in the allotment, Patsy could make out a soft glow of light and a faint movement.

'Look at that silly old sod,' Nell tutted, 'sleeping out there in his shed. This rain is in for the night now. Blue, why don't you see . . .'

Nell turned back to Blue, but his eyes had closed and his breathing had grown deep and heavy.

'Oh Mrs Gunn, I'm sorry, I'll wake him,' gushed Patsy, leaping to her feet.

A soft smile spread over Nell's face.

'Let the poor lad sleep. I'll wake him in a bit.'

'Oh thank you,' Patsy said.

'Nothing to thank me for. I'd like to think if my Frankie were fighting a war in a strange land, some other mother would treat him with kindness.'

Nell fetched a candlewick blanket from a neatly stacked pile in a linen store under the stairs and softly drew it over Blue.

'You go on home, love, I'll look after him.'

Patsy stopped at the door and felt her heart expand with love. She had seen another side of Blue this evening. Deep down, he was just as scared as she.

Outside, the rain had stopped, but the darkness was penetrating. She counted to fifteen to allow her eyes to adjust to the blackout and spotted Snowball, smoking on the old bench outside his shed. A man pursued by demons born in the trenches of the last war, or so they said. Maybe everyone was hiding an invisible trauma?

She opened the front door to her house and unbelted her mac, suddenly panicking as to whether her mother could have heard her voice through the walls. She needn't have worried. Queenie looked up, with something almost approaching a smile.

'You're home. Good. I do worry about you, Patsy. You're working so hard between that factory and the WVS.'

Patsy nodded and turned her back on her mother to hang up her coat, sharp beaks of guilt piercing her.

The room was cold and the air seemed thinner than next door. Her mother sat knitting by a weak gas lamp, her bony fingers working the needles jerkily.

'Jimmy in bed?'

'Turned in hours ago.'

'Yeah, think I need to climb the wooden stairs to Bedfordshire an' all.'

'Stay and talk for a while,' Queenie urged. 'I scarcely seem to see you these days.'

In the half-light, Queenie's face looked almost skull like. Her long, black skirt had ridden up and her ankles were tiny. Her mother had lost so much weight since her father's death, Patsy felt she could trace her bones. Having just come from the company of two women of a similar age, it was impossible not to draw comparisons.

Esther's mother Julia wore her age easily. The skin around her eyes, which had wrinkled with decades of wear, told a story of love. Even Nell, freighted with loss, retained a warmth and empathy in her eyes.

'Did you hear about that disgusting play they're putting on down the Theatre Royal?' Queenie said suddenly, as if her brain had been searching in the silence for some source of unpleasantness. Her mouth tightened, puckering the skin around her lips. Like most women of her age, Queenie had had her teeth removed when she was sixteen, to save on dentistry costs, and had false teeth fitted. Patsy had only seen her the once without her teeth in. Her face had looked like an empty envelope.

'It's a fucking disgrace.' Her voice fired into the room like a bullet. Why was it every time her mum opened her mouth, it was like a declaration of war?

Patsy breathed in through both nostrils, trying to quell her irritation.

'I think the point is to warn people of the dangers of venereal disease, Mum, not to encourage people to hop into the sack with a stranger.'

'Your language is terrible since you started at that factory,' she snapped, oblivious to her own cursing.

'Sorry, Mum,' Patsy said, desperate to keep things on an even keel. 'Talking of the factory, Yardley's are putting on a Christmas talent show on the twenty-third. Thought I might do a turn and sing.'

Her mother looked up from her knitting.

'Will you come and watch? Maybe give me some tips? You used to be a terrific singer, Mum.'

For a fraction of a second, Patsy thought she saw a quiver of a smile.

'Used to be.'

'Standing room only at Wilton's Music Hall, Dad used to say.'

'Yeah, well, he's biased. But my name was the headline at one point.'

'Oh, tell me about it, Mum, please,' she urged. 'How did it feel to perform? Did you love it? What was your stage name?'

Perhaps, she thought, if her mum opened up about her performing past, she might be able to reveal her second job at The Windmill. But her hopes were dashed.

Queenie flapped her hand in Patsy's direction. 'Enough of the past. So this show of yours . . . Any of the other girls entering?'

'Oh, I should say. Most of the girls are entering the beauty contest, Miss Homefront, they call it. All except Lou, she's my chargehand. She's a case.' Patsy chuckled. 'Apparently every year she dresses up in some madcap fancy dress. One year she even went as a pantomime horse. She's a scream.'

Queenie returned to her knitting, one eyebrow raised.

'I bet she is. Where's she living now since her dad turned her out?' Her voice, as dry as leaves, was designed to be casual, but there was meaning in there that Patsy couldn't decipher.

'How did you hear about that?'

'Gossip grapevine.'

'Her dad sounds like a right nasty piece of work, kicking her out after her mum died. She's got a room in Canning Town now, down Hallsville Road I think. Why do you ask, Mum?'

'No reason,' she replied, setting down her knitting and yawning. 'Right, I'm gonna turn in now.'

'Please come to the show, Mum,' Patsy said, catching her mother's hand as she passed. 'It's all right to laugh again. Dad wouldn't want you to live like this forever.'

Her hand slid up to the black armband her mother wore.

'He'd want you to enjoy the rest of your life.'

'How can I?' Queenie replied, pulling her arm back

abruptly. 'How can I when he's floating around at the bottom of the ocean? Dead from a war what wasn't his to fight.'

'Mum, we've been over this, he wanted to fight.'

'It's the bloody government's fault.'

'No!' Patsy said, exasperated, gripping her mother's arm and squeezing her.

'I'm tired, I'm going to bed,' Queenie snapped, trying to break free, but Patsy wasn't going to let go. Suddenly all the pain and anguish of the evening seemed to rush to the surface. She wanted to shake some sense into her mum, or dislodge some answers.

'What's the story between you and Snowball? Why do you hate him so much? Were you together, before Dad? Did he throw you over, is that it?'

At the mention of his name, Queenie's face contorted into something truly frightening, and Patsy let go of her arm as if it were on fire. Queenie's mouth compressed into a barbed-wire line as she touched the little black cross in the lace at her throat.

'Our pasts will always dictate our future. And that coward's has just caught up with him.'

14

Esther

Saturday morning came in with a proper pea-souper. Esther drew back the blackout blinds to see a freezing grey fog shrouding the windowpane and licking at her ankles. An eerie silence seemed to have descended over all of Stratford.

She dressed quietly so as not to wake Walter. He had a day off and she wanted him to rest. Poor thing hadn't come home from his fire-watching shift until 5 a.m.

Downstairs in the kitchen, she lit the gas and spooned a teaspoon of tea leaves into the pot. She then took some potato peelings left on newspaper on the side and shook them into the fire.

'No no, that's not right,' scolded Maureen, walking in from the scullery. Esther's heart buckled. She had hoped to slip out.

'I can see I've a lot to teach you about the art of home-making,' she muttered. 'And why are you wasting tea leaves when there's already used in the pot? You've just got to let it mash.'

Maureen picked up the discarded newspaper and began cutting it into strips to hang on the hook for toilet paper.

'Oh, will you look at this,' she tutted, her scissors hovering over an article from the front page. 'Barking's appointed its first ever woman mayor. "Treat me not as a woman, but as an equal," says Mrs Engwell. Dearie me, that's all we need, some sort of petticoat government.'

Esther was about to point out the benefits Barking could reap from having a woman in power, but Maureen had spotted another article on which to vent her spleen.

'And what about this?' she screeched, jabbing a finger at the article below. '"Hilda Rose Meadows left her baby in the Rio cinema at Barking. She called the police straight away and admitted to abandoning her child. Mrs Meadows confessed to having had an affair, as a result of which a child was born. When she discovered her husband was freed from a prisoner of war camp, she couldn't face him discovering the truth and so left the infant."'

Maureen screwed up the article and threw it on the fire.

'Hussy! She ain't fit for me to wipe my arse on.'

'You'd have to be fairly desperate to leave a baby,' Esther pointed out.

'The world's gone to hell in a handcart!' Maureen retorted.

Maybe it was the oppressive fog, but Esther had never felt so suffocated. She saw winter drawing in, like a long, dark, narrowing tunnel. Her world was shrinking as her belly expanded, with Maureen watching and judging her every move.

'I-I've got to go, Mum, or I'll be late.'

'It's not right, you know.'

Esther carried on buttoning up her coat. 'What's not right?'

'You working, in your condition. It oughtn't to be allowed. Do you want me to go and have a word with Miss Rayson?'

It was the last straw for Esther. Turning to Maureen, she spoke furiously. 'Oh, I think you've done enough, don't you?'

'Meaning what exactly?'

'It was you, wasn't it? Who put a hole in my cap.'

Esther hadn't yet confronted her mother-in-law – there

had seemed little point as she could never prove it – but her raging hormones had got the better of her.

Maureen made a derisory sound as she poured herself a cup of tea.

'Your generation thinks they know it all.' She surveyed her through the steam. 'It's a fool's errand sending women in to replace the men.'

She sipped her tea. 'Sooner or later, this war'll end and you'll finish up back where you started. It'll be the same for everyone! That lady mayoress'll be kicked out of office; that slut will have to answer to her husband. Women the world over will have to face up to the fact that we are homemakers, not homebreakers.'

Maureen looked her up and down, the edge of her lip curling in contempt.

'My son deserves a proper wife, not some bloody feminist. One who'll give him the stable family he deserves. I just helped him out.'

'Your son married a woman with a mind of her own!' Esther blazed. 'Keep your nose out of my contraception and out of my marriage.'

Walter walked into the room in his pyjamas, groggy-eyed. 'Hey, hey! What's going on?'

At the sight of her son, Maureen burst into tears.

'I was only offering Esther a bit of advice, son. I don't think I deserve to be shouted at in my own home when all I was trying to do was help.'

Walter turned to Esther in surprise.

'Esther, you might be a bit gracious. Mum's only trying to help.'

'I . . . I . . . Oh, for pity's sake.'

Esther picked up her bag and slammed the door shut behind her.

★

The fog, combined with the news of Johnnie's death, cast a sombre air over the factory, with everyone seemingly content to work in silence that November Saturday. For the first time Esther could recall, no one sang along to *Workers' Playtime*.

Esther had begged Joanie to take the day off, but she refused, stating that she would rather be in company. Silence seemed to lend its own solidarity. Not one worker passed the grieving girl without squeezing her shoulder, rolling her a cigarette or fetching her sweet tea on breaks. The usual banter was suspended in favour of a quiet show of sympathy and support. Joanie's loss was felt keenly by all, for as they all knew, in wartime the next person grieving could be you.

'I'm so proud of you all,' Esther remarked when the final bell rang. 'We've met all our targets today. Please get home safe in the fog and see you Monday, please God.'

'PG,' echoed the girls in a muted murmur.

The floor emptied until it was just Esther and Lou left. They went round the floor checking the machinery, fastening the blackout blinds and having a last sweep under the belt.

'I'd really like the girls to win the best housekeeping award,' said Lou, casting her eye over the tidy belt. 'It'd be a nice boost for them all to be sent up to Bond Street for a make-over.'

'And what about you, Lou?' said Esther softly, eyeing her friend with concern. 'Who's looking out for you?'

'Me?' she laughed. 'I'm big enough and ugly enough to look out for myself.'

'I read about those women in the paper earlier. Your mum's . . .' Esther's voice tailed off in embarrassment as she searched for the right words.

'Abortionists you mean?'

Esther nodded.

'Yeah, they both got off with a suspended sentence and

have been bound over for twelve months. The judge apparently took into account their good characters. Combined with the fact that no money changed hands, he was reluctant to jail them.'

'How do you feel about it?"

Lou shrugged.

'Sending them to prison won't give me back my mum. If it weren't them, she'd have gone elsewhere.'

Lou turned to Esther. She looked absolutely washed out with grief.

'I miss her and my sisters so much. I'd never been a day without seeing them, and now it's been over two months.'

Tears began to run down her cheeks and she wiped them away angrily.

'Now their schools have re-opened, I've been going there on my dinner break,' she confessed, 'hoping to catch a glimpse of them.'

She hugged herself.

'I just wanna give them a cuddle, Est, let them know I haven't abandoned them. Goodness knows what Dad's told them.'

'Maybe he'll have calmed down by Christmas,' said Esther.

'Trust me, Est. Our relationship is over. As far as he's concerned, I'm no longer his daughter.'

Esther wondered what on earth could've happened to make him hate his own daughter so much?

'Say, how about you and me go to the flicks?' she said. 'Take your mind off things.'

'What about the fog?'

'We'll hold each other's hands.'

'Won't Walter and your mother-in-law want you home?'

'Trust me, I'm in no rush to get home, Lou. Besides, I'm worried about you, it must be ever so lonely going home to a single room.'

'Do you know what? I'd love that. I was supposed to be going to see a show at the Theatre Royal with Martha. *Round the World in Magic*, featuring an Australian escapologist and a human pincushion, would you believe? Only she's just cancelled as she's got to work.'

Esther winced at the thought of the show.

'Trust me,' Lou remarked. 'One prick's bad enough, never mind a dozen.'

'Reckon I've saved you in that case,' Esther laughed. 'There's a new flick on down the bug hole on Broadway. *Millions Like Us*, all about women doing their bit for the war effort in factories. Fancy that?'

'Yeah, why not?' Lou replied, buttoning up her coat and winding her scarf round her neck.

'Do you reckon there are millions like us?' asked Esther as they clocked out and ventured out into the smog.

'Bloody hope not!'

Even though the film was supposed to reflect the grind of their own lives, it was the perfect escapism, Esther thought as they as walked out of the pictures. The newsflash at the end of the film showing Bomber Command raining hell on the enemy had even got a standing ovation. The fog had lifted a little by the time they emerged on to the Broadway, but the girls both tasted soot and metal in their mouths.

Esther took a step, but Lou wrenched her back just as a bus slid out of the gloom.

'Mind yourself,' said Lou. 'I reckon more people have been killed by the blackout than by Nazi bombs.'

'Thanks, Lou,' Esther gasped. 'Since I fell, my head's been all over the place.'

'Hormones!' Lou chuckled. 'I once saw Mum make a whole meat pie and forget to put the meat in.'

'Yeah, my memory's shocking at the moment. Oh crumbs,'

Esther blurted. 'I've just remembered. I promised to drop Yardley's Wings for Victory contribution into the town hall at lunchtime. It needs to be registered by Monday.'

'You could drop it round now?' suggested Lou. 'Dad's usually at the Two Puddings with his tart on a Saturday night.'

The thought occurred to them both at the same time.

'I'll knock and check the coast's clear first, and if it is, you can see your sisters.'

'Oh, thanks, Est,' said Lou, her eyes shining in the smog. She thought about the prospect of seeing her sisters. 'I feel quite nervous. Daft, ain't it?'

Within a few minutes, they'd reached Gibbins Road. Esther knocked, and Lou hung back.

'Is your dad in?' she asked little Elsie Button. With her stubborn chin and wavy blond hair, she was the spit of Lou.

'Sorry no, he's out. Wanna come in?'

Lou stepped forward out the fog and Elsie's eyes grew wide.

'Lou!' She tore up the passage and threw herself with a great rush of breath at her sister.

Esther felt a lump in her throat as the two sisters clung to one another.

'Come on, let's go inside,' she suggested.

Once inside the front parlour, the rest of the Button girls charged in and fell on their big sister.

Lou laughed and sobbed as she fell to her knees and grabbed as many of them in her arms as she could.

It was hard to see where one Button girl began and another ended – all was a great tangle of limbs and blond hair. Eventually, Lou came up for air and kissed each girl one by one on the forehead.

'I want you all to know that I love you and miss you so much,' she cried.

Elsie looked up through a bramble of hair, big eyes hopeful and fearful all at once.

'I thought you left because I told you I hated you.'

'What? When?'

'When I had that row with Maisy in the backyard and I pushed her. I told you I hated you, and I wanted Mum back. I thought after that you didn't want the bother of us . . . At least . . .'

'No! No, not ever,' Lou interrupted fiercely. 'At least what?'

'That's what Dad said,' Maisy continued. 'He says you didn't want to look after us anymore, and that that's Nancy's job now.'

'No,' Lou wept, gripping Maisy's cheeks so hard she looked scared. And then in a softer voice: 'That ain't true. You must believe me. One day I'll explain why I left, but it wasn't because I don't want to be with you girls. I love you to the moon and back.'

'Dad said you're dirty and not to be trusted,' said Maisy.

Lou looked like she'd been kicked in the stomach.

'Well . . .' Lou began. 'What do you think?'

'I just want things back to normal,' Maisy replied, 'back when Mum was alive and we all lived together.'

'Oh sweetheart,' Lou said, folding Maisy into her arms. 'I can't bring Mum back, but I promise you, one day, you will all live with me and my friend Martha. Would you like that?'

All the girls nodded solemnly.

Esther felt him before she saw him, a chill sweeping through the tiny parlour.

'Lou . . .' she warned. 'I think we better go.'

Lou's father was standing motionless by the door, the bald patch on his head shining white like bacon fat.

'Well, well, well,' he said eventually. 'I pop back to get my wallet and look what I find.'

No one said a word.

'This is why, girls, I told you she's not to be trusted. I expressly forbade her from coming to this house, and the minute my back's turned, she comes creeping back.'

'I-I brought her with me, Mr Button,' Esther said. 'It was my idea.'

'In which case, Mrs Smith, I shall thank you to keep your nose out of my family affairs.'

'With respect, sir, it's not right,' she said, feeling a wave of indignation rise up inside her. 'Lou loves her sisters, and whatever she may or may not have done, they are family at the day's end!'

'That's right,' said Lou. 'Please, Dad, I can't live without these girls. We need each other.'

His sickly smile spread over his face, as he looked from Lou to Esther.

'Tell your friend, Mrs Smith, that she's not wanted round here, and if she comes again she will leave me with no choice but to call the police.'

'Come on,' Esther said, glaring at Lou's father. 'Let's get out of here.'

They walked in silence for forty minutes to Canning Town, where Lou's new home was, their footsteps echoing off the deserted cobbles. The encounter – the shock, perhaps – seemed to have taken everything out of Lou.

As they drew level with the public hall, Lou slowed down. A poster outside proclaimed a public meeting was happening inside, calling on anyone who objected to the release of the fascist leader Oswald Mosley from prison.

Finally, Lou broke her silence.

'In 1936, when I was fourteen, I went to the Battle of Cable Street and stood up against that man and his blackshirts. And now look: he's being freed from jail, while the very war he and his fascists helped to stir up is still going on.'

'Awful, isn't it?' Esther agreed. Lou turned to Esther, her voice raw in the moonlight.

'Why are there men like that getting away with it time and time again?'

Esther shook her head. She had no answer to that, leastwise not one that made sense.

They turned down Hallsville Road, where Lou's lodgings were. They passed the school were Renee had been killed and Esther felt as if someone had just trailed an icy finger down her spine.

The school was sealed off, the gaping chasm of its fractured walls shrouded in mist. It was hard to imagine a more desolate place. Esther shuddered as she wondered how many of the dead still lay tangled and entombed beneath their feet. She tucked her arm tighter through Lou's as they walked up the long and heavily bombed road. It felt like a ghost town.

She'd heard many colourful stories about the docklands. Tales of dogfights and legendary bare-knuckle boxers, of loose women and Chinamen with silver pigtails. Now it was every shade of grey, a community disembowelled.

'Oh, Lou,' Esther cried as they walked, 'there's got to be something better than this.' It's almost as if her friend were punishing herself, choosing to live here in purgatory. What had her father found so awful that she'd been banished to this godforsaken place?

Lou didn't reply. Instead, she stopped and pushed open the door of a badly damaged house. The passage smelt of cabbage water and gas. Esther felt her stomach heave.

'Miss Button,' called a reedy voice from the front room. A woman peeked her head round the door, and looked at Esther with suspicious eyes.

'I'm sorry, but you'll have to go. You and your lady friend, I shan't have those sort of goings-on under my roof. I run a respectable establishment.'

'Excuse me?' Lou exclaimed. 'I'm up to date with my rent.'

'Listen, love, I don't want no trouble here.'

Lou closed her eyes.

'Has someone been to see you about me?'

'As a matter of fact, I did have a visitor this morning, but she was only being friendly, warning me about your sort. Go on, get your stuff and then sling your hook.'

She closed the door silently between them.

'What on earth . . .' Esther began. 'What does she mean, "your sort"?'

Lou leant back against the faded wallpaper of the passage and ran her fingers over the sockets of her eyes.

'There's something I have to tell you . . .' she began.

Despite the gloom, Esther suddenly saw her so clearly. She wasn't blousy Lou, the flamboyant blonde mouthpiece, all bold and brassy; she was someone quite, quite different. Someone who had worked so hard to carve out an identity for herself, in order to try and conceal who she really was. It struck Esther in a shattering moment of dream-like clarity.

What was it she'd said earlier? *One day you will all live with me and my friend Martha.*

'Of course,' she breathed. 'You're in love with Martha.'

In her room, Lou sank down on to her bed, utterly defeated.

'Yes, I am. Have been for years.'

'And does Martha love you back?'

'For some strange reason known only to her, she really does.'

'And your father discovered this? That's why he threw you out?'

'Thanks to Patsy's mum, Queenie. She spotted us kissing down the Cut. She could hardly wait to tell my dad, and now it looks like she's been at it again.'

Lou looked at her and Esther saw how terrified she was.

'I think she means to ruin me, Esther, truly I do. She wants to drive me out the East End altogether.'

'Well, she's come up against the wrong woman this time,' Esther said, sliding her arm round Lou.

'You ain't scared I'm gonna ravish you?' she joked feebly. 'You know what beasts us lesbians are.'

Esther snorted. 'Hardly, look at the state of me! Swollen ankles, varicose veins and I can hardly hold a thought in my head.'

They both laughed.

'But seriously, Est. You don't care?'

'Why would I care who you love? We're all free to choose who we want to love. Isn't that the reason we're fighting this war? The freedom to make and stand by our choices?'

Lou nodded thoughtfully.

'Perhaps, but some people's choices are more acceptable to society than others'.'

'Well, it makes no difference to me if you love Arthur or Martha.'

'I'm scared, Esther,' Lou said huskily.

Esther placed her hand on her tummy, thinking about the little life she never planned for but that was busy growing all the same.

'I'll let you into a secret,' she whispered. 'I'm scared too.'

The two friends leant into one another and sat shoulder to shoulder. In the silence, the landlady's radio programme, *It's That Man Again*, drifted up through the floorboards.

'*Top-up you say? I don't mind if I do,*' was followed by the landlady's nicotine-wracked laughter.

'Colonel Chinstrap,' Lou explained wearily. 'It's her favourite character.'

Esther sat up and patted Lou's knee. 'Come on, let's get you out of this fleapit. Get packed. I'm taking you to Nell Gunn's.'

Back in the Shoot, Nell was unfazed about being asked to put Lou up, and about the reason why.

'Of course you can stay, ducks. You were always such a good friend to my Renee.'

'You don't mind my . . .' Lou tried to find the right words. 'Preferences?'

''Course not, I always knew you were that way inclined, known since you was knee-high actually. So did your mum, God rest her soul.'

She picked up Lou's suitcase. 'Nearly went there meself back in '21.'

Lou and Esther stood open-mouthed as she walked up the stairs.

'Wait. M-mum knew?' Lou stammered.

'Course she did and it didn't bother her none. She loved the bones of you,' Nell replied.

Lou looked lost for words, until another thought occurred to her.

'I should warn you, Nell, that Queenie has taken against me. She'll cause no end of trouble when she finds out I'm living next door.'

Nell stopped at the top of the stairs, her bulk almost blocking out the light and her dark eyes flashing.

'I am ready for anything that woman throws at you.' Her knuckles gripped the bannister. 'If it's a war she wants, it's a war she'll get.'

Lou swallowed uneasily.

'Oh please, Nell, we're already fighting one war. I don't want you starting another on my account.'

Nell sat down abruptly at the top of the stairs.

'Except it's not just you, Lou. That woman's hellbent on causing trouble with me and mine. I don't know what history she has with Snowball, but the sight of her and he starts shaking in his boots. And now the silly sod's living in the shed in the middle of bleedin' winter.' She rolled her eyes. 'I ask you!'

Esther felt the rush of cold air from the door. Snowball was standing on the doorstep, shivering from the cold.

Nell hadn't seen him and ploughed on.

'I thought we loved one another, but he's more under her spell than mine and . . .'

'Nell!' Esther said sharply, gesturing to the door.

'Snowball!' Nell breathed, looking uncertain of herself for the first time ever. 'I didn't mean that, love. Come on in, sit by the fire.'

She held out her hand, entreating him to come into the warmth.

He shook his head and stumbled back.

'I'm sorry. I . . . I'm more trouble than I'm worth.' He wheeled round and headed back to the allotment shed.

15

Esther

Wednesday 22nd December 1943

Esther shivered and pulled her winter coat about her as she trudged through the Shoot. The snow was starting to fall more heavily now she'd left the factory, concealing the oily waters of the Cut and spiralling over the streets and markets of Stratford.

This was their fifth – *fifth!* – wartime Christmas and the doldrums of the long, cold winter, the most heavily rationed since war began, had well and truly set in.

There'll always be a Christmas! exclaimed Boardman's on the Broadway, but there were no turkeys to be had and what gifts there were on sale were expensive and nasty. Last week, a rumour went round that someone down Angel Lane had tinned turkey, but it came to nothing in the finish.

To make matters worse, a terrible flu epidemic was sweeping London, and had already claimed the lives of two babies and an elderly woman down the Shoot. So many women of the square were now laid out with it that, in desperation, Nell and Julia had been forced to call upon the WVS to help the neighbourhood with shopping and childcare. For the first time ever, the Shoot's communal restaurant and crèche was forced to close its doors.

Esther couldn't ever remember Nell Gunn calling on

outsiders for help. Was she losing her grip? Had Snowball's decline and Queenie's eagle eye undermined her power?

The horrible thought nagged at Esther, as it did increasingly these days: just what sort of homefront was she bringing a baby into?

Hoisting her string bag on to her shoulder, she realised how much harder things were going to get.

'Cooey, Snowball,' she called when she spotted him digging over the potato patch. She waggled the flask over her head. 'I've brought you some soup.'

His lovely, craggy old face could scarcely raise a smile when he saw her. Was it really only five months ago that she had married Walter and he had given her away? Was this the same man who gave a heartfelt speech in the square, told her how proud she made him? He was a husk of his former self.

'Thanks, love,' he said without looking up, 'pop it down there, will you?'

'You're chilled to the bone,' she said, taking his chapped hands and rubbing them between hers. 'You'll catch this flu if you don't wrap up warm.'

He shrugged her off and carried on digging. Esther pushed down her hurt. 'I had a midwife's appointment earlier. They can never be too sure, but they think the baby might come in June.'

'June, heh? The allotment should be at its best by then,' he grunted, pushing his pitchfork deep into the sodden earth.

'Exactly, I thought we might have a little welcome party in the allotment after he or she shows up.'

He looked up, alarmed.

'I don't like the thought of lots of people in here.'

'Oh, all right . . . Well, we don't have to. That's not really what I wanted to talk about. I wondered whether you might agree to being the baby's godfather? Officially in Judaism we don't have godparents, but I'd like you to play a honorary role in his or her life.'

'I don't know if that's such a good idea . . .' Snowball replied.

'Why not?'

A harsh wind blew over the allotment, humming through the spokes of the old bicycle wheels Snowball had lashed together to grow pumpkins against. Her eyes stung and, angrily, she wiped them with the back of her hand.

'I think you can probably do better for your little 'un than me,' he grunted, driving the fork down hard.

'Snowball, can you please stop digging and look at me?'

'Sorry, love, but I'm going to run out of light. I've got to double dig in all this manure otherwise I won't get the soil properly aerated and I've still a load of root veg to harvest.'

'What's happened to you, Snowball? You can't keep retreating from the people who love you. We just want to help.'

She placed her hands gently on his back and immediately felt his muscles tense.

'It's too late.'

Too late?

'It's never too late,' she protested. 'You don't have to isolate yourself.'

Silence; the only sound the rushing of the wind and the thunk of his pitchfork driving into the soil.

'I . . . I know it's something to do with that woman. You changed the moment she arrived. But whatever happened between you and Queenie is in the past. You can't allow her to continue this hold over you.'

Snowball looked like he wanted to curl into a ball and never unfold himself. 'You don't understand, Esther.'

'So help me to.'

'How can I, when I don't even understand myself?'

He shrugged her off and strode to the other side of the allotment, forking more manure from the compost heap before resuming his incessant digging.

Esther breathed out slowly, her breath billowing like smoke in the frozen air. She had come so close to discovering the real Snowball, but now it felt too late. The opportunity had slipped away into the shadows.

She turned and left, heading to Nell's.

Nell was buttoning up her coat when she pushed open the door.

'I saw you talking to him. Any joy?'

Esther shook her head.

'He'll come home when he's good and ready,' said Julia, ever the pragmatist.

'I've warned him,' Nell bristled. 'He's to be home for Christmas or he's not to bother . . .'

She turned her back, supposedly to take some cups out to the scullery, but Esther knew it was to save face, so that they couldn't see her hurt. His rejection of her, her home and the new life they had built sliced deep.

'Come on, Frankie and Lou!' she yelled up the stairs. 'Shake a leg. We don't want to be late.'

'Late for what?' Esther asked.

'Didn't Patsy tell you?' said Julia. 'Her lovely American chap. His unit and the American Red Cross have arranged a party down the town hall for all the kids of Stratford.'

As Esther, Nell, Frankie, Julia and Lou walked up Angel Lane, they bumped into Patsy and her little brother Jimmy coming out of Nellie Maud's dining room.

Patsy looked as lovely as always, her coltish figure trim in a tailored suit, her red lips and dark eyes looking even more exotic among the shabby market.

'Hello, girls,' Patsy said. 'You coming to the shindig Blue and the rest of his unit have arranged? Mum's at one of her peace meetings so thought I'd take our Jimmy.'

'We certainly are,' Esther replied. 'Do you know anything about it?'

'Not much,' she shrugged. 'Think it's just a couple of sausage rolls and a few party games if they're lucky. Still, it's a nice thought.'

'Will Santa be there?' asked Jimmy, looking up at his glamorous big sister.

'Course not silly,' she laughed, ruffling his hair, 'he's busy in Lapland.'

Esther smiled. It often occurred to her that Patsy behaved more like Jimmy's mother than his sister. Must be all that time they spent together during their evacuation. Thank God he had at least one source of love and affection, because it seemed to be in short supply from Queenie.

It took them a full half-hour to make it up the market, with Nell stopping to chat to all the stallholders. Every trader had their own distinctive patter, a polyglot tongue of Yiddish, Romany, back slang and London jargon. Nell seemed to be able to converse in them all, chatting and laughing by the light of the paraffin lamps. Esther had to hand it to East Enders: even in the frozen depths of winter, they still showed their customary enterprise. She laughed at the sight of a little girl who'd dressed up her cat as a reindeer and was dragging it up the market in a cardboard box!

By the time they finally pushed open the doors to the town hall, their cheeks and noses were frozen.

The ration-book party Patsy had predicted was nowhere to be seen. The whole place dazzled under a shimmering curtain of tinsel, Union Jacks and Stars and Stripes. In the corner stood the biggest Christmas tree Esther had ever seen, strewn with glittering silver chaff – the thin strips of metallic foil thrown out of aircraft to confuse German radar during a raid. A trestle table groaning with cakes, jellies and sandwiches was already being plundered by sticky little fingers.

'It's magical,' said Julia.

'Cor,' breathed Jimmy, his eyes wide as pebbles. 'Santa's here! And look, Patsy, he don't come by sleigh, he's only come on a bleedin' Jeep!'

Esther, Patsy and Lou glanced at each other in astonishment. Next to the tree was an actual American Army Jeep, with a suitably jolly Santa Claus sitting behind the wheel.

'Who wants a sweet?' boomed Santa in an American accent, standing up behind the wheel. He reached into his bag, pulled out fistfuls of sweets and threw them in the air. A chorus of squeals filled the air as a hundred or so kids scrabbled for brightly wrapped toffees.

Frankie and Jimmy dived into the crowd and Lou's eyes lit up when she spotted her sisters in the fray.

'This is your perfect chance to talk to the girls,' Esther grinned, squeezing Lou's hand. 'I can't see your dad anywhere. Go, quick!'

Lou hurried over to her sisters.

'Can you see Blue anywhere?' Patsy asked, scanning the hall.

'No, but it's so busy,' Esther replied. 'Every single child in Stratford seems to be squeezed in here.'

'Say what you like about the Yanks,' remarked Nell. 'They've done our kids proud.'

The crowds seemed to part as Santa made a beeline for them.

'Oi, Santa,' Nell heckled, clearly enjoying herself. 'Where's Rudolph?'

'I put him into retirement.'

Santa stopped right in front of Patsy.

'Say, how about a kiss from the prettiest girl in Stratford?'

'Do I know you?' she asked.

'Sure you do, it's the chump who's in love with you.' Santa pulled down his beard and winked. 'Remember, this is the exact same spot I laid eyes on you, five months ago at the dance. I got the knock-back then, so how about a kiss now, baby?'

He pulled a sprig of mistletoe from behind his back and crossed his fingers.

'Blue!' Patsy laughed. 'You're barmy! You're—'

But she didn't get to finish her sentence, as Blue pulled her into his arms and kissed her deeply on the lips.

All the kids went wild at the sight of Santa Claus in a clinch with Patsy, whistling and jumping up and down around them.

'It's so romantic,' Esther sighed, holding on to Nell's arm.

Nell smiled sadly and Esther knew her thoughts were with Snowball, the man she was in love with yet couldn't reach. If Esther were being honest with herself, the sheer heady romance of it all made her heart ache a little too. Had she and Walter ever romanced each other like this? They certainly wouldn't now with the spectre of Maureen hanging over them.

Finally, Blue let Patsy up for air.

'You didn't have to arrange all this for me,' she said, her face radiant.

'Sure I did. You told me that time we had the picnic in the park that your brother deserves to be made a fuss of.'

'But that was ages ago.'

'And I never forgot it. Jimmy is important to you, so he's important to me.'

He kissed her again, with such tenderness that Esther found herself swallowing sharply.

'I want to prove to you how much I love you, Patsy Jacks,' he murmured throatily.

A silence fell over the group.

'Bleedin' hell Santa, you got an older brother in Lapland?' piped up Nell, breaking the spell.

Blue burst out laughing and slung his arm around Nell.

'I also arranged this for you, Mrs Gunn, my British mom, to say thanks for putting me up last month while I was on leave.'

She waved her hand. 'It was nothing.'

'No, it wasn't nothing. I'd lost my buddy, I was in a bad place and you looked after me. I'll never forget that.'

'Well, you're always welcome in my home, son. You boys are making so many sacrifices for us.'

'Come on "Mom",' Blue grinned, leading her towards the trestle tables. 'You can give me a hand, I think I'm gonna need protection.'

'You're on, son,' grinned Nell, rolling up her sleeves.

'I'll help too,' Julia said.

'All right, kids, it's chow time!' Blue bellowed.

There was an enormous stampede as the kids tucked into jellies, blancmange, jam tarts and other rationed treats that many of them hadn't seen in years.

'Don't make yourself sick,' Patsy called after Jimmy.

'Amazing, isn't it?' Esther remarked to Patsy as she watched the GIs blowing up balloons and pouring out glasses of sticky orange squash. 'They seem to be enjoying it as much as the kids.'

'I think this party will pass into legend,' Patsy smiled fondly as she watched her little brother cram one biscuit in his mouth and another into his pocket. Esther had to agree. This would bring such pleasure to these wartime children, for whom fun was pretty thin on the ground.

Esther realised with a jolt how many of the kids here had been deprived of a parent. There was Frankie, Nell's son, who'd lost his father in the first week of the Blitz; Jimmy, whose father was killed in an Atlantic convoy; and the Button sisters, whose mother had lost her life in circumstances no less tragic, but certainly less openly discussed.

When this terrible war was over, would historians ever study the homefront like they would the battlefront?

Would they ever appreciate the richness and complexity of their lives, the relentless suffering of working-class women like Lou Button and the solidarity shown by women like Nell Gunn? The battles that went on not just in combat, but behind closed doors? She supposed not.

'You all right, Esther?' Patsy asked. 'You seem out of sorts tonight.'

'Yeah fine . . .'

'Thinking of the baby? This time next year, you'll have your own little nipper at Christmas.'

Esther blew out slowly.

'Blimey, yes.'

'You sure you're all right, Esther?'

'Do you ever worry about what's round the corner, what else this war has in store for us?' she asked suddenly.

'How do you mean?'

'Hitler's secret weapon, it seems to be all anyone talks about these days.'

'If it's got my name on, what can I do?' Patsy shrugged. 'We've gotta live for the day. Enjoy our pleasures where we can find them. For tomorrow, as they say, we may die.'

As she talked, she couldn't keep her eyes off Blue, who was performing a card trick for Jimmy, Frankie and the Button sisters.

'True,' Esther replied, wishing she shared Patsy's sangfroid. 'Sorry to be maudlin, must be my hormones. Least we have the Yardley Christmas party to look forward to tomorrow.'

'Aaah yes, about that, Esther . . .'

'Why do I get the feeling I'm not going to like what you're about to say?'

'This is terrible timing, but The Windmill are doing a tour of US Army bases, morale-boosting performances and all. Would you believe it but they're visiting Station 162, Willingale, in Chipping Ongar tomorrow.'

'Is that supposed to mean something to me?'

'It's where Blue and the rest of his unit are based. I have to go. I'm part of the performance.'

'Oh Patsy . . .'

'Oh please, Esther,' she begged, her voice husky. 'If you can let me off my shift a couple of hours early, then I'll have time to travel to Essex and be back in time for the show.'

'Patsy, do you remember when we first found out you were holding down two jobs? I warned you it couldn't continue. I'm terribly short-staffed as it is, I need all hands on the conveyor belt.'

'I promise to sort it all out soon, Esther, truly, but just for tomorrow could you please be flexible? Especially after all Blue and his unit have done here today.'

Patsy was clutching her arm. Her ridiculously beautiful face was so disarming. Esther felt in that moment she couldn't deny her anything.

'Very well, but please be back for the Yardley talent show. Miss Rayson wants to open with your number.'

'Oh, thanks, Esther,' Patsy gushed, hugging her tightly. She smelt delicious, ever so faintly of greasepaint and Evening in Paris. 'I won't let you down.'

'Patsy!' barked a voice and they all jumped.

'Mum!' said Patsy weakly as she turned round to find herself staring down the barrel of Queenie Jacks. 'I thought Jimmy deserved a treat so I brought him along to the party. He's having a smashing time.'

'So I see.' She flicked at a length of silver chaff that seemed to have attached itself to her collar. 'Another sign of the world gone vulgar.'

Blue appeared by their side and Patsy stared at him, trying to warn him off with her eyes.

'You must be Mrs Jacks,' he smiled, unperturbed, holding out his hand. 'Jimmy and Patsy's mum? It's a pleasure.'

'The pleasure's not reciprocated.'

She unpinned her hat and shook the snow off it, clearly impervious to Blue's charms.

'Please allow me to take that, and can I fetch you a drink, Mrs Jacks?' he persisted.

'We're not stopping. We don't need Yank charity. Jimmy!' she yelled. 'Get over here now! And how do you know my kids?' she added suspiciously, rounding on Blue.

'I've seen your Jimmy around the streets. He's a terrific little guy.'

'So it's you who's been giving him them comics?'

Patsy looked like she might have stopped breathing.

'Sure ma'am, yes, that was me.'

Queenie stared at Blue for what felt like a very long time.

'Come to think of it, I recognise your face. You stayed with Nell Gunn recently, didn't you?' Her voice was like ice. 'Stay away from my kids. I only warn the once.'

'Mum, please can we stay?' Jimmy begged, reluctant to leave his place at the table.

'Go on, Mum,' Patsy said. 'He's having such a smashing time. Just five more minutes.'

'Don't create,' Queenie warned. 'Jimmy get here now unless you want a clump.'

'I hate you,' Jimmy yelled, scraping back his chair. 'I wish it was just me and Patsy like before.'

Queenie paled, clamped little Jimmy's hand in hers and ushered him and Patsy from the town hall.

At the door, Patsy turned round briefly, her scarlet lips vivid against the curtain of snow falling behind her head.

'Sorry!' she mouthed. 'See you tomorrow.'

'Wow, some broad, Patsy's mum,' breathed Blue. 'Guess she don't like us Yanks.'

'I don't think she likes anyone much,' Esther murmured.

She had watched the scene play out in amazement. Patsy was playing a dangerous game. How much longer before all her carefully constructed worlds collided?

16

Patsy

The next morning, Patsy watched the clock nervously. She had to report to The Windmill by 11 a.m., so they could make the coach that was to take them to Chipping Ongar to perform at the USAAF station.

She'd come in even earlier than usual, battling through the snow to arrive at Yardley's by 4.30 a.m. to clock on.

At times, her whole life felt like one long, dizzy whirl between East and West London, and she dreaded the day she clocked on at the factory wearing little else but a scrap of chiffon, or appeared on the famous glass stage in her factory turban and overalls. With up to six shows a day and two separate companies, they were forever performing or rehearsing, and Patsy's war was whipping by.

She smiled at the memory of yesterday's party and Blue's sweeping kiss, before her mother had marched her home. The appearance of Blue in her life was what made her feel alive and in just a few short hours, she'd see him again.

There was something irrepressible about him. He had worked his way into her affections and every time she saw him, he seemed to leave an even deeper imprint. She knew it was a reckless game, but it was also one that, at the moment, she seemed powerless to stop.

'Pull out, Patsy,' said Esther, interrupting her thoughts with a tap on the shoulder. 'Emily here is going to take your place. You can clock off now, but be sure to be back here for six p.m.'

'Thanks, Est,' she said. 'You're a pal.'

Outside, the snow was falling thickly and the sky was so heavy and white, you couldn't even make out the factory rooftops or the tips of the cranes.

The number 25 seemed to take an age as it crawled its way in the direction of West London.

Patsy had to laugh as they finally turned into Oxford Street. String bags were a common-enough sight in the streets of the East End, but never seen in the grand streets of the West End. But now that the Board of Trade had forbidden the use of wrapping paper and bags for anything except food, smart ladies in snoods pedalling through Piccadilly clutching string bags was a common sight too.

The bus belched to a stop outside the bombed-out remains of John Lewis.

'All change, all change!' yelled the driver.

'Why do we have to get off?' Patsy asked a passing clippie.

'Road's closed off,' the young woman replied. 'Ministry of Food are putting on a Christmas fair, sponsored by Potato Pete.'

'You're joking?' But as she looked out the window, she could see a strange sort of grotto had sprung up in place of the gutted shell of the John Lewis windows.

Father Christmas was giving away hot baked potatoes and, incongruously, there was even a real baby elephant being led up and down Oxford Street.

'I can't be late because of an elephant. They're never gonna buy that one!' she cried to the bemused clippie, leaping off the bus.

By the time she skidded up Shaftesbury Avenue and around the corner into Great Windmill Street, the coach full of Windmill girls and boys was already idling by the kerb.

'Chop-chop, Patsy. Can't keep the troops waiting, darling,' Kitty called, sliding back the window and elegantly blowing out a plume of smoke.

'Coming!' she called.

Patsy was about to board the bus when a gentle hand pulled her back.

'Mrs Henderson!' she panted.

The owner of the theatre was eighty years old, a little unsteady on her feet but held upright by an iron will. Despite her somewhat formidable reputation, Patsy liked her enormously. Fortunately for Patsy, she seemed to have taken a shine to her too and she often found a little gift of a bunch of carnations or some caviar on the dressing table.

'My little sparrow. You're late,' she scolded. 'Again.'

'I know, I'm so sorry, Mrs Henderson, it won't happen again,' she gushed.

'I won't be able to stop the Old Man sacking you, my dear, which would be a shame as I think you're marvellous. Get your house in order, dear.'

Patsy nodded and boarded the coach, her heart still thumping from her dash.

As the coach passed through the bomb-shattered districts of London and the grimy streets gave way to the flat snow-covered fields of Essex, Patsy felt so torn. Her two worlds were pressing in on her now, demanding more and more of her time. She wondered if she'd have to give one of them up. But how could she turn her back on this life, which nurtured her creative soul? And how could she turn her back on the Lavender Girls?

The girls and boys of The Windmill were in high spirits as they travelled: smoking, warming up their vocal cords and trading gossip.

'Ooh, I do so love our trips to the US bases,' Kitty said. 'All those heroic men in uniform.'

'Give me the French Free Forces,' chipped in Mags, arching one brow. 'Ooh la la. *Très galant*.'

'Give me a Norwegian any day, darling,' laughed a camp Windmill boy behind them. 'Tall, blond and brooding.' He sniffed. 'Terribly outdoorsy.'

'Boring,' Mags yawned.

'Least they don't go to bed with their hairnets on,' he quipped, before winking at Patsy. 'Nothing like conforming to a national stereotype.'

'Not that it's terribly sexy performing on these bases,' Kitty added.

'True,' Mags agreed. 'Last week, I had to perform on a makeshift table in a hangar, with the headlamps of army lorries as improvised spotlights.'

'You should've been on my trip, Mags,' said a girl called Moy across the aisle. 'I performed in front of Clark Gable.'

'As in *Gone with the Wind* Clark Gable?' Patsy asked, finally able to squeeze a word in.

'The very same,' Moy nodded. 'He's stationed with the 351st Bomb Group at Polebrook in Northamptonshire. A right dish.'

'I was fourteen when that picture came out,' said Patsy, once again having to pinch herself at the world she found herself in.

Kitty smiled at her fondly. 'I forget how young you are. Well, you're part of the war effort now, doll.'

Patsy smiled back at Kitty and, feeling a little bit in awe as she always did around her, pushed back her hair nervously.

The older woman laughed huskily. 'You might well be our most wholesome, naïve nude yet, and I really do mean that in the nicest way. I adore you, Patsy.'

Wholesome? Naïve?

Patsy wanted to laugh at the absurdity of that comment. If only she knew. Finally they pulled through a set of heavily guarded gates. So this was Blue's world, this sprawling place of flat, endless fields, runways and Nissen huts stretching as far as the eye could see.

Every hangar they passed contained the dark hulking silhouette of a heavy B-17 Flying Fortress bomber, and the stench of gasoline and mud permeated the air.

'Look at the size of them,' whistled Kitty.

In that moment, a macabre thought hit Patsy. All it needed was four silver handles on it and it would be a giant coffin.

'Apparently they send up a fighter patrol to ward off enemy activity while the boys watch our show,' said Moy. Patsy shivered.

'They're going up on a sortie in two hours, so come on girls,' Mags remarked. 'Let's give them a show to remember.'

Like an unravelling cinema reel, Patsy heard the roar of applause, like the thundering of a waterfall, as she and the girls took to the makeshift stage.

She saw no individual faces, just a blur of outlines framed against the falling snow outside, a sea of vital, bright-eyed young men who in a matter of hours would take to the skies, some never to return. Men like Johnnie. The Windmill girls may be the last thing of beauty or joy that their eyes fell upon. The thought was a sobering one.

Her tableau was entitled moonlight and roses, and Patsy was swathed in garlands of white silk roses and chiffon. Bizarrely, she felt no trace of cold as she arched her back and held her arm aloft. Because somewhere out there in that sea of young men, *he* was watching her, loving her.

The final applause was even more deafening, wolf-whistles echoing round the vast container.

An army compère took to the microphone to thank the Windmill Theatre, but all of a sudden the mic broke.

Groans rang out as the compère tapped the microphone

somewhat theatrically. Strangely, there was music drifting from outside and, in the distance, Patsy could make out a figure standing on the flat top of a building outside the hangar.

A stagehand rushed forward with warm coats for the girls and they were helped off the stage.

'What's going on outside?' asked Kitty.

'Go take a look,' said one of the army personnel standing nearby.

They walked into the snow, following the rush of GIs into the field and craned their necks upwards.

'I don't believe it,' gasped Moy. 'Is that who I think it is?'

'Pinch me, I must be dreaming,' said Kitty. 'Is that . . .'

A pair of strong arms slipped round Patsy's waist and she whirled round to find herself staring up into a pair of bright blue eyes, smouldering with love.

'Bing Crosby,' said Blue.

And it was, it actually was the famous American singer.

Patsy didn't know what she found more astonishing. That she was here, in Blue's arms on base, or that a hundred feet away, Bing Crosby was standing in a long white sheepskin coat serenading thousands of GIs.

Patsy felt she'd wandered into a strange parallel universe. A pure silence cloaked the base as he sang 'White Christmas' on an Essex rooftop.

All around, young uniformed men wept openly as the raw and melancholy notes slid over them, each one wondering whether this might be their last Christmas.

Blue's fingers tightened around the belt of her mac and she felt his chin rest on the top of her head as they swayed to the music.

She turned and pressed her fingers softly to his frozen cheeks, nuzzling into the warmth of his sheepskin flying jacket.

'You must make it home,' she breathed into the space between them.

He was blinking back tears now and, suddenly, she saw how afraid he was. She knew it was forbidden but hang it all . . . Patsy pressed her lips to his and kissed him, so she wouldn't have to witness his fear, and to distract him from the horrors unfurling in his head.

He kissed her back, clutching her face between his hands as if she was made of porcelain. 'I'll come back for you.'

'Goodbye,' she whispered.

'Never goodbye,' he replied. 'Just cheerio for now.'

Darkness fell as they bumped their way back through the countryside to London, all of the girls silent, wrapped in their own thoughts.

Patsy fell asleep with her head resting against the glass window of the coach. She slept fitfully, dreaming of floating white elephants and Bing Crosby serenading the Lavender Girls on the conveyor belt. By the time the coach shuddered to a halt, she yawned and stretched her arms.

'What time is it, Kitty?'

She looked at a delicate wristwatch.

'A little after seven p.m. It took an age getting through some of those country roads. Amazed we made it at all in this snow.'

Patsy clutched her head in her hands.

'Oh no . . .'

'Where are you dashing off to, Cinderella?' Kitty's voice called through the snowy Soho night. 'We're back on stage in a half an hour.'

'Please, Kitty, tell them I don't feel very well. I'll explain later.'

By the time she reached Stratford, she was sodden and her hair was plastered to her face. She clattered up the metal stairs to the top-floor canteen, and she could hear laughter and applause ringing out behind the double doors.

On impulse, she ducked into the lavs to fix her face. She could hardly sing looking like a drowned rat.

Inside she saw a flurry of movement as factory girls changed and chatted away excitedly between acts.

'Lou, is that you?' she exclaimed as she spotted the back end of a pantomime horse backing out the cubicle.

'No, it's Black bleedin' Beauty,' Lou huffed. 'You're in big trouble. Your name was announced to come on stage to sing but you was nowhere to be seen.'

'Oh no,' Patsy cringed.

'It's all right, Esther covered for you. Told the audience you had some stage fright, but you'd hopefully sing later.'

'Oh thanks, Lou,' she said, digging around in her purse for a comb and some lipstick.

'Don't thank me, Pats, thank Esther. Oh, and by the way, your mum's in the audience.'

Lipstick restored, Patsy edged her way into the crowded canteen. The Yardley Follies were just finishing off their dance routine on the stage and the crowd were well warmed up. Esther sidled up next to her.

'Where have you been?'

'I'm sorry, it took an age to get back. I promise it won't happen again.'

'No, it won't, because it's time to choose, Patsy. Yardley or The Windmill.'

'Please don't make me choose, Esther,' she pleaded. 'I love both my jobs, I'll work harder. I'll find a way round it.'

Esther's face softened and, for a moment, Patsy thought she had relented.

'I'm sorry but no, I need girls fully committed to Yardley.'

'In that case, I'm so sorry Esther, but I . . . I can't leave my life at The Windmill.'

The two women stood staring at one another in the dark silence at the back of the hall.

'Very well, I'll take that as your resignation.'

Patsy went to answer, but the compère spotted her.

'She's back, the factory glamour girl, Patsy Jacks from the lipstick room. Come on, folks. Give her a big, warm Stratford round of applause.'

Patsy walked to the stage in a trance.

'No need to feel nervous, love,' he said when she climbed up. How could she tell him she'd just performed naked in front of nearly two thousand men?

'What are you going to sing, Patsy?'

Her mind was scrambled – oh God, what was she going to sing?

'"White Christmas" by Bing Crosby,' she said shakily.

'Great choice, love. Take it away, Patsy.'

As she sang, she thought of all those young men, now flying back from their mission, some limping across the channel with smoke streaming from their engines, some drifting down on parachutes into occupied Europe and what-ever fate lay ahead. Some who wouldn't have survived at all, their remains scorched into the earth; some whose last memory would be the Windmill girls and this song.

Please don't let Blue be one of them.

Her silken voice floated over the room, weaving a magic spell as the snowflakes drifted down silently outside the factory windows. Her voice captured the hopes and fears of everyone there as they faced their fifth Christmas at war. Emotions bubbled close to the surface, as so many in the audience, torn apart from those they loved, wondered if life would ever return to how it was before.

Tears tracked down Patsy's beautiful face as she finished the song, and the whole canteen got to their feet in a thunderous standing ovation.

17

Lou

'Don't know how you're gonna follow that, Lou,' muttered the compère, handing her the microphone. 'Good luck.'

Lou stepped into the spotlight, dressed as a pantomime horse, beads of sweat forming on her temple. She cleared her throat nervously. Performing had always come easily to her. What was wrong with her? Why couldn't she just slip into 'the act'?

Patsy's luminous beauty, the aching emotion of that song, had exposed her vulnerabilities like never before. Bubbly old Fat Lou, the girl she'd been before – that girl seemed to have vanished along with her mum.

Three tables from the stage, Queenie smiled coldly.

'I'm going to sing a song now . . .' Lou faltered, fumbling with the microphone, nearly dropping it.

'I wish you would!' yelled a wag.

Blind Eric the pianist sat expectantly at his piano, waiting for her to tap it for him to start. But her arms were paralysed, the room lurching and tilting. People were starting to pull faces.

'Hurry up, Fat Lou!' yelled a voice from the back of the canteen. 'The war'll be over at this rate.'

She drew in a breath to apologise, but another voice cut over hers, shrill and accusing.

'For a girl whose whole life has been a charade, you'd think this would come easy.'

And then all eyes swivelled from Lou to Queenie.

'That's right, ain't it, Lou?' Queenie said querulously. As she spoke, she rose up slowly, hands on her hips.

'Why don't you tell them who you really are, beneath the silly costume?'

'Mum, sit down,' hissed Patsy, pulling on her mother's arm. 'You're making a show of yourself.'

'Making a show of myself, am I? It's not me who cavorts down the Cut.'

Lou felt the blood in her veins turn to ice. Please God, not here. Not like this.

Queenie turned to the crowds. 'Oh yes, didn'cha know? Lou takes her pleasures in women.'

A few people started to laugh nervously, others exchanged startled looks.

'That's right, after dark, I saw with my own eyes. She and a woman kissing, pawing at each other.' Her face shrivelled in disgust. 'It's a disgrace and decent people have a right to know when her kind are around.'

'That's enough, Mrs Jacks,' ordered Miss Rayson, striding up to the stage and taking the microphone from Lou. 'This is a talent show, not a scurrilous coffee morning. You are ruining this for everyone. Please leave.'

'With pleasure,' Queenie snapped and, picking up her black shawl, she swept from the room.

A terrible silence fell over the canteen.

'Would you like to sit down, Lou?' asked Miss Rayson, concern etched on her face.

'Yes,' she mumbled, feeling like the floor beneath her feet was crumbling away. Lou began to slink off the stage – but suddenly, she stopped.

Five hundred stunned faces stared back at her. Since when did Lou Button shuffle anywhere? Where was her chutzpah? Out of nowhere, she heard Renee's voice in her ear.

If you don't speak your truth, Queenie Jacks will.

'Actually no. No, I wouldn't like to sit down. I've got something to say!' She took the microphone back from Miss Rayson and jutted her chin out.

'I don't love women. I love *a* woman. And it's a pure, kind, non-judgemental love, the best I've ever known, in fact.'

Her heart pounded fiercely in her chest as she looked around at the sea of open mouths.

'I watched my mum trodden down into the ground, so far down in fact, she'll never emerge. By a man who was supposed to love her. So I think I know a thing or two about what constitutes love. Real love, that is.'

Her voice rose sure and strong above the crowd.

'If the love I feel is wrong, just because it comes from a woman, then so be it. Maybe society's out of step with me!'

She handed a flabbergasted Miss Rayson her horse's head.

'I'm sorry for interrupting your night, folks. Happy Christmas!'

As she walked down the stage steps, Esther rose to her feet and started to clap furiously. Joanie and Joycie rose up too, closely followed by Little Irene and Betty. Soon, all the lipstick room and Nell Gunn and Julia were on their feet applauding wildly.

They kept on clapping until she reached them all. She felt giddy, high from the relief of unburdening herself.

'My hands are shaking,' she said, holding out her palm.

'I ain't surprised, Lou,' said Little Irene. 'I thought you was just gonna sing "Knees up Mother Brown"!'

'Your mum would be proud of you, love,' Nell said.

Lou felt her throat tighten with emotion. Discovering her mum had known about her sexuality all along, and yet had still loved her unconditionally was so bittersweet. Never had she needed her mum more.

'Can we go home now?' Lou asked, suddenly feeling all her fight desert her.

Back in the Shoot, the snow was so thick it had collected in great drifts on the window ledges. Still it fell, tumbling from the skies overhead, coating the church roof, the allotment and the houses. An eerie silence had descended over all of Stratford, as if Mother Nature herself was trying to muffle the shock of Lou's confession.

As they crossed the square, the euphoria subsided. The enormity of what she had done hit Lou. She hadn't named Martha, but it wouldn't take people long to work it out. They went everywhere together.

Stratford was a closed shop, a small insular world, particularly down the Shoot. You only had to buy a new pair of shoes and word got round so fast, the whole neighbourhood would turn out for a look.

Then there was the authorities! Stepping outside the normal rules of convention would bring their scrutinising eye on her and Martha. Rumour had it you'd get a capital L under your name if they discovered your sexuality.

'What have I done?' she asked, stopping abruptly in the middle of the deserted square.

'I'm sure you ain't the only lesbians in Stratford,' Nell said.

'Maybe not, but we're about to be the most notorious,' Lou murmured, her face so pale it was almost invisible against the snow. 'I can't go into the factory tomorrow. I can't!'

'Listen, it's important we don't panic,' said Julia.

'Mum's right,' Esther agreed. 'I'd stay away from work tomorrow though, Lou. I'll go and see Miss Rayson and see how the land lies. Things will blow over and after Christmas, there'll be some new topic of gossip. You'll see.'

How Lou hoped she was right. They trudged on in silence, but when they reached Nell's front door, Lou's hand flew to her mouth and she knew with a certainty: this was never going to go away.

'Who's done this?' cried Esther.

Nell traced her finger down the door and stared in disbelief at the black tar on her skin.

'I'll give you two guesses.'

The front door had been daubed with a big black L. Drips of thick tar stained the pristine snow beneath.

Lou's face emptied. 'I'll leave tomorrow, Nell,' she said quietly. 'It's not fair to bring scandal to your door.'

'You'll do no such thing,' Nell replied fiercely. 'That poisonous bitch.'

Esther was the only one not looking at the door. She was staring in the other direction.

Aside from their own footprints in the snow, another solitary set led away from the allotment.

'What's wrong, Esther?' Lou asked.

'I've got a terrible feeling . . .' Her voice trailed off and then she started to run.

'Esther, don't be silly, you'll slip and fall,' Julia called after her, but she ignored her mother, slithering through the snow until she reached the shed.

By the time the rest of them had reached her, she shook her head.

'I found this pinned to the shed door. It's from Snowball.'

Nell took it and read out loud.

'*I'm sorry.*'

She turned the note over. 'Is that it? Sorry for what?'

Esther pushed open the door to see Snowball's scant possessions were gone. The only thing that remained was a small but distinctive anchor-shaped button, which she scooped off the floor.

'For leaving.'

PART THREE

18

Esther

May 1944

It was a Saturday in the middle of May and spring was performing its alchemy. The flu epidemic had at last subsided, and people were beginning to remember they had feelings in their fingers and toes. Nature was waking up too. The dull, brown earth had begun to warm, and a blanket of green was spreading. Everything was bursting into bloom, including Esther.

Eight months gone now, even she hadn't been able to persuade Miss Rayson to allow her to carry on working at Yardley. In a bid to avoid her mother-in-law, she spent most days here down at the allotment, doing what she could to keep Snowball's plants ticking over.

She looked down at the worn shell button in her fingers and rubbed it, as if somehow it might unlock the mystery of Snowball's disappearance. She missed him more with each passing day. Spring was his favourite time in the allotment. He should be here, sewing out his beetroot, runner beans and winter veg. Only yesterday, she'd spotted a little hedgehog snuffling about the compost heap as she'd planted out tomatoes and had gone to tell him. All these little miracles he was missing. She sat down on the old bench outside the shed and took a breather, pushing back the soft tendrils of brown hair from her face.

Pouring some tea from a flask, she settled back in the spring sunshine. It had rained last night and now everywhere smelt of damp soil and green shoots, the air sweet with birdsong.

Everywhere she looked, the ghosts of the past gilded the air. Snowball's favourite pitchfork, wrapped with red string, propped up against the shed as if he'd only just left it. The bands of copper round the herbs to ward off slugs, glistening in the crystalline light. Scraps of white rags fluttered from the fruit bushes to ward off the birds. Snowball was everywhere, but nowhere. He had gone, but the world had gone right on turning.

'Morning,' called a man's voice.

'Morning,' Esther smiled back, squinting against the sun.

She watched as Mr Mahoney, back from prisoner of war camp for six months now, trotted across the square, holding the hand of a small dark-haired girl who almost certainly didn't share his blood.

'Not long now for you, heh love?' he remarked, tapping his belly with a rolled-up copy of the *East London Advertiser*.

'Nope.'

'Hope it's a little smasher like ours. We're just off to the market. You need anything?'

Esther shook her head. 'No thanks.'

It was astonishing. Mr Mahoney knew that child wasn't his, but to save face, or perhaps because the truth paled into comparison next to the horrors he had faced in a German prison camp, he had said nothing.

Silence was the currency with which the East End dealt with its secrets. Mrs Button's death from an abortion and her husband taking up with a woman just weeks after her death? Not discussed. Mrs Mahoney's illegitimate child with a Polish airman? Off limits.

Lou's relationship with Martha Robertson from the

woodmill? Now that was a different matter. Poor Lou was struggling. Five months on, she and Martha couldn't walk down the street without constant nudges. The curtain-twitchers were getting to her now. Yesterday, one of the girls in the lipstick room had even tended her notice. Her mother didn't want her being around Lou, apparently. A corrupting influence. She had a feeling that might prove the final straw for Miss Rayson, who up until now had been supportive.

Esther wished she could do more to help Lou, but what? She had enough of her own problems to deal with, anyway. Snowball's disappearance and . . . She looked down at her tummy and heard the nasty voice of self-doubt whisper its foul truths in her ear.

Can you truly love a child you'd been tricked into conceiving? Could she show the same compassion and unconditional love that Mr Mahoney had offered up to his little cuckoo child?

Twenty minutes later, they were back.

'Mr Mahoney!' she called.

'Yes, my ducks,' he said, wandering over.

'Might I ask you something?'

'Anything, darlin'. Be a good girl, Emily, and take these home to your mum.' She took the bag of doughnuts and fresh bread from him.

'Ooh, better keep this one aside,' he grinned, handing Esther a doughnut, 'now that you're eating for two.'

He watched Emily scamper home, his eyes shining with love.

'You love that little girl.'

He nodded. 'The bones of her.'

'And was it always that way?'

He thought carefully before answering.

'Not always. Between you and I, it was quite a shock when I got home . . .'

He turned his thin face to the sun.

'I was very bitter when I came home from that camp. I didn't want to live. But then I looked around me. At the beauty of this allotment, the communal restaurant, the way Nell and all the women round here looked after my missus while I was away.'

Nell's door opened and she appeared, beating the dust out of a rag rug. She looked over and waved.

'But more than anything, the innocence of that little life.'

'Is that what changed you then?'

'Sort of. I realised that I owed it to everyone, most of all myself, to love, not give in to hate.'

He tapped her gently on the knee with his paper.

'So you love that little one with everything you've got.'

'Thanks, Mr Mahoney,' she said slowly. 'It just feels a little overwhelming, bringing a new life into a world at war.'

'Of course it does, but all that baby needs from you is love.'

He stood up and left his paper on the bench.

'I've read this; expect you'll want it for the compost.'

She stared after him in amazement, then looked down at her tummy, which looked ridiculously large with her skinny ankles poking out beneath. This baby deserved a far better mother than she. She had stood up to all of life's trials – and there had been many in her young life – but this one felt bigger than her.

'I'm sorry,' she whispered, feeling her eyes fill with hot tears. 'I'm so sorry.'

A voice sounded on the far side of the square.

'Come inside, Est, cup of Rosie here for ya.'

'Coming,' she replied, heaving herself up and brushing her eyes with the back of her hand.

Nell watched her waddle her way across the square.

'Girl,' she declared.

'How can you tell that just from the way I'm walking?' she laughed.

Settled at the table with one of Nell's extra-strong brews in front of her, Esther spread out the paper and warmed her fingers on the cheap china.

The face staring back at her from the front page was so familiar that, at first, it didn't even strike her as odd. Then her brain caught up with her.

'Nell,' she said, putting her tea down so abruptly it sloshed over the sides.

'It's Snowball.'

Nell looked up, relief flooding over her face as she stared expectantly out the window.

'No, here, in the paper.'

Together they stared at the photograph on the front page, over an article on the opening of a new hostel in Loughton for aged homeless men and women.

'The new lady mayor attends the official opening of an accommodation scheme for the elderly, run by West Ham Council and London Civil Defence, to help those who find themselves vagrant,' Esther read out loud, astonished.

Snowball stood at the outskirts of the group, together but apart from them, looking as if he'd been coerced into posing for the photograph.

'Th . . . that's the place he was on the committee for last year, and now he's living there.'

'Stands to reason, 'spose,' said Nell, affecting her air of indifference once more.

'But, Nell, this is a terrific breakthrough. Why didn't I think to check there before? Now we can go and talk to him, bring him home.'

'You can, love. I've no intention of going over there.'

'B-but why?'

'He made his choice. I tried to help.' She shook Vim on

to a damp cloth and started vigorously mopping up Esther's spilt tea. 'I have my pride, Esther, I shan't beg him to come home.'

Her jaw was set rock solid.

'It's done.'

Esther knew it was pointless trying to get Nell Gunn to change her mind. She'd have more luck prising open Tower Bridge single-handed.

'I understand, sorry, Nell,' she said, touching the older woman on the arm. 'I didn't mean to upset you.' She drained her tea. 'I'll be off.'

'Don't stray too far from home,' Nell warned without looking up from her scrubbing.

Outside, she wrapped the knocker of number 12.

'Patsy,' she breathed in relief when she opened the door.

'Esther!' she exclaimed. 'Come in. Oh, I can't tell you how good it is to see you. I miss you and the girls so much.'

'What's wrong?'

'Nothing, I'm tickety-boo,' Patsy replied, but in the dim light of the passage her eyes were glassy, as if she'd just been crying.

'No, you're not.'

She burst into tears.

'Come on,' Esther soothed, leading her out to the allotment. 'Let's sit out here and talk.'

The whole story spilt out and afterwards, Esther chose her words carefully in order to assuage Patsy's fears.

'It's the post, it's getting harder to get through.'

'Esther, it's been four months and three weeks. He used to write to me so regular. I have to face facts. He's either thrown me over, or . . .'

Her voice tailed off and Esther shook her head.

'Don't you dare talk like that!'

'But what else am I supposed to think, Esther?' she wept,

her beautiful face etched with despair. 'He usually gets a weekend furlough every month. I haven't seen him since I performed at his base, just before Christmas.'

She bent down, plucked a wild bluebell from beneath the bench.

'I think he's decided he can do better than a show girl.'

Esther breathed in slowly.

'Why don't you go to his base, enquire?'

'And look like some dizzy camp follower?' she scoffed. 'Besides, they won't tell me. Maybe that's all I am – a silly girl who fell for a line.'

'I don't believe that and nor do you,' Esther replied. 'You must hold hard to hope.'

They talked some more until Patsy had to leave for her shift at The Windmill.

'The girls all really miss you.'

Patsy took Esther's hands in hers.

'Not as much as I miss them.'

'So go back. The door's always open.'

'I think it's too late.'

Esther wasn't sure if she was referring to Blue or her job.

'It's been so good talking, Esther. Thanks.'

'It's not just the girls who miss you,' Esther replied with a smile. Then, trying to keep her voice casual: 'Oh, by the way, where was it your mum lived in Poplar, before she was relocated here?'

'Gough Street. Not sure how much of it's left, mind you.'

In Poplar, Esther found a typical East End street, a long road of soot-covered terraces. It was a stone's throw from the busy East India Dock Road.

The docks weren't far from here and she could smell salt and oil on the breeze. What was she doing here, digging into the tangled threads of Snowball's past? What right had she?

Nell had given up, accepted after everything that perhaps Snowball was a man who couldn't lead a conventional life. Why could she not just do the same? She should be at home, knitting baby booties and resting. Not hunting down a man with no name.

Every so often, the long row of terraces would be inter-rupted by a gaping gap of sky. The remnants of a home long since turned to a mass of willow herb, dandelion and chick-weed. The Blitz had caused extensive damage to Poplar, which, being situated so close to the docks, was a major target for the German bombers. She had read that of the twenty thousand buildings in the borough, half had been destroyed or damaged. But Gough Street wasn't a statistic. These were people's homes, reduced to rubble and dust.

She thought she heard children's laughter and she stared up at a bombed building. Pairs of dark eyes peeked out from the charred edges of a first floor. A rustle and they were gone. Esther had the strangest sensation she was being watched. Wearing a mackintosh, her jacquard headscarf knotted loosely beneath her chin, she supposed she could look like someone vaguely official.

'Can I help you?'

Esther turned and took in the cigarette clamped between full red lips. Other details crowded in. Strong inhalation. Flinty green eyes. Turban set at jaunty angle. She'd come across Poplar's answer to Nell Gunn.

'Good afternoon. I was wondering whether you could help me find someone?'

The woman said nothing, just kept on staring at her.

'Do you know this man?' Esther fumbled in her bag, producing the front page of the paper with Snowball's face on it.

The woman glanced at it, then shook her head, blowing out a strong stream of blue smoke from her nostrils.

'Very well. Might you know Mrs Jacks? I think she used to live here. Queenie Jacks.'

The woman removed the cigarette from her lips and cupped it inside her palm.

'Who wants to know?'

'Queenie's my neighbour.'

She raised her eyebrow a fraction.

'How's that working out for you then?'

'Not that well. She's put a lot of people's backs up. I'm just . . .' She searched for the right words. What was she doing here? 'I want to try and understand her a little better.'

'Poplar Recreation Ground,' she replied, flicking the butt on the floor.

'Sorry, I don't understand.'

'Go. It'll tell you what you need to know.'

'I-I still don't . . .'

But the woman had clearly tired of their conversation and, turning her back, she disappeared inside her home.

Retracing her steps, Esther turned back on to the East India Dock Road. It was late Saturday afternoon and the street thronged with shoppers coming back from Chrisp Street market. Dodging them, it was a relief to turn into the cool green space of the park.

She looked about her. What was she supposed to be looking for exactly? The park showed the usual scars of war. Holes where the ground had been dug for sandbags, trenches where people had cowered at the height of the Blitz. Around the edge of the park, handsome almshouses stood, built for the East India Company merchants. St Matthias Church, its stained-glass windows boarded over and its bells silenced by war, stared back reproachfully.

Esther was about to turn back when she spotted a tall white stone memorial near the gate. How had she missed it? She walked towards it. An angel in mourning, wings outstretched with clasped hands, standing on a three-staged Gothic structure, gazed down mournfully at her.

There was an inscription. She read it out loud. '*In memory of 18 children who were killed by a bomb dropped from a German aeroplane upon the L.C.C. School Upper North Street Poplar on the 13th of June 1917.*'

'Oh no,' she murmured.

Suddenly feeling hot, she unknotted her headscarf. There was a list of names and ages on the sides of the memorial and she murmured them under her breath.

> '*Louise Acampora, aged five years*
> *Alfred Batt, aged five years*
> *Leonard Bareford, aged five years*
> *John Brennan, aged five years*
> *William Challen, aged five years*
> *Vera Clayson, aged five years…*'

Her throat tightened. She couldn't bear to read another name on the list. The headscarf slipped from her fingers.

How could these tiny children be casualties of a bomb, and from the first war? How had she never heard of this? Why had she imagined that bombs falling from the sky were exclusive to her experiences?

'Oh Queenie,' she said. 'Did you lose a child to this bomb? Did little Louise or Alfred belong to you?'

She looked up at the tattered clouds scrawling across the sky.

The angel above her head suddenly seemed to spin and for one horrible moment, Esther thought she was about to faint.

Clutching the stone memorial, she breathed slowly until the world stopped lurching. Then she was walking, as fast as she could, away from this grotesque reminder of the war that was supposed to have ended all wars. She knew the fields of France held the limbs and souls of men, boys really, whose lives had ended before they had even begun. But children? On the homefront?

Her hands rested on her tummy and she wanted to scream. Wars equalled death; cold stone memorials where there should have been playgrounds.

Damn Maureen, damn her for tricking her into bringing a life into war. In that moment, she was filled with impotent rage.

She walked fast, shopfronts blurring, until something caught her eye.

William Whiffin Photographic Portraiture. 237 East India Dock Road.

Esther wasn't sure what it was that had made her stop. Perhaps it was the sepia faces in the display, faces from happier times looking down at her, a window into the past.

Dozens of parlour portraits and enamelled postcards dotted the display. Families and children posing proudly in their Sunday best, East Enders who, despite having so little, would have saved hard for a cherished portrait.

She pushed open the door and a bell tinkled softly. An elderly man, immaculate in his sharp-creased suit and half-moon spectacles, emerged from a door at the back.

'I'm sorry, dear, I don't do portraiture any longer. I only work for the war office, photographing bomb damage.'

He sighed and spread fingers stained purple from chemicals over the counter.

'That's all right, I'm not here to have my photo taken. I have some questions, if I may?'

He smiled encouragingly.

'How long have you been running this business? Were you here during the first war?'

'We've been here since 1905,' he said proudly. 'During the

first war, I enlisted, of course, but my wife and son took over the running of the studio. Why do you ask?'

'I've just come from the park, and I was looking at the memorial.'

'To the children from the bombed school?'

'That's right. Do you know much about it?'

'I know everything that happens in Poplar, we've photographed it all – weddings, christenings, even the General Strike. And alas, funeral processions.'

'I hope this doesn't sound macabre, but might I be able to take a look at any photos you have of the school funeral?'

'Of course, but are you quite sure you want to be looking at such sad photographs in your condition?'

'Please, sir, I can't say why, but it's important.'

He disappeared out the back. When he reappeared ten minutes later, he placed a fat dusty manila folder on the counter.

'I lost thousands of negatives and photographs when my shed at the back of the yard was hit by an incendiary. Fortunately, this folder was down in the basement.'

He opened the folder and Esther immediately sneezed from the release of dust motes.

'The funeral was the largest the East End's ever seen. There were thousands of floral tributes laid along the route. They were sent from all over the place.'

He opened the folder, and dozens of shiny black-and-white photos slid across the counter.

'It felt like the whole world was mourning our murdered babes.'

Esther started leafing through the images and felt her heart clench.

'Oh my,' she breathed, holding her fingers to her mouth in shock.

The crowds stretched all the way up the broad East India

Dock Road, six deep, all with their necks craned in one direction.

'There must be thousands of people here,' she murmured.

The photographer nodded.

'All stood in perfect silence as those little coffins passed by. The Bishop of London led the service, said that in all his twenty years with the church he'd never seen a more touching sight.'

It felt like all of East London and beyond had turned out to escort the children from the church to their final resting place, their banners proudly held aloft. Boy Scouts and Girl Guides, wounded soldiers and sailors, the Stevedores' Union, firemen, the Union of Railway Men, French Marines and even representatives from the Australian Navy, all of them following the bodies in a protective guard.

But it was the sight of the little white coffins that Esther couldn't tear her gaze from. She had so many more questions, but the photographer shut the folder quickly, as if he could no longer stand the reminder. A photograph slipped out and skidded over the parquet floor.

With some difficulty, Esther bent down to retrieve it.

'Leave it, miss, I'll pick it up.'

'No it's all right, I can manage,' she puffed, clutching her back with one hand and the photo with the other.

'There now, I've g . . .'

Her voice vanished.

'Th-this woman,' she stammered. 'I know this woman.'

The photographer leant over the counter.

'Aah, yes, I think her name's Queenie.'

Esther stared at the tinted parlour photograph in disbelief. Was this young woman sitting straight-backed on a chair, chin proudly jutting forward, a full head of flame-coloured hair, really the same woman she knew?

'I remember the name because if ever a woman had a

more regal bearing,' he smiled. 'And that hair. It took me hours to hand tint her hair auburn, and even then, I don't think I did it justice.'

Queenie might not have been smiling, but her demeanour was soft, every fibre of her being seemed to be saying: 'Look at my daughter.'

Perched upon her lap was a dainty little girl, no more than two, with her mother's direct gaze and fiery red hair, swept back with blue ribbons. Her eyes were clearest blue. Her summer frock was in a matching shade of cornflour and the buttons were made of shell and fashioned like tiny anchors.

With horror slithering over her, Esther reached into her handbag and pulled out the tiny anchor button Snowball had left behind in the shed.

Gently, she placed it next to the photograph. The button in her hand and the one on the little girl's dress were one and the same.

'Who is this girl? Why is her photograph in this folder?' she gabbled, already knowing the answer.

'I photographed her and her mother the year before the Great War was declared,' he replied, his voice laced with sorrow. 'It's Queenie's daughter, Pearl. She was one of the little children killed in the bombing.

'Pearl's dad left her, run off, so I heard tell, and Queenie remarried a coloured chap, a sailor I believe.' He took the photograph and placed it back with the others. 'A tragedy for that young family.'

Pearl's dad had run off?

Esther's head raged with thoughts that wouldn't quite connect. Could it be that Snowball was Pearl's dad? He would be the right age. It would also explain the cause of Queenie's vitriol and hatred towards him. What was it she had said that day down the Shoot?

'That's it, run away, you always was good at that!'

It would also explain Snowball's reaction when he saw Queenie again on Esther's wedding night. She could still see his face when Queenie had appeared at the doorway. He'd looked like a ghost train had passed through him. He'd looked like a man ridden with guilt. And why would he have held on to a button from Pearl's dress all these years if he didn't have a strong connection to her? If he wasn't, in fact, her father?

Little red flecks of anger danced in front of her eyes. If that were true, then little wonder Queenie was bitter. Her daughter had been killed at school, where she should have been safe, and then she'd been abandoned.

Questions ricocheted around her mind. What kind of man was Snowball? Did Patsy know she'd once had a half-sister?

Esther felt like someone had pierced a hole in her heart, punctured her, and everything inside was deflating. Snowball was an honourable man, wasn't he? Or perhaps she had been so desperate to find a father figure in him, she had created a man who had never existed?

'I said, are you quite well, miss?' The photographer's voice jerked her back to the present.

'Yes, sorry. I'm fine,' she replied.

'Did I answer your questions?'

'Yes, I think possibly you have. You've been most helpful.'

And with that Esther stepped outside into the spring sunshine, shattered.

19

Patsy

Talking to Esther earlier that morning in the allotment had cheered Patsy up, but by the time the evening's performance finished, she felt the familiar foreboding.

She was sitting at her dressing table after the show in her robe, wiping the thick coating of pancake off with cotton wool soaked in witch hazel. All around her, Windmill girls chatted and laughed, bathing in the usual post-show euphoria.

'Are you all right, sweetheart?' asked Kitty, glancing over as she clipped her stockings to a suspender belt. 'Man trouble?'

Patsy nodded. What was the point of denying it?

'Oh, darling Patsy, what did I tell you when you first started here about getting involved?'

Why had she? Got involved, that is, offered up her fragile heart to Blue. This silence was killing her. There had been no telegram from his superiors, no word from any of his buddies, despite them knowing about Patsy. It could point to only one logical conclusion: she had been a flash in the pan, a bit of furlough fun. She'd believed all his heartfelt proclamations of love, truly believed them. Maybe even he had as well. But love in wartime was a fickle beast.

She was a walking cliché. And to think that she had opened up to him, nearly told him about her past and . . .

'Men can be such terrible bastards,' Kitty declared.

Patsy tried to reply, but to her mortification felt her eyes fill with hot tears.

'Do you know what I think, sweetie?' Kitty went on. 'The safest place to be is on that stage. Real life is so messy and fraught with danger.'

Kitty glanced at the walls above the mirror, smothered in foreign banknotes, from French to Spanish, American to Burmese. The currency may have been different, but the sentiment was the same.

'We're a lovely face in a foreign place, a dash of escapism and glamour to blot out the darkness,' Kitty said, lighting a cigarette and holding it up between slim fingers. 'To them, we're pin-ups. We're not reality, darling.'

She stood and cupped Patsy's chin in her fingers.

'Chin up, darling, tomorrow's another day.'

Patsy was the last person in the changing room, and was still sitting there when Mrs Henderson walked in.

'Why hello, my little cockney sparrow,' she said, surprised to see Patsy still there. 'Fabulous show this evening, one can always tell when the Americans are in, can't one?'

She tottered a little as she stepped down into the basement changing room with her dachshund Gilpin cradled against her chest. The doyenne of the theatre might have been frail and a little unsteady on her feet, but Patsy didn't dare to presume to help her sit down. Since her warning outside the theatre last Christmas for being late, Patsy had been the model of professionalism and had won her way back into the old lady's good books.

The polarities between their lives were staggering. Mrs Henderson was from a different generation, born into wealth and privilege. Patsy tried to imagine her in the Shoot, talking on the doorstep with Nell Gunn . . .

But despite this, in a queer way, Patsy sensed a kindred spirit.

'You were seen kissing a GI at Chipping Ongar, I hear.'

Patsy tensed. Relationships between performers and members of the Forces were strictly forbidden.

'Relax,' she smiled, feeding a biscuit to her dog. 'I might have snow on the roof, but I'm not old. I too have stories to tell, my dear.' Her blue eyes twinkled mischievously.

'Do you love him?' Mrs Henderson asked.

Patsy stared at the concrete floor.

'I think so.'

'So tell him.'

'He's gone, thrown me over, or . . .' Her voice trailed off.

'Aah, I see. Then you must comfort yourself with the pleasure you brought him while he was in London.'

Patsy knew, everyone did, that Mrs Henderson's son Alec had been killed by poison gas in the trenches of the first war. After he died, she found a French postcard in his belongings. He had died without seeing a naked woman in the flesh. It was what had led the elderly woman to spend her money buying an old theatre and filling it with beautiful nudes. Other women may have made shrines of their sons' graves, but Mrs Henderson showed her love in other ways.

Patsy was doing exactly what she was supposed to.

'You are a gift of joy,' Mrs Henderson sighed. 'You have a beautiful body and a divine face. You are a pearl, my dear, and pearls are supposed to shine.'

She was right. By the time Patsy left, the stage door Johnnies were still very much in evidence and a small cheer went up when Ben held the door open for her. She smiled her performer's smile – dazzling, bright, fixing on no one in particular.

Patsy went through the motions, signing souvenirs, smiling, chatting with the eager hordes of servicemen clustered around the door.

They thrust gifts in her hand, presents of chocolates, stockings and, optimistically, offers of dinner. The night was dark and faces were reduced to blurred outlines, which made it easier to politely decline.

At last the queue thinned, but Patsy felt another souvenir being pressed into her hands.

'Who shall I sign it to?'

'Your nincompoop,' came the gravelly American voice.

'Blue!'

Her heart soared for a moment but then her joy gave way to anger.

'Well, that's a fine way to treat a girl. I haven't heard from you in months.'

But then he stepped closer to the small pool of light from the stage door and Patsy saw his face. Her heart shattered and her mouth fell wide open in shock.

'We need to talk,' said Blue eventually. 'Can I buy you a cup of tea in our cafe?'

Sitting opposite one another in the corner of the tiny cafe, Patsy could not take her eyes off his face.

'You should see the other guy,' he joked lamely.

'W-what happened?'

'It was the mission I went on, right after you left last Christmas. We'd gone to attack a fuel dump in Amiens. Our plane had its right wing blown off after it was hit in the fuel tanks. Pilot could do nothing to save it so we all bailed out.'

He paused as the waitress came and set down two mugs of tea. She smiled in recognition when she saw Blue and then her face froze in alarm. She recovered herself quickly and patted him on the shoulder.

'It's on the house,' she said. 'I'll bring you some cake to go with it.'

'Jeez,' he laughed as she walked off. 'If I knew getting my face burnt off would mean folk'd treat me this good, I'd have done it ages ago.'

Patsy couldn't share in his grim humour. Instead, she reached out tenderly and traced the lines of his scars. They started midway down his cheek, and the angry red scarring extended down his jawbone to the delicate skin of his neck.

At her touch, his eyes flickered shut.

'You don't know how long I've dreamt of that.'

'I don't know what to say.'

He shrugged. 'I have my eyesight, handy for a navigator. And my life, of course, which is more than can be said of my three buddies who bailed out at the same time.'

His blue eyes stared back at her, haunted. He was no longer the cocky young man Patsy met last July at the dance hall. His swagger had vanished along with his innocence.

'Oh Blue, I'm so sorry,' she said softly. 'Why didn't you tell me before? Why didn't you write? You can't imagine what I've been going through.'

At this, he shook his head and she could see he was wrestling with his words.

'I'm so sorry, Patsy. I . . . I wanted to. But I figured, why the hell would someone as perfect as you want to be with a freak like me?'

'What?' she exclaimed. 'Do you really think I'd be that shallow?'

'No . . . No. Only . . . all those months in hospital, in my head, I dreamt of you, of the last time I saw you at base and I kissed you in the snow. All I could think of was how absolutely perfect you are.'

'No one's perfect. You're putting me on a pedestal I don't deserve to be on.'

'But you are on a pedestal, Patsy, each and every night. Men adore you. You deserve to be with someone as astonishing as you.'

'I thought I was with someone pretty special, Blue,' she

replied softly. Setting down her cup, she threaded her fingers through his.

'I don't care what you look like. I didn't fall in love with you because you've got a cute face, which by the way you still have. I fell in love with you when you stood up to Lou's father at the sports gala, when you made the effort to tell Joanie face to face what happened with Johnnie, when you arranged that magical Christmas party for all the kids in Stratford . . . I fell in love with your kindness and decency.'

Blue looked at her, astonished.

'Wait, you're in love with me?'

'Yes, you big chump, I am!'

'Only you've never said it before, even when I've told you. Say it again?'

'Come here and shut up,' she grinned, and bending forward she gave him a long, slow kiss.

As they broke apart something occurred to her.

'But surely this means you can go home now?'

'They said I could.'

'Wait, you're staying because you want to?'

'I always wanted to. I want to see this thing out, Patsy, and I know this sounds crazy, but at least I'm in the same country as you.'

They talked for another hour, until the free fruitcake was demolished along with another pot of tea, and the cafe had emptied of late-night customers.

'Come on, folks,' sighed the waitress, a woman in her fifties who had worked in the cafe for fifteen years and seen it all. 'I've got a husband to feed.'

They stood up and Blue helped Patsy into her coat, before going over to the tired waitress. He tipped her handsomely, before reaching over the counter and, to her astonishment, kissing her on the cheek.

'She loves me!'

'You Yanks. You're all as mad as a box of frogs. Now go on, clear off.' But she was laughing as she shut the cafe door and locked it behind her.

They stood facing one another in the chill of the Soho night. Standing in the deserted street, Patsy felt her heart begin to thump.

'When do you have to be back at base?'

'I've got to be on the first train out of Liverpool Street on Monday morning.'

'It's Saturday night . . .'

'Sunday morning actually,' he corrected, glancing at his watch.

'So we don't have much time left.' She paused. 'I don't want to go home,' she said, watching as the implications dawned on Blue's face.

'What about your mum?'

'I don't care,' said Patsy impetuously. 'I'm fed up of living in the shadow of her grief. This is my life to live.'

She reached up and touched his face, her voice husky.

'I don't want this night to end.'

'Are you sure?' he asked, pulling the collars of her coat up.

'Never surer.'

The small room was up in the eaves of a creaky hotel, high above the rooftops of Piccadilly. Patsy switched off the light and drew back the blackout blind. She could just make out the swooping beams of the searchlights criss-crossing the West End.

The room was damp and smelt of old cooking oil. Patsy shuddered to think how many wartime couples had used this place, snatching moments of love and lust, casting aside convention. This room had seen the nooks and crannies of many a wartime love story.

'This isn't the sort of place I wanted to bring you,' he said throatily, coming up behind her at the window. Without turning, she reached behind and threaded her fingers behind his head. Instinctively he dipped down and kissed the soft skin on the back of her neck.

'It's away from Stratford,' she murmured. 'It's perfect.'

They drank brandy from a toothbrush cup and carried on staring out the windows, making up imaginary stories about the people who walked below.

Finally, with the heat of the brandy sluicing through her veins, Patsy put down the cup, led him to the bed and kissed him. Blue responded instantly, gathering her in his arms, his whole body tense with desire.

She felt her pulse race as, slowly, he took off her clothes, starting with her blouse and then unbuttoning her skirt. She felt nervous, shy even.

This is ridiculous, she thought. *He's seen you naked on stage.* But this was no stage-managed, softly lit affair. He was seeing her in the raw, exposed. She shivered and he held her with aching tenderness, slowly kissing the edges of her collarbone down to the dip in her throat, until a warmth pooled in her stomach. Her fingers stroked down his back and he winced, drawing back as she touched the rough milky scar tissue that stretched over his spine.

'I love you, Blue. I want you,' she whispered in his ear.

After they had made love, they lay pressed against each other in the darkness.

Huddled in the rooftops, Patsy felt safe and cosseted in his arms.

'I love you, I love you,' he said over and over. 'I don't care what it takes, after the war is over, I'm going to find a way to be with you forever.'

'I can't live in America, Blue.'

'Then I'll live here, on this tiny island where it rains all the time.'

'With my mum's blessing?'

'Then we'll elope, and we'll go live in one of those little villages I passed through with names like Little Plumbottom.'

She laughed and playfully punched him on the arm.

'I'm serious,' he said, taking her hand and kissing it. 'Why not?'

'Because I'm not leaving the smoke again.'

'So we'll stay in London and your mum'll have to face up to the fact that you're a woman now. The point is, when we've won this war, we'll have the freedom to be together. Isn't that what we're all fighting so hard for? Freedom of choice?'

'It's more complicated than that.'

'Then let's uncomplicate it,' he replied, yawning. 'Do you remember the first time we sat on the steps to Eros?'

She nodded, tracing her fingers lightly down his back. 'How can I forget?'

'You promised me that when the war is over, we would meet again on those steps and you'd kiss me. That's just about the only God damn thing I hold fast to. We can plan the rest of our lives then, but that's as good a start as any isn't it?'

'I suppose so,' she whispered, snuggling in closer.

'Then let's make a promise, that no matter what happens, we'll both be there,' he said sleepily, stroking back a strand of her long dark hair from her face. 'And the rest can sort itself out.'

Finally Blue surrendered to sleep, but Patsy couldn't. Her mind was running alive, trapped in a delicate balance of love and fear. She was caught in the darkness of the past, yet fearful for the future.

Getting out of bed, she peeked out the window and saw the lacy light of dawn spreading over the jumble of rooftops.

Suddenly feeling the need for a smoke and some fresh air,

she dressed quietly, took the key and her purse, and padded downstairs, past the night receptionist.

Outside, she lit a cigarette and stood in the empty Soho street. The ripe stench of beer and carbolic cut through the nacreous light.

Disbelief dawned. She had professed her love, given herself fully to Blue. He had a right to know.

You have to tell him.

Quite suddenly, she found herself face-to-face with a fox. His glossy pelt glowed red in the first rays of the sun. They both stood frozen. Up above, a window banged and the fox leapt on to a bin lid and then on to a wall up above. The bin toppled, disgorging rubbish at her feet. The moment felt freighted with symbolism somehow.

Patsy bought two coffees from a stand in Piccadilly Circus before taking them back to the hotel room.

'Thank God,' smiled Blue sleepily as she let herself in. 'I was beginning to think I'd dreamt the whole thing. Come here, beautiful.'

She set down the coffee and he pulled her into his arms, kissing her deeply. But the morning light was not so conducive to romance.

'Come on,' she laughed, flinging his pants at him. 'Get dressed. I need to get home before Mum notices I'm missing.'

'Only if you promise to see me later.'

'Where are you going to be?'

'Well, seeing as it's Mothering Sunday in America today, I'm going to be with my British mom.'

'You're going for Sunday dinner at Nell Gunn's?' she exclaimed, sipping at the coffee in amusement.

'Please join us, Patsy. I leave tomorrow morning and I don't know when I'll next get leave.'

'Very well,' she promised, 'I'll think of something.'

They checked out and walked east, down by the embankment.

Swollen by the May rains, the turbulent brown Thames flowed through the ethereal dawn light.

On Blackfriars Bridge, a couple embraced as if they might never see one another again.

'You said you don't know when you'll next get leave,' Patsy remarked as they walked. 'But surely you must have some idea?'

'An order went round our unit last week, forbidding requests to marry,' Blue said casually.

'Meaning?'

'I think you know, Patsy,' he replied, clearly unwilling to spell it out.

She did. They were readying themselves to invade Europe. The possibility of it, along with talk of a secret weapon attack, was all anyone could speak about these days. In fact, the whole country felt poised on the brink. This very moment, walking hand in hand with her lover by the Thames, was a dreamlike pause. Patsy tightened her fingers round his.

Back in Stratford, she slipped in through the door, and tiptoed up to her bedroom. Half an hour later, she heard her mother stir, and start to scrape out the ashes from the fire.

'Morning,' she said brightly, as she came down the stairs in yesterday's eye make-up.

'You all right, love? You look done in,' her mother remarked.

'I got back late from the WVS and I didn't sleep all that well,' she replied, hating herself for the deception.

'I said you've been working too hard,' Queenie muttered.

'In fact, Mum, I don't feel all that good this morning. I've got a terrific headache. Would you mind if I skipped church?'

Queenie held her palm to Patsy's forehead.

'You do feel hot. You best go back to bed. Only I promised I'd help run a jumble sale back in Poplar so I'll be out with Jimmy the best part of the day. Can you manage?'

'Yes course, I'll get a milky drink and take myself back to bed.'

Lie after lie. Patsy was beginning to surprise herself with the ease with which they slipped out.

The moment she heard the door click shut and her mum and Jimmy set off for church, she tore back the covers and started to freshen herself up. A freezing cold strip wash in the backyard did wonders for waking you up. She chose her frock carefully. Easing herself into a simple coral-pink tea dress, she pinned her hair back – no time for any elaborate victory rolls today. Save for a little Vaseline on her lips, she kept her face naked of make-up. It was ironic, Patsy thought as she dabbed bicarbonate of soda under her armpits, that now she finally had some money of her own, there were virtually no cosmetics left to spend it on.

At midday, there was a discreet knock on the door.

'Blue,' she smiled cheekily. 'Fancy seeing you here.'

He was clutching armfuls of red carnations and a brown paper PX bag.

'My God, I swear you get more beautiful each time I see you.'

'I only saw you five hours ago, you berk,' she laughed.

Checking no one was looking, she briefly pulled him into the passage and kissed him. When their lips broke off, they stared at each other, as if neither could believe their luck.

'Last night was the best night of my life, Patsy,' he said, gazing at her in wonderment.

'Come on, you soppy chump,' she grinned, giving his bum a cheeky tap, 'you don't want to keep your British mum waiting.'

Next door, Nell Gunn was full of it as Blue emptied his bag of hospitality ration on the table. There were goods Nell had forgotten even existed. Tinned fruit, corned beef, dried prunes, coffee, lard, evaporated milk, chocolates and candies spilt out. There was even a bar of *scented* soap with a pretty wrapper.

'You didn't have to do this, son,' Nell said in amazement, slapping her own son Frankie's fingers as they crept towards the candies.

'Sure I did,' he replied.

'She'll only share it with the neighbours,' said Julia smiling broadly as she walked in the room.

'Esther and Walter are joining us in a bit, if that's all right.'

'Smashing,' Patsy enthused. 'No Lou?'

'She's out with Martha,' Nell replied.

If either Nell or Julia seemed alarmed at the scars on Blue's face, they hid it well, and neither made a single remark on it.

'Sit down, sit down and, for goodness' sake, Patsy, put the wood in the hole,' Nell blustered, pointing at the open door.

Once seated by the fire with a cup of tea, Julia was all questions.

'So what's all this Mother's Day business?'

'Well, ma'am, back home in America it's a big deal. President Roosevelt wants us to express our love and reverence for our mothers, both at home and here,' he smiled at Nell, 'with our adopted mothers.'

He plucked a red carnation from his bag, pinned one to his chest, then handed one to Nell.

'We're to wear carnations in tribute to our mothers. Red if she's alive, white if not. I hope I'm not overstretching myself to say I feel blessed to have two.'

Nell looked deeply touched.

'Come here,' she said, pulling him to her apron-clad bosom and giving him an enormous hug.

'I think you're going soft in your old age,' said a voice from the door.

'Esther,' Patsy cried, leaping to her feet. 'I'd give you a cuddle, but I'm not sure I can get close enough.'

Esther winked.

'I told you not to give up hope.'

A happier day Patsy could not remember. They feasted on Nell's oxtail stew with suet dumplings before tucking into the candies Blue had brought. Frankie beat them all at Scrabble, then Blue regaled them with tales of his childhood in Boston. Even Walter, not the fondest of Americans, loosened up and poured Blue a glass of porter; perhaps because he could now see he bore the scars of war.

Patsy felt there was a single shimmering thread connecting her to Blue. The intimacy from their night together meant that neither of them could help but sneak little looks at one another, and whenever his fingers accidentally brushed hers, she blushed.

'For goodness' sake, you two,' Nell had said when she'd caught Blue winking at Patsy, 'I've never seen such a daft loved-up couple.'

'What can I say, Mrs G?' Blue grinned lazily. 'I'm hopelessly in love with this beautiful lady. And for some reason, she seems to love me back.'

Julia and Esther both sighed and even Nell looked a little misty-eyed.

'Isn't it wonderful?' said Julia softly. 'That war cannot kill the blossoming of new love. I wish this young couple every joy in the world.'

Blue set his glass down and stood up. Then, all of a sudden, he was down on one knee. An electrified silence fell over the room.

'B-Blue, what are you doing?' Patsy's words were more of a warning than a question.

'I'm doing something I should have done months ago.'

He took her hands in his and coughed nervously.

'Patsy Jacks. I don't think it's possible to love a woman more than I love you. I know the future's uncertain, I know the US Army won't allow me to wed just yet, but hang it all. I need something to live for. Please will you marry me?'

The whole room seemed to hold its breath. The old clock on the mantel ticked out the seconds.

'Please?'

Patsy shook her head and choked back a sob.

'I . . . I'm sorry, I can't.'

She ran from the house and out into the allotment. Blue followed her, a look of hurt on his face.

'But why?' he cried. 'You do love me, you said so yourself.'

'Because I'm not who you think I am.'

'Sure you are.'

'I'm not, I'm just not,' she protested, angrily plucking leaves from the redcurrant bush and stripping them between her fingers.

'You've put me on an impossible pedestal, like I'm some sort of deity, or goddess. You're not even my first.'

Blue looked taken aback. 'W-well . . . that's all right,' he said eventually.

'You wouldn't say that if you knew the truth.'

'The truth about what?' he yelled, frustrated now. He tore the leaf from her hand. 'Please just look at me. Ever since I met you, I know you've been holding something back from me. I have laid myself bare to you, do me the same courtesy. Please, Patsy.'

'When I was in the countryside, the man I was billeted with . . .'

Patsy felt oddly calm as the words she had bottled up for so long released themselves.

'. . . he took advantage of me.'

'Took advantage?' Blue's voice was laced with anger. 'What do you mean?'

'I mean he raped me.'

'Oh God.' Blue ran his fingers through his hair, as if this would somehow help the news sink in. 'Oh God, Patsy.'

He stood stunned into silence. She could almost hear his thoughts turning over.

'But . . . but you were still a kid, weren't you?'

'I was thirteen, which was old enough for him apparently.' Her voice dripped with sarcasm. 'But it's all right, it was my fault you see, for being too pretty, I "led him on".'

'Jesus. How long did it go on for?'

'Two years give or take. When I turned fifteen, he lost interest.'

'Was there no one you could tell?'

'I tried. His wife, she ran a local dance school. Going there became my escape, I used to dance every night, and one night I told her he was coming into my room. Do you know what she said? "My husband is a complex man."'

'A sick fuck more like,' Blue snapped. Patsy winced. 'Sorry, that's not helpful.'

'I wrote letters home too,' Patsy went on. 'I never spelt out what was happening, just said how desperate I was to come back to Poplar.'

'Why did your mum not come and get you?'

Patsy shrugged and wrapped her arms about her. 'She has this thing about kids in war, that I had to be far away from the danger zone. Even when the Blitz ended and the other children billeted nearby started going home, me and Jimmy still weren't allowed back. She had no idea I was in the worst danger zone of all.'

Blue scrubbed his face despairingly.

'Jimmy?'

'No. He told me if I ever told a soul he would start to visit Jimmy. After that, I put up and shut up.'

'Does your mum know?'

'God no,' Patsy said, alarmed. 'Jimmy and I came home in the winter of forty-three, about six months before I met you, but only because I was seventeen, and it was obvious I couldn't stay there any longer. I don't want her to know now. It would destroy her.'

'But what about you, Patsy?' he said, taking her fingers softly in his.

'What about me?' She felt a huge sob tear out of her. 'What about me? I'm tainted.'

Shame. Humiliation. Guilt. Sometimes, inside, she still felt like that thirteen-year-old girl laying in terror in the dark as the door handle slowly turned.

'I'm so sorry,' she said, swallowing down a sob.

'Whatever for?'

'Because I wanted you to be my first. But even when we made love last night, all I could think of was what a fraud I am.'

Blue's jawbone clenched and he blew out. She could she see he was trying very hard to hold down his anger.

'You're *not* a fraud. That man raped you. He didn't ask. He took. What happened last night couldn't be more different. It was an act of love.'

'Maybe so, but I can't shake off my past. What that man did to me, what he made me do to him . . . His fingerprints are all over me.'

Blue was crying now.

'So we both have our scars. You didn't run at the sight of me, so why should I at this?'

'All the same,' she wept, 'I see it in your eyes. I'm not the girl you thought I was.'

'You're right!' he cried. 'You're not . . . You're even braver and more remarkable than I imagined.'

A chill spring wind swept through the allotment, and Patsy in her thin summer frock shivered. Blue took off his jacket and draped it round her shoulders before moving closer to her, his eyes searching hers.

'I swear to God, Patsy, I will spend the rest of my life looking after you and keeping you safe.'

'But how can you do that, Blue?' she replied sadly. 'When your own safety isn't even certain?'

There was nothing Blue could say to that, for they both knew the invasion was coming. Instead, he pulled her tightly to his chest. Resting his cheek against her hair, he breathed in the sweet smell of her.

A tarnished sliver of moon rose slowly over their heads. Woodsmoke curled through the chill evening air. Patsy wasn't sure how long she stayed that way, nestled in his jacket, his arms locked around hers, keeping the rest of the world at bay.

Blue was saying something in her ear – 'I still want to marry you' – but she couldn't focus because a figure had come into her peripheral vision.

Her mother stood motionless at the gates to the allotment, Jimmy's hand in hers.

'You've recovered from your headache, I see.'

'Mum . . .' She sprang out of Blue's arms and he whirled around, straightening himself up.

'Mrs Jacks. I love your daughter and I mean to marry her.'

Queenie didn't even look at him.

'Patsy get inside. Now.'

Slowly, Patsy took off Blue's jacket and handed it back him.

'Patsy . . . You have to tell her about us.' He gripped her wrists, his heart shattering. 'Please.'

'Blue,' she said, gently prising his fingers from her wrists. 'Let me go.'

'I can't leave you like this.'

'You have to. Please, Blue, just go.'

He looked from her to her mother, his face a picture of abject despair.

'I'll be in our cafe tonight. Waiting for your answer. I'll wait all night if I have to.'

Patsy left him staring after them as she turned and walked into the house. Strangely, there was no screaming or hysterics when they got inside. Because she had decided the time had come.

'Jimmy darling,' she said, bending down to kiss him on the forehead, 'be a good boy and run upstairs to your bedroom.'

When he left, she patted her mum's chair.

'I've something to tell you, Mum and you're not going to like it, but it needs to be said.'

Queenie's expression flickered from rage to confusion.

'What can possibly excuse the lies and the deception?' she said coldly.

When Patsy had finished – and she spared no detail – Queenie crouched down into a ball on the floor. A low keening noise, the sound a wounded animal might make, broke out of her. The sound was grotesque.

Patsy gently pulled her from the floor and sat her back in her chair. Her mother's arms were so cold and rigid, they felt like they might snap.

'I thought I was keeping you safe. Oh dear God, when you came back I even accused you of being spoilt in the countryside,' she said at last. 'What kind of mother am I?'

Queenie's bony fingers worked at a stray thread on the arm of her chair.

'The protective kind,' Patsy insisted. 'You wanted what's best for me. I can see that now. You might've gone about it the wrong way, but you were only trying to keep me safe.'

'I was, I truly was,' said Queenie, a glimmer of relief in her face.

'But I can look after myself, Mum. And now *I* have to do what's best for me.'

She stood up and reached for her bag and coat.

'I'm going to Blue now. I'm going to accept his proposal.'

Queenie was on her feet in a flash, her face a ferment of emotions.

'Please, Patsy, no! You can't leave me. Please don't go.'

'I'm sorry, Mum. I know you don't like Americans, but Blue is the most astonishing man I've ever met.'

Queenie was sobbing, reaching her arms towards her. But despite the pitiful sight, Patsy's resolve stayed strong.

'You felt that way about Dad once, didn't you? Please give us your blessing, Mum, because I am going to marry him when the war is over.'

Her fingers reached for the door handle.

'I can't lose another daughter!' Queenie's voice tore through the terrace and Patsy turned round slowly.

'What did you say?'

Her mother's face was as white as a shroud.

'Now it's my turn to tell you a story. Sit down. This could take some time.'

Patsy hung up her coat, her heart buckling.

Queenie began, staring at the floor as if searching for the lost threads of her past. 'Fourteen years before I had you, I had another daughter. Another life.'

By 4 a.m., they were still talking, Patsy floored by the appalling tragedy of her mother's past. When at last she finished, Queenie clung to Patsy as if the memories had chilled her blood, as if she never wanted to let go.

Patsy was torn. Should she stay or go? Every fibre of her being was telling her to go to Blue, to feel the comforting warmth of his arms, bathe in his acceptance of her and her past, to plot a future together.

The voice in her ear was almost primal. *Go. Go. Go.*

A thin sliver of grey light slid in under the blackout. Horses' hooves outside. Birdsong. The Shoot was stirring. Time was running out.

'Mum,' she whispered as the gaslight finally spluttered and died. 'I-I have to go now. Blue needs me.'

Her mother looked up sharply, her eyes haunted in the gloom.

'But I need you, Patsy. I'm so scared.'

Patsy knew how hard this confession would have been for her mother. For a woman who didn't talk about emotions or feelings, much less air them, this evening was momentous. She'd lost a child and in the most horrific circumstances possible. How could she turn her back on her when she'd exposed all her vulnerabilities? To walk out now would be astonishingly cruel.

'I'll put the kettle on shall I? Just one more cup?' Queenie asked, her voice pleading. 'Please don't leave me. I . . . I don't know what I'll do if you go.'

Patsy nodded, speechless with despair, and Blue was left waiting in a cafe for a girl who never came.

20

Lou

Wednesday 14th June 1944

'Please tell me you're joking,' Martha exclaimed, dropping the spanner with a clatter on the floor of the yard.

Lou shook her head, hating the unavoidable pain she knew this was going to cause her girlfriend.

'But tomorrow? It's all so sudden.'

'Trust me, Martha, it's not. I've thought of nothing else for the past five and a half months, since that night Queenie outed me. I've realised now, this ain't going to simply fade away. Last month, one of the girls in the lipstick room handed in her notice; apparently her mum worries I'm a corrupting influence. And I reckon there've been more who've left on account of me, only Miss Rayson's hiding it. She tells me to ignore the narrow-minded bigots, but I'm putting her in an impossible situation and that ain't fair.' Lou's rehearsed speech didn't come out as she planned; it sounded cold and clumsy.

Martha pulled off her headscarf and wiped her hands despairingly through her mass of curly hair. It was 5 a.m. and she was just coming off a nightshift. The other workers had already clocked off, but knowing how conscientious she was, Lou knew she'd still be there and that they'd be alone for a precious fragment of time. The rising summer sun glowed like burnt amber through the yard and Martha's chestnut curls lit up like a rich cinnamon-coloured headdress.

'I'm not making a good job of this am I?' Lou sighed, taking Martha's work-roughed fingers in hers and pressing them gently. Her touch was more articulate, more intimate than anything she could express through words.

'I understand you wanting to leave Yardley, Lou. But Scotland? Why . . . why so far? There's plenty of jobs you could do here in Stratford where people don't know you. You could walk into another factory job this afternoon if you wanted to.'

'But that's just it, Martha,' Lou said. 'It's hard to explain, but all my life, I've been gobby Fat Lou, queen of the conveyor belt. I don't want to just go into another factory job where I'll have to act the card to fit in. I want a life beyond clocking on. To see what other versions there are of me . . . see what I'm capable of.' She trailed off, desperately trying to find the words to articulate the emotions that were tightening her chest.

'I suppose it comes down to freedom, autonomy . . . the choices that this war offers to women like me. Now the invasion's underway it can only be a matter of time before the war's over, then you can bet your life all the women'll be turfed out their jobs and their worlds will shrink to the size of a pram. Back to being nothing but bloody walking wombs!

'Don't you see, Martha? This is my last chance to travel, to take on a job that only used to be open to the boys. And now I can't even see my sisters anymore since my *dear* father's put a ring of steel round them, you're the only thing keeping me here.'

Lou's unfiltered gush stopped as abruptly as it had started. A single tear rolled down Martha's cheek and Lou felt something break inside her.

'You know he's even moved them to new schools in case I try to approach them? Being so near to them, but not being able to see them, or look after them, is killing me, Martha.'

Lou was crying too now, pain and shame ripping through her at the thought of leaving this beautiful woman.

'But please believe me when I tell you I'm not leaving because I don't love you. I'm leaving because I do. I don't want to turn into some horrible bitter woman like Queenie, always looking back and finding nothing there but resentment. As soon as the war's over, I'll be back. And I hope you'll be waiting.'

Martha stared at the floor, her tears dripping on to the wood shavings.

'You will wait for me . . . won't you?'

Lou held her breath, until Martha looked up.

'You daft cow, you know I will. There's never been anyone but you, even when you used to nick my bloody scooter when we was kids. You're the only woman I've ever loved.'

'Thank God,' Lou breathed, hugging her tightly. 'I promise I'll write and visit every time I get leave.'

'Yeah you better,' Martha said, wiping her eyes. 'Honestly, Lou Button, you as a lumberjill in the Timber Corps? You don't know one end of an axe from the other!'

Lou laughed. 'I'll learn though.'

They hugged each other again, savouring the intimacy and warmth of the embrace in the solitude of the quiet yard. Neither of them knew how long they stood that way, though Lou knew it was enough time to mark the passing of one era and the beginning of a new one. A shiver of excitement rose in her at the prospects life suddenly held now she had Martha's blessing.

'You better go before the rest of the lads clock on,' Martha said, reluctantly drawing back. 'I can't be doing with long goodbyes, so I'll see you at the train station tomorrow.'

Lou nodded and kissed her forehead gently.

'I wouldn't have gone you know, without your blessing.'

Martha nodded.

'I know. Until tomorrow.'

'I'm so proud of you,' Lou smiled, picking a wood shaving from her lover's hair.

'I'm so proud of us,' Martha replied.

The next day in the factory canteen at dinnertime, a sombre air had wrapped itself around the Lavender Girls. It had been nine days since the Allies had landed on the beaches at Normandy. The whole country held its breath as news gradually began to filter back. Lou, like everyone else, devoured every last scrap of information she could.

'On D-Day, the 387th Bomb Group of the US Air Force attacked three coastal batteries at Beau Guillot, La Madeleine and St-Martin de Varreville,' said an antiseptic-sounding BBC news reporter over the wireless. 'Congratulations were offered to our tenacious American allies when, two days later, they again flew in hazardous conditions to hit a fuel dump south of Caen, destroying enough fuel for an entire panzer division. Their heroism will have saved an untold number of Allied soldiers' lives.'

'That's Blue and Johnnie's unit,' remarked Joanie dully. 'Well, *was* Johnnie's. Guess that means Blue won't be getting leave anytime soon. Poor Patsy.'

Lou reached over and closed her palm over Joanie's, gazing out the window at the brilliant blue sky, so clear it looked like it had been freshly painted.

'Odd, ain't it?' remarked Little Irene.

'What is?' Lou asked.

'How the weather can be so at odds with what's occurring across the channel,' she said, pulling a fag from under her turban and lighting up.

'Blue skies here, yet a stain of red spreading across France.'

Lou stared at Little Irene, astonished. The youngest Lavender Girl usually only opened her mouth if it meant stirring up a bit of gossip about sex, boys or actresses.

No one very much had the heart for frivolities these days though. It felt wrong somehow to be going to dances or pubs with so many young men breathing their last.

'Listen up,' said Joycie, pinching Little Irene's fag for a cheeky drag. 'It's Lou's last day, but it feels more like we're at a wake.'

'I don't want no fuss,' Lou warned. 'In fact, I can't. Miss Rayson wants me to leave the factory as unobtrusively as possible. She's been so good letting me go at short notice. I don't want to upset her.

'Which reminds me.' She dug around in her overall pocket and fished out a brown envelope.

'Joycie, I know you've taken over the collection fund from Esther. Next time you're dropping off at my dad's, do me a favour and see if you can sneak this to the girls.' She handed Joycie her final pay packet.

'Tell them it's from me and to treat themselves to something nice.'

'But you'll need this when you leave,' Joycie protested. 'For the future.'

'Please, Joycie. It's important. 'Sides,' she added, attempting to make light, 'no sense saving in wartime, no pockets in shrouds.'

'Oh Lou,' said Little Irene, bursting into tears. 'I can't stand to think of you not being here. First Patsy, then Esther and now you. You *are* Yardley's!' She trumpeted loudly in her hankie.

'Come here, you daft sod,' Lou said, putting her arm around her. 'We'll always be pals wherever I am.'

'So when are you leaving Stratford?' asked Betty.

'Tonight. I'm on the last train out of Liverpool Street. Sounds like a film, don't it?'

'Tonight?' Irene screeched, ignoring her lame joke.

'But that's so soon,' protested Joycie.

'There's no point hanging around like a bad smell on the landing,' Lou shrugged. 'Besides, I've got to report for training in Shandford Lodge near Brechin day after tomorrow. Any of you know how far it is to Scotland?'

A table of blank faces stared back.

'Blowed if I know,' Little Irene remarked. 'Just the thought of it scares me.'

'That's 'cause you need an overnight bag if you go to Plaistow,' teased Betty.

'Oh, eff off,' she grinned, getting Betty in a headlock.

'Lou Button, a lumberjill,' said Joanie shaking her head. 'Bit different chopping down trees to packing lipstick.'

'I always was more of a dungarees kind of girl than a turban-clad glamour puss.'

Everyone laughed, but no one really felt it. The bell for end of dinner sounded.

To her surprise, the girls respected her wish for no fuss, and when her shift finished, everyone had to rush off to various places anyway. And so it was that Lou found herself quite alone as she crossed the cobbled yard.

She paused at the gates and turned back to look at the old factory that had played such a big part in her life. Renee Gunn's voice echoed through her mind.

Welcome to the East End's finishing school.

What times they'd had. She loved all those girls to bits. The job may have been tedious, but it was the people who had made it all so special.

Stratford, like the rest of East London, was a big, old, mucky place, which smoked too much, stained your neck brown and gave you a formidable education in the ways of the world. But she wasn't half going to miss it.

'So long,' she whispered, before passing under the archway for the last time.

Outside, a figure in dungarees was leaning against the high brick wall, smoking a cigarette. Her uncontrollable curly hair had sprouted out from her turban, and one of her thumbs was heavily bandaged.

'Martha! I thought we was saying goodbye at the station later?'

'We was. Only I had a fight with a saw and came off worse,' she grinned ruefully, holding her thumb aloft.

'So the boss said I could take the rest of the evening off.'

'That's big of him.'

'What's nearly losing a digit for the final victory?' Martha joked wryly. 'Come on. Hurry up.'

She slung a bag at Lou.

'What's this?'

'I went shopping and bought you a going-away outfit. I thought we could nip to the Two Puddings for a cheeky rum and black. You can get changed there and then we'll head to Nell's. She's invited me to your leaving tea.'

Lou looked at the woman she loved and felt her eyes mist over.

'Don't start,' Martha warned. 'I'm not sacrificing my last bit of mascara to you, Lou Button.'

The pub, nicknamed the Butcher's Shop on account of the punch-ups that usually occurred on a Friday and Saturday night, was unusually quiet and subdued.

Lou nipped to the loos to change into the outfit Martha had bought her. 'Oh, Martha,' she breathed as she pulled out a black Max Cohen double-breasted suit, crisp white shirt, black tie, cufflinks and highly buffed brogues.

Martha had chosen these clothes with love and care, replacing the items her father had cut up. By the time Lou had put the outfit on, teased her custard blond hair up into a high victory wave and painted her lips with two layers of stark vermilion red, she felt ready to take on the world once more. It occurred to her, as she postured in front of the cracked mirror, that these clothes – the androgynous way she presented herself to the world – gave her a more powerful identity, a transformation out of the everyday, even a way of getting her own back on the patriarchy. She thought of her father's cheap council suits and dandruff.

Lou smoothed down her lapel, straightened her cuffs and joined Martha at the bar.

'Martha, you shouldn't . . .'

'Don't start,' she said, pushing a drink along the bar. 'My leaving gift to you.'

She appraised Lou with admiring eyes.

'Garbo or Dietrich, can't decide which one you look like?'

'Both?'

'I'm serious. You look beautiful. I do hope I'm not going to lose you to a lumberjill?'

'Never!' Lou giggled. 'Keep your voice down.'

But Martha was in no mood to play it safe.

'Your mouth looks like strawberry jam,' she whispered, 'I wanna kiss you right here and now!'

'Behave you saucy cow.'

They raised their glasses and clinked them softly.

'To your mum; she'd be so proud of you,' said Martha, growing serious.

At this, Lou could not stop her eyes from filling up. She pressed her hands into the sockets and sent her thoughts rushing through the narrow streets of the East End, to the door to where she saw her mum standing in her faded wrapover apron. Lou couldn't remember a time growing up when Flo Button hadn't waved her off from the doorstep.

Love you, Tin Ribs.

She'd had so little of anything, yet her capacity for love was endless. Lou knew this sense of loss was not something that would ever fade over time. She would just have to learn ways to live with it.

'I miss her so much, Martha,' Lou confessed. 'I'm scared.'

'You don't have to go,' she replied, moving her hand across the bar and letting the edges of her fingers touch Lou's.

'You and I both know that's not true. Just sitting here, we're taking huge risks. The sooner I'm out of Stratford and we let things calm down, the better.'

She took a big swig of her drink and felt the heat from the rum numb the back of her throat.

'Now the invasion's begun, we'll see a swift end to the war, surely?'

'Not if you believe those folk in Bethnal Green who swore they saw some sort of new rocket missile a couple of days ago,' Martha replied.

'What? Where?'

'Grove Road, six people killed apparently. No pilot, just came out of nowhere, its tail end on fire.'

'Christ alive,' Lou sighed. 'Just when you think you've seen it all.'

It took a while for this news to sink in, and when it did, a thought suddenly hit Lou.

'My sisters! If London's under fire again, I can't leave them.'

'About that, Lou . . .' Martha looked uneasy. 'I heard on the grapevine, your father and Nancy...'

'Go on.'

'They've married apparently.'

'Didn't take the sneaky bugger long.'

'And they're moving to Norfolk. Fresh start for everyone. Stratford has too many painful memories, leastwise that's the story he's putting about.'

Lou drained her drink in one go.

'Why is my life so bleedin' shit? Why can't God give me a break? First my education went, then my mum, followed by my home and job, and now it looks like my sisters are lost to me forever.'

'Wouldn't life be dull if it was peaceful?' Martha teased gently. 'Surely you and I, our type, we're made for complications.'

She touched Lou's cheek. 'This world will never be kind to us, so we must be kind to each other.' She smiled, her kind hazel eyes threaded through with flecks of gold.

'You are right as always, Martha Robertson.'

Martha drained her drink. 'Come on, you don't want to add Nell Gunn to your list of complications.'

At number 10, it was unusually quiet when Lou pushed open the door.

'Cooey,' she called up the passage. 'Anyone home?'

She grimaced at Martha. 'Maybe she's forgotten.'

Suddenly, the front parlour burst into life, with Lavender Girls appearing from behind chairs and furniture.

'Surprise!' yelled Little Irene, her face lit up like an irreverent street urchin. 'You didn't really think we were gonna let you go without a fuss.'

'I'm going to miss you something rotten,' said Nell, appearing at the doorway clutching a freshly baked batch of her famous sausage rolls. She was still wearing her apron, but she'd taken off her turban and applied a little coral-pink lipstick. Lou loved her for it. She hugged her tightly. Nell smelt faintly of Yardley's Lavender, the scent her mum had worn.

'Right,' said Joanie, advancing at her with balloons, paper streamers, ribbons and a silly hat made out of old back copies of the *Yardley News*. 'Tradition dictates . . .'

'That we make you look like a proper 'nana!' Betty shrieked, pinning a bow to her lapel.

Soon the tiny room was filled with laughter and smoke,

the wireless was cranked up, drinks were poured and Nell found her good rug transformed into a miniature dance floor, with all the girls linking arms and kicking up their feet to 'The Lambeth Walk'.

'Esther sends her apologies for missing it,' said Julia, who'd got back from work. 'She's finally seen sense and is resting.'

'I know,' smiled Lou. 'I said my goodbyes after work yesterday.'

'This looks like far too much fun,' said a husky voice from the door.

'Patsy!' Lou cheered, pouring her a drink and going to greet her. 'Come on in, girl. No work tonight?'

'Nah, night off.'

'Your mum doesn't mind you being round here, with me?' Lou asked cautiously.

'She's all right with it.'

Lou raised one sceptical eyebrow.

'No honest. Me and Mum . . . Well, we had a heart-to-heart recently.'

She looked thoughtful.

'I think we both see each other a little differently.'

'And you and Blue?' Lou ventured. 'Any word?'

She shook her head. 'No, but it's not hard to work out why. You've only got to listen to the BBC to know it's a round-the-clock effort, but I'll find him, Lou, explain to him why I had to stand him up. There's so much I need to tell him in fact.'

'That's the ticket, Pats,' Lou grinned, clinking her glass against Patsy's.

'*Slàinte*, as they say where I'm going.'

Patsy took a sip of Lou's drink and shuddered.

'Hell's teeth, Lou. Is there any orange in this gin?'

'Not really,' Lou admitted. 'Drink up, girl, reckon we need all the spirit we can get.'

'Come on, you two, it's a bloody party, not a WI coffee morning,' yelled Betty.

Two hours later, the gin had been drunk and the food devoured.

'Lou!' yelled Martha over the music. 'I hate to break up the party, but you've got a train to catch.'

'Just one more song,' pleaded Joycie. 'Patsy, how about you sing us a song, for Lou?'

'Yeah all right,' Patsy replied. 'I know just the one.' *Me and My Girl* had been a popular musical before the war, but was enjoying a comeback and, besides, the track seemed very fitting. Patsy's smooth, silky voice did it justice as Martha held her arms out and Lou stepped into them.

The faces of the girls she adored flashed past her as she and Martha danced together one last time.

'Please come back to me, when the war is over,' Martha whispered in her ear.

There were cheers and tears as Lou gave a final bow.

Bundled up in her coat, with her worldly belongings tucked into a tiny suitcase, Lou stepped into the summer evening with Martha by her side.

The window flung open.

'We love you, Lou,' cried Little Irene, tears mustering in her eyes. 'Be lucky.'

Lou held up two crossed fingers.

'Please God.'

They walked in an emotional silence, cutting down the turning that led to a small pedestrian bridge over the tracks. Another quarter of a mile and they'd be at Stratford train station and the awful moment where they'd have to part. Lou was saying goodbye to her whole life and all that was precious in it, to step into the unknown. It felt so wrong, yet somehow, her feet kept right on walking.

Coming down the steps towards them was a man.

'I don't believe it,' Martha said under her breath.

'What is it?'

'It's your dad.'

And astonishingly, it was. John Button was walking towards them with an unbearable expression of smugness and a slight swagger.

Lou tightened her grip on the suitcase handle.

'Just keep walking, Lou,' Martha muttered. 'You don't have to talk to him.'

They drew level by the tracks.

'You're really going then,' he said, with a sanctimonious smile.

She nodded.

'I think it's for the best, don't you?' He looked her and Martha up and down. 'I mean to say, you've caused quite enough trouble.'

'Me?' Lou exclaimed. Martha laid a warning hand on her arm.

'You do realise that what you are both doing is entirely unnatural? God will judge you.'

Lou spluttered, her laughter disbelieving.

She went to reply but, in that moment, a peculiar thing happened.

Out of the sky fell strips of silver paper. They fluttered over the tracks, snagging on the steps to the bridge and dancing in the wind.

In the distance, a long slow whistle shrieked; a heavy goods train was chuntering up the line. The tracks seemed to vibrate, the odd silver paper catching the light and gleaming, flashing like a semaphore signal.

Lou was filled with the most terrible feeling of uncertainty. The air was electric. Her skin prickled and her heart began to beat uncomfortably. Yet her feet were glued to the spot, like invisible roots were sucking her ankles down into the ground.

'Come on, Lou,' Martha was saying, tugging her. 'Your train.'

The grey smudge of the goods train grew closer, kicking up dust and billowing clouds of smoke as it picked up speed.

Ba-boom. Ba-boom. Ba-boom. Her heart mirrored the motion of the train.

Her father had his back to the tracks and seemed reluctant to let the chance encounter go.

'Don't think you will ever see your sisters again,' he gloated, picking a strip of silver foil from his shoulder. 'You're dead to them now.'

A spark flashed off the track. Noises mushroomed through Lou's head. The beat of her heart, the screeching of heavy metal, the long shrill whistle. Martha saw it first, her eyes widening in horror. Her mouth was moving frantically, but her words were lost to the noise of the train. Then Lou spotted it.

Out of the heat and smoke, a stray barrage balloon, designed to keep enemy aircraft from flying overhead, had torn loose from its moorings and came at them in a great rush of silver, like a giant leaping fish, billowing over the roof of the train. Its trailing cable sliced through the trackside bushes like a scythe.

'Get down!' Martha's blood-curdling voice was the last thing Lou heard as she pushed her to the concrete floor in a great thud. A tearing noise, a grunt, then silence.

Hot metal. Smoke. Chaos.

Lou tried to lift her head up but a bolt of pain in her diaphragm crushed her back down again. She needed to breathe desperately, but every time she did, she felt red-hot particles burn in the back of her throat.

Further up the tracks, she could hear ambulance bells clanging, screams tearing through the air.

'Lou,' groped a voice. 'Lou where are you?'

Martha looked like some sort of apparition as she appeared out of the smoke, her face entirely covered in soot, her hair standing on end with static.

'Martha,' Lou tried to say, but her tongue was fat and heavy, her head full of fog.

Martha laid her into the recovery position, took water from a bottle and dabbed it on her lips.

'I'm all right,' Lou gasped, struggling to sit up and pressing her fist into her side. 'I'm winded from the fall.'

'I'm so sorry,' Martha cried. 'I pushed you to the floor too hard, I just wanted you out of harm's way . . . My God—' she broke off in dismay as the smoke over the tracks cleared. 'Lou, look!'

Ten yards from them, her father lay half on, half off the tracks.

He opened and shut his mouth in silent agony, his body jerked and bucked then slumped as if a current had run through it.

'I'm going to get help.' Martha staggered to her feet.

'Martha,' Lou choked, managing to pull herself on to all fours. 'It's too late.'

Her father's body had stopped its strange dance and he was now lying wet and lifeless, his eyes staring vacantly ahead.

In the distance, a colossal boom sounded. Lou and Martha stared at each other.

Lou watched, dream-like, unable to move her limbs, as two ARP workers ran over the bridge towards them.

A hollow sensation spread through her stomach as she looked at her father's body. He was dead. No doubt about it. Part of his scalp had been ripped clean off by the cable. The other half of his head was untouched. Flecks of soot fell softly on to his brilliantined hair. His staring eyes looked up at her, still reproachful.

Lou leant back on to her haunches and vomited violently.

Nine days later, they buried him and no one was any closer to understanding the strange and brutal way John Button had been cut down.

'Death by misadventure' was the verdict at West Ham Coroner's Court. One of the new rockets coming down had sliced through the cable, cutting loose the barrage balloon, which had swept him up and slammed him down on the railway tracks. Just one of those awful wartime accidents, folk said, like getting run over in the blackout.

No one deserved to die in such a gruesome way, but she would not mourn his passing, any more than she would miss him. She was only at the funeral to see her sisters.

They stood on the other side of the grave to her, bewildered little girls in black, and Lou longed to vault the grave and pull them into her arms. But she had to go about things the right way. Flanked by Nell and Julia, with the Lavender Girls and Miss Rayson behind her, they had all warned her to keep a cool head.

Lou looked about the huddled group. Strangely, considering how high up he was at the town hall, there were only a few friends and colleagues of her father's present.

Lou couldn't see Nancy's face as it was shrouded behind a black lace veil, but her hands kept a tight grip on Lou's sisters. She only let go of them to allow them to step forward to the graveside and throw a small flower on top of his coffin.

The priest was talking, but Lou wasn't really listening. She was gazing at Elsie as she stepped forward with a single white rose. Lou willed her to look up and see the love and pain etched in her face.

It was Nell who noticed it first, her eyes lifting up to the blue June skies overhead. A strange spluttering sound broke open the still summer air.

The priest tailed off. The congregation looked at one another nervously.

'What is it?' she heard Joycie say behind her.

The noise grew more persistent. The green leaves on the tree trembled. The sound rose up from the bowels of the graveyard, growing from a dull throbbing to a full-throttle staccato.

'Doodlebug!' Lou yelled.

A huge black rocket was heading unswervingly in their direction. A tremendous noise rose up over the neighbourhood. The pom-pom guns started firing, the siren wailed . . .

Silence. The engine had cut out.

'Take cover,' someone yelled. Some people dived behind gravestones, others stood stock-still by the freshly dug grave.

Lou ran as fast as she could towards her sisters. Wrenching them from a stunned Nancy, she pushed them down and tried to cover them as best as she could.

A dark shadow swallowed the graveyard. Lou's heart punched in her chest. *Please don't let my sisters be killed.*

She closed her eyes, but when she opened them again, she could see the rocket lurching, changing course. All of a sudden, it nosedived with terrifying speed straight into a street of houses about half a mile away. A thick, choking cloud of smoke mushroomed into the sky, followed by the loud hiss of a fractured gas main.

Lou lifted her head up. All around, people were holding on to one another, faces ashen. Her sisters were crying now and she gathered them in her arms.

'It's all right, girls. You're safe, you're safe,' she murmured over and over.

But were they? What the hell was happening? First the rockets in the East End, and then, six days ago, the Guards Chapel in Westminster had been hit. Herbert Morrison had even had to make a statement in the House of Commons admitting the existence of Hitler's new terror weapon. The doodlebugs, as they had already been nicknamed, were claiming innocent lives and to Lou's mind, they were way more terrifying than anything conjured up in the Blitz, coming as they did straight out the blue.

'Everyone all right, girls?' said Nell, helping Lou to her feet. Julia rushed over at the same time as Nancy, who had recovered herself.

'Girls, into the church now,' she flustered, pushing back her veil.

'Please, Nancy, I'm a nurse,' Julia said calmly. 'Just let me check them over.'

'Very well, but then I want to get them home.'

Lou knew it was now or never.

'Nancy, we need to talk,' she blurted.

Nancy hesitated.

'Please,' she begged.

Nancy looked like she didn't have the strength to argue. Lou guided her to the nearest bench and lit two cigarettes.

'What the hell is happening to this world?' Nancy muttered, lifting the cigarette to her lips. Lou saw her trembling fingers and, now that her veil was drawn up, the deep circles under her eyes.

'I'm sorry, Nancy, for your loss.'

Nancy turned to her, suspicion and shock registering on her face.

'No matter what my father might have told you about me,' she went on, 'I'm not a monster. You must be devastated.'

Nancy's face softened.

'I am. I loved your father very much.'

She drew deeply on the cigarette and seemed to relax.

'I know he had his faults, and I can't say I agree with the way he treated you, Louise. But when all was said and done, he was good to me.'

Lou couldn't help herself.

'Did you know he was married, when you started up with him?'

'He told me it was a marriage in name only, that your mother never understood him.'

Lou laughed sharply and blew out a cloud of smoke.

'That's original.'

Nancy looked wounded.

'Look, I'm sorry. I've no grouse with you.' And truly she hadn't. To her mind, Nancy was just as much a victim of her father as her own mother had been.

'All that matters is the safety of the girls.'

'Now, on that, I do agree with you,' Nancy replied. 'Which is why I still plan on going ahead with the move your father planned.'

'Where?' Lou asked.

'Before his death, he'd bought a cottage, not far from Hunstanton in Norfolk. I'm taking the girls there next week, they're already enrolled into local schools.'

Bought? Lou hid her surprise that her father had enough money to be buying houses, especially when he never seemed to have enough to give her own mother housekeeping when she'd been alive.

'I think the girls'll like that,' she said softly. 'Might I visit them, when you're settled?'

Silence as Nancy surveyed the glowing tip of her cigarette.

'I miss them so much, Nancy.' She held her fingers to her chest. 'My heart aches for them.'

Nancy dropped her cigarette on the floor and ground it out.

'I'd love to say yes, Louise, but I'm sorry. It'd be disrespectful to your father's memory. He made his wishes very clear to me.'

She stood up and brushed down her skirt.

'For what it's worth, I'm truly sorry. You can write and I'll pass the letters on. That's about as much as I can offer.'

Nancy returned to Lou's sisters, whom Julia had finished checking over. She chivvied them back into the church and Lou stared out over the wreckage of her life. The pallbearers were hastily filling in her father's grave as a shell-shocked congregation recovered themselves.

The bastard was still controlling her, even from beyond the grave.

Lou stood up shakily and walked back to the graveside. She had delayed her training with the Women's Timber Corps, but now, she supposed, it was time to leave.

A crushed white rose lay discarded by the graveside, its petals brown and bruised. She picked it up and tossed it on the mound of earth.

'You win.'

21

Patsy

Patsy was standing in front of the mirror, pinning her black pillbox hat on, when she became aware of her mother standing motionless behind her.

'Mum!' she gasped. 'You gave me a right fright.'

'Terrible business about John Button.' Queenie stared ahead, a dullness to her eyes that unnerved Patsy.

'You'll be careful, won't you?'

Patsy met her gaze in the mirror.

'Mum, there's not a whole lot I can do if one comes down and cracks me on the head, is there? There's either one with my name on or there ain't.'

Queenie's eyes immediately filled with tears and Patsy regretted being so flippant.

'Sorry, Mum, course I'll be careful. Where's our Jimmy by the way?'

'He's staying over at a pal's house in Epping for a few days. I arranged it.'

Queenie saw Patsy's surprise register. 'I thought it might be safer,' she said defensively.

With Jimmy away, this would be the perfect time to talk. Patsy swept her long, dark hair into the chenille fishnet snood and played for time as she wondered how to broach the question.

It had been six weeks since Patsy had confessed to Queenie

about her abuse, and Queenie had in turn revealed her shocking secret about Patsy's sister. Patsy still had so many questions about it. Her mind simply could not comprehend the enormity of the loss, or that her mother had had an entirely separate life before she met her father. She still didn't know who Pearl's father was, or even where Pearl was buried.

Queenie had never indulged in feelings, or even found the words to express her loss. Pearl's death, followed by her father's, had built up a solid wall of pain inside her mother. Breaking through the surface of twenty-seven years of stiff upper lip felt rude and invasive. Instead, Patsy resolved to try and find chinks, softer moments in which to explore her mother's past and tease out the truth.

'D-do I look like her? Pearl?'

Queenie sat down at the kitchen table, surveyed her calloused fingers.

'No, you were very different. Sometimes I can't see her face at all.' Her voice broke off, impossibly raw.

Queenie spread out her fingers on the table before her, almost as if taking part in a seance, and her eyes flickered closed. Patsy knew she should bring the conversation to a close. In the weeks since their double disclosures, Queenie had seemed to age, shrinking deeper into herself. Simply knowing about Pearl was enough, for now.

She opened her eyes abruptly.

'What time are you off to work?'

Patsy drew in a quick little breath. She hadn't yet told her mother where she was working; Queenie thought she was still at Yardley's. One step at a time.

'I'm leaving now. Why, do you want me to stay here, with you?'

'No, you go, love.'

Patsy hesitated at the door. 'You sure?'

'You're so much better with Jimmy than I am, more like

the mum he really deserves,' Queenie went on, ignoring the question.

'What? Don't be ridiculous,' Patsy scoffed. 'He adores you.'

'It's you he adores,' her mother whispered, drawing ever-decreasing circles through some stray grains of salt on the table. 'He's made that obvious.'

Patsy stared at her mother for a long time. She was acting very strangely, even more so than usual. She seemed vague and washed out, like she had slipped into the shadows of herself. Not at all like the fierce matriarch Patsy knew.

'Mum,' she said cautiously, 'I can see you're upset. I can stay here today, Yardley's will understand,' she went on, hating the lie.

Queenie waved her hand in the direction of the door.

'You get off. I'll be fine.'

Eventually, Patsy reached for her handbag.

'I'm sorry,' Queenie whispered, 'for not coming to get you. For not being a proper mother to you and Jimmy.'

Patsy moved to her mother's side and took her cold fingers in her hand.

'How many times must I tell you until you stop blaming yourself? What that man did to me – it's not your fault.'

Queenie raised her daughter's hand to her mouth and kissed her fingers.

Her lips felt dry and powdery, like a butterfly wing.

'A mother should know.'

Patsy looked searchingly into her mother's eyes, and what she saw there frightened her. She was sodden with pain. The wounds she'd had for so long were festering.

'We'll talk later, Mum, when I get back from work, all right?'

Queenie nodded. 'A mother should know,' she repeated.

Patsy left, secretly relieved to get out from the air of tragedy that seemed to permeate every corner of their home.

Outside, everything felt sharpened to a dazzling focus. Events were moving at a dizzying speed. The invasion, swiftly followed by the new menace in the skies, Lou's father's death . . . The spectre of loss was around every corner. But there was only one absence that occupied every corner of her mind.

By the time she reached Piccadilly, the reminders of him were everywhere. The doorway where Blue had tricked her into their first kiss, the steps to Eros where they sat and shared a revolting egg sandwich. She forced his beautiful face from her mind and kept walking. The streets around Rainbow Corner seemed desolate without the light and vigour, the gaiety of the Yanks.

It was as if the Pied Piper had come and led them all away. Restaurant owners stood in their empty doorways, taxis formed queues once more. Even the Piccadilly Commandos, as the working girls were called, looked at a loose end.

A queer hush had spread like a blanket over the streets of Soho. Flag-sellers for the American Red Cross seemed to be on every corner. Patsy bought one and pinned the tiny Stars and Stripes paper flag over her heart.

The door to the American Red Cross club opened and a man emerged on to the pavement in front of her. His hair was so dark, it was the colour of a raven's wing. The broad shoulders . . . It could only be . . . Suddenly, she felt his presence, got the sense of him, his laughing eyes and potent smile – he was so fantastically real to her.

'Blue!' she cried, her throat choked with emotion.

The man turned and looked at her quizzically.

'Sorry,' she mumbled. 'I thought you were someone I knew.'

'Say, are you all right, miss?' He reached his hand out towards her but Patsy wheeled round and stumbled in the direction of The Windmill. By the time she reached the theatre, she realised she was fifteen minutes early.

She pushed open the door to the cafe opposite the theatre

and ordered a cup of tea. Her hands were still trembling, and gratefully, she wrapped them round the warm mug the waitress set down in front of her.

'It's you, isn't it? You work in the theatre.' Patsy looked up and recognised the older woman's face.

'You ain't been in for ages.'

'I've been busy.'

The woman glanced at the flag pinned to her blouse.

'Look here. I don't usually get involved, love. Working here I've seen it all, but your American chap . . .'

Patsy's head snapped up.

She smiled and crossed her arms over her pinny. 'How could any woman say no to blue eyes! I kept the cafe open until three a.m. that night. He offered to pay me to stay open later. I got in no end of trouble with my old man, but he seemed so desperate.'

Patsy's eyes filled with tears. 'How long?' she blurted. 'How long did he wait?'

The waitress shook her head.

'Not sure, darlin'. I had to lock up eventually and I left him sitting on the doorstep. He said he planned on waiting until he had to get his train at seven a.m.'

Patsy couldn't speak.

'Never mind, ducks,' said the woman, patting her briefly on the shoulder. 'Let's hope he comes through it, heh?'

The waitress turned and then stopped suddenly.

'Oh, I nearly forgot.' She rummaged behind the counter and pulled out a dollar bill.

'He asked me to give you this.'

She set down the note on the tabletop. Patsy picked it up and turned it over. Words written in black ink: *I'll never regret loving you. Your nincompoop.*

The pain was so raw, so acute that, for a moment, she felt she couldn't breathe.

How could she sit here drinking tea when Blue, the man she loved, was fighting over the skies for all their future? She knew she'd had no choice but to stay with her mother that night, but the thought that he'd sat here all night long in the cold and dark waiting for her, hoping she would come, hoping she would say yes . . . All he'd wanted was the reassurance of her love, that she too saw a future for them both, but she'd rebuffed him. And now he was where?

The heartbreak of loss settled over her. For a long while, Patsy sat searching her memories, wondering what she could have done differently, but it all came back to the same point. Family came first. And yet . . . Fleets of regret seemed to pin her to her chair.

Eventually, she picked up the dollar bill and headed to The Windmill.

The theatre was quiet that evening, and for the first time, there were spare seats. It was almost like being back in the Blitz, Kitty told her.

Before the performance, the Old Man had given them a pep talk, reassured them they had bomb-spotters with klaxons situated on the reinforced roof should a rocket come over ahead.

'You're not scared are you, Patsy?' Kitty asked as they waited in the wings to go on.

After what she'd been through? At least this enemy didn't sneak in insidiously in soft slippers speaking in hot whispers.

Patsy stuck up the 'V for victory' sign and winked.

'That's the spirit, darling. Nothing keeps The Windmill's sails from turning.'

Kitty glanced out to the stage beyond the darkness.

'Set designer's gone to town tonight,' she remarked. 'Very desert chic, darling. Maybe Valentino will come and whisk me away on his white horse and ravish me.'

Patsy looked at Kitty's face, her scarlet Cupid's bow lips

and impossibly high cheekbones. The sheer golden glamour of her was mesmerising. She was like a beautiful painting or a sculpture. Patsy felt a sudden surge of gratitude that this creature had taken her under her wing.

'Wouldn't you get sand in your bits?' Patsy quipped. Kitty tipped her head back and roared with laughter, earning her a disapproving glare from the stage manager.

The seats may not have been full to capacity, but those who were there made enough noise to raise the roof, and little wonder. The theatre was doing what it did best, pure escapism. The Windmill girls looked exquisite this evening, Patsy thought, like graceful hummingbirds aquiver with feathers.

Patsy wore nothing but an enormous picture hat and a long, orchid-mauve velvet sash that skimmed her breasts. The stage background was one of Eastern opulence: couches of roses, ropes of pearls, glinting jewels and draped tiger skins. The scent of Phul-Nana and Californian Poppy lingered. The whole stage was steeped in glamour.

Patsy loved this world, the ability to transform, to shake off her past and create a new identity for herself. She had learnt that shedding identities was easy. While in Suffolk, she had been a victim, somewhere for that man to lay his hot heavy body and foul breath night after night. Back in Stratford, she was a dutiful daughter; at Yardley's, the war worker. On stage, *she* was in charge. For the first time ever, she was the author of her own life story.

Patsy was about ten minutes through her nude tableau act when the pedestal began to shake ominously underneath her feet. Overhead, the rattle of a klaxon started, but it did little to drown out the drone of the doodlebug as it sliced its way over the Soho skies. Her mouth turned dry. *Stay calm, stay calm*, she told herself, keeping her arms held aloft. The Windmill girls kept on with their dance act without missing a beat. *If they weren't moving, she sure as hell wasn't going to . . .*

A deafening silence as the engine cut out.

'Keep going,' Kitty muttered out of the corner of her mouth.

The colossal bang nearly deafened her and the stage shook. A cascade of dust and debris streamed from the stage lantern, showering Patsy's naked body.

An audible inhalation of breath from the audience, followed by a deathly hush.

Everyone craned their neck skywards to where a great chunk of masonry had dislodged from the ceiling. The V1 hadn't hit them, but it had been a damn near miss. Patsy glanced over to where Kitty lay sprawled on the glass stage.

'I wanted to be swept off my feet, not knocked off,' she said coolly. 'You all right?' she mouthed to Patsy.

In a fit of pure spontaneity, Patsy nodded then slowly, yet gracefully, thumbed her nose up towards the roof of the theatre in a gesture that said: 'Sod you, Hitler'. By moving, she had breached the Lord Chamberlain's strict ruling that nudes should remain motionless – but Patsy didn't care.

A silence, in which Patsy felt a vein in her forehead throb. The sound of clapping reverberated up from under the seats, rose up over the spotlights and engulfed her.

The audience was on their feet, wild with applause at her gesture of defiance. Patsy looked out over the sea of smiling, whistling faces, scanning for just one face she instinctively knew in her heart of hearts wasn't there. Blue.

Then her eyes *did* connect to a familiar face. Patsy was drawn to her because she was the only person in the entire theatre not giving her a standing ovation. The only person not smiling.

'Mum?' she gasped.

From the second row, Queenie's brittle eyes seemed to

bore into hers with such intensity that Patsy instinctively covered her modesty with her purple sash.

Queenie rose and stalked from the theatre, her body as rigid as a concrete post as she barged her way past the ecstatic audience.

Patsy's stomach lurched with acid bile and for a dreadful moment she thought she was going to be sick. Should she follow her? Try and explain? She stood on the plinth, frozen with indecision, her hands still clutching the sash.

The music struck up again and Patsy became aware of Kitty nudging her.

'Patsy darling, drop the sash,' she muttered. 'Show must go on, poses please.'

How Patsy retained her professionalism and continued with the show she had no idea, but the moment the curtain went down she tore to the dressing room and bundled on her clothes.

'Whatever's the matter?' Kitty asked.

'No time to explain.'

Patsy raced out into the hot, dusty night, her heart banging in her chest.

Nothing registered. Not the smoking remains of the Regent Palace Hotel, women in blood-stained cocktail dresses being treated next to the wreckage, nor the glittering shards of a smashed chandelier. She had to get home, find her mum.

Her blood raced as she ran down Cat's Alley, the roar and applause of the audience still thundering through her veins.

She pushed open the door to number 12 and the bang seemed to echo through the darkness. Patsy groped for the gas lamp.

'Mum . . . Mum . . .' she called, braced for a tidal wave of anger. She had been lying to her mother for the best part of a year. The fallout would be apocalyptic. Patsy had betrayed her trust. The thought caused a fresh wave of panic to spiral through her.

As a dim light spread over the parlour, Patsy knew instantly that her mother wasn't there. Sometimes you can just feel the presence of others, but this house was cold and empty.

'Mum,' she whispered, creeping up the staircase. She pushed the door to her mother's bedroom and it creaked slowly open. The room smelt of mothballs and Vim.

The floor had been cleaned, the bed linen stripped and the cupboards were empty. A fire was dying in the grate.

'Oh Mum,' Patsy wept, her panic turning to fear. Was this why she had sent Jimmy away? Please God don't let her have done anything stupid.

Then she spotted it. Propped on the mantel by the mirror was a letter. She tore it open and sank down on to the empty bed.

Dear Patsy,

Twenty-seven years ago this month, I lost my Pearl. I tried to carry on, but my pain is poison. I allowed my grief over losing Pearl and your father to blind me to your suffering. A good mother would have guessed what was going on. I should've known and I must shoulder the blame.

I no longer have the right to call myself your mother and it's better for you and Jimmy without me. Don't waste your energy trying to find me for I'm long gone. Don't mourn my absence. Trust me, it's better this way.

I followed you this evening. I wish I had asked you to stay after all, maybe I half-hoped you'd talk me out of leaving. I can't say I approve of your choices, nor could I deny my shock at your nakedness, but I have relinquished the right to cast judgement. Maybe it is I who is out of step with this new world in which we live? One thing is certain however, the way you reacted to that rocket made me realise that you're far stronger than me and Jimmy's in safe hands.

*I know it won't always be easy, but Nell Gunn will
make sure you are looked after. I've written my own letter
of apology to her, to Lou Button and to all the people
whose life I've made a misery since we arrived in
Stratford. I've inflicted suffering to match my own. I've
twisted the knife so deep that I don't expect, nor do I
deserve, their forgiveness.*

*You are and always will be my precious girl. I love you
and Jimmy more than I can express. I hope you can find
it in your heart to forgive me for leaving.*

*In the top left drawer of my chest is a brooch, which
belonged to my mother. I used to wear it as a good luck
talisman when I was performing. When you wear it I hope
you'll remember me as I was when you were young, not
the dreadful woman I allowed myself to become.*

Do not live as I have. Live well. Live for Pearl.

*Your mother,
Queenie Jacks.*

Patsy put down the letter and pulled the drawer open. Sure
enough there was a silver-and-amber brooch nestled in a silk
scarf. She lifted it out and rubbed it between her thumb and
forefinger. In the dim and distant past she could recall her
mother wearing it, but she hadn't seen it in years. Patsy held
the amber up to the firelight and it glowed. In the sudden
prism of light a tiny fly was suspended in the jewel. Trapped
forever, hopelessly frozen in time, a little like her mother.
Queenie's life had stopped the moment the bomb dropped
and killed her daughter. She had been confined in a bubble
of grief, until it had slowly calcified her.

Patsy suddenly felt the heavy burden of her mother's pain.
It seemed to coat the walls, her anguish gilding the airless
space.

'Oh Mum . . .' she murmured, pressing the brooch to her lips. With Queenie gone, Patsy no longer felt frustrated or contained. Just horribly sad.

In the fire, a few cooling coals collapsed. Patsy's tears began to fall.

22

Esther

Queenie Jacks has gone. Queenie Jacks has gone.
The thought took hold and ran on a loop in Esther's
sleep-deprived mind.

She drummed her fingers on the bus seat.

'Come on, why so slow?'

It was early Monday morning and Esther was on the
trolley bus to Plaistow, on her way to the hostel where
Snowball was staying. As soon as she'd heard of Queenie's
moonlight flit, she knew she had to tell him. She had tried
to push him to the back of her mind since her dreadful
discovery in the portrait studio in Poplar, but he had a right
to know that his estranged wife, if that's what she was, was
finally gone.

The bus hit a pothole and they lurched forward. Esther
clutched her enormous tummy and felt her baby give a startled kick.

Walter had left her tucked up in bed that morning with
orders not to get out – the midwife would be calling any
minute for a check-up.

The last six weeks had dragged on indeterminately. They
had expected the baby to make an appearance in the middle
of June, but it was now two weeks past that. The midwife
had assured her it was perfectly normal to go over your due

date with first babies and that delivery dates weren't an exact science But whether it was normal or not, she was bored, fed up of waiting and being fussed over by Maureen.

Guilt tugged as she realised how reckless she was being leaving the house. In these final days of confinement, she knew she really ought to be resting, but as soon as Maureen had gone to Angel Lane Market, she'd made her escape and hoofed it, or rather waddled it, out of there.

Maureen would be ages. The market would be alive with gossip this morning over the discovery that Queenie had done a bunk, leaving little Jimmy to be raised by Patsy.

There were many who would say 'good riddance'. Queenie was a tyrant, yes, but now that Esther knew about the loss of her first-born daughter, she felt nothing but pity. If her suspicions were right, how could Snowball have left her like that and run off? Stupid, feckless man.

A white wall of anger rose up in Esther and she did her best to quell it. Confronting him in this hostile state would not serve either of them. She wanted to untangle his past, not tighten the threads.

She stared out at the streets of East London as they flashed past. Since the doodlebugs had begun dropping, London had emptied again. Another round of evacuation trains had taken the children off to places like Leicester and Birmingham, out of range of the rockets. The patched-up, scruffy streets were taking a bashing once more, and every so often, the bus would trundle past an enormous crater or a roped-off pile of rubble where once a row of houses had been. Homes had been opened up like dolls' houses and the streets glittered with powdered glass.

Esther sighed as she listened to the couple in front discuss the new menace. *It's like the Blitz all over again.* After five years of war, though, it felt worse than the Blitz. Most people's reserves of resilience had dried up all together. It was

Churchill who'd said: 'War is full of surprises, mostly unpleasant,' and Esther was inclined to agree.

It was the sheer randomness of it that got to her the most. Yesterday, Stratford had been alive with talk of the poor folk watching *Gone with the Wind* in a soundproofed cinema when a rocket came down. The entire back row was still sitting in the cheap seats with their heads blown off. Noises took on new meaning. One hardly dare fry an egg for fear that you'd miss the sound of a rocket's approach.

Finally at her stop, she got off and walked slowly and stiffly down an unremarkable street.

Once at the door to the hostel, she stopped. What exactly was she going to say to Snowball? Why didn't you just tell us about the bomb that hit the school, that you lost a daughter? *Why did you run and leave us?*

War is an uncomfortable business, not suited to the black-and-white certainty of the past. They had been so busy looking at the trenches of the first war, they hadn't even entertained that Snowball's trauma could have come from the homefront.

She knocked on the door. No answer. On instinct, she followed a path round to the back of the hostel. A small but lovingly tended allotment dominated the entire back garden. At the end of the garden ran railway tracks. Tomatoes and runner beans had been trailed up the high brick wall leading to them. Every spare inch had been thoughtfully and imaginatively utilised. A flash of light drew Esther's eye to a patch of herbs. Coppers bands to stop the slugs. Red string round the fruit bushes.

Mr Middleton's Dig for Victory radio show crackled from a wireless next to an open window. Next to a pitchfork sat a half-drunk mug of creosote-strong tea.

'This is your allotment, Snowball,' she breathed out loud.

Sitting down slowly on an old bench outside the Anderson shelter, she reasoned she might as well make herself comfy while she waited. It looked like Snowball had been gardening here only moments before.

An uncomfortable tightening clamped her abdomen.

Esther gripped the edge of the bench and tried to breathe deeply. The feeling passed in ten seconds or so and she removed her cardigan. It was so hot. She massaged the back of her neck and blew out slowly. Come on, Snowball. She felt ever so peculiar.

Away from the clamour and bustle of Stratford, Plaistow was so quiet and still. A fly buzzed lazily overhead and she batted it away. The fly grew louder, more persistent and she got up clumsily.

'Esther?'

Snowball was standing at the old garden gate, shambling in his torn, old, frayed grey cardigan, rag-tag trousers held up with string. He was clutching an old wooden pallet of seedlings. And just like that, there was no anger, only a huge surge of inarticulate love.

'Snowball,' she breathed in relief, 'I'm so happy to see you.'

'What are you doing here?' He glanced at her enormous belly. 'You look like you're about to pop.'

'I . . . I had to come and see you. Queenie's gone. She's left.'

His face seemed to collapse and he dropped the tray of seedlings.

'It's all right. You don't need to pretend anymore. I know everything. About Queenie and your daughter.'

'My daughter?' he repeated in a trance, staring at the smashed plants and spilt earth at his feet.

'Yes, Pearl and the school bomb.' She waved her hand in agitation. 'This bloomin' fly won't leave me alone. I swear it's following me.' Its buzzing filled her head, louder, louder, more invasive. Her brain felt soupy and detached from her body, all that mattered was Snowball, getting him home. If she could only stop this wretched rattling in her head.

Snowball was trembling. But then again, so was she. As one, they looked from the ground to the juddering grey skies. A black blur was streaking through the clouds.

'Esther,' Snowball said slowly, 'it's a doodlebug. RUN!'

The shimmering heat of the still summer morning seemed to break open.

Her world was reduced to rudimentary senses, the scratchy fabric of Snowball's cardigan as he bundled her into his arms and dragged her towards the Anderson shelter. Then she was falling, tumbling, screaming into the darkness.

The explosion seemed to rip a hole in her head, deafening her.

The ground jerked and the walls around her shuddered, causing a vacuum, followed by a hot rush of air. Darkness. Smoke. Heat.

She coughed and lifted her head off the ground. Saliva spooled from her mouth.

'Snowball . . . Snowball . . .' She groped her hands out into the inky pit, her voice fading into the repercussive air.

Esther felt hot corrugated iron, then the compacted earth of the floor. She was trapped. Underground. Panic closed in, a silent scream trapped in her throat. *No. No. No . . .*

She hauled herself to her knees and pushed weakly on the door of the shelter. It was stuck fast. A soup of smells filled the darkness, the sticky sweet metallic smell of blood, dust and burning.

Behind her came a rustle.

'Esther.'

'Snowball . . . Thank God! You're here.'

In the darkness she could hear scratching, a bang, and she half wondered if he hadn't keeled over. But then came the sudden crackle and flare of amber. A soft glow illuminated the shelter and Snowball's face appeared out the darkness.

'Just as well I kitted this Anderson out last week,' he said, blowing out the match. 'Are you all right, love? I think I've cut my arm.'

He guided her slowly on to a narrow bed and once her heart had stopped thumping, she took in her surroundings. A small chair and a narrow makeshift bed, made from what looked like an old door, lined the sides of the underground shelter, which stood about six feet high and six feet long. Esther had never been in an Anderson before. In Stratford, few people had the gardens to dig them into, and it was an unnerving experience, a little like sitting in a small, dark bicycle shed. A dull static heat cloaked the tiny space. A hurricane lamp sat on top of a camping table next to a flask, and a stack of Dig for Victory leaflets.

Snowball was busying himself pouring water from the flask into a kettle and lighting the gas under a primus stove.

'I got a bit of stera but no sugar I'm afraid.'

She laughed hysterically.

'You're making us a cup of tea?'

'Why not?' He walked to the tiny door and pushed but it was jammed solid. 'Reckons as how the rocket must've hit the train tracks and dumped a ton of debris on us.'

Suddenly, the walls of the confined space seemed to slide even closer together.

'Will they find us?' Esther gibbered, gripping the edge of her seat.

'Course they will, love. Someone from the hostel will raise the alarm. They'll have heavy rescue out for us.'

He sat down next to her and patted her arm. 'We've just got to sit and wait it out. Stay calm like.'

'H-how long?'

He shrugged. 'How long's a piece of string? Depends on how busy they are. But don't worry, they'll come for us.'

Esther shifted and felt a sudden hot warmth seep down her legs.

'I'm not sure I can wait all that long, Snowball.'

'I'm not sure we've any choice, love.'

'No, you don't understand, the baby – I think it's coming.'

'A-are you sure?'

She hauled herself up and the patter of hot liquid spattered on to the floor.

'Quite sure.'

For a long time, Snowball sat, stricken. He rubbed his head with both hands, as if assembling his thoughts.

'Well, we better get ready then.'

Esther felt a calmness descend that she was quite sure wasn't warranted by the situation.

'Have you ever delivered a baby before?' she asked.

'No. But then, I've never been trapped in an Anderson shelter either.'

For a long time, nothing happened and Esther began to wonder if she hadn't accidentally wet herself. Snowball made them tea and cut up an old fruitcake, feeding her a few nibbles at a time to keep up her strength. She was so hot. Gently, he dabbed at her forehead with a hankie soaked in cold water.

'Where's Nell Gunn when you need her?'

'I'm so sorry that you're stuck with me, love.'

'Behave. If it weren't for you getting me in this shelter, I mightn't be here at all.'

The familiar tightening of her stomach began as the contraction began to build inside her.

Esther held her breath, willing it to pass.

'I don't know much about labour, love, but I do know breathing is necessary,' Snowball urged, taking her hand in his.

As it dissipated, Esther felt overwhelmed and burst into tears.

'I don't know if I can do this! Not like this.'

'Don't talk daft,' he scoffed. 'You're the strongest girl I know. Look at what you've already faced up to in your young life.'

In the darkness, with fear curdling her insides, she blurted the whole sorry truth, about Maureen tricking her into having a baby, her doubts and worries about motherhood.

'Maybe this is my punishment, for not wanting this baby?' she whispered, her grey eyes pale in the confined space.

'Now you listen here, my girl. Don't believe any of that fatalistic rubbish. It mightn't have been the start you wanted, but now he or she is coming, you'll love this baby with the whole of your heart.'

'Do you really think so?'

'I know so. There's nothing but goodness and love inside you.'

'I'm sorry, Snowball.'

'Whatever for?'

'For snooping into your past.'

Snowball patted her hand.

'It's me who should be saying sorry. For running away like that.'

'It's all right,' said Esther, drawing back to look at him. 'I understand, really I do. You were grieving for your daughter.'

He gave her a sad complicated little smile.

'Pearl wasn't my daughter. She was my niece.'

Esther stared at him.

'Are you trying to tell me Queenie Jacks is your sister?'

He nodded.

'But that photographer, he told me that's Pearl's dad left her.'

'And so he did. He worked on the railways, fly-by-night. Nasty piece of work, he was. Did a runner soon as he heard Queenie was having his child, which is why I moved in with her, to help her face the scandal.'

He dabbed fresh water on his hankie and drew it over Esther's brow.

'By the time she was five, I came to look upon Pearl as my own. I loved her as much as any father would've. By 1917, I was the caretaker at the school she went to, Upper North Street School, so I got to see her every day.' He smiled at the memory. 'Walked her to and from school so Queenie could work. Little poppet.'

'You were a caretaker?' Esther asked, her mind tumbling with questions. 'I thought you were over in France!'

'I was until I got shot in the foot and invalided out.'

Suddenly the light guttered as the gas lamp died.

'Oh no,' she gasped, gripping his hand.

'It's all right,' he puffed. 'I've candles here.' He lit one up and Esther stared at the fragile flame.

'Please go on. Tell me the rest of the story.'

'Oh love, not here, not now.'

'Please,' she urged. 'If you don't keep talking, the panic will set in.'

He sighed, a deep rumbling sigh, which seemed to reach to his very bones.

'The funny thing is, for so many years, I couldn't really remember what happened. I must've buried it in a place far deeper than we're buried now.'

'And?' Esther asked, hardly daring to breathe.

'When Queenie moved to the Shoot, it brought it all back, big visions, flashbacks, not sure really what you'd call them, but suddenly I was back there in the school on the day the bomb hit.'

He gripped the edge of the bed as if for support, the blue veins on his hands like old rope.

'Extraordinary what I suddenly remembered. Smells. Sights. Strangely no sound though. It's silent in my memory.'

'Tell me.'

'I daren't.'

'I've lived through the Blitz, Snowball. I'm not green to total warfare.'

He laughed suddenly, softly.

'Pearl had the brightest red hair, stubborn little creature she was, just like her mother. On the day . . .' He broke off, the breath leaving his body in one great big rush. With a Herculean effort he composed himself.

'On the day the bomb hit, they were to make paper lanterns in class. Beautiful summer morning it was, all the kiddies turned out in their best summer frocks. Was Pearl excited, not many!' He chuckled. 'Held my hand all the way to school, chattered non-stop about it. Proper little chatterbox was Pearl.

'Anyway, I gets her to the school gates, gave her a kiss and told her I'd pick her up later as Mummy was working. At mid-morning, I was pushing a broom through the school playground when suddenly the whole yard went dark. Strangest thing, there must've been an explosion, but like I say, I don't recall. It was as if someone had switched off the sun. After that . . .' He drew a trembling hand over his mouth.

'Go on,' Esther urged.

'Out the darkness, I saw great clouds of smoke and dust coming from the school so I started to run. As I got closer, it looked like the whole school was imploding in front of my eyes.

'Seemingly a squadron of Gotha aircraft was overhead. The bomb dropped through the roof, through the girls' classroom on the top floor, through the boys' it went, not exploding until it reached the infants on the ground floor.

'In the classroom . . .' He squeezed his eyes shut, his voice no more than a whisper.

'God it was a massacre. Children trapped under desks, debris and timber, some driven clean into the earth by the force of the explosion.'

He began to weep.

'I started pulling kiddies out. Some dead, some alive, and I carried them into the playground where I laid them out, before running back inside.

'Oh Esther, some were disfigured beyond recognition, torn to pieces, their faces stained yellow from deposits of TNT.'

He held his hands to his cheeks, the memory of the event suddenly so lucid, it was as if it was happening here and now. Esther didn't dare interrupt him. He had lived with this secret for twenty-seven years.

'Then the mothers started arriving and now here I can remember the sounds. Weeping and screaming as they searched for their children. Queenie was hysterical. Poor Miss Ely the infants' headmistress tried her best to calm her.

'The teachers were the heroines that day. They pulled those bodies from powdered brick, wood . . . human flesh. So many poor little mites you couldn't put a name to.'

'And Pearl?' Esther ventured, tears rolling down her cheeks.

He shook his head.

'I dug through that classroom. And I dug. And I dug.'

And you're still digging all these years on, she thought sadly, thinking of all those times she'd found him half-crazed, digging relentlessly in the driving rain and snow.

'Eventually the police and Miss Ely stopped me trying to find her. Told me I was wasting my time. That Pearl's complete body would never be found, the force of the explosion was too great, but I never forgave myself.'

And Queenie never forgave you either.

'On the day of the funeral, the largest the East End's ever seen, we buried our murdered babies.'

His jaw set in rage.

'What kind of bloody war is it that sends hordes of men to slaughter little children? Innocent children making paper lanterns at their desks.'

Esther shook her head. She couldn't speak, her throat was clogged with horror.

'Those kiddies suffered for their country, as much as the men what fought in the trenches, on the seas or in the air, leastwise that's what the Mayor of Poplar said. Happen he was right.'

His emotions were vacillating now between anger and despair.

'They buried fragments of what they hoped was Pearl in with another broken child. Fragments. Like a handful of dust.' He stared at his palm, stained with mud.

'The only thing I found was the button from her dress.'

'This one?' she said, pulling it from her pocket. He nodded.

'All that's left of a life. One pathetic button.'

'So when did you leave the East End?'

'Directly after the funeral. I knew my sister would blame me with her dying breath for not finding Pearl so I left her a note saying sorry and I joined the navy. They were so desperate by that point, they didn't care about my injury. I weren't alone. Hundreds of young East End men were so shocked by the bombing of the school, they were queuing up to fight.

'The difference is though, I was running away. I never really stopped running all those years . . .'

'Until you met Nell and found a home,' she interrupted softly.

'She showed me acceptance and love I never thought possible.'

'Until Queenie showed up out the blue and derailed the lot?'

He nodded, tears coursing down his cheeks.

'And now I've let down the one woman I've ever really loved.'

'Nell will forgive you,' Esther soothed. 'Once she knows the whole story.'

'But Queenie won't,' he said, his voice a hoarse whisper. 'I can't blame her. I had a job to do. To bring that little girl home safe.'

'But don't you see, Snowball? Her grief and anger were misplaced. The only people responsible for the bomb that killed your niece was the German pilot who dropped it and the Kaiser. Not you.'

He carried on staring at the button in Esther's hand.

'Besides, I don't think she blamed you,' she went on, 'not really. I think she blamed herself in many ways. She wrote letters to everyone she'd ever crossed before she left, apparently. To Nell and Lou. I'd be willing to bet there's one for you back at the Shoot.'

He shrugged. 'Not sure I deserve her forgiveness.'

Esther gazed at this man whose entire life had been blighted by one traumatic experience. A bomb dropped twenty-seven years ago had reverberated, sending cracks and fissures down the decades.

He had carried the death of his niece with him around the world, the secret laying softly and silently within him, but each year stealthily taking over more of his heart and mind. It had soured every job, shrivelled every relationship, turned him out of every comfortable bed, until he was reduced to a man who existed on the outskirts of life. He never felt he was worthy of any comfort, wandering about instead in a kind of purgatory.

Esther longed to shake this gentle, kind soul, help him to see with the clarity she could. But that kind of insight could only come with help, support and love.

'Please come home,' she begged. 'We all need you.'

Just then, they became aware of banging overhead. The noise made her jerk and almost instantly, she felt another contraction gather inside her. Dust showered from the ceiling.

'It's rescuers!' he cried, sitting up as she bent over.

'Hold tight, my love,' he urged. 'They're coming to get us out.'

She cried out as pain ripped through her body, her tears for Snowball and the eighteen children who'd never be rescued.

Forty-eight minutes after they were helped from the darkness of the Anderson shelter, blinking, into air still thick with acidic yellow smoke, Esther gave birth in the back of the ambulance parked outside the hostel, the most dramatic birth the paramedics could recall. A perfect little girl, though quite the whopper at 9 lb 2 oz. And after Esther, Snowball was the first person to cradle the fresh new life in his arms.

'Oh, love,' he said choked with tears. 'She's just terrific, a little smasher.'

He could hardly take his eyes off her baby's little wrinkled face, marvelling at her perfect rosebud lips and minuscule fingernails. Esther watched them both in a kind of awe.

Maybe new life and love was the best kind of healing there was. All her doubts melted to nothing. After the story she had just heard, she knew she would treasure this baby with everything she had.

Snowball put his arm around her and tenderly kissed her forehead. 'I'm so proud of you, love.'

'You the grandfather?' asked one paramedic as they readied themselves for the journey back.

Snowball hesitated.

'Yes, he is,' Esther replied.

'Close shave that, sir,' he grinned. 'You nearly ended up delivering your granddaughter.'

As the ambulance drove them both back slowly, Esther didn't ask whether he was going to make his peace with Nell, but when they pulled up outside the London Hospital, just as a precaution to check mother and baby were well, Snowball slipped away.

'Never been inside a hospital in my life, not about to start now.'

'I'll see you down the Shoot then?'

'Please God. We'll see what Nell has to say. I've some explaining to do.'

'One more thing I meant to ask,' she called after him as she gingerly sat down in the wheelchair a hospital medic had brought out. 'Why "Snowball"?'

'Market traders down Angel Lane saw me having a snowball fight with some nippers. The name stuck. But my real name's Alfred Tanner. Alfie for short.'

'Suits you,' she said with an exhausted smile. 'Oh, and Alfie? I'm so proud of . . .'

'ESTHER! ESTHER! ' Esther and Alfie turned suddenly to see Walter pegging it up the road, still wearing his Yardley overalls and clutching his clipboard.

'Oh love I came as soon as I heard,' he sobbed, colliding with a medic as he skidded to a halt.

'Sorry, mate,' he puffed.

His face was bright red and tears streamed down his cheeks.

'I've been such a stupid, selfish berk. If I'd lost you and the baby I'd never have forgiven myself. I don't know what's come over me this past year. I haven't stopped to put your feelings first, I allowed my mum to call the shots when I should have listened to you . . . Can you ever forgive me? I-I'm such a wally.'

'Walter lad,' Alfie chuckled, laying a hand on his shoulder. 'Breathe!'

'He's right,' added the medic, 'or there'll be two of you in a wheelchair. Now, we need to get these two inside.'

'I do forgive you,' Esther said wearily, 'but things are going to have to change.'

She kissed the top of her baby girl's head.

'I'm a mum now and that means we need our own space to be a proper family.'

Alfie winked at her as he watched the medic push her and her baby into the hospital.

Something told him that Esther was going to be just fine from now on.

A couple of days later, once Esther and baby Louise, as they had decided to call her, were declared to be in good health, they were both discharged from the London into the care of the nearby Jewish Maternity Home in Whitechapel. It was here that Esther fell even deeper in love with her baby girl, if that were possible. Walter visited daily, as contrite as it was possible to be. Coming so close to losing them both had helped to focus his priorities. He genuinely seemed to be the man she had first fallen for: sensitive, humble and full of love.

Her stay in the maternity home had given her time to think with clarity. Esther vowed to never tell her husband the truth about the timing of baby Louise and his mother's meddling hand in it. He would be shocked, angry and hurt. Some secrets, Esther concluded, were best kept that way.

On the day of their discharge, Yardley's had given Walter the day off on full pay and when he came to the ward he was hopping with nervous excitement.

'You look very smart,' Esther grinned, taking in the suit and tie.

'Well. It's a very special day,' he replied, bending down to kiss their daughter first, then Esther.

'I've got a taxi waiting outside, ready to take us home.'

Esther mentally prepared herself for a return to the house she had last seen when she had fled in search of Snowball. Maureen would be waiting, no doubt with plenty of advice.

But once settled in the taxi, it sailed past the turning they needed and drove further into the guts of Stinky Stratford. The familiar smells of hot grease, stagnant water, spilt beer, leather and boiling bones gusted through the car window, causing the taxi driver to wrinkle his nose.

Esther turned to Walter and raised one eyebrow. But he was staying silent, a big daft smile plastered all over his face.

'Walter . . . what's going on?'

He grinned and tapped the side of his nose.

'Wait and see.'

As the car drove slowly into the Shoot, swerving to avoid the potholes, Louise woke with a start, her big brown eyes snapping open in surprise.

'That's it, my darlin', take a good look at your new home,' Walter murmured.

Esther was flabbergasted as they pulled to a stop and a sea of familiar faces stood waiting to greet them on the kerbside.

Across the doorway of number 12, a big 'Welcome Home' banner was flapping gently in the breeze, along with dozens of white paper storks which had been cut out and pasted on the windows.

Nell and Alfie were there, arm in arm, and so were her mum, all the Lavender Girls, Miss Rayson, Patsy and little Jimmy.

'But this is Patsy and Jimmy's house?' she exclaimed.

'Was,' Walter corrected. 'Patsy and little Jimmy have moved in next door with your mum, Nell and Alfie, as we're all to call him now. Soon as I heard, I asked Nell to put in a word with the fella from the council and it's all arranged. We're now officially tenants.'

'But didn't Patsy mind?'

'Not a bit. I think the old place contained too many memories of her mum, and now she and Jimmy have Nell and your mum to fuss over them. I'm going to give the place a lick of paint, but you can give it a woman's touch once you're all settled. For now though, it's a home. *Our* home.'

Walter held her gaze, his gentle eyes scanning hers for approval.

'And your mum,' she asked, 'she's all right with this?'

'You leave her to me. She's my mum, and of course I'll always love her, but it's time I put you two first. You're the most important people in my life and I'd be lost without you. You were right. We need our own space so we can be a proper family.'

'Oh Walter,' Esther cried, unable to stop her tears. 'You don't know how long I've waited for this.'

Walter leant over Louise, who had drifted back off to sleep. The leather of the taxi seat creaked as he kissed Esther softly on the lips.

'I love you, Mrs Smith.'

'Oi,' yelled a voice like a klaxon from the kerb. 'Get your mucky paws off her and get out that taxi so as we can all have a cuddle with that beautiful baby.'

Esther and Walter burst into laughter.

'You don't want to upset your neighbour,' Walter winked. 'I hear she rules the roost round these parts.'

Esther got out the car and the girls fell on her and baby Louise, oohing and aahing over the Shoot's tiniest resident.

Over the sea of excited faces, she locked eyes with Alfie.

'Welcome home,' she mouthed.

Esther felt a bolt of pure relief. It would take time to shake off the guilt and horror of losing his niece, but for the first time in decades, Alfie could now stand still in his own skin. The neighbourhood might be poor, smelly and bomb battered, but oh was it ever rich in love! There was nowhere else she'd rather be right now. Try as you might, eventually all roads led back to the Shoot.

23

Lou

Saturday 26th August 1944

Two months later, on a sweltering hot late-August day, Lou's train pulled into Liverpool Street station. The whole place was awash with tricolour flags, fluttering from every hoarding.

She emerged on to the sticky, hot platform and grabbed a nearby porter's arm.

'Hey, pal, what's with the French flags?'

'Didn'cha hear? Paris was liberated yesterday. *Vive la France*, heh?'

He grinned jubilantly. 'Our boys'll be in Berlin next.'

Lou felt like she was coming back to civilisation, of sorts. Nine weeks now she'd been in the wilds of Scotland, working for the Women's Timber Corps, helping to saw down trees, measuring logs, peeling off bark and generally avoiding being hit by fallen timber. The majesty of the Scottish forests had proved to be the perfect escape from her problems. By nightfall, she was so exhausted, she was asleep before her head even hit the pillow. She was fitter, leaner and healthier than she'd ever been in her life.

When Martha had written to her to tell her about Nell and Snowball's hastily arranged wedding, she had managed to swing a forty-eight-hour pass. She'd have to turn around no sooner than she'd arrived, but it would be worth it to see her old friends and of course . . . *her*.

She slung her duffel bag over her shoulder, rolled a cigarette, popped it behind her ear and set off to do the hour-and-a-half walk back to Stratford. Her legs felt springy and for the first time since her mother's death, she felt a lightness in her chest. She would never stop grieving for the woman who gave her life for her daughters, but instead of drowning under it, her grief was something that could be lived alongside.

She strode through a forest of fluttering handkerchiefs, waved as women bade farewell to sweethearts; past soldiers and sailors lazily rolling up cigarettes as they waited, and mothers fussing over children boarding evacuation trains. For the first time ever, Lou felt separate to the detritus of war, not hemmed in by it.

An extraordinarily loud wolf-whistle tore through her thoughts.

'Blimey, you really are Tin Ribs now!'

She turned and Martha's gap-toothed smile emerged through the smoke, a Craven 'A' dangling from the corner of her mouth. She looked just as dishevelled as usual. Her cloud of chestnut hair was barely contained by a red polka-dot headscarf and she wore dungarees with patched knees. Lou's heart cartwheeled with joy. Martha didn't give a rat's arse about her appearance, and she was all the more beautiful for it. Lou flew into her arms with a solid thump, hugging her as tight as she dared.

'Steady on, people are staring,' Martha laughed, as a woman clutching the hand of a gawping child tugged her past.

'Two old friends hugging, where's the harm?' she replied with a complicit smile. 'Now come on, we've got a wedding to get to.'

Back in the Shoot, Lou was greeted like the prodigal daughter.

From the moment she emerged from Cat's Alley, the

Lavender Girls descended, hugging her, ruffling her hair and jokingly squeezing her wiry arms.

'Check out skinny here,' said Betty, with a caustic grin. 'Seriously, I've seen more meat on a butcher's pencil. Look at yer arms, like a couple of sparrow's kneecaps.'

'Shut up,' Lou laughed. 'Just 'cause you couldn't knock the skin off a rice pudding.'

'Here, Lou, heard the one about Hitler's revenge weapon?' chipped in Little Irene. 'They're thinking of renaming them Hitler's Virgins . . .'

'Why?'

''Cause they've never had a man in them. Mind you, nor have you for that matter!'

Lou rolled her eyes. All those weeks of missed banter.

'Shut your yak, Betty,' ordered a deep voice. 'And move out the way so I can take a good look.'

'Nell.' Lou grinned, as the shadow of the Shoot's chief female fell over the cobbles.

Nell held her at arms' length, while she appraised her. 'Don't they feed you in Scotland? You're too skinny,' she said bluntly. Then she hugged her, the tightness of her grip telling her everything Lou needed to know.

The door to number 12 opened and a very happy looking Esther emerged with a tiny sleeping baby swaddled in a blanket, nestled in her arms.

'Esther!' Lou exclaimed. 'Let me have a cuddle with this little one. You're looking ever so well. What's her name?'

'Louise Julia Smith,' she smiled shyly, handing her very carefully to Lou. 'Lulu for short.'

'You named her . . .' she broke off, her voice incredulous.

'Yes, after you.'

'She was gonna call her Andy if it was a boy,' piped up Little Irene. 'You know, after the Anderson shelter, where she was nearly born.'

'Shut up, you cretin,' said Nell, clumping her round the back of the head.

Lou looked at the tiny little girl in her arms and felt an emotion she found hard-pressed to put a name to. She knew she'd probably never have a baby, but loving this little girl was not a bad consolation prize.

'I'm so touched, Esther.' The two women locked eyes and Lou felt a current of love and understanding flow between them.

'Anyway, how comes you're coming out of number twelve? I thought Patsy and Jimmy lived there?'

'Not anymore,' said Esther. 'Many changes since you went away. After little Lulu's dramatic entry, Walter told his mum we needed our own space and arranged it all. Patsy and Jimmy have moved in with Nell, Snowball – sorry, Alfie as we call him now – and Mum."

She tucked little Lulu's blankets up under her chin, unable to tear her eyes from her.

'How's that gone down with the mother-in-law?' Lou asked.

'You can imagine,' Esther replied, lifting one eyebrow. 'Actually, not all that bad – she's round most days offering up her pearls of wisdom on childrearing.'

'Lucky you,' Lou grimaced.

'It's all right, she leaves by three p.m. most days so she can get to the front of the queue down to the Underground. She's only happy when she sleeps deep. Even manages to smuggle that vicious cat of hers in with her sometimes.'

'One good side effect of the rockets then,' Lou replied wryly.

Both girls burst into laughter.

'Don't, Lou,' Esther giggled, her grey eyes shining in the August sunshine. Lou reflected on how happy and content she looked. Being a new mum suited her.

'And how is Patsy, since her mum done a flit . . .'

Lou's thoughts trailed to the letter which had been forwarded to her from Queenie Jacks.

'Queenie wrote to me you know, apologising for telling Dad about me and Martha and her display at the Yardley Christmas show.'

'She wrote a lot of those kinds of letters,' Esther replied. 'One to Nell and Alfie, a few to different women down the Shoot – basically to anyone she'd crossed.'

Their eyes turned to Nell and Alfie. Nell was fussing over her husband-to-be, straightening his tie.

'I still can't believe they're getting hitched,' Lou said. 'About time.'

'Yes, we all need to start looking forward, not back. To life after—'

'Don't say it,' Lou interrupted. 'I swear every time someone says "after the war is over" it delays the end by one more month.'

'I never had you down as superstitious,' Esther remarked. 'But you have to admit, with Paris liberated, it does feel like the end is in sight.'

A cautious hope prevailed and in a funny way, Lou felt a tinge of sadness, not that she dared voice it. *When the war ended*. What then? The men would come home, want their jobs back. Women would be back in dresses and back in the kitchen, leaving her where? All her life, she'd felt out of step with society. War had aligned her, helped her to feel strong and purposeful.

When it ended, you could bet slacks would be placed to the back of the wardrobe, and she'd go back to being an anachronism.

The ache she felt for her sisters – the one hard work and exhaustion, to say nothing of black market Scotch whisky, kept at bay – how would she cope when that returned, when she had to return to these dusty old streets?

'I thought I heard a familiar voice!' Patsy tore across the cobbles and kissed Lou on her cheek.

'Patsy, I'm so sorry about your mum leaving. I wrote, but I'm not sure if you got it.'

'Thanks, Lou. It's a big shock. Not sure I'm still any closer to understanding it if I'm honest.'

She ran her fingers through her dark, wavy hair, clamped her bottom lip between her teeth.

Lou gazed at her and felt taken aback at the change in her friend. She was still glamorous of course, but her eyes looked older, freighted with the losses she'd endured, smudged with yesterday's eye black. She was a girl, really, when she'd joined them thirteen months ago. Now she was what could only be described as war weary. Mind you, they all wore that familiar look, so scoured by war that no amount of Max Factor could fix it.

'Any word from Blue? Did you find him like you said you would, explain why you never showed at the cafe?' She hadn't intended to bring it up for fear of upsetting her, but somehow the question slipped out. Immediately tears filled Patsy's eyes.

'Oh God, I'm so embarrassed,' she said quietly, stroking baby Lulu's velvet cheek to avoid having to look at everyone.

'Whatever for?' Esther asked.

'I did the one thing I vowed I'd never do. I acted like some silly camp follower. I went to his base in Chipping Ongar last week. A train and three buses it took me! Anyhow, I just wanted to see if he was still alive, or if I could get any news of him. More than anything, I wanted to say sorry. For turning down his proposal, for leaving him in that cafe all night long.'

'And?' Lou asked.

'They're not there anymore. The 387th Bomb Group flew their last mission out of Chipping Ongar in July and now they've moved. The fella I spoke with didn't know where to. The base has been taken over by Air Disarmament Command.'

'Oh dear,' said Esther.

'Quite. He's probably completed his missions, if he's even still alive, that is, and he's back home in Boston. I'm sure I'll always just be a wartime fling he'll chuckle over with his buddies out of earshot of his wife. I guess I just need to forget Blue ever existed.' She hugged her arms about herself. 'Move on. Plenty more fish and all that.'

She smiled with a fake brightness, her eyes as flat as the Cut.

'The irony of it. I kept him waiting so I could stay with Mum, and now she's left me. Serves me right heh!'

Esther reached out and squeezed her arm. None of them were fooled. Her heartbreak was palpable.

'But one positive . . .' and here her smile was genuine. 'Yesterday, I had a meeting with Miss Rayson, cap in hand, and asked for my old job back at Yardley's. Told her I'd pack anything; soap, lipstick, bullets if needs be.'

'What?' Esther and Lou said at the same time.

'But Patsy, you loved your job at the theatre,' Lou protested.

'I know, I did . . . I do. Mr Van Damm and Miss Henderson were wonderful, told me I'm welcome back any time, but little Jimmy needs me closer to home.'

'But still,' Esther said, 'you have a gift. It would be a crime to squander it. You don't light a lamp then hide it under a table.'

'I don't know about that, Esther,' Patsy chuckled. 'But don't worry too much. I've already enquired about joining the Yardley Follies dance troupe and they said they'd love to have me. In fact, they've already signed me up for rehearsals for a new show at the Theatre Royal, so theatreland ain't seen the last of me just yet.'

'Phew,' Esther replied. 'If you need anyone to look after Jimmy for you, I'd be happy to help.'

'That's kind, but Alfie's already volunteered to look after

him when I'm at rehearsals. Reckons as how he's going to make a proper gardener of him down the allotment.'

'He seems to have found himself a very attentive uncle,' Lou remarked, pointing to the allotment where Snowball, or rather Alfie, was risking Nell's wrath by playing football in his suit with Jimmy and half the neighbourhood nippers.

Lou still couldn't wrap her head around Snowball's turbulent past, or the fact that he was Queenie's older brother, but he had clearly cemented a place in Jimmy and Patsy's heart.

'That's been the only good thing to have come out of Mum's disappearance,' Patsy said, smiling and waving over to them. 'Discovering Alfie's our uncle and having the freedom now to get to know him. He's such a lovely man.'

'Shame your mum could never see that,' Lou sighed.

'I know,' Patsy replied. 'If she could only have forgiven, she could've stepped into the present, rather than being anchored in the past. Forgiveness is everything, I reckon, and that's something Mum ultimately couldn't allow into her heart. Her sense of bitterness, like her grief, swamped her in the finish.'

The trio fell silent as they digested Patsy's words, gazing out over the square, at Alfie and Jimmy sowing the tentative seeds of a new relationship, at Mr Mahoney keeping a watchful eye on the daughter that wasn't biologically his but whom he adored all the same.

'Forgiveness is everything,' Esther murmured. 'I like that.'

Lou's eye was drawn to the woman she loved, who had stuck with her through thick and thin. Martha was busy carrying out plates of sandwiches and helping the women of the square set up the wedding breakfast buffet in its centre.

Maybe she should forgive her father and Nancy for judging her so harshly for loving a woman? It wasn't really their fault. Let's face it, how many others had gladly stood in condemnation of her relationship with Martha? When it came to same-sex relationships, there were no polarities of light and shade, just an ocean of ignorance.

If nothing else, forgiving them would put her one step closer to accepting the loss of her sisters. She had to hope that one day they would come looking for her, intrigued over the big sister they would have only the vaguest memories of, and she could set them straight. It was her only hope.

'Right you lot!' Nell's voice ricocheted round the square. 'Don't just stand there like a tit in a trance, there's bread what needs buttering here.'

'Better go,' Lou grinned, carefully handing back little Lulu into her mother's arms. 'Duty calls. Come on, Patsy.'

The wedding ceremony in the Shoot's church was short and sweet, just as Nell and Alfie wanted. There were no readings or bridesmaids, there was to be 'none of that malarkey, not at my age' as Nell had said. And it being a rationed wartime wedding, there was to be no confetti (it was now illegal to manufacture it), cake (who wanted iced cardboard?) or presents. But despite all that, as the congregation spilt out into the summer sunshine, they all agreed it was the best wedding they had ever attended.

It had all the ingredients of a truly great East End wedding. Everyone had raided their larder, pooled their rations and pitched in with whatever they could contribute. At least two pianos were rolled out on to the cobbles. Mr Mahoney played the spoons – well, two old bits of hammered metal he'd fashioned into spoons from his time in the Nazi prison camp. The Lavender Girls entertained everyone with a peppy Andrew Sisters number and Mrs Barnett, who fancied herself the next Vera Lynn, sang 'We'll Meet Again'. The guests roared with laughter when Lou stuck two rolled-up napkins in her ears.

'You saucy cow,' Mrs Barnett said, screeching with laughter.

And then Nell was rising and tapping a spoon against her glass.

'I know it's not customary for the bride to make a speech, but I got something to say.'

'That ain't like you, Auntie,' Little Irene heckled.

Everyone laughed good-naturedly, including Nell. Suddenly, a distant drone had everyone looking to the skies as one for uninvited guests. But the skies were clear, only a few indolent clouds piercing the blue.

'It's all right,' yelled down Mr Mahoney, who was posted up on the church roof. 'It's a motor vehicle on the Broadway.'

'Don't even think about it, I don't wanna be a doodlebug bride,' Nell said, pointing a warning finger overhead.

'I just want to say I never thought I'd see myself getting married again at my age, and to such a good man.'

'Hear hear!' chorused the guests.

'I look out at all our beautiful Yardley girls and to me, my own youth seems like yesterday. Except, I bet none of you youngsters can imagine me as anything other than an old battleaxe.'

'Never, Auntie,' Lou called jokingly.

'When you grow old and your hair grows grey, life gets more difficult. Then the war comes along and smacks you about a bit more. Ageing is a little bit like getting slowly rubbed out – all your achievements, your strengths, all pale into invisibility.

'But,' she eyeballed the now silent crowd, 'one of the strengths of the Shoot has been our great community. We have stood and fallen together. When this war's over, and someone finally tops Hitler, please God, let's keep it that way. Let's keep this community allotment and restaurant going, let's carry on eating, loving and living as one. God knows, me and my husband have lost more than our fair share of loved ones, as indeed have many of you. But we've kept going because we've got each other. So, a toast,' she raised her port and lemon, 'to neighbours and family. May they always stay one and the same.'

'To neighbours and family,' Lou chorused, realising in that moment that this ramshackled community down the Shoot were her family now. She gazed about the wonky, dusty square with its patched-up houses and the allotment, church and communal dining hall at its matriarchal heart. All of it seemed to be bound together by the long garlands of faded bunting.

Nell sat down and Alfie placed one hand over hers. No words were needed. Lou knew how much trauma the old man had lived with over the years, how frozen he had been in the past. Julia reckoned he'd suffered a total nervous collapse when Queenie had shown up, and looking back, they wondered what more they could all have done to reach him.

It would take a while to untangle still, separate the memory from reality, but she had a hunch that, with Nell's love and acceptance, Alfie would heal. Tending to his beloved allotment, teasing life from the soil instead of fruitlessly searching for the dead, would help him slowly recover. Maybe that's what working in nature was doing for her? One thing was for sure: she would never again look at the vagrants sleeping rough in Itchy Park the same way. If it hadn't been for Nell, she too would have ended up homeless. It was the finest of lines between respectability and destitution.

'And now our Lavender Girl Patsy's agreed to sing a special song,' Nell went on.

Patsy stood up and, after blowing a kiss to the newlyweds, sang a faultless rendition of 'Shine on Victory Moon' that had more than one guest dabbing at their eye. Her voice was strong and emotive, capturing perfectly the mood of hope and fear down the Shoot.

So spellbound were the bride, groom and guests, they

didn't see a familiar figure emerge from Cat's Alley. But Lou did, and she braced herself for the reaction.

The pretty young dark-haired lady placed her case down gently on the cobbles before covering Nell's eyes with her hands.

'Surprise!'

Nell's face was an absolute picture as she wheeled round. 'Lily!' she gasped.

'Hello, Mum. Sorry I missed the actual wedding, but the crossing took longer than expected, it's a long way from America.'

'Oh my days . . .' she stuttered. 'W-what are you doing here?'

'Coming to spend some time with my lovely mum and stepfather,' she grinned, pulling Alfie into their hug. 'It's good to be back.'

Nell Gunn was, for once, rendered speechless at the surprise appearance of her eldest daughter Lily, the Stratford success story who had emigrated to New York to work for the Yardley salon on Fifth Avenue.

'Anyone else ever seen my mum lost for words?' Lily called out.

'NO!' chorused back every single guest. Glasses were charged and Lou had a hunch the wedding party would now go on long into the night.

She was still smiling at the reunion when Martha tapped her on the shoulder, her face grave.

'Martha, what's wrong?'

'Lily's not the only surprise visitor. There's someone to see you, she's in the church.'

'Who?'

'You better go and see.'

Lou walked into the Shoot's tiny church. After the dazzling sunshine, the dim light inside was so dark, she could barely see. Splotches of yellow and red burst across her eyes as she walked blindly up the aisle. A woman was sitting on the front pew, with her back to Lou.

'Can I help you?'

The woman turned.

'Hello, Louise, I heard you'd be here today. How you keeping?'

'N-Nancy.' Lou's mind stumbled to the worst conclusion. 'The girls, what's wrong?'

'They're all fine, don't worry, a neighbour's looking after them. Please sit down.'

She patted the cold wooden bench next to her and, warily, Lou sat down.

'We need to talk.'

'What about? You made it clear at Dad's funeral the time for talking had passed.'

Nancy had lost weight since Lou had last seen her and her face seemed to have folded in on itself.

'I made a dreadful mistake in trusting your father.'

Lou snorted. 'A fancy woman come out the woodwork?'

'No, nothing like that. They say you know where you stand with a thief, but you never know where you stand with a liar.' She sniffed. 'In my opinion, they're both as bad as each other.'

Lou knew her father was a liar, but a thief?

'What are you saying?'

'It's been a nightmare since we buried your father, Louise,' she said shakily. 'I should've taken that rocket dropping nearby as the bad omen it was.'

The air between them thickened.

'I got a visit from a detective soon after we arrived in Norfolk. Seems to think your father was embezzling funds from the council's Wings for Victory fund. Hundreds of pounds' worth.'

Lou was staggered. 'How did they find out?'

'There was a periodical check into the fund by inspectors and the shortfall came to light. They were on the point of arrest when he was killed.'

'Was it true, do you think?' she asked, already knowing in her heart the answer.

'Well I don't like to speak ill of the dead, but the detective seemed to think they had enough evidence to put him away for a long time. And I just can't explain how he came by the money to put the down payment on the house in Norfolk.'

She looked at Lou, her pale eyes watery.

'I never had anything to do with it, you must believe me. I've lost everything.'

'Don't worry,' said Lou, thinking of the lies he told at the time of her mum's death, 'I know all too well how duplicitous my father could be. What I don't understand is why none of this has been in the papers?'

'Council wanted it kept hushed up for morale. There'd be an outcry. Him being a former mayor, all his awards and what have you.'

Lou couldn't keep the bitterness from her voice as she thought of the unnecessary deaths of Renee and all those hundreds of other East Enders in the council rest centre during the Blitz.

'Stands to reason. West Ham Council are getting pretty good at sweeping scandal under the carpet. When we move the carpet, we'll be sneezing for a month!'

A tense silence fell between them.

'I'm so sorry, Louise,' Nancy said, twisting a handkerchief between her fingers.

'What for?'

'For believing the horrible things your father told me about you and for not letting you see your sisters.'

Lou's first reaction was to bite back in anger. Sorry wouldn't mop up all the tears she'd wept, nor vanquish the poison, vitriol and condemnation. Then Patsy's words drifted through her mind, curating themselves in her heart:

Forgiveness is everything.

'S'right Nancy, you weren't the first woman he lied to. So what now?'

'I asked your sisters the other day who they'd like to live with.'

'And?' Lou felt her blood begin to pulse in her ears.

'They miss you, Lou. They miss Stratford. They're scared and confused and I don't know what to do for the best. It's not as easy bringing up kids as I thought.'

She started to cry.

'I'm not a bad person, Nancy,' Lou said softly. 'There's no one who could love those girls more than me.'

Nancy pressed the heels of her hand into her eyes and nodded.

'Then they should be with their sister.'

For a while, Lou felt incapable of speech, but common sense cautioned her.

'It'll take a while to sort, I'll have to explain why I need to be exempt from war work, that could take some time, and find us lodgings. I have to return to Scotland tomorrow and . . .'

'I know, I know, and don't worry, the girls'll be safe with me until you're ready to take them.'

She pressed a piece of paper into her hand. 'This is my address, come and visit on your next leave, write to them. They'll be thrilled to bits to hear from you.'

Lou placed her hand over Nancy's in silent gratitude.

'I'd like to stay in their lives in some way after they're back with you, would that be possible?' Nancy asked.

'Of course. I don't blame you.'

'That's more than I deserve.' She made to stand up. 'I must go, I've a train to catch.'

'Won't you stay, come and have a drink?' Outside, the piano-playing and singing was growing louder.

'The party's just warming up,' Lou smiled, jerking a thumb towards the church door.

'That's so kind but I really must be on my way.' She bent down, placed a little dry kiss on Lou's cheek. 'God bless.' Then the small, broken woman scurried from the church.

Lou looked up at the altar. A shaft of light hit the crucifix, and it lit up like burnished gold.

'Did you hear that, Mum?' she whispered reverently. 'The girls are coming home.'

That night, after blackout fell and the sky was blistered with stars, Martha took Lou by the hand and they slipped down the Cut for five minutes alone. The moon was a huge luminous disc, shimmering off the greasy surface of the canal.

Martha's lips met Lou's and she felt a shiver run through her. She could hardly bring herself to believe that happiness was within her reach.

'This could be it for us, Lou,' Martha murmured, reading her mind. 'I want to help you raise the girls, far away from here, where we can start over. Be who we want to be.'

Lou wanted to believe in nothing more, but the memory of Queenie waited in the knife-edged shadows like Banquo's ghost. After all she had endured, she couldn't completely allow herself to believe in a normal life.

'What's that?'

'Don't be so jumpy,' Martha scolded, but Lou pressed her finger to Martha's lips to silence her.

A muffled sound came from about a hundred yards up the towpath. Lou's heart smashed against her ribs as she edged along the path.

There on the concrete steps leading down to the Cut, under a *Players Please!* cigarette hoarding was a slight girl, with her knees drawn up under her chin.

At the sound of Lou and Martha's steps, she glanced up, her eyes glistening with tears.

'Patsy, what's wrong?'

'I'll see you back at the Shoot,' Martha said tactfully, melting into the night.

'Budge up,' Lou ordered, lighting two fags and handing one to Patsy. 'Here you are, you look like you could use a gasper. Blue?'

Patsy nodded.

'I didn't buy that nonsense earlier about moving on.'

'Nell told me she'd written to Blue at his base, before he moved, to tell him she was getting married today. She even asked him to give her away. She was hoping he'd turn up. Right up to the last minute.'

'And so were you?'

Patsy nodded and drew on the cigarette, sending skeins of smoke drifting across the water. 'I've been looking for him all day, waiting, hoping that at any minute he'd come through the alley. But he didn't show so . . .'

She tailed off as more tears consumed her.

'I feel like I'll spend the rest of my life looking for him, hoping he's still alive.'

Lou glanced up at the huge milk-coloured moon overhead.

'He'll be somewhere, looking at the very same moon, thinking the same thing about you, mark me.'

'Except, I've a horrible feeling in here that he's not alive no more.' She touched her chest. 'I read somewhere that the USAAF raised its mission count to thirty last year, so what are the odds, Lou? Really.' She stubbed out her cigarette on the step. 'How many second chances can one man have?'

'Oh Patsy,' Lou wept, folding the shattered girl in her arms. There was nothing to be said. Love in wartime was the most fleeting, fragile kind there was.

Patsy curled herself into a ball, as if her pain was physically crushing her into the ground, and let out a gut-wrenching sob.

'I miss him so much. Why didn't I just show up at the cafe that night, tell him how much I truly loved him? If I'd have accepted his proposal he may have fought harder, he may have been here today.'

'You can't know that, Patsy,' Lou soothed.

'No, but at the very least I could've given him one last kiss.'

She looked up suddenly, still hugging her knees. The look of bewilderment and fear in her eyes hollowed Lou out. 'But I didn't, and now's he gone.'

24

Patsy

Ghosts everywhere. At times, Patsy felt like she walked among the dead more than she did the living. Two wars had decimated her family. Her father, the half-sister she never knew, Blue... her mother wasn't dead, but she may as well be. Patsy hadn't heard a whisper from her. True to her word, she had vanished, so mentally Patsy had consigned her to the grim roll call.

Last night at the pictures with the girls, Patsy had fled in tears after seeing the Pathé News footage of walking skeletons liberated from the Nazi concentration camps. She had looked into their eyes to see what horrors they must have witnessed and saw only blank hollows staring back from the screen.

Gas chambers. Piles of bodies. Children reduced to shuffling bones.

The unfathomable scale and depravity of the Nazi plan had been laid bare. It should have made Blue's death feel justified, but somehow, it had only compounded her pain.

She wasn't alone in her rage at seeing images from Auschwitz and Bergen-Belsen. Yesterday morning, Harry Tunnocks, a dispatch driver at Yardley's, whose son was being held prisoner in Japan, had tried to set fire to the German POW camp down Carpenters Road. 'Why should those Nazis sit there growing fat in British camps?' he'd said. Miss Rayson had brought him to his senses, pointing out that revenge wouldn't solve anything.

People's worlds had fallen apart and, naturally, the human desire for retribution was overpowering. But Miss Rayson was right. They *all* had to work out a way to piece themselves together, find a way back to the person they'd been before the war.

Last week, Patsy, Jimmy, Alfie, Nell and the Lavender Girls had held a peculiar little ceremony in the allotment. Esther had visited the photographic studio in Poplar and explained the story to the photographer, who in turn had given her the portrait of Queenie and Pearl. How queer it had felt to Patsy to see her mum, so young and brimming with pride, clutching that little red-haired girl on her lap. She had been forced to reappraise her own mother, accept that she only knew a fraction of who she was really was, or had been.

The photo had been buried in a special part of the allotment Nell called the memorial garden, along with the button from Pearl's coat that Alfie had carried all these years.

Pearl had been killed by a bomb dropped on a school in the first war. Renee by a bomb dropped on a school in the second. This grim fact united them all and helped to join the dots of Nell and Alfie's relationship.

They had hoped there was some symbolism in burying the link to Alfie's painful past, that her uncle would stop punishing himself. Though Patsy had a sneaking suspicion that being around Jimmy and baby Lulu was what was really helping to bring him back to life.

Where the keepsakes were buried, they had planted orange nasturtiums and lilac sweet peas. Bright and pretty flowers could stand as a reminder to the atrocity of Pearl's death. But there was nothing Patsy could do, and nowhere she could go to mourn Blue. A shop doorway, a tatty hotel room or the corner table of a cafe could hardly serve as a memorial. No, she would have to carry her memories of their blistering encounters in her heart and mind.

'Are you sad?' came a small voice from the doorway, making Patsy jump.

'Jimmy,' she said. 'Come here darlin'.' He came and curled up in her lap, his warm, sticky hands wrapping round the back of her neck.

'Uncle Alfie says we're to go downstairs as the street party's starting soon.'

With a jolt, she realised he'd lost another tooth and somewhere along the way, his face had slimmed out. In and among all her trauma, her little brother had been busily growing and she'd scarcely noticed his childhood flashing past.

'Oh, Jimmy,' she sobbed, hugging him tight. His skin was so warm and biscuity smelling, and she buried her face in his curly dark hair.

'Will I have to go back to the country to live with Mr and Mrs Smythe?' he asked, alarmed at her tears.

'No, not ever,' she said fiercely, and then a darker thought slithered over her. 'Did Mr Smthye . . .' she swallowed. 'Did he ever come into your bedroom?'

Jimmy shook his head.

'Promise?'

'Pinky promise,' he said, holding out his little finger. 'Can we go to the party now? I'm starving.'

She started to laugh. 'Of course we can little man. Do you know how much I love you?'

'The whole wide world?'

'That's right, and the universe too.'

'So how comes you were crying?'

'I'm happy is all. Happy 'cause the war is over.'

He nodded seriously.

'I can't replace Mum, I know that, but I'll try my hardest.'

'Does that mean I don't have to go back to school again?'

'Don't push your luck pal,' she said, poking him in the ribs and making him laugh.

'Come on, I think I can smell a bonfire getting lit, which means . . .'

'Baked potatoes!' roared Jimmy, slithering off her lap and charging headlong down the stairs. Oh, for the resilience and hunger of youth.

Patsy pulled open her drawer and surveyed her treasured lipsticks. Victory Red would certainly be apt, but no. Burnt Sugar? A pretty pink shade Elizabeth Arden had created to accessorise with khaki – definitely not. She doubted anyone would ever want to wear khaki again. There was only one that would do on a day such as this. Yardley's Renegade Renee. A red as eye-popping and bold as the woman it was named after. She wound the stubby tube up and carefully slid it over her lips, pressing them together before dabbing at the corners of her mouth. Next, she pinned her mother's brooch on the space over her heart.

Behind her, suddenly and inexplicably, she felt the presence of others. Women the world over, grieving, fighting down losses, painting on their faces and finding the strength to put one foot in front of the other. Women just like her. She would be all right. She would damn well have to be.

Patsy missed Blue with a pain so fierce at times it left her speechless. She would never forget the man who burnt through life like a flame, but she had Jimmy, Alfie and Nell. Her friends. Plus she was loving being involved in the theatre again with the Yardley Follies. She had life! Yes, she had much to be thankful for. The best way she could honour such a remarkable man was by living her life to its fullest, seizing it in the way he had done. She looked into the vertiginous chasm of her grief and tried to imagine a time when she wouldn't miss Blue or regret not showing up at the cafe. Maybe that would never come. But it was better to live alongside it. Better to just keep waking up each day and finding something to be thankful for, no matter how small the joy.

Patsy put the tube of lipstick back in the drawer and went down the stairs to join her friends.

Outside, after a tremendous thunderstorm in the night, the Shoot had woken to cerulean blue skies on this momentous national holiday. What scenes!

The Lavender Girls were out in force, stringing up bunting from every upstairs window ledge and gas lamp. Flags saved from two coronations and a jubilee bedecked the square in a blaze of colour. All the women of the Shoot were out helping to prepare for the biggest street party the square had ever seen.

'Come on, Auntie Nell,' Patsy called in through the open kitchen window, which for the first time wasn't covered in anti-blast tape.

'Just gotta get me windows gleaming now I can see out the bleedin' things,' she huffed. Her whole body wobbled as she polished the glass with vinegar and vigour. In the background, her favourite wartime companion was broadcasting his show on the wireless – the Radio Doctor's fixation with regular bowel movements mirrored Nell's.

'Careful, there'll be no glass left the way you're going at it,' chuckled Alfie as he walked past carrying old bits of timber he'd salvaged for the bonfire.

'I just can't seem to remove the stains.' Nell worked at the glass, her fingers white from the strain.

Alfie put down the timber and placed his hands on Nell's shoulders.

'Come on, love. Sit down and rest for a bit.'

Patsy knew Nell's mind was, like so many others on their first morning in peace, half here and half with the ones she'd lost. By rights, Nell's daughter Renee should have been outside larking about with all the other Lavender Girls. *By rights . . .*

'I'll take this, Uncle, and you make Nell a cup of tea.' She took the wood and left the two alone.

Outside, she joined Jimmy and all the other kids in stacking up wood for the bonfire.

It wasn't just Nell sprucing up. The whole Shoot was attempting to cast off nearly six years of horror and gloom.

Every window was filled with pictures of the King and Queen, red, white and blue streamers fluttered from the allotment, and the trestle tables were being set up for as much food as could be mustered. Baby Lulu was fast asleep in her pram outside number 12, while Esther and Walter helped make sarnies.

'Oi, Patsy, go and get dozy drawers to help!' shouted Joanie from the top of a ladder, as she attempted to pin up yet more bunting.

Patsy walked over to where Little Irene was sitting with her back to the allotment shed, her nose deep in a book.

'What you reading?'

Irene looked up.

'Got me hands on this mucky book everyone's on about, *Forever Amber*. Banned in fourteen American states for being too pornographic. Full of glamour, sex and scandal, it is. T'rific stuff!'

She sighed and wiped her nose. 'I'm hoping some of it will rub off like.'

'You nit,' Patsy chuckled, leaving Little Irene to her potboiler. Even the end of the war couldn't deter the factory girl from her endless quest for glamour.

Patsy looked around affectionately at the rest of the factory girls she now saw on a daily basis.

Joanie, Joycie, Betty, Little Irene and Mavis, like her and Esther, had suffered their own losses on the homefront, but never failed each day to brighten up her life with their own brand of humour and courage. She loved them for it.

'Look who it is!' yelled Joanie suddenly, squinting into the sun from the top of her ladder.

Out of Cat's Alley emerged some familiar faces.

'Lou!' screamed Esther, looking up from the mountain of bread she was buttering. It was Lou and Martha, laden down with suitcases, and trailing behind them were the five Button sisters.

The Lavender Girls and Lou fell on each other in a tangle of limbs. It was a while before Patsy could squeeze in to give Lou and Martha a cuddle.

'Please don't tell me you're going today of all days?' Esther said.

'Sorry, Est, we need to collect the keys from the landlord tomorrow.'

'So you're really doing it?' Patsy ventured. Lou shot a secret smile at Martha.

'Yep, we've been saving up our wages and we've scraped enough to take over the running of a little B&B in Brighton.'

Everyone oohed and aahed at the thought of living by the beach.

'It's not on the seafront, a couple of roads back,' Martha interjected, 'and it needs a fair bit of work to bring it up to scratch after the bombings . . .'

'But it'll be our little slice of paradise,' Lou smiled, unable to wipe the look of adoration from her face as she gazed at Martha.

'Are you excited to live by the sea, girls?' Joycie asked Lou's little sisters.

'Not many,' Elsie replied. 'Lou's said if I work really hard to get into grammar school, I can carry on and she'll help with the books and uniform.'

'I want her to have the opportunities I never got,' Lou said, putting her arm around her sister's shoulder.

'Now, that is good news,' said Julia, who had wandered over.

'You got your own hands quite full by the looks of it,' Martha remarked, pointing to the two skinny girls whose hands Julia was holding.

'Who are you then?' Lou asked them brightly.

'They don't speak English,' Julia replied, gently smoothing down the youngest one's hair. 'They're Dutch, from the liberated countries. I'm looking after them until someone can find their parents.' By their dreadful grey pallor and wary eyes, they had seen things no child in Stratford had.

One of the girls had an entire leg in plaster.

'Poor tot no sooner gets here than she got caught up in the wreckage of a rocket attack in Whitechapel. She got an infection which most likely would have killed her except she was given penicillin,' Julia explained. 'Previously it's only been available to the military, but now it's more widely available, so that's one good thing to have come out of the rockets.'

'Sure Nell's cooking will build her back up too,' Lou remarked.

'You can count on it,' she laughed. 'And now tell me, Lou, is this the right move for you? Sometimes our problems can't be solved by moving to a new town,' Julia said knowingly.

'I understand what you're saying,' Lou replied carefully. 'But I – *we* – think a fresh start is what's needed. There are too many painful memories in Stratford. No one knows us in Brighton, so we can start peacetime with a clean sheet.'

'Plus, it will be a wonderful place for the girls to live,' Martha said.

'I think it's a great idea,' Patsy said.

'Thanks, Pats,' Lou said, reaching over to squeeze her hand. 'I just hope Mum approves.'

The sudden ringing of the Shoot's church bells took everyone by surprise, for no one had heard them since they were silenced in the summer of 1940. The noise pealed out over the square and an impromptu cheer rang out.

'Think you can take that as a sign,' Esther smiled, her eyes shining. 'Oh, I never thought church bells could ever sound so good!'

'Right, Lou, we best be off then,' said Martha glancing at her watch.

Patsy felt overwhelmed as she hugged her old friends goodbye.

'Ta-ta, beautiful girl,' Lou whispered in her ear. 'Never give up on love.'

'Can I visit?'

'I'm counting on it. And make sure to tell us next time you're performing with the Yardley Follies. We'll all be there cheering you on in the front row.'

Patsy smiled, suddenly remembering something her mother used to say in the old days, before grief and anger consumed her.

'See you later, alligator.'

'In a while, crocodile,' Lou grinned back.

The old saying cheered her.

Small joys.

And just like that, Lou Button was gone, and this time, Patsy knew she wouldn't return. The Lavender Girls threaded their arms round each other and watched as their old pal went off in search of her bright tomorrow.

By mid-afternoon, it was fair to say everyone was pretty pie-eyed, drunk on watered-down beer and black market rum.

The dancing and singing was almost frenzied as joy and relief exploded. The milkman had lent his cart as a platform and the Lavender Girls were all up doing the can-can, while the men of the square stoked up the mother of all bonfires. Walter and Esther sat in the shade of the allotment sharing a private joke. Baby Lulu was fast asleep in her pram, oblivious to this historic day.

Patsy noticed Mrs Barnett, usually the life and soul of these things, sitting quietly on the steps to the church.

'Oi, Pats, get up here and give us a song!' yelled Betty.

'In a bit,' she called, walking over to the church.

'You all right, Mrs B? Can I fetch you anything?'

'Just sitting it out for a while is all. I still got a son out in Burma. The war ain't ended there yet, so don't feel right to celebrate. Not that I begrudge the others mind, but it's nice to have time out with your thoughts. I feel closer to him that way.'

Patsy knew exactly what she meant and, in that moment, felt the same burning desire to do just that. Once she'd asked Nell to keep an eye out for Jimmy, she slipped away. He was so busy tucking into jam tarts (eight at the last count) and dancing round a burning effigy of Hitler, he wouldn't even notice she was gone. She had no conscious awareness of where she was going. Her feet moved as if of their own accord.

The streets of Stratford seemed to be having a competition for who could have the highest bonfire. Even telephone kiosks had been raided for their directories to heap up on the fires. Patsy couldn't blame people. After so many years of darkness, it was good to see the light. Music burst from pianos, accordions and radiograms – anything people could turn into an instrument was being played.

Stratford had spontaneously erupted and Patsy smiled at the sights. Bells pealed, car horns tooted and all the East End girls looked so ravishing with red, white and blue ribbons streaming from their hair. People were going mad with joy.

On Stratford High Street, she could scarcely move for the crush of people waiting outside the town hall for the prime minister's 3 p.m. speech, which was due to be relayed by giant speakers specially rigged for the occasion.

She pressed on, past the parish church, the sounds of 'Land of Hope and Glory' pouring from its open doors. They were holding continuous services all day. Patsy hesitated, unsure of whether to go in, but then she remembered another place that had offered hope and sanctuary.

It took her a while to remember where it had been, but eventually she found it. Canning Town, close to the docks, was even noisier than Stratford.

All the ships in the docks, from the largest container ship to the smallest tug, were sounding their horns and flashing swooping V signs through the sky.

Patsy cut down Bethell Avenue, smiling at the nuns waving flags from their badly bombed convent, the noises growing louder as she drew closer to the docks. Finally, she reached Tidal Basin Road. The buildings were so badly bombed, she scarcely recognised anything.

In front of a punch-drunk shipping office stood the place once occupied by the Coloured Men's Institute, until it had been demolished in 1930 to make way for road widening. Community eviscerated in the name of traffic flow.

She closed her eyes and allowed memories to seep in through the cracks.

A tall, smiling man opening the door and welcoming her in. Her hand dwarfed in her father's.

She could only have been four, certainly no older. They weren't fully formed memories; more like snapshots, fragments of a contented life she had once known. She pictured them now as photos in a black-and-white scrapbook.

Dark-skinned sailors everywhere, just like her dad, sitting at tables writing, playing billiards and reading the paper. Every tide brought coloured men in, every tide sent them out again, but for a brief time, it represented sanctuary from racism.

In her mind, she opened the door to a modest canteen,

and there was her mother, alongside other white women, serving up plates of hot spicy food, wavy red hair framing her like a halo in the light. Her father's arms were wrapped around her. Kissing her, protecting her, holding the pain over Pearl at bay.

Their love had been all-consuming. Certainly enough for her mum to go against her own family's wishes. They must have used that love like a shield against the outside world.

Why was she here, trying to walk down memory lane to find it bombed beyond recognition? Because she wanted to make sense of her mother's secret past, the secret that hadn't faded but festered.

Patsy saw it all so suddenly, with blistering clarity.

The death of her father, the stabilising factor in Queenie's life, had shaken free all the old grief and it had come pouring out of her, her anger unleashed, more potent than ever before. Patsy began to understand, to enumerate the complications.

How must her mum have felt when she set eyes on her brother, whom she'd not seen since the bomb had split them apart all those years ago?

Where was she now? Wherever it was, Patsy prayed she'd found some peace. And what of poor Alfie? A lifetime running, hiding, trying to obliterate the memories, until his past had caught up with him. A sense of understanding dawned and with it, a visceral desire to help heal him.

A crowd of sailors snaked past, clutching bottles of beer, each hand in hand with a girl. The girls wore poppies and cornflowers in their hair, ribbons round their bare ankles. Their joy was unconfined as they sang 'Happy V Day to You'.

Just like that, the door to memory lane slammed shut in her face and Patsy blinked, snapping back to 1945.

The group paused while one stopped to do up his shoelace. One of the sailors took the opportunity to kiss his girl, doing so so passionately, the flowers fell from her hair. As Patsy watched them, a sharp burst of emotion lodged in her throat.

When the war is over, I'm going to kiss you again, Patsy, right here on these steps.

The words resonated in her head, powerful as a vapour.

'Cheer up, love, didn't no one tell you? The war's over.'

A sailor was tugging at her hand. 'Come with us. Come and kick your heels up girl.'

'What? No . . . No. I-I can't.'

'Why, you got some place else to go?'

'Yes, yes I have,' she replied, the words surprising even her.

And then Patsy was running, bumping into crowds in her haste to get to Piccadilly. This was madness. Blue was gone. Why was she running for a date with a ghost? But she'd made him a promise hadn't she? And even if he wasn't actually here anymore, it was dishonourable not to keep her word.

Tears slid down her cheeks as she ran. The memory of his kisses, his touch, the intimacy they had shared in that shabby little hotel room on the eve of D-Day – it all seared through her, propelling her forward.

The crowds in Soho were even crazier and, at one point, Patsy found herself jammed solid, moved along by the sheer weight of bodies.

'Kiss me, beautiful,' begged a soldier over the roar of voices, but Patsy managed to pull herself out of the stream and, with some effort, manoeuvred herself into Great Windmill Street. The queue for the theatre was the longest Patsy had ever seen.

She stood by the stage door gasping for breath. Her frazzled brain was working out which route to take to avoid the crush, when she heard a familiar voice: 'Patsy sweetheart, you're back!'

Kitty was leaning jauntily against the doorframe, wearing nothing but a white silk robe and an enormous ostrich feather plume.

'Kitty,' Patsy cried, overwhelmed at the sight of her old theatre friend.

'What are you doing here? Looks like you're needed on stage.'

'B company on at the moment. I've just popped out for a quick gasper, darling. Manning the door while Ben nips to the lav. Absolute madness here today, back-to-back free shows for servicemen and women. You heard about Mrs Henderson?'

Patsy nodded. She'd read of her death at the end of 1944 in the paper.

'So sad.'

Kitty blew out a stream of blue smoke, which set her ostrich feathers quivering.

'At least she got to see her beloved theatre make history. Do you know what her last words were? "If I die, the show must not stop on my account."'

She struck a dramatic pose.

'And so we dance on.'

Patsy laughed at her exuberance. 'God I miss you.' She stared longingly backstage at the dark, scruffy corridors, at the promise of what was beyond. She missed the sweat and greasepaint, but mostly she missed the girls.

'So come back, darling.'

Patsy shook her head.

'I know, I know. Family first.' A bell sounded from within the theatre.

'Look here, I really must go, but come for supper,' said Kitty.

'Tricky with Jimmy, why don't you come to me?'

'I've never been further East than Aldgate. What fun!'

She ground out her cigarette. 'Ooh, while I remember, Ben wanted to get a message to you.'

'Any idea what?'

'None whatsoever, but it seemed to be terrifically important. So long.'

She vanished into the darkness in a swish of silk. The door closed.

Patsy took a deep breath and ventured back into the fray. The encounter with Kitty had taken the wind out of her sails, and suddenly she felt unsure of herself. Alone. Vulnerable. She was part of the crowd, but somehow separate to it all. How could she feel this lonely in the midst of so many people? When she smiled, she felt like a bad actress, imitating a feeling that ought to have been cascading through her. But she could find no joy, no common ground with the crowds she mingled with. She couldn't even stand to look at the cafe, *their* cafe, turning away as she walked past.

Patsy was jostled and bumped about like a tiny pebble in an incoming tide of human emotion. She had never seen British people behave in such an unrestrained way. It was extraordinary. Conga lines, glassy-eyed kissing as strangers locked lips, noisy, ribald singing.

At 6 p.m., the crowds thinned, a great surge of people swarming in the direction of Whitehall as rumours spread that Churchill was to be speaking.

For the first time, she could see the steps to Eros, and the boarded-up pedestal. She stepped up tentatively, squinting against the sun as she stared up at the empty plinth and the seamless blue skies beyond.

A scuffle next to her as an officer from the tank corps scrabbled up the stacked-up sandbags and leapt on top of the empty pedestal. He stood on tiptoe and aimed an imaginary bow. The crowd roared their approval.

'Oi Eros, where's Aphrodite?' yelled an Australian voice.

Soon he was joined by a paratrooper in a maroon beret, who then hauled up a young blonde woman in a very tight pair of green slacks.

Patsy cried out. Suddenly, she was flying. A pair of strong hands had hooked under her armpits and raised her up off her feet. She felt like she'd been thrown in icy cold waters, her breath coming in short sharp gasps as she clung to the paratrooper on top of the plinth. Coming here had been a mistake. Grief had derailed her. She should be back down the Shoot with her brother and friends, not chasing the nostalgia of the past. The crowds of Piccadilly Circus began to spin, the view vertiginous. Faces, voices, laughter spinning round and round like a child's top. The bells of St James grew louder and louder in her head.

The paratrooper plonked his cap on her head, pulled her into an embrace.

'Patsy . . . Patsy . . .' A voice was calling her. An American voice. She whipped round so fast, the paratrooper nearly fell.

'Steady on . . .'

Her eyes roamed the crowds, but she couldn't locate the voice. Hysteria started to beat in her breast, she was going mad. She had heard him, hadn't she? She had heard Blue calling her name.

'I say, are you all right?' asked the officer, spotting her distress.

'I'm looking for an American . . . I . . . I need to find him . . .' She was weeping now, aware of how barmy she must've looked.

'I thought I saw him.' She put her hand on her forehead. 'I-I thought . . .'

'That one?' asked the paratrooper, pointing his finger to an airman who had climbed up a nearby lamp post.

She turned. Something cold crawled up her spine. Her whole body started to thrum.

'Patsy . . . Patsy, I'm going to get you!'

'Blue!' she screamed, a sob tearing through her. 'Blue!'

She turned to the officer. 'You have to help me. Help me to get down!'

He let rip an ear-shredding whistle to the crowds. 'This lady needs to get to that GI over there,' he yelled. Blue was shinning down the lamp post.

And then Patsy was being helped down, invisible hands supporting her as she was lowered down off the pedestal then hoisted high up over the crowds, bumped from hand to hand, surfing over the tops of heads.

She closed her eyes for fear of falling, and his voice came to her in the darkness. *Patsy. Patsy.*

With a sudden rush, she came tumbling down, delivered into a familiar pair of arms.

She looked up. 'I-is it really you?'

Her heart smashed against her ribs. His eyes were huge. Pale. Haunted and brimming with love.

'Patsy,' he wept, gripping her face, and at the touch of his fingers she shuddered.

'Oh God, Blue . . .' She ran her hands over his cheeks, his lips, his eyebrows. 'You're alive. *You're alive.*'

He crushed his lips to hers. The relief was scalding. Patsy was aware of nothing else: not the jubilant applause of the crowds, the pop of a press photographer's flashbulb. Just the familiar feel of Blue's lips, the smell of him. Her head was telling her this was madness, things like this didn't happen, but her heart sang out. Some things are just too much to compute and her brain simply wouldn't form the words to convey what she was feeling.

Tears slid from her eyes, soaking into her hair.

'I went to the Shoot,' he said, drawing back. 'I missed you, then I went to The Windmill, but Ben hadn't seen you, then our cafe . . .' He gripped her shoulders. 'I thought I'd never find you . . .'

She tried to drink in every detail of his face. His eyes were like bruises, his cheekbones gaunt, the bright blueness of those eyes dulled, like a stream gone murky.

'Come on,' he urged. 'Let's get out of here.'

She gripped his hand tightly, reaching over and closing the other hand over his knuckles just in case, and they began to run.

On the middle of Westminster Bridge, they felt like they were suspended in time as the ancient river flowed thickly beneath them, the two of them, alone at last, marooned on their own island in the dusk. The evening was as warm as midsummer and London's shabbiness was hidden by the rows of blazing bonfires along the banks.

For a long time, they clung to one another, for fear that they might melt away, just staring at one another, hopeless with relief and love. Patsy felt as if she were floating above herself, looking down on the rooftops, the bonfires, the bridge and a wartime couple embracing.

'Where have you been?' she ventured finally. 'I-I thought you were dead.'

'So did I,' he rasped, his voice rough.

'I came to see you at your base, there was so much to say, to tell you.'

He looked at her curiously.

'We moved to the New Forest six weeks after D-Day, then France and then, well . . .'

Time stretched and contracted. Before D-Day. After. She sneaked a look at his face, and saw fatigue and fear. His eyes were haunted by the death and destruction he had witnessed.

He dipped his head and stared at the water flowing under the bridge. 'I got Nell's letter about the wedding, but I couldn't come. I'm sorry.'

'It's all right. I understand.'

'No, I don't you think do, Patsy.' He stared out towards St Paul's Cathedral, its silvery dome now a symbol of defiance and deliverance.

'When you turned me down, I was destroyed,' he said quietly. 'I waited for you. When you didn't come, I realised I owed it to my crew to focus on the job in hand. On staying alive. On just getting through it.'

'Getting through what?' she asked fearfully.

He turned to face her at last and she wished she hadn't asked.

'How can I begin to describe what's in my head, Patsy . . .?'

She waited for him to fill the silence.

'Whole cities engulfed in firestorms. Factories, schools, churches, museums and air-raid shelters turned to vast crematoriums . . .'

He broke off and began to cry.

'How did I walk away from it alive when so many other good and fine young men didn't, Patsy? Some didn't even survive their first mission, never mind thirty. God I even became some sort of lucky mascot to the newer recruits.'

He broke off and wiped his eyes with the back of his hand, his fingers trembling violently.

'In my darker moments, as we flew over burning civilisations, I wondered if I hadn't actually died and this wasn't hell itself. You think I'm crazy don't you?'

She realised she was crying herself now as she took out her hankie and gently held it to his cheek.

'No, I don't think you're crazy, Blue. War is . . .' She trailed off, trying to find a way to articulate how diabolic and brutal the past six years had been. But nothing she could say could assuage his trauma, or sense of guilt that he had lived when so many other men hadn't.

'I don't know why you survived,' she said instead. 'I only

know I'm awfully glad that you did. And that you're here today. With me.'

He nodded and blew out slowly.

'But what happens now, Blue?' she asked, hardly daring to breathe.

She had crushed his heart, sent him into total war without a scrap of hope. What right did she even have to ask that question?

They both fell silent, gazing out at the huge Union Jack on top of the House of Lords. After years of darkness, the lights suddenly seemed dazzling, the searchlights swooping and falling, making a kaleidoscope of the sky. Big Ben towered over them, floodlit by columns of light.

'Now, I'd like to go home.'

Patsy nodded. She felt a tidal sob rising up inside her. She had suspected this was coming, she deserved it even, but the pain at the thought of losing him again was savage.

'I understand. It's been nearly two years now, you must be . . .' Her voice cracked and she brushed her eyes angrily. 'You must be desperate to get home to Boston.'

'No. Not Boston. Home to Stratford, Patsy,' he said, turning to face her. 'To Nell and the Shoot, and then we can work out where we go from there. Together. Deal?'

She nodded and he looped his arm around her shoulder. Patsy thought her legs might buckle and she pressed herself into the nooks and crannies of Blue's familiar body. Together they walked off the bridge towards the embankment.

Patsy had so many more questions, her fractured mind span with them. *Would he stay here in England permanently, would he take on Jimmy, could he ever forgive her for leaving him waiting that night?* But he was with her now, and that was all that mattered. The time for talking and plans would come later. They had a tomorrow. They had hope. Like old

London town they were bruised, broken and battered, but in time they'd recover.

The darkness of the night was held at bay by the blazing bonfires, the orange flames silhouetting the outlines of noisy revellers. In the warm glow Patsy paused and Blue pulled her into his arms, kissing her gently.

The raucous singing of the crowds and the tooting of the tugs on the river melted away as she savoured the feel of his lips on hers. Hot tears of relief slid down her face and she tasted them in their kiss.

When he pulled back, his pupils were so large they were like two blots of spilt ink. Behind him the moon rose, like a huge luminous disc shimmering off the flat surface of the Thames. The sky was blistered with a thousand brilliant stars.

'Thank you for keeping your promise to meet me,' he said, pulling her collar up around her neck and drawing her closer. 'And now I'd like to make one to you . . .'

'Go on.'

'I'm going to devote the rest of my life to loving you, Patsy Jacks. After all, I told you the first time I saw you that I'd met the girl I was going to marry. And I keep my promises too.'

Patsy leant her head on his chest and drew that love around her like a warm blanket. The small joys she had vowed to find in the everyday suddenly felt infinite.

'Come on,' she grinned, tugging him eastwards. 'Let's go home to the Shoot.'

Further Reading

Meet the Windmill Girls

I have long been fascinated by the daring and high-voltage glamour associated with London's most famous wartime theatre. Patsy's hidden life as a revudebelle at The Windmill Theatre was a way of injecting a much-needed shot of escapism, allure and exoticism into the plot. I admit, I was also intrigued by the notion of mixing up two worlds – the drudgery of Stinky Stratford and the impossible glamour of the little Soho theatre, a place where soldiers from all around the world flocked to find solace from their respective theatres of war.

As Kitty tells Patsy: 'We're a lovely face in a foreign place, a dash of escapism and glamour to blot out the darkness.'

But when I started plotting this book, I was worried, eighty years on, that there'd be too little left of the iconic theatre to get an authentic feel of its past.

Enter Jill and Joan, two fragrant yet formidable former Windmill girls who kindly agreed to take me on a tour of their Soho streets one bright and breezy March day . . .

We arrange to meet at a posh Soho hotel opposite the stage door where they made their first tentative steps into show-business.

It isn't hard to spot them as I walk past the endless vape

and coffee shops. They are both immaculately turned-out grandmothers, and their poise and deportment seem incongruous among the herds of tourists who scuttle along, viewing London through their mobile phones.

'It's so different now. This used to be a filthy back alley back in the fifties,' Jill says as we walk along in the direction of the theatre.

It takes a certain amount of chutzpah to knock on the door of a West End theatre and ask for an audition. Even more so when you're a fourteen-year-old schoolgirl! Armed only with a bucketload of swagger and a red hat set at a jaunty angle, Jill walked up to one of the most legendary theatres in Soho and had an interview that would change her life.

'The enormity of what I was doing didn't hit me at the time,' says Jill.

The year was 1958 and The Windmill Theatre in Great Windmill Street was a celebrated hotbed of British talent, launching the careers of Peter Sellers and Bruce Forsyth. But it was most famous for its wartime activities.

By 1940, as a blacked-out London faced the full onslaught of the Blitz, forty-one theatres in the West End dimmed their lights, then closed. Only The Windmill remained open, determined that war-weary civilians and servicemen should find joy and entertainment despite – or maybe because of – the constant fear of death. It earnt itself the immortal slogan 'We Never Closed' (sometimes referred to by cheeky journalists as 'We Never Clothed') and high-kicked its way into the history books.

For a young schoolgirl in drab, post-war London, a place of bombsites and fogs, Soho was the epitome of glamour, and The Windmill Theatre its glittering heart.

And now?

The little shop opposite the stage door where the Windmill girls used to go to buy pan stick and carmine lipstick is now closed, under development. The deli where they went for the best salt beef sandwiches outside of Whitechapel is a bar. And The Windmill Theatre itself? Jill shudders.

'After The Windmill closed, it had various different incarnations. At one time it was a TV studio, then it became a cheap lap-dancing club. See how they stuck nasty black cladding over the beautiful arched doorway. But look,' she says, 'my little cherub is still there.'

Peeping with a mischievous grin over the top of the cladding is the face of a slightly impish carved-stone cherub. The face feels symbolic of the era in which Jill and Joan worked there. They both insist that although the theatre was best known for its nude tableaux vivants, or living statues, who famously posed motionless on pedestals, it was naughty but nice, an altogether more innocent time.

The Lord Chamberlain had decreed that nudes be allowed on stage – provided they did not move. This was strictly adhered to, otherwise The Windmill would have lost its theatre licence and been shut down.

Patsy's gesture of defiance after the doodlebug dropped nearby was based on a true story of a nude who broke her pose to issue a 'long nose' salute to the enemy overhead.

'After I knocked on the door, I was shown up to see the manager, Vivian Van Damm, or as he was known, the Old Man,' Jill continues. 'I remember running up flight after flight of stone steps, past a flurry of frilled and feathered Windmill girls, impossibly glamorous with their carmined lips.'

'What did it smell like?' I ask.

'Perfume, sweat and greasepaint,' she replies. 'But it was the noise that was most overwhelming. The sound of tap shoes up and down the stairs, the humming of several old Singer sewing machines from the wardrobe department, composers in the music room, and the clatter and chatter of the canteen. Over it all, a tannoy relayed the sound of the show. It was very noisy!'

Once inside the Old Man's room, Jill found herself under the hawk-like gaze of Van Damm.

'He wasn't a man who wasted words,' Jill recalls. '"Can you sing and can you dance?" he asked me. I'd worn out my mother's parquet flooring practising my steps, so I answered yes. He paused, looked me in the eye and said: "I like you. I'm going to take a chance on you." When he produced a contract, I had to confess that I was still at school. He sent me home with the contract and I promised to return.'

And return she did. For another five years.

'It was gruelling. We performed six shows a day, six days a week. The revue featured non-stop shows from midday until eleven p.m. There were two revolving companies, so one day we would rehearse, the next day perform.

'Soon after I started, The Windmill's press office leaked my arrival to the press. "Convent Girl in Windmill Show!" screamed the headlines, and I was summoned to the Old Man's office. Van Damm had received a letter of complaint from the Mother Superior of my old convent school. The sisterhood of St Mary's no longer wished to be associated with me. He was furious. "They are ashamed of you, but they should be proud of you. I am." With that he dismissed me and continued to issue press releases to the newspapers proclaiming: "It's a far cry from her Woodford Convent School days . . ."'

Van Damm was nothing if not a canny marketing man. It was he who dreamt up the concept of continuous revue, mixing a recipe of magicians, comedians and ballet with beautiful dancing girls and nudes. And he who came up with the immortal slogan 'We Never Closed'.

'I was a Windmill girl, which meant I had to dance and perform better than anyone else out there,' she says. 'I was trained by Keith Lester, a leading ballet dancer who had trained in the Diaghilev tradition of Russian classical ballet and partnered some of the greatest ballerinas of the 1920s and 1930s. But by 1958, he was trying to get my legs to do things they had never done before! He terrified me. He puffed out his chest, flared his nostrils and shouted at me.'

Keith had created The Windmill's famous fan dances in the 1940s. The only nude the censorship law permitted to move on the Windmill stage was the principle fan dancer. Staying within the law required considerable skill on the part of the dancer, as she had to remain covered while manipulating the huge ostrich feather fans.

'Have you tried lifting one of those?' Jill asks me. 'They're heavy!' It wasn't much better if you were one of the nude living statues who posed as part of the tableau. The revudebelles not only had to have a flawless body, they also had to stand frozen, with one arm held aloft, for twelve minutes, multiple times a night.

'How did they do it?' I ask.

'Theatrical discipline and stamina. The statue effect was achieved by subtle stage lighting. The pose was never head on but faced towards the wings. When the curtain came down between scenes, the stage hands stepped on to the stage with the girl's dressing robe and handed it to her while looking away. It was respect for the girl, and Van Damm was very strict about that.'

'How did they achieve the look of a marble statue?' I ask, for the photos of the revudebelles look like they are covered in chiffon or gauze.

'Make-up, careful posing and they always made sure to shave their midlands,' she says with a wry smile.

Amazingly, the theatre never took a direct hit, despite London being bombarded nightly for eight months.

'One of the most famous Blitz Windmill girls was a blue-eyed, blonde, husky-voiced woman called Maggie McGrath. We met later in life and became good friends,' says Jill. 'Boy, was she a force to be reckoned with.'

Wartime Windmill Girls, Peggy, Sonia, Gerry, Margot and Rene at the theatre in 1943. Reproduced with kind permission of The Windmill Theatre Collection.

Maggie would often repeat the famous escapade where she and another Windmill girl rescued six terrified, panicking horses from a burning stables during a raid, rounding them up and leading them to safety through the middle of Piccadilly Circus while singing 'I've Got Sixpence'. When they weren't dodging bombs, the Windmill girls were out on the road, performing to troops in aircraft hangars, drill halls and canteens. Maggie remembered performing in the open on a table at one outpost with headlights of army lorries as improvised spotlights.

A parody of a Churchill quote is attributed to an unknown officer at RAF Hornchurch, who quipped: 'Never was so much shown by so few to so many,' following a 1942 performance by the Windmill girls. Little wonder the girls had such an army of devoted fans. During the war, queues of servicemen stretched back to Shaftesbury Avenue and, nightly, the seats were packed with Allied soldiers from around the world.

One wonders how many of these men saw out the war alive.

'It's terribly sad,' says Jill. 'There was one young soldier who had fallen in love with one of the Windmill girls. He waited every night in the cafe over the road. After D-Day, he was never seen again.'

This heart-wrenching recollection is in part what inspired the character of Blue, although for creative reasons, I gave him and Patsy a happier ending!

It was a desire for young men to get the opportunity to see a woman naked that brought about the formation of the theatre in the first place. The Windmill was indeed owned by an eccentric, iron-willed and wealthy widow by the name of Mrs Laura Henderson, who had a stormy working relationship with her manager Vivian Van Damm. Mrs Henderson enjoyed going around London in her chauffeur-driven, canary-yellow Rolls Royce, or looping the loop in her aeroplane. But behind the dynamic and forceful personality lay a secret sorrow.

'Mrs Henderson lost her only son in the Great War,' Jill explains. 'After his death, she discovered a French postcard of a naked woman among his belongings and realised he had probably gone to his death without ever seeing a naked woman in the flesh.'

Maybe she saw the face of her son in every soldier who passed through her doors during the Second World War? She was certainly a woman ahead of her time. It's a little-known fact – and not touched upon in the film *Mrs Henderson Presents*, in which Judi Dench plays her – that in real life, she raised money to set up a string of contraception clinics across the country to support her friend Marie Stopes, as well as employing unmarried mothers to ensure they had money and a roof over their head. This remarkable woman never got to see VE Day. She died in 1944, aged eighty-one.

After nearly three hours of chatting about the past glories of this unique theatre, I realise, with a jolt, the time. Jill and Joan are such raconteurs that I have been utterly transported back to the mid-twentieth century and am reluctant to drag myself back to 2019. We stand outside the entrance to the boarded-up theatre and I feel a pang not to have shared in their visceral memories myself.

Oh, to have heard the clatter of hooves as Maggie steered horses along the cobbled back streets of Soho against the flash of fire and crump of bombs; to have heard the applause and laughter echoing from the little theatre; to have had the opportunity to listen in on the conversations of the queuing servicemen, many of whom didn't survive the war.

But I can't. Instead, all I can do is write about it. So that's what I've done and I really hope you've enjoyed it.

Left to right, Joan, Kate and Jill in Soho.

Author's note:

For the sake of accuracy, I should point out that although to the best of my knowledge, everything relating to the wartime Windmill is true, there are two areas where I have used creative licence. Firstly, it's unlikely that a girl like Patsy, with some West Indian heritage, would have been able to find employment in a West End theatre. Not impossible, but in those highly discriminatory times, certainly difficult. Hearteningly, research shows that The Windmill did employ some women of colour. A stunning Chinese woman by the name of Moy Wong worked as a Windmill girl during the war.

Secondly, Patsy holding down two jobs would in reality have been impossible. The Windmill obviously had a ferocious work ethic, requiring all its performers be stage ready by 9 a.m. for rehearsals, before the start of the first house (show) at noon. The last performances of the day began at 7.45 p.m. and ran until about 10.30 p.m. when the final curtain went down. It really was a non-stop revue, meaning Patsy would never have had time to dash from East End to West. I hope readers and former Windmill employees forgive the creative licence I have used here to make Patsy's double life work. Everything else is deliciously true.

*

Jill's glossy book, *Remembering Revudeville: A Souvenir of the Windmill Theatre*, compiled by Jill Millard Shapiro (Obscuriosity Press), is a treasure trove of memories and was a great help to me in researching this book.

In Search of the Lavender Girls

I love archives and libraries. Carefully untying the cream ribbon of an old file and catching the scent of eighty-year-old dust motes is a thrill. More than once, I've found hours can slip away leafing through yellowed newspaper reports and witness accounts from the Second World War in the silence of a reading room.

But nothing beats what historians call 'primary sources' and what I prefer instead to call 'magnificent women'. I love sitting down face to face with a wartime survivor and listening to the unfiltered gush of personal history. For me, history when viewed up close and personal takes the true temperature of the times. From the brand of hearthstone women used, to the market they haggled in, wartime civilians' lives are more telling in the detail, which is why I'm always happy perched on a sofa with a cup of tea and notebook, just listening.

I spoke with some remarkable Yardley workers in researching the first book in this series, *Secrets of the Homefront Girls*. Women like Eileen McKay, who proudly told me: 'I may have snow on the roof, but I'm not old, I have stories to tell.'

But I hadn't managed to find anyone who worked at the Yardley factory during the war years. Eileen's recollections were of the immediate post-war years which did, of course, give me an incredible flavour of the old factory in Stinky Stratford, but weren't able to fill in the tiny details I'd craved.

Then, shortly after the book came out in August 2019, I received a beautiful handwritten letter in the post.

'I was a wartime Lavender Girl, I read about your book in a magazine,' wrote Joan Osborne. 'Yardley was the most wonderful years of my life. I am now 91.'

Yardley has the most wonderful years of my life

I got in my car to drive down to Hullbridge in Essex to see Joan at the first available opportunity. Meeting her was pure joy. All the vibrancy, hopes, dreams, fears and tiny day-to-day details of her wartime existence were brought to life.

'I was born in Barking in 1927,' Joan told me in her immaculate bungalow. 'I was the youngest of ten. I was evacuated when war broke out but came back when school finished. I started at Yardley aged fifteen in 1942. My dad didn't want me going into a factory – that was too good for his girl. He wanted me in an office, but the lure of Yardley was too much.

'It must have been the glamour. I remember travelling from Stratford to Ilford on the bus and the conductor opening the window so everyone could smell the lavender blowing from Yardley.

'Carpenters Road – or Stink Bomb Alley – was famous for its smells. Seven different types of air flowed down there, depending on which way the air was blowing. I can still smell the lavender,' she smiles.

Joan was sent to work in the top-floor perfumery department, where she was given a broom to sweep the floor.

'I thought: "I haven't come here to sweep floors," so they moved me to bottle-filling, where I was putting the skin and caps on bottles. They were losing so many girls to the services, I don't think they wanted to lose any more, so they kept me sweet.

'I earnt eighteen shillings and something a week and my clocking-in number was 157. I've still got the card.

'They were dangerous times, especially when the flying bombs started up, but being young I didn't think that much about it. I was more upset by how cold it was in the factory. The heating was rarely on and we were always freezing. They used to give us cups of Oxo to warm us up. At least the room always smelt lovely from the lavender, freesia and April violets perfume.

'Sometimes people would go home and you'd never see them again. My supervisor, a nice lady who used to check our work, went home one night, let herself in and a rocket dropped on her house. These things just came over night and day. No warning at all as to when they were going to drop. I remember crouching by the side of bushes a lot.'

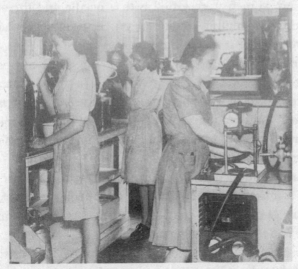

Joan's big sister Millie working in the perfume department at Yardley.

Joan's life was lived out against cataclysmic world events: the terrible waiting for D-Day, followed by the remorseless raining down of Hitler's revenge weapon. Many people I have interviewed describe the falling of the V2 rockets as psychologically more shattering than the Blitz, as they arrived without warning, with no chance to seek shelter. The outskirts of London, like Croydon and West Ham, received the most. But for a young girl like Joan, it wasn't the shadow of death under which they lived that would prove most memorable, but the small joys.

'Us East End girls were obsessed with glamour. I never went down the shops without my make-up on,' she laughs. 'Once a month, there was a staff sale and I used to queue for my lavender soap, talc and lipstick.

'We all did our hair nice. I used to go to bed with my dinky curlers in and do my face out with Yardley's pancake make-up. We all took such pride in our appearance and loved to sing along to *Music While You Work*.'

The East End obsession with glamour also came from being raised in the heartland of the schmutter (rag) trade. East End women were gifted with a needle and thread and could buy a length of material on their dinner break and have run it into a nice blouse by teatime.

Care over their appearance took on extra importance during the Second World War, when Churchill declared that 'Beauty is your Duty'. There was a genuine fear that if women lost their femininity and, God forbid, were seen looking a little scruffy, it would lead to a collapse in morale that would be detrimental to society.

Britain's oldest cosmetics firm, Yardley, rose to the challenge, telling their customers that 'good looks and morale go hand in hand'. *Vogue* told its readers that 'a woman past caring is a woman past repairing'.

These powerful messages were underpinned with a sophisticated pseudo-military marketing campaign for cosmetics, which saw the weaponisation of lipstick. There were shades called Auxiliary Red, Victory Red and Homefront Ammunition. There was even a shade created called Burnt Sugar, said to go perfectly with khaki. The message to women was clear. Lipstick is your weapon and you are a soldier on the homefront.

Red lips became a potent symbol of wartime glamour and defiance. It was rumoured too that Hitler hated women with red lips.

Yardley would reward workers who kept a tidy conveyor belt with a free makeover at its Bond Street Beauty School.

'I was sent up there,' recalls Joan. 'I came back looking lovely. What a treat in wartime.'

But looking at Joan's photo, what strikes me most is not the make-up, but the naturalness of her beauty. It's the same with so many of her generation. It goes beyond skin-deep to their poise, the tilt of the chin, the swagger of their expression.

Joan aged 20

One day, she told me, Joan drew the eye of an admirer.

'I met Reggie at the wedding of one of the Lavender Girls I worked with, in 1948. He'd just been demobbed. His sister, Ivy, was my chargehand in perfumery.

'Reggie had had a rough time during the war, I know he crossed the Rhine, but he didn't ever talk to me about it. All my brothers came home from the war so I was lucky, but I did learn that when a man goes in the army, he doesn't come home the same person.'

Joan and Reggie did their courting at the picture houses of East London, before marrying in 1953.

'Money was tight, so I wore my big sister Millie's wedding dress. She'd worked in perfumery too and we were very close. She was seven years older than me and, in many ways, like a mother to me.

'Millie was a beautiful woman, very popular in the perfume department too. I remember when she won a competition to name a Yardley lipstick. She was so proud and her lipstick Gypsy Rose was a beautiful pink.'

And here is where the story takes on a serendipitous twist. While I was researching *Secrets of the Homefront Girls*, I was reading through a back copy of the *Yardley News* (the factory's own magazine) and my eye was drawn to an article congratulating a couple, who met working at Yardley, on their marriage.

'Arthur from dispatch married Millicent from the perfume room.' Just a paragraph nestled among many other marriage notices, but I loved their names, so I included them in *Homefront Girls*.

Millicent was Joan's older sister.

'She died many years ago, aged fifty, of breast cancer. Seeing her name in your book made the hairs on my neck stand on end,' says Joan.

Joan was devastated by the loss of her lovely big sister and missed her as much as she missed the camaraderie of her days in the factory.

'After I started having children in 1955, I left Yardley. Being at home on your own with children was hard. You missed being part of a big group of women.'

Now, sixty-five years on, I got the sense she still does.

'I'm only an ordinary working girl, but the years I worked at Yardley made my life. It taught me the value of hard work and how to manage in the war years. I met lifelong friends and my husband through Yardley. It gave me everything I could wish for.'

It was a pleasure to meet Joan and listen to her reflect on a life well lived. Let's keeping listening to the voices of this unique generation, while we still can!

92-year-old Joan, all smiles as she reminisces about her past.

Slaughter of the Innocents

Heartbroken Benjamin Batt, digging through the ruins of the bombed school in 1917. Copyright William Whiffin. Reproduced with kind permission of Tower Hamlets Local History Library and Archives.

Have you ever seen a photo that has stopped you in your tracks? This black-and-white photo sparked the plot line of Snowball's story. I came across it at Tower Hamlets Local History Library & Archives and found myself transfixed. The story behind it is as haunting as the image.

Benjamin Batt was the school caretaker for Upper North Street Elementary School during the First World War. He was on duty one warm summer's day in June 1917 when, according to an eyewitness, 'the sun had been shining, then it seemed to go out in a roar of thunder.'

Overhead were a squadron of fourteen German Gotha bombers, circling over London looking for targets. Choosing a clear day, the biplanes had taken off from Belgium, looking to bring to the war away from the western front to the heart of Britain. Their casualties here were not soldiers, but tiny children.

In an attack that seems to defy all belief, one of the German bombers dropped a 50 kg bomb on the junior school in the country's first daylight bombing raid.

The bomb crashed through the roof injuring many and killing three older children on an upper floor. But it found true devastation on the ground floor where the infants, mainly aged five, had, according to one newspaper article from the time, excitedly been making paper lanterns.

It must have been chaos and terror on a scale unimagined. The blast brought tonnes of masonry, bricks and debris crashing down on the children and teachers.

Caretaker Benjamin rushed in and together with teachers Gertrude Middleton, Mary Philomena Cunnington, Annie Elizabeth Allum and Emma Watkins (who all later received an OBE for their heroism) helped to extricate tiny bodies, both living and dead, from the rubble. Children were said to be stained yellow by the TNT from the bomb. This was the detail I found most harrowing of all.

'Ghastly sights,' said the mayor who arrived on the scene. 'Infants laying across their desks with terrible wounds, writhing in pain, others dead, their bodies mutilated.'

Panicked mothers arrived too, each desperately hoping their child was not one of those caught in the blast. As quickly as possible, the bodies of the children who were killed were taken to the mortuary, and the injured were cared for by nurses and surgeons, and taken to hospitals.

One little boy on the upper floor recalled: 'We were doing our sums when we heard a whirring in the air. We looked up and all of sudden there was a big noise. Something came right through the ceiling. It was a bomb. Such a lot of stuff came with it. When I picked myself up I saw the headmaster all covered with ink. Tables and desks and things had been knocked over, and there were two large holes where the bomb had come and gone. We were all frightened but the teacher helped us to get away, and we ran off home.'

Eighteen children were killed that fateful morning, mainly aged five. A further thirty-seven were badly injured, with limbs torn off. You will find the full list of the victims' names at the front of the book. I dedicate *Secrets of the Lavender Girls* to them, for as the Mayor of Poplar, Mr Will Crooks, said at the time: 'These boys and girls truly suffered for their country as any man who has perished in the trenches, on the high seas or the air.'

The suffering must have sunk deep into the soil of Poplar. Benjamin Batt remained on the scene for many days digging for bodies. *Digging. Digging. Digging.* Among the bodies found in the ruins was Benjamin's own son, Alfred, known to all as Alfie.

This grief-stricken man never recovered from the mental wounds of what he saw, smelt and touched in the days after the bomb hit, or the sheer horror of pulling his own son from the wreckage. Five months later he took his own life. His heart was broken.

I had this heroic man's name in mind the entire time I was writing Snowball's story, trying to fathom how much trauma and suffering the human brain can absorb before the fuse box blows.

But from horror came slender shafts of hope.

The world shared in the East End's grief and there was an international tidal wave of revulsion and shock at the bombing of the school. Hordes of young East End men clamoured to sign up to the army, and it is rumoured that the bombing was one of the reasons why the royal family changed their name from Saxe-Coburg to Windsor. King George V made the announcement one month after the raid.

As I wrote in the prologue, there was an enormous outpouring of collective grief at the funeral cortège. Hundreds of floral wreaths from around the world, from Buckingham Palace to small country village schools, and some from as far afield as New Zealand, lined the route, which was ringed with thousands of silent spectators. The docks ceased work for the day, shops shut and blinds all over the East End were drawn as a mark of respect.

Two years later, a marble memorial was unveiled to the eighteen children in nearby Poplar Recreation Ground. This memorial serves as an eloquent witness to the tragic impact of world events on the tight-knit East End community. It was completed only five days before the Treaty of Versailles was signed, formally ending the war between the Allied Powers and Germany.

The 100th anniversary of the bombing was marked in 2017, two years before I began writing this book. As part of my research, I went along to the school, now called the Mayflower School, to interview headteacher Dee Bleach. The entire school was rebuilt after the bomb and outside the front door there is a plaque, which reads: 'Learning from our past can lead to a more peaceful future.'

I was fascinated to hear how the headteacher commemorated such a tragic event and taught the school's pupils about it, without scaring them.

'It was quite an undertaking, especially when we learnt two weeks before that the Queen and Duke of Edinburgh would be attending,' says Dee. 'The most important thing was to help the children have an understanding of the past and the extraordinary history that their school represents and why the East End community was so strong. We wanted them to try to imagine what life in wartime was like for children back then at the school they now attend.'

All year groups spent months producing poems, artwork, paper doves, diaries and creative writing to fully explore and bring to life the worlds of the children who went to their school one hundred years ago. They were also taken to the Imperial War Museum, the Stow Maries Great War Aerodrome in Essex and the memorial to the bombing in Poplar Park. Teachers also took some children on a walk of nearby streets with a map of Poplar from 1916, to try and locate the homes of the children who died. This is imaginative teaching.

Crucially, the children were also taught the realities and hardships of a life lived in the grinding poverty and slums of East London, and how different a classroom education was in 1917. Pupils were told how boys and girls were taught separately after the infant classes, and how they entered through different entrances. All children were taught reading, writing, maths and singing, with girls learning laundry and needlework skills and boys woodwork. As part of their homework, girls sewed pillowcases for the nearby London Hospital. The school was equipping them for a life in service, or one of the many factories and sweatshops in the local area.

Punishments were severe. Naughty pupils could expect the cane or a slap round the back of the hand with a ruler, and if you played the fool, the 'DUNCE' hat, lines, detention or all three were a ritual form of discipline.

On the day itself, the school children took part in a moving memorial march, on the original funeral route, to All Saints Church on East India Dock Road.

This day was the brainchild of local historian Stan Kaye, who spent four and a half years researching and organising the commemoration event and astonishingly managed to contact the surviving family members of every single child who died – some of whom had never even heard of the bombing, much less that one of their ancestors died in it. 'It was a labour of love,' Stan reveals. 'I even dreamt of it, you could say it got under my skin.'

I understand this passion to shine a light into the dark recesses of forgotten history.

'Those children are a part of me,' he continues. 'Having Her Majesty at the commemoration ensured that these children will never be forgotten.'

The names of all the children were read out in front of the Queen, as was this beautiful poem written by Boyce class, Year 6, Mayflower School.

Under the Blanket of Summer

Under the blanket of summer
Children's laughter drifts on the breeze
Their innocence wrapped in the safe arms of tranquillity
Under the blanket of summer
A sound splinters the air
Roaring fire enveloping the light, burning the sky
A few seconds, a few heartbeats
And then silence.
Never again will you meet a new day
Never again will you rise from rest
Never again will you laugh with friends
Each day the sun will shine
But for you, never again.
Under the blanket of summer
Eighteen blessed coffins lie
Laden with pink and white petals
Under the blanket of summer
The poppies shine a little brighter

Each one a reminder of a life lost, a life remembered
Under this blanket of summer
We will never forget.

What wonderfully talented children, and how heartening to
see them turn a commemoration of a historical disaster into
a message of hope.

Select Bibliography

The following books and pamphlets gave me a good insight into the time period.

Barbara Bell, *Just Take your Frock off: A Lesbian Life*. Our Story Books, 1999.
An authentic and funny picture of lesbian life in the 20th century.

Mike Brown, *The 1940s Look: Recreating the Fashions, Hairstyles and Make-up of the Second World War*. Sabrestorm Publishing, 2006.

Carol Dyhouse *Glamour: Women, History, Feminism*. Zed Books, 2011.
I gleaned so much from her insights into the working-class thirst for tinsel-town glamour.

Juliet Gardiner, *Over Here: The GIs in Wartime Britain*. Collins & Brown, 1992.
A revealing insight into the time when, at its peak, there were a million and half young American men living in Britain.

Mike Hutton, *Life in 1940s London*. Amberley Publishing, 2014.

Norman Longmate, *The Doodlebugs: Story of the Flying Bombs*. Arrow Books, 1986.

Mollie Panter-Downes, *London War Notes*. Persephone Books, 2015.

A razor-sharp observation on London life in wartime.

Jill Millard Shapiro (ed.), *Remembering Revudeville, 1932–1964: A Souvenir of the Windmill Theatre*. Obscuriosity Press, 2014.

A lush hardback which brings the glory days of the Windmill Theatre vividly to life within its glossy pages.

Julie Summers, *Fashion on the Ration*. Profile Books, 2015.

Liz Tregenza, *Style Me Vintage: 1940s*. Pavilion Books, 2015.

Sarah Waters, *The Night Watch*. Virago Press, 2006. One of my most favourite novels. Waters gives a beautifully written insight into the lives of gay women in wartime.

The Other Eastenders: Kamal Chunchie and West Ham's Early Black Community. Eastside Community Heritage, 2002.

A fascinating insight into the pre-war, black dockside communities.

Revudeville Souvenir. Various editions. Collection held at the British Library.

For more information on Yardley and the war in Stratford, I visited Newham Archives and Local Studies Library, which holds a collection of back copies of the beautiful old *Yardley News* as well as back copies of the *Stratford Express,* all of which were invaluable and authentic sources on wartime life in Stratford and the Carpenters Road factory.

For more information on the war in East London, I visited Tower Hamlets Local History Library & Archives.

For more information on beauty and fashion in wartime, I paid a visit to the treasure trove that is the archives of the Fashion Museum in Bath, and spent many a happy hour browsing through back copies of *Vogue* and *Woman & Beauty*.

Acknowledgements

I would like to express my heartfelt thanks to a number of people.

To Mary Ashmore, whose brave recounting of her life and her mother's life growing up in Poplar opened my eyes to the struggle women endured during the Second World War.

To former Windmill girls Joan Bravery and Jill Millard Shapiro. I'm eternally grateful to these wonderful women for sharing with me their Windmill story and the place that extraordinary little theatre of dreams held in their hearts. Thank you for reading through extracts of the manuscript and setting me straight. You are both fabulous guardians of the Windmill legacy.

To the original Lavender Girls: Joan Osborne, Eileen McKay, Ann Roper, and Irene and Dorothy Green. They all brought the Yardley factory in 'Stinky Stratford' to life with eye-watering detail. They don't make them like that anymore.

To Karen Cullen, Head of Marketing for Yardley of London, for allowing me to delve through the cupboards of their archives in Windsor, which I was delighted to see groaning with the most beautiful old Yardley perfume and make-up bottles and pots. The evocative smell of Yardley's English Lavender these empty bottles still contained after more than fifty years did more to transport me to the

Carpenters Road factory than any time machine could have. Reading *The House of Yardley: 1770–1953* certainly helped too.

To Canning Town local Stan Moore and Stratford local John Moore, whose lively storytelling opened a magical door into the past.

To Hoxton girls Flo, Linda and Kelly, for sharing their East End and showing me how to eat jellied eels. Thanks for the stories and the laughs.

To local historian Stan Kaye, and to Dee Bleach, Headteacher of Mayflower Primary School (formerly Upper North Street School), for sharing with me the poignant way they chose to mark the commemoration of the school bombing.

To Doreen Jacks, for telling me what it was like to grow up as a mixed race child in wartime East London.

To Jennifer Daley, university lecturer, for her expertise about the lives of GIs in the USAAF.

To Gloria Spielman, for setting me straight on Jewish weddings and a whole lot more besides. Your humour, attention to detail and flair are very much appreciated.

To early readers Lor Bingham and Amy Condon for offering me their much-valued opinion.

To Sarah, Mandy and all the hard-working staff of Canning Town Library, for letting me conduct interviews there, finding me women to interview and allowing me to take over the library for the launch of *Secrets of the Homefront Girls*. A special note should be made here about all the incredibly hard-working and dedicated librarians I've had the pleasure to meet this past year.

To the inimitable Vivian Archer, from Newham Bookshop, whose enthusiasm for East End history, bookselling and reading is infectious. Thanks for your support. www.newham-books.co.uk

To my inspiring writing gang, Dani Atkins, Sasha Wagstaff, Faith Bleasdale, Fiona Ford and Jean Fullerton, who make this writing lark just that bit more fun.

To two of the most passionate, driven and dynamic women in the business: my agent Kate Burke and editor Kimberley Atkins. Thanks, Kim for your support and always encouraging me in the nicest way possible to dig deeper.

To my side-kick Sarah Richards, for helping transcribe interviews and generally making my life easier with such effortless skill and ease.

And finally, saving the best till last, my dear and very inspiring readers, who offer me such wholehearted support, in the form of letters, emails, treasured family stories and drawings. It changes what can be a solitary process into a vibrant conversation.

Please do get in touch. I'd love to hear from you.
www.katethompsonmedia.co.uk
www.facebook.com/KateThompsonAuthor
@katethompson380
katharinethompson82@gmail.com

This book was created by

Hodder & Stoughton

Founded in 1868 by two young men who saw that the rise in literacy would break cultural barriers, the Hodder story is one of visionary publishing and globe-trotting talent-spotting, campaigning journalism and popular understanding, men of influence and pioneering women.

For over 150 years, we have been publishing household names and undiscovered gems, and today we continue to give our readers books that sweep you away or leave you looking at the world with new eyes.

Follow us on our adventures in books . . .
🐦 @HodderBooks ⓕ /HodderBooks 📷 @HodderBooks

HODDER &
STOUGHTON